The Spirit of Life:

The Legend of Xavier

Britney A. Matejeck

Dorrance Publishing Co

585 Alpha Drive

Pittsburgh, PA 15238

Visit our website at *www.dorrancebookstore.com*

ISBN: 978-1-6393-7200-3

eISBN: 978-1-6393-7879-1

The Spirit of Life:

The Legend of Xavier

Prologue
Krakaten

I remember sleeping, but my broken memories have taken over. I am surrounded by my past. What an idiot I was. To let these bastards abuse my reputation. But that is what I favor, to be abused and raped. I want more, though my nightmares haunt me. Sometimes I wish I have never existed in the first place, but . . . I remember . . . my baby.

I awoke before I can make out a scream. I feel the sweat dripping on my skin. Skytra is still asleep, but I have business to do. I slip out of bed, hoping to not wake her. I change silently. As I exit my room, I make my way to the room we were supposed to meet at. This room is a large bedroom with large windows and draping curtains, but I use it to meditate. Once I walked in, I am baffled to not see him.

"Where are you?" I said out loud, questioning, waiting for an answer as I scan the dark room with my eyes.

Before I would have guessed it, a large shadow appears behind me.

"There you are . . ." I said, not settling for anything yet. We are just getting started.

"Krakaten Malick . . ." his deep dark voice calls me.

"Arban Surly . . ." I darkly call back. I will not settle this time.

"You're late . . ." I start.

"And—"

"We made a deal," I break in.

"And yet we have another to discuss . . . remember?" Arban's voice stings at my heart.

"Yes," I let out.

I will not settle. No, not yet. Arban's fingers reach my skin. I feel gravity pulling me back. I slowly back down, but my upper body slightly up. His fingers lightly touch my neck.

"I don't need your fingering to make an agreement . . ." I said. Arban laughs shallowly.

"So, you either fall under my rule or your son, Xavier will die," Arban said. His voice echoes into the heart of my soul.

"Xavier doesn't want your bullshit, just leave off," I call out, trying to defend all I have. Arban gives another shallow laugh. I do not think I will ever agree with him, now. Never.

"It's your choice, Krakaten. you can either bow down to me, or the baby dies . . . and you will never be the same, no one will," he said, raising his voice.

I take a moment. Only one moment, I close my eyes. I breathe. I can feel the dark gaze of Arban fallowing my private thoughts.

"Never."

Then I am pulled back. Arban grasps my neck tightly. My face burns and I feel the blood rushing through me. Pressure builds up around my head and I begin to choke. Arban begins to hiss, and I am pulled back to my greatest fear. My baby boy now must be killed, and I will fall in a pile of bones, in the ashes of my family. The dark will now rise, the cold will now freeze the suns and they will turn to black holes. My crown will be broken, my son, Xavier will be dead, and the truth will be exposed. My bare-naked body fading away . . . my face forgotten, and I will be forever lost in my psychotic mind.

Before I could make another thought out, the vile dark king

begins to rape me, and I will forever be forgotten.

~

I make my way to the war room, classes about to start. My armor is fixed tight to my body . . . and for some reason I can still feel Arban's grasp around my neck. It is 07:10. Almost late, I watch the clock on the wall as I enter the room.

"Good morning, class. I am sorry for being here a bit later than usual, I must have woken on the wrong side of the bed," I said lifting my head up a bit higher than I usually would.

Each student dressed in their own fixed tight armor, in position and ready for orders, await me.

Classes continued through quite well. Today, students were leaning how to fight their weaknesses, or other students that target them. My students did quite well except for Gradius, who was complaining about a foul made by Alicia.

"That was not fair. No way!" he protested.

"So what? just accept it. Your loss," Alicia groaned, rolling her eyes.

"Just quiet! We can redo the match tomorrow, there are others who have not had a turn yet," I yelled over the commotion.

Besides that, for each class I had at least one student glare at me, probably noticing my new scar from Arban's touch. I got nervous. At every student noticing and making the comment: "What's that scar on your neck from?"

I responded in a chattering tone; uneasy at first, rushing at the end, "Oh, nothing. Do not worry about it. Let us get back to class, thank you," I would said clapping my hands together, trying to rush though the day.

After classes I found myself more exhausted than usual. I never get this tired after half the day. I change to my usual clothes—or casual royal wear. Not too fancy, but comfortable. I slowly took a seat in my office. I lay back all the way against the seat, almost till my head would probably fall off. My desk was filled with scattered parchments of documents and other matters. The desk was large, but still I could not see its dusty wood surface.

By this point, I did not want to do anything. But soon enough, I slowly started to get things done (the simple, easy things first), then I got myself to focus. After about an hour or so, I had done quite enough, and I started to rest my head on the desk (which was now somewhat clear), until a knock became present on the door.

I looked up at the clock on the left wall before I could think about answering. 19:00. "Who is it," I called tiredly.

"It is just me, Zynix. Can I come in?" My son, Zynix called from the other side of the door.

"What is it? I am terribly busy right now, in fact . . . you should be getting ready for slumber," I called.

Zynix opened the door only a bit, where I could see his face and a letter in his hand that is out to me. "I have to give you something, I am not allowed to open it . . . it is for you," Zynix said shyly.

"Come in," I said strictly.

Zynix came in slowly, closing the door softly behind him. I motioned him to give me the letter into my hand.

"Who gave this to you?" I asked keeping the same tone, pressing my fingertips on the letter. Zynix did not respond.

"Who gave this to you?" I said, raising my voice.

"Mother wanted me to give it to you. She does not feel too well," Zynix said in his shy low-tone voice.

I took a closer look at the letter. I expected it to be from Arban, but that is not the name listed here. Zxarvixar?

"You should not have this," I said quickly and strictly.

"But—"

"Go, go take care of your mother! I don't have time to deal with your shit," I said, warning my son.

He nodded shallowly without a word . . . and left.

I sighed, stress piling up on me. I really hoped my baby was okay.

Once it was 19:30 I went off to check on my love and rest for the night.

The words of the letter appeared in my mind. A brutal war was coming. The first thing that came to my mind was my baby. Skytra, my wife, was pregnant. My second baby boy was waiting till the day he will join the rest of the family.

Before I went to sleep, I had asked Skytra about Zynix with the letter, but she simply pushed the matter aside. She had thought nothing of it. "Give him a break, he's just a boy," she said every time I seemed to have something against my own son. I just agreed with her like always. What was the point? What mattered more than having rubbish toward my own son was my baby boy that I knew . . . would shine brighter than billions of stars in a galaxy. Any galaxy. He is my precious. My precious little angel.

I awoke early, already suiting up in my armor.

"Love, the war starts now, but you must stay, I will have one of the guards—"

"What?! I am fighting, for everything I got."

"Love, I won't let you do that! Our child will die, you are not . . ." I tried to argue, but Skytra already was suited up before me a raced down the stairs.

I sighed. I wanted to scream. I was ready to have a fit like a small child. I-I need my baby to live.

"What in the name of Hell are you doing!?" I yelled, catching up to Skytra.

"Xavier will die if you go out there! He is everything to me, to us and to this family. Please, love, Xavier must live," I pleaded before Skytra could rush out the doors.

"Don't do this . . ." I added.

She slowly turned her head toward me, leaving her hand flat on the door as if it were part of the design.

"I want him to live too. I want to live. But this is what I feel that I need to do. This war needs me. This family needs me. I will fight no matter what will block my path. I promise to protect Xavier. Don't worry, love," Skytra explained softly to me.

My thoughts filled my head about this.

"Please . . ." Skytra added, which lightened my spirit, my dark thoughts fading away by her voice, the voice of a young girl who wanted the young boy to be happy just once in his life, and I will never forget what she has done for me.

Skytra was that young girl who thought I should be happy. I shall always live up to that voice.

"Protect Xavier, promise that. I just want you to know that I worry about you. I worry that you will suffer much more than I will. I hope you will be safe," I finally responded.

"I promise . . ." Skytra started turning away from the door and walking toward me.

"I love you so much, Krakaten," she said wrapping her arms around me.

"I love you too, Skytra," I respond hugging her back, embracing her.

"Be safe," she said.

"Always," I said kissing her forehead.

She is shorter than me anyway.

The brutal war broke out. Zxarvixar sent out his army hoping he could destroy our country's spirit. Never. I looked past all the fighting just to make sure Skytra is okay. I wanted my baby to live. She might have fell a few times, but she is my girl and she stood back up and took back what was rightfully hers. She smiled after taking down an enemy. I always had hope in her. There was something she had that I knew my baby might just acquire. No, he would. He would.

Enemies fell, blood spilled on to the ground, staining the grass with its deep red color, painting it like a masterpiece. A masterpiece of war. Months and months passed, filling in the details. Most of us could not handle it any longer, even though we had fought extremely hard since it all started. We have already been through many wars; it seems as if the people just want to get it over with.

"Come, Krakaten, let us give an olive branch," Zxarvixar's voice echoed through my mind.

I began to follow the voice, stepping over dead bodies that were left to rot. Wind started to pick up, engulfing me inside a tornado of such. The wind was hard to get by; with all my strength I make my way to the center. Out of the ground a glowing green mist grew high, forming Zxarvixar.

"An olive branch?! We are at two opposite sides of this planet! No agreement will make this work, trust in my words," I argued.

"Well, there are other ways we can agree, right?" Zxarvixar suggested.

"No. you just want my soul. You just want to feed yourself . . ." I said in a shaky tone.

"Well, all of us got to eat, even if we have the same diet . . ." Zxarvixar went on.

"I am sorry, I won't let you take my life away from me. I need my baby." I defended my life desperately.

"Very well then. Let this war be over. You win . . . and you will have your baby, but be warned I will be back . . . Xavier has much to look forward to," Zxarvixar stated as he faded away once the storm had grown in enough to pass over him.

I was left in the middle of this terrifying tornado. I was not left to die, but worse, I was left to rot . . . to be nothing, to be the worst that has ever happened to this family because I was selfish.

About five or six months passed since the war. So much blood. We pretty much killed off Zxarvixar's army, but we had not lost any major family members. The feeling of being back home was the best. I put on my nightwear and I made some tea for myself, and I saved some if Skytra would like some. I made my way up to our room, slowly trying not to spill the tea.

"Love, are you not well?" I asked in case.

"I will be fine. I promise. I am just sore," she said tiredly as she lay on her back in bed.

"Well, feel better, love. I brought some tea if you like," I mentioned kindly.

"Yes, I would like some, but I need your help to sit up," she replied. I come over to help her, then placing the hot tea on a tray laying on the corner of the bed. "Thanks, love," Skytra said as I settled in for a nap.

"You are very welcome," I replied before drifting off into a deep sleep.

"Just wait, I have plans for your boy, Xavier." The voices of Zxarvixar and Arban resounded at almost the same time, but slightly off, making it seem like an echo lost in a cavern. "You are nothing . . . your kingdom will fall. You let your own family down. What were you thinking, going off with your little girl friend . . . letting those who abuse your power rape you . . . and you will fall. Not like a great king, not like an ordinary one, but one who falls from failing to keep your own mind sane! You are nothing . . ." These words echoed through my mind repeatedly till morning.

A couple of weeks later, I was tired from tending my love and work at the same time, but my eyes were wide open, aware of everything happening around me. Well, my wife was pregnant . . . so I must help her. It was morning and I had much to do. I headed down the stairs, surprised to see my wife's older sister, Styre.

"Oh, good morning, Styre," I greeted her.

She did not seem to be happy or in the mood. Her arms were still crossed, and her expression barely changed at all.

"What is wrong? Did I upset you somehow?" I ask confused.

"No, not at all. It is just that we do not have enough medical staff to tend the wounded," Styre started, sighing in between.

"I can't believe we are even short for students who plan on

going into medical, no wonder why we do not have enough," Styre continued mumbling.

She paused, and we were flooded by background chattering. But then she broke it, relieving me.

"Anyways, our people are losing hope. We need you to bring back our country's spirit. Please, Krakaten. Will you do that for us? For our country?" she asked with wide eyes that hope to grab anything left in me.

Right when I was about to reply a familiar voice echoed as a scream throughout the palace.

"Skytra," I said before I make a run for it.

As I ran to the steps and up, I pushed people aside to get through.

"Excuse me, excuse me," I said, racing up the steps.

I ran down the hall, swung open the door of our room, and once I stepped inside, I froze. I did not blink or move. Skytra continued her whining.

"Krakaten, don't just stand there! Help me," she screamed at me.

"Oh, okay . . . everything is going to be okay," I said under my breath.

I rushed around the room. First, I shut and lock the door, then I got some extra pillows out of the closet to support Skytra. I knew this was going to happen soon. Why didn't I prepare for this? Skytra had gone into labor, soon after the womb has broken, creating a mess of water on the bed.

"Ugh, I don't have time to clean this up," I mumbled about it.

Skytra continued her whining pains. I let her tightly hold my hand. It was now or never.

A loud and rushing knock was present on the door.

"What?! My baby is going to be born!" I yelled across the room, too stressed out for this.

"Krakaten, I only want to help!" Styre yelled back.

I almost wanted to whine myself this time.

"I can do this, myself!" I yelled back, wanting her to leave me alone.

"Y-you are so selfish! I can't believe my younger sister would marry a man like you!" Styre yelled. Her words stung at my heart. I began to forget about everything that was going on, until Skytra began to speak.

"Krakaten, I love you because I know that you want the best for this family. You may be a bit selfish, but that does not mean you are not a great leader . . . or a sweet husband," Skytra explained under pressure.

She continued, "That does not mean you are not going to be an amazing father to Xavier."

I continued to hold her hand, but passionately this time. She was the most amazing woman in the world. She was going to be an amazing mother as well. After one long yelp, I checked on the baby. His head was already starting to come out.

"His head is coming out!" I said loudly.

Behind a stressed and sweaty face, I could tell that Skytra was glad to hear it. As I was guiding Xavier's head out, I heard screams come from downstairs. Faintly I could hear my name from multiple voices trying to reach me. I looked both at the door and Skytra. I decided to take the wiser decision: Skytra. I stayed with her, trying to forget about the screams. It cannot be real, it is my own mind, just ignore it. The voices slowly became louder, and louder . . . until, people banging on the door. My name was being called.

"Krakaten! There's a fire, a fire is starting to grow!" Styre yelled.

Before I could respond, her voice faded as the flames reached our room.

"Oh no, this must be Arban's or Zxarvixar's doing!" I shrieked.

"Krakaten," Skytra calls me. I looked her in the eyes.

I was afraid, and so was she.

"I need you to protect Xavier. please let him live, even if it means risking everything at this moment," Skytra explained.

I was so afraid of losing her.

"Skytra, no. Do not say it, please. I know what is going to happen. I don't want it to happen," I said as tears swell up in my eyes.

"Xavier will know everything one day. For now, we must do what we can," Skytra continued. I nodded. I never wanted this day to come. I wished it never did.

"Krakaten, I love you," Skytra's voice echoed through the room.

"I love you too, Skytra, my girl," I said, not being able to see much because of the tears.

By memory and my studies, I began to perform a soul transfer. A type of magic used in emergencies. It was time. I spoke the words from my mind to my lips, as I motioned my hands around Skytra's external belly. I will have only sixty seconds to hold my son before he is reborn, safely in a friend of Skytra's. I will send a note and some goodies, hopefully soon enough. As the fire crawled on the bed and devoured Skytra, Xavier faded out into my arms like a figure made of dust. He looked as if you could blow his figure away. He was pale white, with light pink hair, that glittered silver and gold. He slowly opened his bright magenta eyes. Though, with such a horrible background, he began to cry. Surprisingly, it was soft, or maybe the flames were louder. The flames came up from between the floorboards and were now slightly taller than me.

"It's okay, my little angel. Soon, this will be all over," I said, trying to calm him.

As I looked at him in my arms, I saw the cross necklace I was wearing. I was unsure when I might see son again . . . maybe this was my last chance. I took the necklace off and put it around his neck. The cross was about as big as his head. Right away, Xavier put his mouth on it. Well, he was a child, and I was giving it to him. Oh well. I heard a quick thud; I looked up, unsure of what to expect. A hooded man, wearing all black, even his hands. He stood like a spider balanced on the railing of the balcony. I could not see his face at all.

"Who are you?" I asked.

There was no response. All I could hear were the flames growing louder and louder. He jumped down and walked straight through the flames, toward me. He must have drunk potion, unless that was his talent. Slowly he slipped a dagger from his cloak.

"Xavier, I love you," I said kissing him on the forehead.

"So does your mother and the rest of your family . . . so much. Be safe my boy." I really hated this moment.

Once the man pounced in the air, Xavier faded away, and the dagger went straight into my chest.

I tried to get the man off me, though he was much stronger than he looked. He was not even near to my height; he was so much shorter. I could not believe that he was beating me. The man dug the knife deeper in me. I blacked out, and everything disappeared.

Chapter One
Xavier

I awoke, with bright sunshine heating my face. I turned over, wanting to sleep in longer.

After a few minutes, mother called, "Xavier, breakfast is being made!" from the kitchen.

I got up anyways and dressed quick. I love the breakfast mother makes me.

"Coming!" I call as I slipped on some jeans. I ran into the kitchen, jumping right into a wooden stool.

Mother giggled, "Well, someone's hungry".

"Very," I said.

My mom hassled a bit with the jam, mixing it hard.

"Can I help?" I asked, unsure if it would splatter everywhere.

After a moment of continuously mixing she finally responded, "Sure, how about you taste this for me?" she said, lending the spoon to me.

Just as I pressed my lips on to the spoon, I fell in love with it. I slid the spoon out of my mouth.

"It's perfect!" I said, ready to spread it onto my toast.

"All right, here you go," my mom said passing the bowl of

jam and a couple plates of food, so I could pick what I want and what amount I wanted.

"Thank you," I said, happily taking some toast, and fruit and putting it on my plate.

As I ate, Mother started cleaning up some dishes.

"Where is dad?" I ask after a moment.

"He's out gathering." It was another moment of silence.

"Can I go gather?" I ask shyly.

"No, honey. You are too young to go out in the woods all by yourself. Also, it is not easy. You need to learn a lot of basic things first, before I even let you go out on your own," Mom said, making herself clear.

"Can I at least go out with you?"

"Okay, what would you like to find?"

I thought for a moment, then quickly replied, "Oh, I know! Remember those flower crowns I started making?" I burst out.

"Yes," Mother said slowly, making it sound more like a question.

"Well, we could go out and find more pretty flowers!" I said, as if I were throwing my arms up into the air.

Mother smiled.

The forest was what Mom called: "A dark and scary place with lots of beautiful wonders." The forest was beautiful indeed. Mother said it become very dark at night, and the scary part is when you get lost . . . but I did not mind that when it was broad daylight.

"What about that one?" I asked, pointing at a dark red flower in an unusual looking tree.

My mother squinted at the flower in the tree.

"I don't think so. Many flowers that look like that may be poisonous." She said it as if she is warning me about something dangerous.

I grabbed on to her hand tight. She looked down at me with a graceful smile. In the corner of my eye I spot something glimmering pink. I turned around quick with a gasp at the sight and run towards it.

"Oh, look, Mom!" I called while I make a stop at the site, squatting to glare at it.

Mom turned around and gave me a surprised look. I examined the flower I stopped upon. It was pink and glimmered in the sun. The cherry blossom flew in the wind and fell upon a small puddle of water-like a mini lake. I figured that the flower can only survive in this type of water, rarely. I wanted to pick the flower up from the water, but I was afraid to kill it. I was always afraid of harming life. My mother walked up behind me, placing a hand on my shoulder.

"Mom, if I pick it up, I may kill it," I said with worry in my tone.

She gave me another smile.

"That's okay, we don't have to pick the flower up out of its source to obtain life, do we?" she said looking at me like I knew this already.

"What do you mean?" I looked up at her. She continued smiling at me and bends down to touch the flowers petals.

"Do you know what type of flower it is?" My mother asked me.

"Tell me" was all I could say.

"This is an exceedingly rare flower. And this is no ordinary Cherry Blossom. It's called the Blossom of Life." My mother looked back at me with open eyes and gave me a feeling I never had before.

A feeling of life.

My mother focused back on the flower but kept glancing back at me.

"Come. Feel the petals." My mother continued the flower, the tone in her voice forcing my hand to reach out and feel the petals.

I gently, with a shaking hand, bent down and reached towards the soft touch of such a sacred flower. It's beautiful.

I leaned forward and kissed the petal. I found comfort

within and I felt like I have been blessed with its sacred power. The soft touch left my lips and the feeling stayed within my heart for eternity.

"That flower will stay with you in your heart forever, and that flower will never die out. As long as you'll live."

I did not realize my mother was speaking again, so I looked at her, trying not to look confused.

"It will?" I asked.

My mother looked back at me and places a hand on my heart.

"Of course. If you keep your beautiful heart open and full, yes. Yes, it will."

My mother's voice was soft and warming. A tear dripped down my cheek, and that was when I felt so much, I lost my head and my heart controlled me now.

I almost did not hear a roar in the air. I thought I was dreaming now until I feel the ground start to shake.

"What's that?" I intended to ask, but by that second, we were running to safety.

My feet started aching with pain and all I could do is run, which made it worse. Trees passed by me, and I never felt this lightheaded in my life. We made a striking pause, and I looked over to a group of glowing purple eyes. Before I could feel fear grow on my body, we ran once again with my mother pulling me along the way. My mother trips on the run. I turn and pause.

"Mom!" I saw the glowing violet eyes once again, six of them. I looked back at my mother.

"It's okay, just keep running," she said to me, trying to stay calm.

"No, I won't leave you here!" I yelled out to her.

"Go!!" she screamed, waving a hand for me to go.

I stepped back a couple of steps, not wanting to leave my mother's side and realizing the beast was coming out behind her. My eyes became wide. Tears ran down my cheeks, while the beast came into the light. At the same time, I realized my mother was stuck, with her leg tied into a large tree root that stuck out of the ground. I could not help her now.

The beast was larger than I ever expected, and its six eyes glowed violet, three on each side of the head. Black scales cover the body and long silver horns shines in the light. Once its violet, transparent wings shook out, my eyes grew open again. I realized that this is no ordinary dragon. It is the largest dragon ever discovered and it had its own lair where he would sleep. He was a shape shifter and he killed anyone that tried to kill him or discover his home. He was the Night Shifter dragon. The black dragon stared into my soul and licked his pearly white teeth. It looked as if it was ready to kill.

The dragon's eyes turned a deep violet and prepared for his charging position.

"Run now, Xavier!" my mother screamed, pleading—no, praying for me to live.

I took as many steps back as possible. I took ahold of the nearest tree before I could faint. The beast gave its last look at me with a charging position that almost made me jump. For the last time, I looked down at my poor mother. She could no longer scream, and she cried in front of me.

"Please, stay alive. For me. For everyone. Stay alive." These words sank into my soul deeply. My mother gave me the look like this is the last time she would ever see me again. And it is true.

"Xavier, listen to me. We all love you. I love you. Live. Just live for me. I love you." She said into my heart and I knew these would be the last words to be said by her.

The beast charged with all his might and landed with its jaw clamping on what was to be my mother. With the beast's claws outstretched, I almost thought I would be the one to die. But no, the blood drained out of the dragon's lower jaw. I could see blood slipping between his teeth. My vision blurred of the sight and that was the last I could see.

I awoke quick and alert. The dragon sat across from me, with a dead body between us. It was hard not to look. All the blood leaked and stained the grass, yet strangely the dragon was quite pleasant with the sight. I was terrified. The dragon sat meters above, taller than the trees we have here.

"Why would you do such a thing?" I asked the dragon shakily.

His eyes glowed into mine, and he walked toward me with his eyes widening curiously. I feared the beast with its hungry eyes. Although the beast was starting to haunt me, I felt strong, but I knew I could not take this beast down all by myself, so I had only one choice: live.

The beast stopped in his tracks in front of me, nose to snout. I carefully took a gentle look into the dragon's eyes. They glowed violet into my soul. The center was a leafy, nature green. The dragon gave a look that indicated sorrow, but it was hard to believe that the dragon was sorry for anything. The dragon was calm, and it was hard for me to be the opposite of calm. I placed a hand on the beast's snout. I felt a lot now, but still, I did not trust this life. Just not yet.

I took slow steps, backing away from the beast. Luckily, the beast stayed still. I sat down on the side of another tree. I buried my face in my arms with my legs curled up. I started crying once again, with tears burning down my cheeks. I wished this never happened in the first place. I lifted my head a little so I could wipe my fiery tears. A white glint caught the corner of my eye. I looked up in curiosity. The dragon was gone, and there was a young girl standing over my dead mother. I stood and took small steps closer. As everything came into view, despite my tears, the girl was blond with light skin, wearing a silk white dress.

"Uh, hello?" I said randomly, not thinking.

The girl turned around and smiled.

"Oh, hello," she said back.

Her voice was light and pretty. I stepped next to the girl and we both looked down at my dead mother.

"So, this is your mother. Dead, right?" her ghostly voice and the word "dead" shook me.

"Yes. How did you know?" I ask softly.

The girl kept looking down at my dead mother. I studied her, and she looked even younger than me. About half my age.

"Well, I was walking in this forest alone and I stumbled upon this dead woman, and I turned and saw you crying so, I figured she was your mother."

Once she finished, she turned toward me, bright green eyes shined upon me that I have not noticed before.

"So, what's your name?" she asked me with another smile.

I took a long pause before I could answer. I did not even know why.

"I'm Xavier," I finally responded.

"Oh, you're an angel living in this area. I heard you hold a magnificent legend. Wow, I am Sarah. Also, an angel," she said cheerfully, letting her wings open behind her.

"You look like a nice person," Sarah said softly, letting her head drop.

I felt something warm and soft slip into my hand. I looked down surprisingly, Sarah had slipped her hand into mine. I started to blush, not because I was embarrassed, but because I admired her kind heart. I close my hand around hers.

A growl echoed in the distance, and I pulled my head up in alert.

"I don't think it's the perfect time to make a friendship," I said, seeing the beast appear out of the dark parts of the forest.

"Oh, no. Xavier run!" Sarah yelled, pushing me aside.

The beast charged, and I knew that I have only one choice now.

I put my feet to it, running. Running for all I have left. The beast started to follow my lead, and obviously the dragon was faster, so I had to run twice as fast. I ran, trying not to look back at the beast charging at me, getting closer. I ran deeper into the woods, with the beast on the trail behind me. Trees appeared in my way, so I made a few sharp turns to not get hit, and to get ahead of the beast. But for all, the beast was smart, changing shape to pass though trees and branches.

"Oh, no," I said, eyeing the beast, in the corner of my eye.

Realizing branches, vines, and other nature, this game of tag became an obstacle course. Within seconds I slide under a tree root, and a snatching bite came up behind.

I kept running trying to get away, find a hiding spot or anything that would keep this monster away from me. I can hear rustling trees not far behind, falling and hitting the ground. This beast was angry. With a millisecond glint, I found a place to keep safe, not anything I could stay in, but something that will give my feet a rest. I jumped into a bunch of roots under a tree, which luckily had enough room to fit my small body. I covered the back of my head with my hands, feeling the shaking of the beast wanting to grab ahold of me. Small pieces of bark and moss shook off upon me. I knew I could not stay when the dragon's growl and roars got louder and angrier. At perfect timing, I made a run for it. This time my whole life ran past me and the air got thicker, and I felt a burn in my heart.

The world around me changed from a bright day to a haunting nightmare. I ran past trees and jumped over roots. Everything became a challenge to me. Life is something we were born to, but you must work your heart into it to keep it. I thought my world would end. But I knew that would not happen . . . until I made my mistake.

I turned my upper body back to my left. The beast had his jaws ready to snap me in half. Within seconds the dragon's jaws came at me. I tried to run them out, but I was too late. The dragon's jaws went right into me. The upper jaw went through my left eye, and the bottom jaw went right into my left hip. I became blind. Blood went everywhere, and pain shocked though me. I screamed in pain. *I am too young to die.*

I fell to the ground in pain. I felt my blood still pouring out of me. I placed my hand over my left eye that was cut open. I cried. Tears of blood came out of eyes of beauty. I thought everything would fade away. Life felt like it was over. I cried from the pain in my hip. I placed my other hand in between my legs where the pain in my hip spread. I screamed some more with bloody tears coming out. The most pain came from my hip, and electric bolts pained me in several areas, some worse. It hurt so bad that I thought I would fall apart by now. I thought I was dead.

As I lay on the ground, I am sure the beast had flown off somewhere, but either way I was only glad I was not going to be chased any longer. I tried to get up with one hand on the ground and the other on my hip. I lifted my body above the ground, and pain grew everywhere on me. I screamed. I dropped myself back on the ground to let my muscles relax. I was left here all alone with no one around to save me. I doubted that my father would find me dead at some point. I reached in my shirt to grasp my necklace. I slipped it out. It was a silver cross. I loved this necklace so much; it always made me feel good about myself, or just made me at peace. This necklace was my only hope right now. I kissed the cross for my only survival. I must live.

I fell asleep where I lay, with the cross charm in my fragile hand. I felt something scoop me up above the ground, holding me in warmth. I still felt blood run down my cheeks. I was crying. I held on tight to whoever was picking me up because that is what I need.

"Shh, you'll be okay. I promise," An adult male voice sounded calm.

I realized it was my father's familiar voice. I guess I was wrong about earlier, my father did come and find me. I place a hand on his cheek, and I peeked open my good eye.

"Dad?" I asked to be sure with my voice shaking.

My father took his thumb and wiped the blood underneath

my left eye.

"Shh, it's me," he said softly.

"What hap—"

"Shh, just relax. I promise. Do not talk. Just relax, okay," my father's voice interrupts, with calmness.

On the way back I fell asleep, not dreaming, but having nightmares.

Chapter Two

I flashed open my one good eye. I was on my bed.

"I'm home?"

I was a bit confused. It was just me. The first thing that popped up in my head was an old box left under my bed. I slid off and bent down to go find it. The old and dusty box was still there, but it had moved farther back. This old box was a gift, but it did not come from my mother or my father. It was unrecognizable to me or my parents, but oddly it had my name on it. I slid it out and sat back on my bed with it. The first couple things I saw in the box were some bottles of medicine and a small container luminescent powder and some other things I could not name. But underneath it all was a leather woven journal, with intertwined straps. In between the straps was a black ink fountain pen. I decided to grab the journal and sit on my bed. I blankly stared at the cover. After a couple minutes, I finally start to write something inside of it. After about fifteen minutes of both thinking and writing, I have written my cover page. Some of the things I included were not only my name but my birthday, the current date, my age, my gender, some other things about me, and most importantly a note I wrote that read: With Love and care, please, do not read. Thanks.

After I read my work over again, the door opened unexpectedly. My father came in and stood beside the bed looking over me. After a long moment of silence, my father finally broke it. "It has been a month since the accident. I finally found you, luckily. I saw that you were hurt badly, so I carried you home so you can relax and heal," my father explained to me.

"Thank you."

My father did not say anything, but he gave a kind look to me. I turned on my back and looked up at the ceiling, I thought about the blood I saw.

"Blood is everywhere, you should take your blood-stained clothes off so, I can fix you up, okay?" my father said to me as he was glaring at the mess.

My father left me alone so I could take my stained clothes off. As I did, I thought about the beast and why it came after me. I had no explanation. Once I slipped off my clothes, looked at my left eye in the mirror. There was a large scar though it. I was scared to open my eye though because of the blood and pain that came with it. Plus, I did not want to see what haunted me most. I could not put on a new set of clothing because of my injuries and the blood all over me, so I had to wait for my father. I sat in the corner next to my bed, and I let my tears pour out.

Several minutes later, I heard the door open again. When my father walked in, his eyes went wide on me. I only looked away because I had too much attention already.

"Xavier . . ." my father's voice held worry.

I did not answer.

"Xavier . . . what's wrong?" he said with even more worry, walking toward me.

I still did not want to answer. I cried harder, trying to hold it in.

"Xavier . . . please—"

"I don't want to talk about it," I interrupted softly, digging my head in my arms.

My father bent down in front of me and placed a hand on my cheek. I cried harder. “She’s gone.” I cry softly.

My father soothed me with his hand on my cheek.

“Shh, I promise she will always be in your heart,” he whispered into my ear. Soon I felt his warm arms around my naked body, keeping me calm. I hold on for dear life, laying my head on his shoulder.

“Help me. Help me, please.” That was all I wanted now, help.

My father stood up with his hands grasping mine, motioning me to get up.

“Let’s get you cleaned up,” he said trying to make me feel better.

I stood up carefully with my father’s help. I let go of his hands and crossed my arms. I felt like I was dead meat. I went to the bathroom to go get cleaned up, with my father there to help me. As I walked in, my father claimed he forgot about the hot boiling water. I waited till my father came back with a large clay water pitcher filled with boiled water. The water pitcher was made by my mother, one of many pieces made and kept by her. They were now memories of her life that had passed.

After checking that the drain plug was in and locked, my father poured the boiled water into the tub, and when it was empty my father set it aside on the corner table by the tub. I waited a couple minutes before I could get in. Once I sat in the tub, the water quickly turned into deep, dark red blood. I quickly got used to the hot water and my father began scrubbing my wounds with a brush filled with soap.

Once it ran across my skin I screamed in pain, “Father!” I quickly yelled with the jolt of pain.

He was trying to wash the scar on my left hip, which hurt the most out of all my wounds, which was also made up of scratches from when I went running. It has been a month, and now I am wondering why they are still on my body. Are they scars? Or did my father lie about how long had it been since the accident? I would probably never know. My father put the brush filled with soap down.

"Okay? Well, I guess we will try something else then now, right?" My father seemed to be confused of my pain. I shrugged. I did not know why I had to suffer. I wanted to live free of pain . . . but God would not let that happen. My father began to look through the bathroom cabinets until he found a pair of gloves. My father put on the gloves and poured some soap on his hands. He scrubbed a bit and dipped his hands in the water. My father began to wash me again. The gloves did not hurt my skin; in fact, it was smooth and not rough like the brush. So then, my father continued with the gloves.

Once my father scrubbed my whole upper body, he used the pitcher to wash me off. He soon left me to dry off and change. I got out of the tub and grabbed my robe and wrapped it around me. I also cleaned up the whole bathroom, so it would not seem like someone died in there. I left to my room and began to put something comfy on, a soft T-shirt and my shorts. I wondered if my eye was better now. I wondered if I could see the the world through broken glass, dying off as its gods vanish. I stood in front of the mirror in my room. I was afraid, but I needed to know now.

Placing my three fingers over my closed eye, I needed to know by now. Though I already knew that even if my eye healed, I would never be the same, because I already am not the same. Sliding my fingers off my eye, a glimmering shine poked out. My eyes opened wide at the site. The sparkles in my eye shined bright, and all the bad spirits within them have faded away to sleep behind my pupils.

"Dad?" I yelled out loud unsure of myself.

No answer. Why does he do this? I knew I have made some mistakes but, he should not be keeping this up constantly. I decided to go find him again. Right at the door of my room about to leave, the door swings open, and the figure of my father standing over me, made me fall to the ground.

"Ouch." I thought I landed on a bruise; I still have not taken any medicine yet.

"Xavier . . ." he said casually.

"Yeah?" My whole body hurt now.

"Let's get some medicine in your body," he said, and now I am thankful; it is all I want. I went to sit on my bed, once I did, I noticed my father already had all the medicine stuff with him in an old box-like a mini treasure chest.

"Oh, thanks," I said relieved of my own pain. My father spreads cream to my skin and got me a glass of medicine to take, which I am thankful for.

"All right lay down and get some rest. Let the pain disappear," my father said as he finished up, and left the room.

As I lay, I stared up at the ceiling. Hoping to understand something clearly at last again. I closed my eyes, but I always ended up opening them a few seconds later. An hour of staring at the ceiling, I finally fell asleep and everything fell to dark.

When I awoke, I do not feel right. Maybe because something is not right. I go to find my father again. "Dad?" I found him outside in the garden maze behind our home. He was planting flowers and other plants in clay pots my mother made. Something my mother would do. He turned around to face me, I could see the hurt of my mother in his eyes. "I don't understand something . . ." I said suddenly. Just about when my father was going to say something, I continued, "I do not understand what happened to mom, and besides my scar, my eye is perfectly normal . . . . unharmed." I said almost traumatized, but calm. Calm, but shaking, I have a feeling of determination, but I did not know to what. Answers? I believe that was it. Answers to my life, how any of this makes sense.

"Xavier . . ."my father started. I dropped my head, because every time someone said my name like this, shallow, almost hallow, they started to tell me something deep, explain almost all my feelings summed up in one person's voice. My father continued, "Life . . . is not always perfect. I want you to understand that life is not going to be the same again. But I am sure you will adjust. Your mother is in peace and happy. Your eye is a gift to still be an open wonder to the world. It's a lot to take in but—" He paused and looked me straight in the eyes. "I'm here for you."

I took it all in while I inhaled. Then I exhaled.

I looked around, the vegetation everywhere. Sunlight shining through the leaves of tall towering plants. I looked back at my father straight in the eyes this time. "I am afraid. Afraid that if all else fails, I might fail too. That I will not make it above all if it falls under, that I will fall under with it. With all of it. I want to live. I want to be a free flying bird; able to fly and . . . . I wish to find someone . . . a mate. I want to heal my pain," I explained through meaning and through my heart which is almost broken or at least starting to break.

My father relaxed his look on me.

"Xavier, your words are full of meaning . . . you speak from the heart. You can help others. Though words," my father explained lightly.

"I am not trying to help others through words, I want to help myself first. And not even with words, with love and care and actually doing something than saying it's all going to be okay when it's not!" I said strongly but I was not yelling.

My voice was rather quiet, but you could still feel its strength.

"Calm down, Xavier. Just—"

"No, I won't calm down till everything stops haunting me. Till I find someone who loves me till they die!"

"Xavier, I do love you . . ." he said trying to get me back, but I was already backing up . . . faster till the point I was going to run.

"No, don't act like that with me . . . I can't stand any of this!" I screamed, making a run for it. I could hear my father calling after me, but I did not care now. I wanted to cry all over again. I wanted to be loved. I wanted someone to hold me in their arms and kiss me. I wanted to feel like I meant everything to that person.

I continued to run until I felt so useless, that I started to cry. I fell apart and started sobbing on the earth. Love me. Love me. That is all that went through my mind. Sure, my father cared, but it was not enough for me. I kept pushing him away. I knew it has wrong, but this kind of love was not my kind of love . . . I was just so afraid to say it to his face. I do not even think I ever will.

I went back home, thinking how running will get me nowhere. All I had ever done was run. That was because I did not know how to handle fear. I could not stand facing it all alone. I at least wanted to have someone stand by my side. I felt so depressed, I was falling apart. I was surprised that I was not completely broken. Probably because there was so much more horror to face. Soon enough I fell asleep and I already knew it was time. I could feel a light chill in the air. I liked the feeling of the nighttime. That is the reason why I like to keep my window open, because I love the chill of cool air touch my skin and tickle my toes. I wished someone could be my starry night.

Chapter Three

One year later, I was thirteen. It was late and I was ready to sleep for the night. I slipped into bed, trying to fall asleep. I closed my eyes and an uncomfortable feeling arises. I tossed and turned. It remained. I had the urge to take off my clothes. Personally, I was unwilling to. But I forced myself out of bed.

"Ugh!"

I hated the feeling that I was getting. I slipped my clothes off until I was just in my underwear and laid back in bed. For a little while I was okay . . . but for some reason I wanted to take my underwear off . . . so I did. For some reason, I felt comfortable sleeping nude.

Once I awoke, I slipped out of bed and examined the scars on my body in the mirror. I placed my right hand on my left hip over my scar. I felt different. I felt change. I felt like a completely different person. There were so many emotions I was going though; I didn't know how I felt. I took some steps back, thinking of so much that I bumped into my bed behind me, and fell against it.

"Ow!" I let out.

Life seemed to get harder by the second. I got up and sat on the edge of my bed. I started getting a mix of feelings. My vision blurred and I was confused on the inside. “Help me.” I softly said into the air. I wiped my tears with my eyes but, more came, like a storm of heavy rain never going to stop. I shifted up to my pillow to lay down in my bed on my right side. I cried.

A knock hit my door. Oh, no . . . my father was going to see what I had been going through. I rubbed my neck, tracing my fingers on young neck hairs and kept my hand their while, I heard the door open.

“Xavier, you okay?” he asked calmly.

I shook my head, but he did not notice.

“Leave me alone,” I said reluctantly.

I felt a hand slide down my spine, which made me shiver. My father came around and sat on the edge of my bed, by my feet. He gave me a calming smile.

“You want to talk about it?” my father asked me softly.

I sat up and hesitantly cried, “No!” My voice suddenly got softer, I didn’t want to yell at my father.

“I don’t want to.”

I cried so much that I could not talk about anything right now. I dropped my head and covered my eyes with my hand.

“Xavier?” my father asked softly, taking my other hand left on the bed, grasping it slowly and softly.

I shook my head once again, while my father took my hand and putting it up to his lips, kissing my hand.

“I love you,” he honestly said by the heart.

I knew it was true, all along. And I knew that I also loved him. But I was afraid to show that now.

I could not say it. I could not love him, yet I couldn’t push him away. I dropped my hand and turned away, so my father did not see my tears burning down my cheeks. My father placed a hand on my shoulder.

“Xavier, I don’t want you to be upset. I want you to be happy, not crying. So, please tell me what is wrong. If you do not tell me, I won't know, and I won't be able to help you. Please Xavier, I am not trying to embarrass you. I want to help you, Xavier," he explained.

I thought about the honest words he spoke, and I knew they were true. Personally, I am afraid to tell him. Honestly, I chose not to tell him . . . . another mistake.

"Dad, I don't want to cause harm, but I need a favor. It would really help if you would give me some . . . . time, space . . ." I lost track of my words and I started to nervously shake.

"Please . . ." I was able to let out hesitantly.

I slid my hand down and I let my father see the tears burning down my cheeks. My father relaxed, while I still was anxious. My father looked worried about me with his calming eyes. He nodded and left the room without hesitation.

So much went through me at that moment, I felt terrible for what I had done. I thought once again: I did not want to push him away. I regretted it, I felt bad for my father, but on the other hand, I had to do it. There was too much pressure that I could not take anymore. I decide to lay back down in my bed and let myself rest in peace. I got comfortable and I felt grief in deep in my soul. My tears where heavy and just even attempting to wipe tears did not help. I fell asleep for a little but awoke when I noticed how cold I was. I sat up and realized that the window was open, bringing in a cold chill. For once, that cold chill made me shiver, it reminded me of my nightmares. I walked up and pulled in the two latches, locking them in the center. I let my hands hang on the latches and I leaned my head against the center border of the two windows. I still cried for my life. I never knew it would fall so quickly.

I had not realized that I was naked this whole time (even when my father was here), but I seemed to have not minded. I finally slipped some clothes on and decided to head out of my room. I entered the main room of my home and headed to the stairs.

"Father?!" I yelled out once my foot touched the first step and fleeing up the rest. "Father!" I cried when I heard no reply once I got to the top of the stairs. I pushed the door to my father's room, running in.

"Father . . ." I said softer once I halted to a stop.

Tears ran down my cheeks as my father sat on his bed with still no reply. No matter how hard I screamed, my father would not have reacted. His eyes held grief and pain with tears of his own. I realized his pain and how much he cared. I realized the connection between us. I did not have to push him away so I could clear away my own pain. I should have let him help me . . . I was just so scared.

"Father!" I cried again with as much tears as possible.

I started to walk towards him, his eyes still looking toward the floor. With no attention, I threw my arms round his shoulders and cried so hard I almost bawled my eyes out. I wanted attention so bad now, I realized myself that I cared all along but just never showed it. With tears and love, my father lifted his head and looked over his shoulder to see me crying on him.

"Xavier . . ." he hesitated. "You know I love you. Please . . . I only want to help you, not embarrass you. Xavier."

My father paused. I let go of him and stepped back in front of him with despair. My father took a deep study of me, like he was searching in my soul for my feelings.

"You're a child growing into an adult—"

My face flushed red.

"And I know it's hard but please, I only want you to be happy..."

My father took another long pause before continuing, "Anything."

Those last words echoed inside me. I was tempted. With more tears, I said the truth from the heart.

"I love you too," I said faintly.

We both joined in a hug while I cried against my father.

"Don't leave me," I said between tears. His hands were soft on my skin and his arms were warm into my soul.

"I would never leave you again," he said softly keeping me calm.

I dug my head into him, showing my love. My father pulled my head back with a soft hand on my cheek.

"I will always love you," he said to me.

I looked deep into his teal eyes. His eyes held beauty and sunk into my heart. My father stepped back and held my hands, his eyes gleaming over me.

"Now, tell me . . . what is wrong?" My father asked calmly trying not to embarrass me. But either way my cheeks burned at the question.

"It's kind of the same as you said . . ." I was not speaking right.

"Um. I'm just having a tough time," I said not complete but at least honest.

"It's okay, I understand what you mean. Life always gets at its hardest at these types of things."

My father's words calmed me. and luckily, I was not too embarrassed. My father ruffled my hair and I put my hands in the way so my long, shoulder-length hair would not get messed up.

"No please, not my hair," I begged.

"Okay fine," my father stopped messing with my hair.

"Well, you know if you feel uncomfortable or something is wrong in that type of manner, just come and talk to me. That is it, even if it's that embarrassing . . . still I need you to tell me these things or else I'm no able to help you, okay?"

My father's words hit me hard in the head, realizing how much he meant. I exhaled while my father started looking at me up and down. My father placed a hand on my shoulder, and I looked up to face him.

"Xavier, no matter what the situation is . . . I will be there for you to help you, promise." My father looked me in the eyes with promise and a caring heart.

"Thanks," I said with a relaxing feeling.

After a while, my father started to understand my need of space and alone time. I explained all I could about how I felt. He said I should get out more . . . maybe that might help lower my depression. I have had practice hunting, using a handmade bow and handmade arrows. I made the set myself . . . though I had help from my mother. I was always good at crafts somehow. I loved sewing things together, colorful beads, and adding final additions to a work of art. I decide that I want to go out and practice with my bow. I got dressed in my hunting outfit, which I also made myself. My mother always thought it was good for me to learn this much, as my father thought it is too much for me.

I got my bow from under my bed with the arrows. Before I left, I let my dad know I would be out with my bow. Once he said okay, I found myself in the wilderness.

Right beside my home, there was a small hut made to, not only store gear, but to fix and modify them. I had not used my bow in a while, so I went there to make sure it was all right, and so it didn't snap when I shoot an arrow. I loosen the twine wrapped around my bow and retighten it. I also tie new string on to my bow because the old one was worn out from shooting many arrows before. Once I thought my bow was ready to go, I made extra arrows, I have always done this when I went out, so if I lost one, I would have plenty more. Plus, when I have a lot extra, I save the rest in my little hut just in case.

My feet ran on the grass with trees passing by me, I withdrawn the arrow locked in place at the string of the bow. I let go and the arrow went streaking the air, until the sharp point strike into a near tree. I ran into the woods for the arrow, having fun along the way. Past rocks fallen branches and other trees; the environment became like the lost woods. Once I stopped in front of the tree I hit. The arrow was rigged into the tree. I pulled hard, even though the arrow came out slick easy, what was left was a deep hole. Almost like my heart.

I stared into the hole that was left with scratch marks. The hole was shaped almost like a diamond, but with sharp edges and thin sides. My eyes widened at the sight. Then I relaxed realizing how much it meant deep inside, instead of another breakdown, I began to run. I did not know where I was going, but if I run, I'll be fine. I knew only to run with my favorite bow and the arrow gripped in my hand. I took another shot. I felt my memories come to me, with that beast chasing me to my death. My haunted scars.

With the pain of running with all of what I have left, I remotely stopped upon a rock wall. A cliff, I thought. I turned to my right to see a ledge hidden by bushes. I ran to it. I stepped on every ledge that came after like stairs built into the rock. Once I found the top, I threw my self against the rock, finally realizing how tired I was from running. With heavy breaths I fell asleep right where I was.

I awoke from my dreams, wiping my eyes. I raise my hands at the sight I came upon. Bright light struck my eyes. I winced and blocked light from my eyes with my hand. I stood up and walked forward to the sight. The morning sun shone, not only in my eyes but the whole cliff glimmered revealing a large pit in the middle. Waterfalls poured its beauty in, and my eyes widened. Dragons came flying around in and out of waterfalls. I stopped walking once I came to the edge of the pit. For some reason, I was not afraid to look down. Even if I fell, I had my wings to save me. I did not fly often, but I knew I have wings in an emergency. My wings opened while I saw the beauty of life in front of me.

I wasn't afraid so I sat on the edge of the pit with my feet hanging in it. I looked in the center of the pit where a huge pool of water settled from the raging waterfalls. Something pink glimmered in my eyes. I couldn't tell what it was at first, until it floated up to me. The blossom of life. It floated into my hands and landed gently. I felt its soft petals once again. "Oh, it's you again. My only friend till the end," I said to myself sweetly and kissed its shimmering petals. I let the soft petals slip against my lips, though the feeling stays with me forever till the end. The flower began to float again, but not away from me. Instead, the blossom of life settled in my hair above my ear. "Now you'll be with me forever." The sight took my breath away. I spent a lot of my time there. In a pocket on my side, I slid out my journal. I wrote the beauty of this place and that I hope to come again one day. I stayed almost all day watching beautiful beasts fly above me. But as the day grew dark, I knew I wouldn't be staying for another night.

Soon enough, I was back to where I was before, the forest of trees surrounding me. Just this time . . . I had my lucky flower with me. This time I wasn't running for my life. I walked slowly and got used to the environment. I knew my father must be worried about me, but I pushed the topic aside in my mind. I felt my instincts come up, and I felt like an animal of some type was nearby. I turned around in alarm. Slithering was silent but present. Before I knew it, a snake popped its head out of a tree branch. Its eyes flamed, staring into my eyes. It slithered around the branch till it could stick his head up to me. I backed up, but the snake slivered all around me. I couldn't go anywhere. The snake's eyes flamed staring into my shallow heart. Tears came falling. Why dose life hates me so much.

"What do you want of me?" I shook, while the snake took a good study of me.

It made its move by wrapping around my neck. I struggled and fell to the ground. It was hard to breathe. As the snake wrapped around me, my movement became slower as time passed. Soon enough, my body went numb. What was wrong with me? Finally, I felt the snake strike.

Chapter Four

Back home again, the last place I would want to be. As I stared out my open window, it was impossible to imagine a perfect life. Sadly, while I was suffocating, I somehow lost the blossom of life and I began to worry. The blossom of life was my only hope I had, and now it's gone. What have I done. All I knew was to blame myself for everything that happened so far.

I almost saw something flash till I knew it was real, flying across the air. I got exited for a moment thinking it was the blossom of life, but once I could catch it, my dreams crashed. It was only another flower that I caught through the air coming through the window. "No. It's not a cherry blossom. I'll never find the blossom of life again." I threw the flower back into the wind again, once my doubt grew, my tears shed and all the hopes and dreams I once had where all gone.

A knock was present at the door.

"Son," my father started while walking in.

"I don't want to talk," I mumbled, keeping my head down in my arms.

My father sighed and came around and stood next to me stroking his fingers between my thick strands of my hair put together.

"I know that life has become harder for you, and I know that your . . . well, going through some changes, but I promise I will be here for you. I don't like seeing you depressed like this. I love you and I want to help you." My father paused from explaining, and I finally lifted my head up from being buried underneath my arms.

My father placed his hand on my cheek and my tears dripped onto his fingertips. My father gave a depressing smile and hugged me tightly so we wouldn't let go.

Once in my father's arms I cried all my tears out on to him.

"Xavier, I love you," my father spoke in a soft voice.

My tears became heavier, and before my tears got to the max, I was able to speak out.

"I love you too."

As my tears hit vary heavily, my father held on to me tight noticing my strong feelings. He started stroking my hair again when I dug my face more into him. My father held me tight for a little while after and let my go with a hand on my cheek.

"You know if you need it, I'm here to help," my father stated.

I gave a short smile and my father's gaze relaxed on me.

"Do you want to talk about it?" my father spoke in a faint voice.

My father noticed my nervous expression.

"Truth is that I have no right to make fun of you," my father stated, making me feel somewhat better.

"Honestly, I don't think there is anything else to talk about since you already know my pain."

"Well, if you want, I could stay here with you to keep your feelings settle," my father suggested.

"All right, as long as it helps."

Soon I was sitting on my bed leaning against my father letting my pain settle.

"Look, I feel like I'm breaking apart. I started feeling like this after . . . . mom died . . . and I just need some hope or something . . ." my words got lost into nothing less.

My father started shifting closer to me.

"I know it seems like a lot but that's why I'm here . . . to help you get through life, to rise."

I took the thought to my head. I wondered when my life will become a miracle.

"I guess I will have to wait then?" I questioned.

"Not really. More like learning and keeping a positive attitude first," my father corrected me.

I lay in bed with tears, but my father was there for me just like he said.

"Thank you." I started to open at a good relaxing time.

"For what exactly?"

"For everything, everything you done to help me get through this tragedy . . ." I continued.

"Well, I wouldn't call it a tragedy . . ."

He paused to let me think about it first.

"I suggest you would not call life a tragedy if you looked more on the positive side," my father corrected me, like usual.

I talked with my father throughout the day and my feelings settled.

"Xavier . . . I think I understand the problem," my father started. And I waited for him to speak what my heart had kept inside.

"It seems like everything that's going on now has struck you personally. Like you can look in the mirror at your changing body and expression and you would just break down . . . like life has taken so much out of you . . . You really just wanted to hide that . . ."

With my father's explanation in hand, I could only say one word to describe me based on that: "Exactly."

I woke up the next morning with a tight feeling in my stomach like something had gone wrong, like if I skipped a day. I slipped out of bed putting on a sweater and fall colored jeans. I ran upstairs to find my father, but as I took each step again my stomach turned, and my senses told me something was wrong. Once standing in front of his door to his room, my feelings felt a drop.

"Father!" I yelled out but there was no answer.

I struggled to open the door as I am terrified. Once opened enough my heart dropped.

The room was full of sorrows: empty and nothing more. Tears where already pouring out of me, but I wouldn't give up, not now. I ran downstairs to every room in the castle. With every room I visited, my heart fell giving me more doubt of finding my father. Once I checked every room my heart sank deep, and my tears grew more painful. Every moment of life that I thought I had had disappeared. When I realized he was too gone, my real pain came.

I thought for a moment what I should do for my life. I can't stay. I need the blossom of life and I will find it, even if I had to use all my luck. I grasped my cross around my neck. This was all I had left and then I took off. "It's time."

I ran back to the spot where I was bitten. A pentagram was drawn where I lay in my own pain. I lined the mark with my fingers, every line was so precise that no man could have done this. A demon. I looked up from the inhumanly mark, searching for any sign of the blossom of life. I squinted at the pathway full of trees, tall grass, and other plant life. I looked around for other signs but what was in front of me hold the path to take. I started at it making sharp turns while am at it.

At one point I thought I saw that dragon again . . . but I assumed it was my imagination because I knew I already had problems. Did my mother really die by that beast? No, it can't be my imagination, right? Problem is that it happened. Again, I was seeing figures. Until the beast stopped me in my tracks.

"Holy—!" I let out, making a sharp stop in front of the beast itself, sitting down like nothing ever happened licking its bloody claws.

The dragon stopped licking his claws and gazed at me curiously like I'm new to him.

"You killed my mother!" I yelled, throwing a threatening gaze back.

The dragon shook his head at me like I was some idiot. I started to argue back but soon I stopped because the dragon did not take any offense. "Why did you come after me?" I asked to the beast that probably thought he knew everything. The beast did not nod or shake his large head; he only signaled me to follow him, and for some weird reason I did.

As I followed this beast that I seemingly could not trust, the beast was still guiding me, hoping that I would follow him all the way. The beast led me through the forest. I did not understand what has been happening since that first death. My mind spun at all I was getting at. As I followed, the beast continued to guide me, slightly off the forest to a cliff that peeked out. The beast eyed me as he continued to walk; my soul tingled.

"Why did you bring me out here?" My mind suddenly cleared at the environment. I started to give thought of my rudeness earlier. I decided that I should be polite and kind to the beast. I wished I had the guts to apologize.

The beast decided to settle by the cliff. I sat down next to him and noticed how he pointed his snout in the air. I looked up where his snout pointed. The sky was turning from a bright sunset to a grey sky. The first drops of water landed on the tip of my nose. As the rain began to make landfall, I slipped on the hood of my sweater and wrapped my arms around my body to stay warm in the freezing rain. The beast that lay next to me had gotten up and started to move a bit. At first, I thought he would be leaving me here, until he lay behind me, wrapping himself around me like he was a nest. I was thankful. The moment the beast put up his wing over me, I lay against him. I guess I should have been nicer at first, even if it was true of what he did before.

"I am going to name you Nightmare."

As the storm made its way through, I somewhat happily fell

asleep dreaming of sunsets, and my favorite . . . the starry night sky. I awoke with bright streaks of light aiming for my eyes. The dragon of the night began to get up while the sun began to rise over the cliffs that soar high in the sky across from our cliff we lay on, which was the lowest of them all, but led down into a deep and dark trench.

Nightmare made his way toward the trench and faced into it. I came over and did the same beside him. In the deep trench a kind of almost glowing pool of water lay far deep in. At first I couldn't tell what it was, but I saw it jump out of the water and back in. After a couple of more did the same, I realized they were fish. I looked back at Nightmare, who watched the fish intensely, without blinking or flinching. I knew that this beast was starving and could eat probably just about anything by now. "Are you hungry?" I asked, staring at the colorful jumping fish. In a millisecond, Nightmare stood positioned behind me. As I turned around, I saw his hungriness. His tongue slid around his bloody teeth. It was feeding time. "Go get it."

Nightmare launched into the air, with a swift spread of his wings, he swooped down and came back up with a dozen fish in his mouth.

"Whoa . . ." I said out loud with amazement.

Nightmare dropped the pile of fish and ate one by one. I watched, exploring the ways of the dragon. Once Nightmare ate, I found myself hungry too. But even so the weirdest thing happened. Nightmare caught fish for me! I didn't know how to react. I thanked him, but was I really going to eat raw fish? Plus, I was more of a vegetarian . . . but I did eat meat sometimes. I awkwardly took a bite and continued. It wasn't too bad. For how starving I was, it was still a meal.

After eating, Nightmare began to walk, and I followed again. He didn't go that far, as I expected. Nearby was a guardian pool, under another cliff which acted as a cave. Beautiful vines hanged down trailing its lovely leaves against my skin. The pool was beautiful. The first thing I thought was to just strip of my clothes and bathe in it. In the end of my thoughts, I did it anyway. I dipped my feet in. it was warm. I loved warm water. It was always soothing and helped me calm down all the time. Once the water was slightly above my waist, I was all the way in. I pulled myself in the water and I thought: Who am I? But then I realized I will not really find out today, but I will know the answer in the future. I might not know who I am today, but one day I will find out who I am. And then I let myself drown in my own future with my last thought: Life can only be tamed if you treat life kindly.

I awoke, naked at the edge of the water. Nightmare hung over me. Protecting me. He was staring, but at what? I realized it when I looked in front of me. A man, watching me. Watching my naked body.

I watched the man, fear within me. I found myself pulling back, closer to Nightmare. Once our bodies touched, Nightmare swung a wing around me. I realized he was trying to protect me, because he was scared for me. Nightmare not only cared about me. But loved me.

Without a word, the man bent down in front of me, holding his hand out to me.

"I'm not going to hurt you. I want to help you," the man said to me in a calming voice.

"Who are you?" I asked, still shocked, and afraid.

"Jacob. Jacob Soars," he replied.

"And you?"

"It's Xavier. Just Xavier."

Warm arms engulfed me. I felt safer now. Now and forever. My life was gone. But a new one replaced it. Jacob wrapped warm towels around me. I was glad he found me. I did not think I would last long in the forest, anyway, eating raw fish. From being out in the woods for a while, I quickly got a fever. I sat on the edge of the bed in my new room. Jacob was going to take care of me now. Now I knew I would never have the chance to see my father again, thank him, or even apologize. Jacob walked in my room with a hot tea.

"Careful, it is hot," Jacob said, although all I said was, "Thanks."

After I took some sips. Jacob carefully wrapped arms around me. I leaned in, careful not to spill the tea.

I came home last night, soaked and shivering cold. Jacob carried me, while Nightmare was to follow behind. Once Jacob got me home and took care of Nightmare, he gave me medicine. I fell asleep immediately. Once that happened, I thought Jacob must have given me a sleeping drug. As I slept, Jacob traced back to my old home to collect my valuable belongings. Jacob told me I would be fine here. I agreed to his word and took all he had within me.

I felt Jacob's heartbeat while I laid my head on his chest. I remember the night he took me in, that I cried so much he had to stay with me. I remember crying so hard, Jacob refused to let go of me. Now, that I'm not crying . . . I feel better. I love the warm touch around me. I wish I could stay like this forever. And ever.

Now that I was awake, Jacob said I should go clean myself, and I did. As I stood in the shower, I let warm water run down my back. I stayed in there for about an hour, until Jacob was telling me to get out before he took me out himself. He almost did, but I already was wrapping a towel on me. Instead, Jacob helped me dry my hair. I told him not to, but he insisted on it. So, I let him. Once I changed, Jacob helped me put my hair in place again. I know it may look dumb, but it was help. All my hair was grouped together like it is.

Once done Jacob spoke again in a soothing voice, "Much better, right?"

I thought back to my life before.

"Yes, much better now."

Jacob nodded.

"Great, you look starved. Now come on then, how about

something to fill up on?" Jacob's accent grew on his lines. I just didn't know where he was from. Something I should ask about.

The smell of food hit me like the roaring tall kingdoms that soar above.

"Wow, you cook?" I let out amazed by the sense of smell.

Baked beans, fresh salad, baked bread with butter, vegetable soup and much more.

"Of course. Why not? I knew you would be hungry after living in the wild . . . for some time," he said, suddenly cheerful.

I hadn't tasted amazing homemade food in forever. Well, it at least felt like it. I eagerly tried not to stuff food in me, but I struggled, even though Jacob said to eat whatever I want since I was overwhelmed by so much food.

I pleasantly ate, without too much conversation. I was too busy eating, then to have a verbose conversation. I loved the tea Jacob prepared. I took a sip while Jacob told me about his life, while I listened and took it all in. I love every herb dropped into hot, almost steaming water. While some people were addicted to coffee, I felt like I was addicted to tea, especially with some sour lemon in it.

After the amazing food, Jacob seated me in his living room. Packed bookshelves and left out books surrounded us. Anxiety took over.

Jacob sat in the lounge chair across from me. I could feel my self-shaking from a space like this.

"Sorry about the mess, I don't have much more room for these extra books, see? I was planning on selling them . . . how bout you help me? then we can move on from there."

My anxiety released, but in a somewhat painful way. I tried to regulate my breathing while I helped Jacob bring books out to his small shop. In and out the door, I felt somewhat dizzy. Once I saw Jacob come back in, I asked for a break. I took to my room and I fell asleep.

I woke to a soft hum, and I thought I was hearing the chirping birds outside, but instead I found Jacob weaving basket.

"Jacob?" I ask softly.

Its later in the day, and clouds block the sun, from what I can see from my window. "Yes?" he responded in the exact tone as mine.

"Why are you here?" I asked, even if he is watching me sleep.

Jacob took a short look towards the window, then back to me.

"Watching you, or at least to be near you, calms me," he said soothingly to the heart. "What for?" I ask.

Jacob took a deep breath before he continued, "You drag unpleasant memories away, and bring a new light . . . I think of you as if you where my own son."

The last words hit me straight in the heart . . . so hard, it felt as if it were swollen and throbbing. I place my hand on my chest where the pain has hit. I just could not believe it.

I let the flow of tears pour out of me. I was engulfed in Jacob's arms. I simply could not let go. Not ever, not now. I wished my father would have felt such a way with me. Maybe he had, and I just couldn't see it before. I wished I would have also felt the same back to my very own father. I wished I could love him the same way . . . maybe even better. Everything I had ever done, to own a father . . . has just vanished. It just wasn't enough. If I just have listened, once more, or thought about it over, said something to the heart . . . just once more before it all faded away to ashes. Even the bones cannot be spared. As every soul fades, the bones are left to rot. Nothing is left. Not ever. And when I fade away just like everyone else before me, who died of lost love. My heart will be the last, after my skin started to peel and flake up like dandruff, and minerals turn to dust within my skin, and its shining snow-white color fades to ash. My hair no longer shines, it fades grey, and soon enough it is pulled from the root. The bloody carcass burns . . . then fading from existence, bursting organs, the color of my eye's fades . . . and then bursts like the rest of my organs. Bones are left with a still beating heart which falls cradled into my pelvis. It crystalizes, and at last . . . breaks into crystalized shards of a broken heart. The bones fade into a storm of ashes.

My body gave a jolt of fear. I was shaking from the horrid image: fading till my own existence has disappeared. Throughout the haunted images flowing though my head, Jacob had me cradled into his arms. I finally felt safe, and what I felt most . . . protected. I dug my head into Jacob's shoulder; he shuddered and then pulled me closer. It was going to be a long life. Just us two and Nightmare. The three of us left alone.

Chapter Five

Finally, Jacob sold the books lying around, and even lent some to me. The shelves were more organized, and the living room was cleaner. I was glad, my anxiety much lower when being in the room. I even decided to tell Jacob about my anxiety. He said he had it too, but I had never seen him get the way I do. I felt much better telling Jacob about my anxiety. It can get bad, and I mean I could die. The fact that I was claustrophobic made it even worse. Even the fact that I was very emotional just added on top of it. I just wished someone could hold me when I was afraid.

I also asked about the basket Jacob was weaving. He told me he likes everything made by his own hand, even he decided to teach me. I loved crafting stuff like that. Not only did I love the result but putting my hands to work calmed me down . . . it was one of the ways I coped with my anxiety. And so, Jacob let me make things. I felt much better with my hands at work. Jacob especially loved to watch my talent in my fingers; I had done things like this when was younger, and now I was learning a lot more.

Jacob showed me every step slowly, and he made sure that I was not confused. Though, I got the handle of it quickly, and I felt already like a pro. The baskets were made of vines, leaves, and even rope, for strong sturdy handles. Since I was so motivated for more, Jacob and I made lots more, till our hands were sore. The technique looked complex, but once you got the hang of it, you would always get it right.

With sore hands, Jacob and I had some tea together; Jacob was thinking hard about something, something I needed to know.

"Xavier . . . I see you are growing up so fast," Jacob said to start it off.

"You think so?" I asked, surprised.

"Of course. And there is something I would want to work on with you. You know you should be schooled and continuing with education. What did happen?" Jacob's tone was curious, full of cautious wonder.

"Oh . . . well I was home schooled. There was no public school near my old home. Remember . . . it was away from everyone else," I said shyly.

"Well, I hope you to continue your education especially with me. And no, I won't pressure you to school publicly. I wish you to continue privately with me as your mentor," Jacob's strong accent showed when he spoke like this. Sometimes I viewed him as a completely different person.

"Okay, where should we start?" I realized Jacob probably did not know my level of intelligence so it might take a few before Jacob could see where I stood academically.

"Well, before we learn of your level and make the first step, I must explain how I will teach it to you," he said.

"Of course."

"First I want to ask about your writing. What do you do, or prefer?" Jacob started. I felt as if his accent was throwing me off the topic. "Well, I actually love to write, mainly in my journal of course. I have been writing in cursive my whole life, I don't know how to write normally. I like to write my own experiences, and I also have been learning a lot of poetry . . . but

I would love if I could write scientific journals . . . I have been reading some over the past . . ." I explained. I was a young teen, and I felt somewhat intelligent.

Jacob's eyes widened, surprised.

"Wow! That sounds genuinely great. You sound like you love to learn . . . yes?" Jacob became more interested in my learning experience, so I told him as much as I could.

"Yes, I love to read and write. I actually have taught myself . . . when my mother passed . . . and my father was left with me," I said, my voice fading at the part of my mother.

"Well, I would absolutely love to teach you. I want you to understand that I want you to show growth academically, but physically and emotionally. So, I maybe a quite different teacher than your parents," Jacob explained. I nodded, showing my understanding.

"All right then, let's get to it."

The power of knowledge and heart. I wrote two essays a day, including studying and reading on the topic, an hour of mathematics including sciences of magic and potions, two hours of physical training, one hour of meditation and empowering motivations, one hour of history and speeches, and I tried to read as much as I can. It did sound like a lot, especially the way Jacob put it, but it was not so bad. Jacob gave me frequent breaks, especially when my brain felt like it was on fire. But the best time to take a break was the hour of meditation. Jacob taught me numerous ways to clear my mind. It took away bad memories and keeps me in a relaxed state. The best place for meditation was out in the wild. I would sit, and close my eyes, while Jacob tells me to listen close. I can hear all the birds chirping and bugs buzzing and just the pure sound of nature.

~

I am fourteen, and I am starting to feel better about myself. My depression had gone down a large amount, my anxiety hadn't shown its face in a long time, and I felt like I was starting to like what I saw in the mirror. Jacob said this was one of the most important things to learn in adolescent life. Every morning I slipped out of bed and walked straight up to the mirror, without attempting to put on my clothes. I carefully investigated in deep detail. For minutes in silence of looking in the mirror, I would tell myself that I was beautiful just the way I was. It's just that I wished I wasn't the only one saying that.

A bright and shining morning came. I opened one eye and found the sun shining towards my eyes. I turned my face into my pillow. My sheets and blanket lay in a mess on my bed, half falling off and half on my bed. I didn't have such an amazing sleep; I could barely sleep at all. During the night I just stared out my window counting stars in the same position as I was now, lying flat on my stomach, legs straight and apart, hands tucked under my crooked pillow, and instead, my head turned to the window . . . the same as I woke up. From almost no sleep I felt tired this morning, I didn't even want to get out of bed, it was 09:00 and lessons started at 10:00 after breakfast.

I began to slip out of bed, and I felt something wet and sticky. I already knew what happened without even looking. If I didn't sleep well one night and I wake up to a bad mood, there always was a pool of semen on the bed. Sometimes even urine, but it was not so likely. For how lazy I was, obviously I didn't want to clean it up, but I managed. I didn't even clean it up that well, but I made my way to the mirror. Dark circles showed themselves under my eyes. I really did have a bad night.

Without putting any clothes on, I went downstairs. I was starving by now. I didn't feel like putting anything on, not even shorts. I did not care this morning and was not the first time I have walked down into the kitchen naked in front of Jacob.

"Morning, Xavier . . ." Jacob said looking up from drinking his tea and reading daily news.

"Something wrong . . . are you okay?" Jacob asked, unsure of what to say of my nude appearance.

"Nope . . ." I said, clearly showing Jacob I was not in a good mood today.

"I have told you before to not walk down here bare so often and . . ." Jacob tried to tell me again. Anytime I did this, Jacob started talking all over again and I hated it.

"Well, why can't I?" I asked over Jacob's words.

"It's just that . . . never mind. If you're just simply being yourself," Jacob said softly as if he was unsure of what he was saying.

"Okay fine, I didn't sleep well. That doesn't mean that you should accuse me for coming down here naked. Why can't I just walk around the house like this? It shouldn't be such a big deal . . ." I explained. Jacob was really getting on the edge of my nerve.

"It's just that . . . not all the time . . ." Jacob was losing his words as he spoke, he can't even make a face to explain himself.

"Jacob, I just didn't feel like putting anything on! I didn't even sleep last night, and I cannot even come down here and relax . . ." I yelled toward Jacob; his hand motion silenced me. I dropped my head in guilt. I felt queasy and sick. I didn't even want to eat breakfast.

"Xavier . . . don't speak to me like that. You know better than this. You should . . ." Jacob's serious tone and words faded at the sight of tears making their way down my cheeks. Jacob hated disciplining me when I cried. He could not stand it. The room was filled with silence, the only words I could form were "I'm sorry."

Jacob did not even say a word. He just bent down, open arms to me. I took a warm hug from him, crying light tears on his shoulder.

"Jacob . . . I don't think I can handle lessons today, I feel sick," I said, which makes Jacob let go of me and take a closer look. He places a warm hand on my head.

"Pretty warm. You should go lay down. I will bring you

something to eat . . ." Jacob started, but I shake my head, "No, I feel really sick . . . I don't think I could hold it in . . ." I said, my stomach beginning to hurt.

Jacob understood what I meant, and I was glad he did because I didn't think I could handle any food right now.

I lay in bed, cold. Jacob placed an extra fluffy blanket over me. He felt my head once more and went off and came back with a hot and wet rag and placed it over my head. I had a headache now, and I was starting to feel worse. My stomach was in an awful lot of pain and I felt like I couldn't even move out of bed. Jacob told me to rest, but I couldn't even close my eyes. My stomach pain felt like it was growing everywhere.

I tried to rest for a little bit, while Jacob stayed with me. I told him to stay . . . I just didn't feel secure by myself this terribly sick. Soon enough, I couldn't stand my stomach pain, I sat up. I started feeling nauseous, and finally made my way to the bathroom across from my bed on the other wall. Jacob said I would be fine and left the room for my own privacy. I was continuously gagging, and I finally start to let it out. I tie my hair up in the process. After throwing up like five times in a row, I made it back into my bed. I still was naked, I just felt so sick that I felt like putting on clothes was a waste of my time now.

I just lay in bed, almost crying now. Jacob came back to check on me.

"Feeling any better?" Jacob asked.

I didn't feel like speaking. I shook my head. I was biting on the edge of my sheet, about to cry. Jacob placed a hand on my head. I lay on my side now towards the window. He moves my hair out of my face. Jacob notices the tears in my eyes.

"Please...stay," was all I asked.

Jacob nodded, and then surprisingly, bent over and kissed my cheek.

My breaths were uneven, and my tears were starting to fall in my slightly parted mouth. Jacob still had his hand over my head, gently watching over me. I have a migraine now. My stomach started churning again. This time when I attempted to sit up, I almost screamed in pain, but I made it. I slowly made my way to the bathroom.

This time when I got out, I felt like I have been in there longer throwing up constantly. Jacob came over and helps me get up on my bed again. He started whispering soothing words into my ear, so I could relax from the pain better.

The entire day I had been stuck in bed, in and out of the bathroom, just simply throwing up in pain. I didn't like to look at it, I just closed my eyes hoping it wasn't from last night's dinner. It was nighttime and I was starving, but every time Jacob offered me something light and small to eat, I refused. I knew it would just come back up, just like the rest of it.

The next time Jacob stopped by was early in the morning, the suns were not even up yet.

"Jacob . . ." I let out softly, peaking open one eye.

My stomach was in the worst pain now. I couldn't even attempt to get up on my own no more. My hand was tightly squeezing my stomach; the pain remained. Jacob placed a soft and warm hand over my head. After a moment, Jacob leaned in and kissed my cheek. I let out a small sob and began to cry softly to myself. This time Jacob wrapped arms around me. He knew he couldn't lift me up to sit, but he still had arms around me . . . holding me till I calmed down.

After an exceedingly long moment, when the medium yellow sun was slowly rising, Jacob let go of me. My tears were damp on to my face, but I was no longer crying. "You know you should eat something, you're probably starved," Jacob finally spoke again.

"I'm just afraid for it to just come back up again . . ." I said unsure.

"Well, how about something light . . . and you don't even have to eat a lot, just something so you are not starving yourself," Jacob said to me.

I nodded and Jacob exited the room.

He came back in with a hot soup. Even though I had been suffering a bad stomach pain, I appreciated everything Jacob had done to make sure I was going to be fine. I really loved to be loved. When I cried in pain . . . I was also crying with appreciation to Jacob's love for me. I might not be his real son . . . but he was right. I really was like his son. Because he loved me like I was, and I loved him like the only father in the world . . . if only I treated my actual father that way . . .

Chapter Six

As a young adult, I was sixteen now. Two years had passed, and they had been full of life. I really enjoyed being here with Jacob, it was just as I grew, more personal things hit me . . . I felt like I was growing more far apart with him, but at the same time I struggled to keep the bond together.

As I dragged my fingers softly against the books I thought, every legend ever told was at my fingertips. Even though I had been here for long, as I dug through this old library, it seemed like I learned more every day.

"It seems you found more interests?" Jacob asked, studying my liking to the old books.

"Yes, wow there really old and valuable books," I said to be honest.

"Even some are ancient," Jacob adds in.

I could only smile at the thought, reading titles of these amazing legends at hand.

"You know, I'm glad you're still able to find an interest after you lost everything you had," Jacob stated. I sighed at the short thought, dropping my head a little, my fingers slipping away from the books.

"Well, I don't see the point for anything else, I mean you already said that I lost my life then, so . . . ?" I felt like a waste of time looking for answers.

"Just because you lost everything doesn't mean you have to give up on yourself," Jacob said to me.

I thought about the words spoken to me. It was hard for me to keep looking up after everything I lost. Family.

We both sat down in a comfy lounge chairs in the middle of the library. With another sigh I made, another rose petal faded from existence. Jacob Soars took a long study of me.

"I can see that expression you have on your face."

No more hiding now, I thought.

"It seems that you can't see the truth. Correct?"

"What truth?"

I felt like I'd given up everything.

"The only truth that stands in front of you."

"You're not even standing," I remarked jokingly.

Jacob gave a short laugh before he could answer, "No silly, I mean look at your most precious value after everything you lost."

"My cross," I gave a lousy answer.

"That too but, most importantly the blossom of life, given to you from the heavens in acceptance."

"And that means . . . ?"

"It means, even though you lost everything out of life, you still have hope in life."

"But I lost that hope multiple times," I took the conversation a step further.

"That's because you lost hope."

I thought about everything I'd been though.

"This blossom will always take after you; it's how you treat it."

I thought about all I have done. Running.

"Then I have to stop running and go through with it."

"Exactly."

Time to time, training to find what was inside me. Who I truly was. With my weapon clenched in my sweating palms, my breath began to slow, eyes on target. Anxiety rushed through me. It always felt like my blood flow or . . . the next thought was one I didn't like to imagine. And it happened. Well, slightly. I just thought of the flow of my own urine. Just a few seconds caused me to spurt a bit. I didn't mean to. I was sixteen, and anyone could think I should still be in diapers, but that's not it. It happened when I feel nervous . . . or anxiety. Even sometimes instead of finding a small urine stain in my shorts I may find a small spurt of semen . . . or even both.

I shook away the thought, but I almost dropped my bow . . . well, I kind of fumbled with it. Jacob gave me a look which caused another spurt. I dropped my bow this time and I fell to sit on the ground, hands covering my eyes. Anxiety rushed through my bloodstream and everywhere else.

"I can't do this, Jacob!" I cried out.

I could feel my hands shaking so much. I felt a hand placed on my shoulder.

"Xavier, please get up. Let's get that anxiety out of you first," Jacob said, offering his hand out to me.

I took it and I unsteadily stood up, in front of Jacob. Jacob placed hands on my shoulders, trying to calm me, "Okay, just take deep breaths. Inhale . . . then exhale."

I breathed slow in and out, and deep.

"I am sorry, Jacob . . . I just freaked out a bit," I said still shaking.

Without a word Jacob brought me in close to his heart. His warm arms wrapped around me, and I listened to the soft, deep, and slow heartbeat. My anxiety seemed to calm down as I listened to Jacob's steady heartbeat.

Jacob let me go after a little bit. I gave a weak smile Jacob accepted it and motioned me continue. I took a sharp look towards my target . . . this time I felt ready. I felt much better now. I put my feet to it, my toes pointed and precise. Bow ready and positioned in my sweating palms. At the end of my trip, I flew just two feet off the ground with my bow and arrow aimed . . . and I released. In milliseconds, the arrow penetrated the target right at its center. Perfect.

I landed with my knees slightly bent, one foot in front of the other, angled. head slightly facing at a downward angle, came up slowly, eyes dead at my target.

Once I fully find my normal standing position, I place a hand on my hip, bow clenched in the other. I froze at what I can do . . . "Wow," my eyes go wide.

"Do you know why I'm teaching you these skills?" Jacob Soars, my instructor, finally spoke again after watching my every move.

"All right, why?"

"You know I was looking for an actual answer, right?" Before I could answer Jacob spoke again, "You give up?"

"On the question, yes. on my potential, No."

"Well, good enough," Jacob decided to accept, (especially that he knew that I can be a bit lousy).

"I'm teaching you, not to be a physical warrior, but to think and act like one. I'm not focusing on the body, but the mind . . . and your 'emotional' heart. It may not seem so, but I want you to believe you can do anything, I want you to be strong (again that is mental/emotional), I want the best out of you . . . Xavier. Please tell me that I was helping with that . . . ?" Jacob explained.

The last question was almost pleading.

"Yes," I firmly replied with a nod.

"Good, I want to see some positive changes then," Jacob said happily and led me inside.

"I need a break . . ." I said heading to my bedroom. Once I got in, I went to the bathroom . . . I really needed to calm myself a bit, even if that meant just urinating, splashing water on my face, and taking deep breaths. I got in and locked the bathroom door. I just didn't feel comfortable with the bathroom door unlocked with Jacob around. Once I was settled in, I let my anxiety rush out of me. I felt like I was just holding it in this whole time, even when I was listening to Jacob's heartbeat. I just felt exhausted. I started to take deep and slow breaths and I whispered to myself that I was going to be fine, multiple times. After I was done urinating, I turned to the sink to splash warm water on my face. I let the water soak in, and I looked at my face in the mirror. I didn't feel like my normal self, I felt like I had taken over another man's body, unable to control myself, unsure of what things wander in this body. Diseases? Mental issues? I was unsure, but it sure felt like it.

After about fifteen to twenty minutes in the bathroom, I left and I grabbed my journal from underneath the bed and lay down comfortably on my side, continuing my journal from yesterday, doing other training. With every word I wrote, my heart latched on, becoming more honest with myself on the way. I heard a knock present, even though I knew the door was open wide. I looked up from my extremely cursive writing, which I started this journal when I was young, so cursive was like my life talent. Jacob Soars stood at the door asking for permission to come in and talk to me. Surely, I agreed, but closing my journal in the process, leaving a bookmark where I left off. Jacob Soars started giving a glare at the shelf full of pictures and things by the door, and soon cleaning a picture frame with a rag during our conversation.

"You know, I have always found something great in you—"

He paused his cleaning looking back at me with a smile, then placing the picture back on the shelf, "Something special in you . . . that not everyone can see, only certain special people . . . and I'm not saying I'm special, but there will always be someone out there that will be able to see that," Jacob Soars explained while taking a seat on the end of the bed next to me.

"Someone that can see through God's eyes, can see perfection in imperfect places." Jacob took a moment to think, letting me have the moment to really take those words in before a next set of words come in.

"Someone who loves you, that can see your sincere heart

that's inside you. Everything I said, remember these words and keep them close within," Jacob said closing his hands on mine for a while.

I took a moment to think before I could speak.

"What if I can't find that special person?" I said in an honest, innocent tone.

"Trust me, you will because God will make that happen. At one moment in your life you will cross that very special person that can mean everything to you, but you have to be careful because this only happens once and will pass without you knowing that person is the one. So, when you cross that person, the choice is yours. You can either accept and realize to see this person as special to you or forget and leave. The choice is yours. If you really believe in what I am saying, then be aware of this. Let your heart chose the one, I promise every word."

We found ourselves staring into each other's eyes like we can see our insides. Jacob Soars took a breath leaving his eyes from mine, letting go of my hands.

"Wait, who is this special person?" I started to ask, getting a bit anxious.

Jacob gave a short laugh again like usual when I said something that sounded stupid for my age.

"I don't know that. It could be anyone, and I don't mean that too literal . . . just with common sense, but God does not chose this person, he gives you an opportunity . . . and then so it's your turn to choose if that person is meant to be." Jacob started to stand up again almost about to leave.

"Wait!"

I ran up to him before he could leave. I latched on a warming hug.

"Thank you, for everything."

"Oh, my pleasure." Jacob seemed to admire my kindness, hugging me back, stroking my hair.

I almost cried this time, just latching on to all that I had. Jacob was my family and I was not planning on losing him too.

"Jacob don't leave . . . please," I pleaded, tears swelling up in my eyes.

I sounded like a child, not wanting his mother to leave him alone in the house. Jacob slowly lifted my head with two fingers under my chin. I looked him in the eyes. I saw his love for me straight through, clear like a window, but reflecting the image of me like a mirror. His eyes softened on me. I was tense, my muscles feeling like a frozen rubber band about to break. My body tensed from head to toe. My eyes were wide, waiting for the unimagined that has been imagined now. First, my cheeks were stuck tight to my face, my lips began to tremble, my eyes burning from not blinking, heat rushed through all my face. Next, my heart raced in my chest, beating hard like a drum. My shoulders were close and tight, while my throat felt like it was closing. Continuing down, my stomach was tight and queasy. With so much beating in my chest, I felt like my ribs were about to crash. Further down to my pelvic area, I was all tight. I could feel the weight of my upper body pressing down on my pelvis. My anxiety loves to roam there, and that's where I find it most often. With so much pressure, my genitals hurt, and I knew the most pain would come when my body started going back to rest. To my legs, it felt like rubber in the mid parts and buckles at the knees.

Jacob's eyes continued to soften looking at me as if I was the most precious person to him. I was. I started to cry, but I was unable to hide it. I was shaking now, unable to control my movements. Everything fell. Jacob did not give me a light kiss on the forehead, but it was almost arousing, and I was somewhat scared. Soft and light as it was, I trembled so hard I was afraid to fall. Both of his hands on my chin, I finally squeezed my eyes shut. Soft lips dragging on my skin. I didn't want to think about it, I wanted to forget this now. I did love Jacob as a father, but I felt like this was too much for me right now. I peeled open my eyes, my vision was blurred, I started to feel somewhat dizzy now. I couldn't breathe, the air became heavy, and it was swallowing me up. I felt like I was falling, and my vision blacked out. I fell not in love but because too much of it.

Cool air crossed my delicate skin. It was cold, but I was sweating, so it feels nice. My breath was slow and heavy. I didn't plan on opening my eyes, I didn't want to know what was happening around me.

"Xavier," I heard Jacob calling out for me.

I didn't make a sound. I didn't even think I have the energy to speak . . . or maybe it was because I didn't want to right now.

"Xavier," Jacob repeated.

I moaned, I couldn't even say a single word. I heard Jacob sigh in the distance. I wished I could say something, maybe make him feel better. I soon felt a light shake on my shoulder. I tried to open my eyes to see Jacob, but I can't get them to open all the way. Instead, I got a blurred figure of Jacob.

"Ja—"

"Shh," Jacob interrupted my attempt to call him.

My voice was hard and cracking up. I felt Jacob somewhat lifting me from laying down in bed facing the ceiling. My back was pulled to my pillow against the backboard. This time I found it easier to open my eyes. I tried to speak again, but I ended up coughing to clear my throat, but I started coughing up blood. Not a lot though. In the end, I was wiping blood off my mouth with a wet napkin. Jacob said not to worry about the sheets, so I didn't. I felt too exhausted to do so.

"Jacob, what happened to me? Did I . . .?"

I was finally able to speak again, not fully well like normal, but much better than before.

"Xavier, your anxiety came over. You panicked and fell to the floor. You were shaking, almost screaming like you were having nightmares. I just didn't understand . . . are you okay?" Jacob explained his worry.

"I-I couldn't handle myself. It was too much for me. I really didn't . . ." I said, my voice trailing off in the end, but by Jacob's expression I could tell that he understood fully.

"It's okay, Xavier. Just calm down," he said to me.

I realized, just by looking out the window, that it was later in the day. It was probably about 18:00. Jacob and I usually ate dinner around that time. Jacob went off to start cooking. He just told me to relax; I took a nap right then.

I awoke right when Jacob said the food was ready. The smell of food felt nice in a while, I kind of wished I had eaten earlier in the day. I sat down at the table, Jacob across from me.

"Are you okay now?" Jacob asked me.

"Yes, much better now . . . I feel like I was starving," I said.

"Well, eat up now, while you still can," Jacob said delightfully. I gave a short smile, showing my appreciation for Jacob being here with me. Jacob's cooking was always good, at least when I was here. My first dinner here was like heaven. Though I felt like Jacob would call me heaven, and said the food was just a taste of it. I partially smiled at the thought. Jacob noticed this and gave me a strange look.

"What is up with you?" he asked.

I could tell he couldn't hide his humor from me.

"Nothing, just stupid thoughts . . ." I said.

Jacob shook his head like it wasn't the first time this happened.

When I was finished eating, I almost leave right away, but I looked back before I could, all I have. I run back, wrapping warm arms around Jacob. Soft sniffles sound in my ear. Jacob was holding back tears.

"Shh, there's no need to hold it in. cry. Just simply cry," I said light and gentle.

Right then, Jacob had to let it all go. He just couldn't hold it in much longer. But I didn't blame him. I felt that way all the time.

Sometimes I think of what Jacob has ever thought of me as. Sometimes I try to see through Jacob's eyes and find myself. But what does he think? Deep inside me, I felt that Jacob would call me a guardian angel.

"Good night, Jacob," I said before I went off to bed.

"Good night, Xavier," Jacob called back to me.

In my room again, I lay naked, on my back, in bed. I let my skin be exposed to the frigid air. It felt nice for a while, just lying down, until I got too cold. I pulled the covers up on me and I tried to relax and fall asleep.

I didn't fall asleep right away. I felt like my eyes were just going to stay open staring around this dark room. I turn onto my side and try again. Still, I felt like I was suffering in the dark. I turned to my other side, still I couldn't fall asleep. After trying too hard, I just gave up.

I sat up in my bed and turned to my nightstand to find my blown-out candle. With a snap on my fingers, the flame came back to life magically. The light was wonderful, but a wave of depression came over me. With a swoop of my hand, the candle blew out. Again, it was dark and cold, I had to keep the light. I swooped my hand again, and warmth returned to me. I continued to do this to distract my feelings. Over, and over . . . until, without a knock, Jacob slowly walked in, surprised that I was still awake.

"Xavier, you should be asleep . . ." he said to me softly.

"And you should be asleep too . . ." I said as a comeback, but softly. I didn't have the guts to yell out at him.

"Okay fine, I came to check on you," Jacob said.

"And you didn't even knock . . ." I said.

"Xavier, stop. Now," is all Jacob said seriously.

I didn't reply, with one wisp of my hand, the flame disappeared, and I dug my head in between my legs, wrapping my arms around me, rocking myself back and forth, before I started to cry.

Tears started to swell up, I began to whisper repeatedly, "It's going to be okay; I am fine. I am fine."

"Xavier . . ." Jacob said softly, reaching out for me. And I cried softly, just holding on. My wings opened behind me and covered around me.

"Xavier . . . ?" Jacob questioned.

I shook my head, "No."

"Xavier . . . you're—"

"I know, I am emotional. Let me be," I said.

"No, I mean you're—"

"I am what?" I asked.

"You're glowing," Jacob said.

"What?" I said not knowing if I should be surprised or confused.

"You're glowing," Jacob repeated.

My crying slowed down to a stop. I lifted my head, wiping tears from my face.

"I am?" I asked.

Jacob just simply nodded. I slowly slid out of bed to the mirror. I couldn't believe it. My skin shone elegantly. My hair and eyes were bright and shiny. What looked like veins in my body glowed a light neon pink, matching my eyes. My wings opened elegantly, shining like my skin.

"Xavier," Jacob said again.

"Yes?" I finally said.

"You're beautiful."

I smiled at the thought.

"Thank you."

Chapter Seven

I dragged my fingers on the chiseled sandstone walls, dressed in rusting armor, feeling stupid on what I was getting into, but I knew on the inside that it was not about just putting yourself in a dumb situation. I was seventeen now, but I didn't feel so mature. Sometimes I still felt like I was twelve.

"Dude, you're in the way," I heard a voice come up from behind; at first, I thought I was lost in non-reality, but then it wasn't my imagination anymore.

A man stood waiting for me to move, making me realize it's time to step to the arena.

"Oh . . . sorry-I didn't mean . . ." I try to make out; instead, the man pushed me aside.

Well, I was trying to be nice. But then I realized, there is no point on being nice if you're just going to fight later. I guessed I might as well get used to it. So, I walked in with others wanting a competition.

I walked through the sandstone arch. Sunlight caught my eye, and I was entering, squinting, with a hand to block the light while everyone didn't seem to mind, staring at me. After a little bit, it didn't seem to be that bright. In fact, the clouds were blocking the shining golden star.

"Hey, you ready to fight, little dude?" a man called out. I

spun around to find a man standing by the weaponry rack, waiting for an answer.

"Little?" I said confused. "Oh . . . yeah, um . . ." I let out, completely in confusion.

"Wait . . . how do you know I am a dude—I mean guy, yeah, how do you know I am a guy?" I asked, wondering how this guy knows my gender when I looked like a complete female. "I mean . . . how does anyone know my gender?" I said more openly.

"Well . . . uh, your edges aren't as female . . . or you got the space for some balls there," he said a bit unsure. He was probably trying to keep it cool with me.

"Oh . . . uh . . ." I didn't know what to say.

"Well, besides that . . . what's up with the glitter and your hair . . . and—"

"I'm an angel," I cut him off, softly.

"You're a what?" he said confused.

I spoke louder this time.

"I'm an angel," I said while opening my wings to prove it, but I closed them up quickly so no one would notice.

But many had seen, muttering things to the others.

"Oh . . ." he let out.

"I really didn't want to have to do that, I wish the others haven't seen," I said watching the others behind my back.

"Well, I'm Jax, how about you?"

Jax let out a hand for me to shake.

"I'm Xavier," I said.

He nodded, and I release my crossed arms and gave him a shake.

Jax was hard to describe. But what I noticed the most were his curves and his cool tone. If I could give one word to describe Jax, I think it would be *slick*. He might be the type that was cool with anything, letting it all slip by. He was tan, tall and bald, but wore a maroon bandana around his head. I also noticed his head was rounded in all edges. But overall, I liked him.

At least I had some respect.

Jax passed me a sword, and he got a long and large axe. And it was time.

"You ready for this, bud?" Jax said to me loudly over all the commotion.

"I don't know . . ." I tried to say over everyone, weighing my sword with both hands clutched around the handle.

"What?" he yelled over the crowd.

"Never mind," I whispered under my breath. We heard a bell. And again, and again. Everyone was frozen. The gates were closed for entry. Metal bars held us back, but then metal bars were what held us forward. So here we were, trapped under the arc. There was some room, for storage of weapons and armor, but the crowd was huge and packed. I spun around to see unfamiliar faces. Where was Jax? I attempted to scream his name, but nothing came out. It was useless. I heard clanking metal. I looked up like I was before. The guardsmen were opening the metal gates. I braced myself as everyone around me gathered as close as they could to the gates. Like animals escaping human hands and back to the wild—their home. As people began to push around me, I was starting to lose my balance. Jax was gone, I had no one. The air became thick and foggy. It felt like thick carbon dioxide to me. I spun around till my vision blurred and I felt like I was falling. I couldn't breathe anymore. Everything suddenly turned black.

Cold metal reached my skin. My vision was blurred but coming slowly back to normal. Cold metal reached for my skin again, until I realized someone was shaking me, but very lightly though. As my vision cleared, I saw a man in a full armored suit, from head to toe. Though I wished I could see his face, but I couldn't see anything from the cage of his helmet.

"Hey, are you okay?" I heard the man's voice come from the metal helmet.

"Huh?"

I started to find myself again, the same place as before but I was lying on my back on the ground this time. I realized the game has begun.

I grabbed hold of his metal arm, just trying to get up.

"Are you okay?" he asked again, placing a metal hand on my cheek, brushing hair from my face. I notice that there was not metal on his fingertips, it was his skin. Medium gray skin. Unbelievably soft skin. I was aroused by the touch, but I tried not to. Then I couldn't help it, I touched his metal hand, grasping it tight. I nodded this time.

"What happened?" I asked breathless.

"You passed out, and before you hit the ground, I caught you and laid you down softly," he said to me. Next, he helped me sit up on the ground.

"Thank you," I said catching my breath finally.

He shook his head while checking that I was okay.

"Thank you," I said again, this time I sound more aggressive, wanting him to accept it.

This time, he looked me in the eyes. The dark cage almost looked as if I was inside it, wanting to find the light.

"There are no thanks inside the ring," he said.

Soon enough before I could say anything back, metal began to clank again, this time the gates were closing. He looked back at me.

"Go, the gates are going to close," he said in hurry, pulling me up and pushing me along.

"But—" I said.

"No, go!" he pointed out to the gate.

As the gate began dropping down, I made a run for it, making it inside the arena. Before I could look around me, I saw him struggle to make it. The gate was almost closed, only about two feet left, maybe even lower. He made a run for it and slid under but got stuck.

"No!" I screamed after him. The guardsmen noticed him trying to make it under. This time they lifted the gate a little bit—what I thought was to let him through was to find guardsmen catching him from the inside, pulling him back, and the gates closed. But before I could feel sorry for him, I heard more metal clanking.

I looked around. The men were ready to fight, but before they could, the other metal gates were opening. The other gates were different from our gates. They were the same metal bars, but the openings were taller and thinner. I also noticed the multiple locks that were used to keep the gates closed, and once they opened, instead of more contestants—beasts. More specifically, Bone-Snapping Dragons. Three gates, each one holding one Bone-Snapping Dragon. Three in total. They exited their cages, their bones rattling, and a metal helmet covering each skull. Also, metal covers the back of their claws, and a metal whipping tail with a mace at the end.

"Oh shit."

It wasn't one big fight that broke out, but many that did. The dragons were what started all the fun—though I was not enjoying it. I was almost terrified, but at first the beasts didn't seem to notice me, they went after those who wanted the attention, snapping their jaws on bodies that they can grab ahold of. That was a lot of broken bones. Until I noticed the dragon on the left was charging at me.

I tried to run, but the beast's teeth caught on to my leather baldric sword belt. It tried to rip it out, but it was useless. I was already being lifted in the air. The beast swung me around into the wall. Pain struck from my spine to my legs. I yelled out in pain. I was almost falling, but I realized, the next moment, I was clawed against the wall. Still I was screaming in pain.

Briefly to the side, silver metal shone. It was hard to focus because of the dragon's rattling bones, trying to take a bite out of me. Finally, I saw something astonishing. The same man whose name that I didn't know, who helped me out, escaped. He was running past the bars coming toward me. What was he doing? He had his sword out by his side, he continued to run until he was feet away from me, jumping in the air, stabbing his sword right in the center of the dragon's neck.

The dragon fell and released me. I fell to the ground, my vision blurring again. I felt cold metal hands reaching my skin again. This time I shook more aggressively, but not meaning to. I tried peaking open my eyes. I was shaking again, and this time, my eyes were wide open. I couldn't believe it. The same man, he saved me . . . again.

"I see you . . . the real you . . ." he said breathless. I already knew what he meant. He saw my wings. He knew I was an angel.

"Who are you . . . ?" I started to ask. He froze completely. He said nothing.

"I want to know your name . . ." I asked more clearly. He turned his head to his left, and the next moment, one of the dragons jumps on his back.

"Run!" he screamed.

I scoot back against the wall. Just watching. Watching him attack the beast. The dragon was about ten feet tall. Much larger than him. He attacked and wrestled with the dragon. Twisting and turning. The dragon trying to take a bite out of him.

"Run!" he screamed again to me.

This time I made a run for it. I hadn't realized what was going on with everyone else. Dead, bloody metal bodies lay down on the ground. Only a few other men remained alive in the ring. But there was only supposed to be one winner.

I continued to run till I reach the other side of the ring. The ring wasn't even that big. It was what you call cheap, but it was the only one close to home. The larger modern ones were held in the kingdoms for true warriors. I looked all around. The dragon taken out by that one man who saved me twice was out, down on the ground. Still there were two more, one on the same man, the other attacking a group of men who teamed up against it. I watched the fighting with minimal fear, but I was paralyzed by it all. The beast continued to attack him, until by the sight of the corner of my eye, I saw a man escape from the group and go to attack him. I tried to scream for him . . . but I realized I still hadn't gotten his name. The man from the group attacked him. A stab in the shoulder. He fell back, and the beast came at him. I ran forth before anything else could happen, before the dragon's jaws could meet him, I slid out my sword and stabbed it in the mouth. The dragon's bones cracked, and it fell back ward. Before I could freak out, the man from the group was running at me; with a swing of my sword I stabbed the man in the chest. He fell and bled to death. One more dragon to go. A handful of men left.

I looked down to see the man's bleeding wound, blood seeping through his armor.

"Oh my god, are you okay?" I said out loud.

He didn't said a word or make a movement. I bent down close to him. The other men were too busy on taking down that other dragon. I brought my ear close to the opening of his helmet. I heard his breathing, heavy and deep. I began to drag him. At first, he was extremely heavy, but then when I had a good hold of him, it was much easier. I dragged him toward the metal bars from which we entered. I laid him against it, and I took a seat beside him.

My heart was racing. I was breathing heavily too this time.

"Are you okay?" I turned to him to ask again.

I took a good look at his wound. He nodded, still breathing heavily too.

"Oh my god, oh my god . . ." I started to panic. I started taking deep breaths. I can fix this; I will help him out.

"I need to stop the bleeding, then clean the wound and then—"

"I'm fine . . . please. I have suffered worse," he said finally.

"Please, I want to help, after all you did for me . . ." I said.

"Please . . ." he started.

"No," I cut him off.

I looked straight into the deep dark cage of his helmet. After a mass of thoughts, I relaxed on him.

"Look, I know a lot about medicine . . . and I really love to help. But first I need you to take off some armor—your helmet . . . and suit," I said calmly.

This time he didn't reply. I really wished he could talk to me more.

"Please . . ." was all I said.

I could feel the tears falling down my face. I clutched both hands on his helmet.

"Please . . ." I said one last time.

This time I laid my forehead on his, and I let my tears drain down on my face.

Seconds later, I felt his metal hand slide onto my back. I pulled away to face him. Before I heard a word come out, metal shook. I stood and turned around quickly, guarding him. Everyone was dead, the last dragon dead. We were the only ones. "Come on, kill him already!" I heard someone scream. I hadn't noticed such a large crowd watching us from above. It was an arena after all.

I turned quickly to face the man again.

"You deserve to win. You can attend to my wounds after. Declare your glory. I am too weak to fight back . . . plus, I have won every time since my first time . . ." he said softly. I latched on to every word. I nodded, tears stuck to my face. As I made my way to the center of the ring, I took a good look at the crowd. They sat still, leaning forward, paying close attention to the angel who ruled the ring.

I stood in the glimmering sunlight. Looking up to the light, I turned to get a word from him. He sat in the dark shadows, bleeding helplessly. No word. And I took a deep breath, holding my sword to the air, letting my heart free. "I declare glory."

Crowd was somewhat confused, but seconds later there was loud cheering. I finally truly realized I won.

This time the gates were open from where I entered. I started to walk backwards toward him. But I kept my eyes on the crowd. I waved lightly to everyone, then I disappeared; I ran back to attend his wounds.

"You did it . . ." he started to say, but I was already dragging him to sit in a chair under the arc. He sat leaning back, like he was going to pass out.

"I need you to take off your helmet . . . you need more air," I said.

"I am fine, just attend the wound . . ." he said to me.

Without asking I rip the helmet off. I couldn't stand to see him suffer. And I was amazed to see his face.

"You look . . . beautiful-I mean amazing—I mean—"

My face burned red.

"Just help me . . . forget it. I shouldn't be showing my face to you, so make it quick before someone sees me," he said softly.

"Okay, I need your armor suit to come off," I said. He simply bent forward. I noticed a band on the back of his neck, and I started to take it off, gently pulling it down. I had never seen armor like this in real life. I heard of it though. From the kingdoms, of course. The armor was skintight. It showed your curves, and it folded in and out. It was made up of small metal, flexible plates which allowed it to fit around the body, move, and fold. Before I got lost in the topic, I quickly attended the wound. He was left in his shorts, lying back. The wound was not in the shoulder, but close to it. More of the chest.

"Black blood . . ." I said out loud.

I had never seen black blood before. I looked up to see if he heard me, but he was still wiped out. On my baldric sword belt, I had a small pack; it was full of medicine and things, just in case I came out of the ring bleeding. But instead of using it for me, I was using it to help someone who helped me more than ever.

As I started to clean the wound, I constantly looked up to his face, I also checked around me, to make sure no one was around. As I looked at his face, I started to catch the beautiful details that made up his face. He was still lying back, but I noticed his eyes were closed. He was resting now. His skin was grey, medium grey. But it somewhat glimmered. His head was somewhat round, and he looked about my age, maybe a bit older, considering that he had some facial hair. but one of the most fascinating things was his hair. Mine was a little past my shoulders, but his was to his mid neck maybe longer because the ends curled. His hair was thick and rounded over his head, and it curled all around, in the same direction—out. The color was my favorite. Black like the night, and wide stripes of blue—sapphire blue. I loved all of it. With his eyes closed he looked so much younger. I was sure I looked similar when I slept. Then I noticed his lips; they were thick and had a tint of purplish-blue. Oh, and now I stupidly knew the color of the tip of his penis. Oh, great. But the one thing I caught that threw my mind off was his eyes. When I saw them, I saw the night that I stare up to when I couldn't sleep. Next time he opened them I want to make sure of it.

I continued with the wound. I lastly, bandaged it, but I let him rest some more. I saw another chair nearby, which I should have grabbed, so I could fix his wound. But I grabbed it anyway, and I took a seat next to him. While I let him rest, I think of what to say, how to thank him, and the so many other things that were left on my mind.

After a couple of minutes, he opened his eyes again. I was right. Exactly like the night I looked up to when I couldn't sleep.

"Your eyes are beautiful . . ." I said.

He stares at me for a moment, then gives a weak smile. How wonderful. I smiled back, but brightly. I just couldn't hold it in.

Before he could make out a word, I continue, "It is the same night I looked up to when I can't sleep at night."

His expression came out surprised. I love to finally see his face and his expressions . . . it was so wonderful.

"Oh . . . that is so sweet for you to say . . . I really appreciate that," he said sweetly, like my mother would.

"I want to thank you . . . and I want to know your name," I let out.

"Oh . . ." he seemed to be thinking now, like I said something that was hard to process. "You don't need to thank me," he said getting up.

"But I want to thank you. You did so much for me . . . and I really want you to know how much it means to me," I said almost pleading.

"Like I said before . . ." he cut himself off and took a good look at me.

"It is my pleasure," he said, his eyes glimmering, with a smile on his face. He really meant it. I smiled back, but thoughts still wandered in my head.

"But I also want to know why. Why did you feel the need to save me . . . twice," I continued.

Without a moment to think, without pausing he said, "Because you are special," his voice was soft, and he turned to face the wall.

"What do you mean that I am special?" I asked.

He turned toward me again. "Because, you're an angel. I can see a lot of amazing things about you that you don't even know about," he continued softly.

I took a moment to think about it. Was he the one?

"Wow . . ." I let out.

"And my name is Xavier . . . And yours is?"

He looked like his universe crashed down on him. His smile faded and his eyes darkened.

"I feel that it is better off that I have no name in your dictionary," he said depressively, putting on his suit and picking up his helmet, ready to leave.

"No, but I want to have a name to remember. To remember this memory. I want to really remember what you did for me. With no name . . . I might . . . forget . . ." I pleaded, my voice fading in the end. He stopped in his tracks. I placed a hand on his shoulder. It was silent. But soon it broke when I heard tears and sniffling. He was holding back tears.

"My name is Isaac."

Isaac started to leave again, but there was still more I needed to let out.

"Wait!" I called out.

Before he could go any further out, I grabbed ahold of him, hugging his shoulders tightly. After a long moment, I slid off a bit, but I still laid my hands on him. His chest.

"I have never met a man who is so . . . attached to me . . ." he started to say.

I was unsure of what he was saying.

"Is that a good thing?" I asked.

"It is the best thing that has ever happened to me," he said brightly, smiling at me. I smiled back.

"It was nice meeting you, Isaac."

"It was a pleasure to meet you too, Xavier."

Before Isaac could take another step, I broke in, "Um, someone once told me that one day I would pass by someone who could see amazing things in me, but that it is my choice to leave it or see through that persons eyes. Share the beauty. A soul mate. I really . . . believe that . . . you are that person . . ." I said shakily.

Isaac smiled at me. "You really are as sweet as you look. Thank you for everything," he said.

"Thank you too," I added in.

"You're welcome," we said at the exact same time. We laughed after that. Isaac really did have a nice laughter.

"Oh . . . and don't forget to tell that person that they really knows the immortal heart."

"I will. I promise," I said. And we both smiled, and Isaac put his helmet back on and finally left. I was left all alone, my heart pounding in my chest. I had never met a man with such beautiful eyes, and such an amazing heart towards me. I feel that I am in love.

Chapter Eight

Walking out of the arena, my head all messed up, I felt pity growing inside me. What happened. I wished it ended different. I wished Jax wasn't dead. Wiping tears away and my wings feeling broken. These wings hurt so badly, I just wished someone could massage my back muscles that come out to my wings, which would really help right now. It was amazing to meet Isaac, but there was so much on my mind, that I didn't know when I will ever see him again. I didn't know where I was going, but obviously I needed to get home.

I found myself walking to a garden—not just any garden, the garden in the village square. By the looks of it, people put more money in it than their own homes. It was incredibly beautiful and more modern than the rest of the village. So, just finding myself here made me feel a lot better . . . like a rainbow after the storm. Letting my heart soar, I lightly dragged my fingers against roses and other flowers that popped up within bushes.

The garden was literally a maze. Tall bushes surrounded me, and it was a matter of making your way in or out. Pathways that lead to other pathways had an arc above. Below, the path was made of handmade grey bricks that were uneven. It probably took the whole village to make the Main Square Garden Maze look this good.

I made my way through, trying to name every flower in my head (sometimes I like to give myself some brain challenges to help me with my anxiety). Something glimmered in the corner of my eye, and I almost thought I saw it before when I was young, though I couldn't even remember anymore what it was. I realized I found my way to the center subconsciously. Then, I remembered that I used to come here with my mother when I was little, and my mother would be at the center and I would have to find her. After a couple times of visiting, I somehow remembered how to get there, and I would never get stuck or lost. And here I was at the center again. I turned around to see a young girl; probably two or three years younger than me. But not just any girl. She was skeletal. Her bones were black as coal and ash. Between the bones, there was this thick green stuff that glowed. It looked like a sticky substance. Slime. And since her long wavy/curly hair was black, it was so hard to notice. But with my particularly good eyesight, I can see she had streaks of dark blue or violet. Then I noticed the flower she held in her hands by the stem, studying it. It almost looked like she lost a loved one or something. I suddenly felt bad and wanted to help . . . but I wouldn't have the guts to make some stranger feel better. So, I went on touching the tips of roses . . . until she started to look up at me and stare, her golden eyes glowing at me . . . like I turned her on just by getting her to look at me. I suddenly felt anxiety, and I wanted to leave the garden . . . and automatically I started off to find my way out of the maze of bushes.

"Wait," she called at me, I automatically stopped, like I was being controlled by some other mind . . . hers.

I looked back at her. She looked as if she didn't want me to leave because if I did everything she ever had would be lost and I would exist no more.

Her eyes were like the last life that existed at the end of the world—she began to speak again, "I would like it if you would stay for a while . . . I am pretty lonely."

I almost began to ask if she lost a loved one, but something kept me from going on to that topic. I sat next to her on the bench and picked off a rose and gently rubbed my fingers on its petals, staring into the dusk of the day—the sky turning from pink and yellow to violet and a light and shady indigo.

"Thanks for staying . . . at least for a little while . . ." she said, giving me a weak smile. "It's not like I have anything much to do anyways," I said still picking at the flower.

"Don't say that . . ." she started, then she paused.

"What happened to you?" she asked me, pointing to my rusting armor. I had scratches on my face, and bruises under the armor.

"Oh . . . I was at the ring . . . and I had a crazy experience . . ." my voice faded out.

I didn't want to talk about it.

"Oh, hey, I go to that ring!" she said all excitedly.

"You fight?" I asked confused.

"Of course! I wouldn't just go there to watch," she said.

She really sounds exited. It's like when you meet your best friend who likes the exact same things that you like. I was sort of liking it.

"Yeah, it was my first time today . . . and—"

"You won," she cut me off.

"Yes," I said.

"Wow. I remember my first time. I was fourteen," she said thinking back.

"And how old are you now?" I asked.

I really was starting to enjoy the conversation. I just hope I don't have to bring Isaac or Jax up.

"I am fifteen. And you?" she continued the conversation. She was only two years younger than me. Well, that was fast.

"I am seventeen," I said.

"Not bad. By the way my name is Bonesella."

"Hi . . ." was all I could say.

"And your name . . . ?" Bonesella asked.

"It's Xavier . . ."

I said unsure of how far this was going.

"That is a nice name. I really have been enjoying your time. I want to . . . get to know you better . . ." Bonesella said.

She simply liked me. It wasn't a bad thought. But when I added Isaac to the pile, I was completely lost in my head. What was my sexuality? I really didn't even know. I was just making connections with people without even understanding my own feelings about it.

"Well, to be honest . . . I really enjoyed your time too. I wouldn't mind talking another time. It was really nice meeting you," I said sort of awkwardly.

I stood up to leave, but she places a hand on my shoulder.

"I . . . uh . . . I—fine, I like you, okay. I really do like you. You seem nice and kind . . . and I am sure a lot of people would appreciate your presence. I really like you," Bonesella forces out.

"I know . . ." I said awkwardly.

I turned around to see Bonesella grinning. She dropped her hand from my shoulder. We just stood there, staring into each other's eyes. The next moment was unexpected.

I closed my eyes, trying not to imagine it. But it was real, and I couldn't help it. The air became thicker. I couldn't breathe. I felt dizzy and queasy. I really didn't think I could handle anymore. Her lips were soothing, but I felt like I was just going to die here. My legs became weak. I lost my balance and blacked out.

I was shaken on the shoulder. I opened my eyes and my vision cleared.

"Xavier, are you okay?" Bonesella asked over me.

She leaned over me. I was lying down on the ground.

"What happened?" I made out.

I wasn't sure if I was dreaming or not.

"Um . . . we . . . kissed and you passed out," she said in a shaky tone.

I sat up and noticed that my hands were shaking rapidly.

"Anxiety," I said.

"What?" I didn't think she heard me right.

"I have anxiety . . . and sometimes I panic . . . and black out," I tried to explain.

I noticed that my tone too was shaky.

"Oh, I am sorry. I didn't know. Are you okay though?" Bonesella asked to make sure I was okay.

"Oh, it's fine. I am better now."

Without a word Bonesella helped me up. We sat at the bench again.

"I am sorry," Bonesella said softly.

"No, it's okay. I just need to . . . catch my breath," I said shallowly.

She gave me a calm look. Inside, I didn't blame her. Outside, I felt weak.

"I really need to get home . . ." I started to say with a hand on my face.

"I could . . . maybe walk with you . . ." she said soft and shaky.

"No, thank you. I am fine," I said quickly, but softly.

Before I could leave, Bonesella said, "It was nice meeting you."

"You too."

I subconsciously found my way out. It was late. I felt stupid . . . and I felt like I needed help. But wherever help was, it was too far to reach from here. I nearly cried on the way back, tears swelling up . . . I tried all I could to stop them. I really hoped I wouldn't see her again . . . but the more I thought about it the more depressed I became. Isaac also roamed my mind. On the way back I was trying to think of something else to cover up the thought. Though honestly, I was wondering though the trees on my own. I thought about my life at where it stood. I didn't even think that I will see Isaac again. Every night I lived through . . . I cried. And I was never sure if I would live though the next. Most nights I dreamed of finding someone who cares . . . pretty much the love of my life. Though I made no imaginary descriptions of such a person. Mainly because this person could be practically anyone . . . obviously not those who bully me . . . but someone who's heart feels mine. Isaac.

Honestly, I never thought about gender when it came to love someone . . . mostly because I didn't care what it would be. I only cared if I loved that person or not. Man or woman or whatever they may be, if it is love, it is love. So, I was stuck between two.

I finally wandered to my home and went straight to my room without saying anything. I began to write my journal entry for June 6, 2800. I soon finished up my journal with some feelings I had kept inside me today. After that I just went to bed without warning.

I finally awoke to the bright sun from my dreams. Honestly, I thought I would have nightmares . . . but instead I dreamed about what I usually dreamed: someone out there loves me. Isaac. I sat up on my bed and started to think what just happened. I blush at the thought. My face burns red. I was falling in love. Torn. I didn't mind Bonesella, but there was something about Isaac that latches on to my heart. His act towards me. Saving me twice. Allowing me to heal his wounds. Allowing me to win. And yet I kissed the wrong person. I started to cry softly.

I slipped on a pair of shorts and a sweater and before I walked out of my room to the living room, my tears were wet to my face.

"Good morning," I said to Jacob who was in the living room sitting on a lounge chair sipping up tea.

"Good morning, Xavier. How was your sleep?"

I looked at him as if he was staring at my nude body. Honestly, I never heard anyone ask me any such a question.

"Um . . . okay I guess—Why are you asking anyways?"

I already began to feel awkward this morning.

"Well, . . . you looked as if you had a bit of an uncomfortable sleep . . .," he said casually taking another sip of his tea without looking up from the ground.

"You mean you were watching me sleep!?!"

"Well, actually I only wanted to say goodnight . . . but you were already deep."

I crossed my arms tightly about to throw a fist—but something about Jacob's calm manner of sipping tea made me stop with a sigh. I decided to sit in the other lounge chair across from him.

Jacob finally put his tea down and began to speak, looking at me finally.

"So, talk to me Xavier, what is bothering you?"

"Everything . . ." I lied. Nothing was bothering me that was present, only what happened yesterday was taking over my mind.

"Please be honest. Xavier, I know you are . . ."

He wasn't lying. I was always honest unless something bothered me bad. Usually something I didn't want to talk about because it brings bad memories.

I just stared into my lap. I didn't think I have the guts to say it. My heart was torn in two. He just stared out the window like he was obsessed with the birds.

I started to cry softly again. I hated the thought of love torn between two. But as I think about it, the only one I really love was Isaac.

After a long silence, I said fine, but I was still depressed. And so, I relaxed back in the chair and talked away ignoring the fact Jacob was there listening to me.

I started telling him about Isaac and how he saved me twice, and the weird incident with Bonesella. Jacob ended up staring into my eyes when I told him that she kissed me. I tried to look away, but it was hard not to realize what just happened.

". . . and now I feel torn. I really feel bad for Isaac though. I wish I could see him again . . ."

I continued. I already felt uncomfortable by it; I didn't want to speak much anymore.

After a while Jacob finally said, "What does your heart tell you?" His tone was soft.

I almost didn't hear him.

"I don't know . . ." I started to say.

"No, your heart. Speak from your heart not your brain," he said.

"Isaac. "My heart said Isaac . . ." I said softly. I couldn't believe it.

After a long moment of silence filled with thought that I had to speak again because the silence hurt.

"You know . . . for how long I've been here and that I'm older now . . . I wish I could just live out on my own . . . find someone just for me . . . . someone who actually cares and loves me over everything . . . that's what I want." Tears started swelling up at my words.

Quickly Jacob responded, "So, that's what you want then, go ahead."

"Are you serious?!"

I looked over at Jacob. He was so calm . . . but he made the best out of my day. I was smiling like crazy now. Jacob gave me a quick short nod.

"Well, you are going to have to work for it," he said.

I still couldn't believe he was being serious.

I ran up to him, giving him the hug of my life. I was practically crying now. Tears ran down my cheeks, with every moment of life I had left in me.

"Oh, thank you so much! I've been dreaming about it for so long!!! Oh, I had this dream last night too . . ." I exclaimed.

I was too excited; I could barely speak.

"Dream . . .?"

I let go. Jacob seemed to wonder what I've been dreaming for so long now.

"What is this dream of yours . . ." Jacob asked with complete interest.

I began awkwardly my story, and I felt weird about the dreams I have at night . . . . but I was still willing to be honest.

"Well, it has been going on for a while. I've been having dreams about what you've said, about love and that special person . . ."

I began to sit down again, and I went straight into the story, with Jacob's eyes at full focus.

"Well, last night . . . and some other nights, I had a dream about it. About someone who really loves me . . . . someone who cares . . . . someone who can see inside of me, and all the pain I went through . . . and take it all away for good . . ."

I broke out in tears then, the story was embarrassing, and I was afraid to continue. I began to chew lightly on the edge of my sweater's sleeve, where my hand was in a slight fist, fingers partially in my mouth, full of my own tears.

Jacob took a long look at me. The tears down my face. The anxiety in my eyes. My body, shivering. I was nothing but a bunny afraid of the woods.

"Xavier . . ."

Jacob got up from his seat and bent down in front of me. He pulled my hands down, his hands grasped around mine. His eyes glimmering in mine.

"Xavier . . . trust me. I understand the pain. The pain of your dead fam—"

"No! you don't understand! You weren't there when they died!" I cried in pain. I was already on the far side of the room, crying against the wall.

"Xavi—"

"Don't call my name! I don't want to hear it!" I was already dead inside.

My heart shattered across the floor. Jacob calling my name. I'm long gone by now and these dreams will forever be locked inside me.

I ran into my room and shut the door. I made sure it was

locked, and I let my tears fall across the floor to the bed. For some reason, I began to take off my clothes. I just needed my time alone. I wanted to forget about the world and be myself with the person I love. Isaac. But by now I already know that won't happen.

I lay in bed crying all the tears that I had left to shed. All the memories. The nightmares. My dreams were all shattered in the beginning. As I cried, I expected another knock on the door from Jacob . . . but none came. I waited another hour. Nothing. Even though I should care about Jacob, I felt better with a little time alone away from him. He's helpful to have around, but that didn't mean he was always right. I suddenly began to worry. After all the pain, I felt like I pushed him to far away. I cried harder, but this time it was because I was blaming myself for everything. Everything I had done to push Jacob away. I wished I could go back and fix my mistakes, but I know I wouldn't be able to.

"Jacob!" I cried out loud.

Tears were streaming down my face like all the streams were draining themselves out. No answer came calling. I wanted to chase after Jacob, but I was afraid of him seeing me like this. My pain. I wrapped my arms around my naked body and wait for Jacob to come in and ask what was wrong, and I'll reply with an extremely emotional apology. But it never came.

I soon couldn't handle waiting any longer, so I left the room to go find Jacob . . . while I was still completely naked. I began to rush around the house worried and trying to hold on to what I have left.

"Jacob!" I yelled.

No reply. I rushed upstairs till I made it to Jacob's room, then I froze. The door was open, and Jacob was sitting at the edge of the bed, crying to himself silently. I saw an image of my father the moment I noticed his tears. It was right before the time I lost him. The last time I got to see my father's face ever again.

"Jacob! Don't ignore me . . . Please Jacob!" He didn't said a word, nor did he look over to me. I ran up to him and I started crying into the back of his shoulder.

"Jacob . . . don't do this to me . . . I'm sorry for what I've done. Punish me any way you want . . . I just want you to forgive me . . . . please?"

Instead of giving me words, Jacob leaned his head against mine. My heart bloomed. In return, I hugged his shoulders. For a long moment we stayed still, until my heart started to get exited again. I let go, and I stood in front of Jacob, wanting him to look at me in the eyes. I was ready to apologize.

Jacob looked up at me, but I could tell that he was trying not to look at me in the wrong area, since I was naked . . . but I was glad he gave no comment about it. Before I could apologize Jacob began to speak for the first time in forever.

"Xavier, you are the most amazing, kind and loving angel there is . . . I just wish you could be the happiest angel too."

I took in his words. I never really considered myself an angel. I was never sure of my identity, but they said I'm an angel from heaven. I'm not directly associated with heaven in anyway nor have I ever been. Though the thought of being one brings me joy. No one ever calls me an angel, the first and last to do so were my parents.

"Wow, I've never saw myself like that before . . ."

The thought began to sink into my heart.

"Well, you should. I've always thought of you like that. A beautiful wonder to the world that is. I just wish you could see that. How utterly amazing you are. You might not see it now but trust me you will see it in the eyes of that special person you have always dreamed about. Trust me . . . and don't forget my word."

Jacob seemed to have eased down about what has happened, and now he's telling me about the gifts of God, that were willing to fall down on me . . . with joy.

"Jacob . . ."

I wanted to be serious now, but still, tears started swelling up again.

"I wanted to apologize to you, but I was so worried and upset . . . I could not handle it anymore. I'm sorry for doing that to you. For pushing you away, just like I did to my father. I felt like I could not accept it. I could not accept my pain. After my mother passed, I was left in pain. I didn't want to talk about it with my father. I tried to keep it in the whole time. Until I trusted his word at the last time . . . .and he was gone. I never saw him again. I wish I could have just trusted him once before it was all gone . . . and now I don't have that. A chance. A father. Trust. I've lost it all."

I stared down at the floor, why have I been so foolish so long. My thoughts wandered back to the times I remembered that I could not trust my father with myself. My own body. My stare wasn't at the floor anymore . . . but I couldn't keep my eyes from staring at my own penis. A hand relaxed on my shoulder, and I suddenly almost jump. I found Jacob's eyes marked right on mine. My face burned a little, but not a lot because I knew guilt was more important right now than embarrassment.

"Xavier . . ." Jacob said to me.

"Yes . . ." I couldn't keep the thought away.

I already felt overwhelmed. As my fingers dragged down to the thought trapped within . . . my hand was caught by Jacob's, before I could fill myself with anxiety and grasp my hand around my penis. It was always stupid for me to do, but sadly this had become a habit for me when anxiety come back to me, or whenever I was afraid or uncomfortable. Though while I thought about my unpleasant habits, suddenly felt glad for my hand to be caught by Jacob's hand . . . or else I would have made a bad embarrassment. Jacob continued, "I really want you to listen to what I said. I know it's hard after all has happened to you . . . but I need you to hold on until you catch that soulmate of yours. Promise you will try to be happy . . . just for me?" Jacob's words were warming, and my cheeks felt like roses. I leaned in, hugging Jacob's body, letting his warmth come into my soul.

"I promise to try my best to be happy . . . though I can't be happy all the time. I'm going to need you to accept my pain when it comes . . . remind me the beauty of life and tell me it's all going to be okay and that you will promise forever that I will catch and hold on to my soulmate one day," my words were soft and light.

A small smile breaches across my face.

"I promise," Jacob replied.

I trusted his word, and I trusted his heart at the fullest.

"Are you ready to continue your story?"

Jacob and I went back to my room and sat on the edge of the bed ready for my story.

I was thinking on where I should start off, but I didn't want the story to turn into the nightmare that happened earlier. So, I started with something simple.

"I feel like for so long I've wanted to hold someone's hand, tell them my long-held feelings of depression and lost love, and..."

I took a moment of thought before I said it. Should I say it? I knew I was afraid to say so, but I had kept this in for so long, it was a secret never told. I decided to go with it because Jacob started to look as if he was getting impatient, and so I continued.

"I have always wanted to have . . . sex with someone . . . and in these dreams, it comes up so often . . . mostly with a man," I said uneasily, and unsure of Jacob's expression and his thoughts right now.

"I have been dreaming a lot about it and sometimes I for some reason I can't imagine myself with a woman and I don't know why. I can't help the thought. Though I doubt I would get the chance to do that with someone I love . . ."

I felt like I had ripped a hole in my heart. I wanted to stitch it back up, but I didn't think I could.

I was glad the silence did not last long because Jacob began to speak . . . but at the same time I was afraid of what he was going to say about it.

"Xavier . . . that's . . . different of you—"

"No, it's not. I have wanted it all my life and I get dreams about it and the next thing was when I wake up there is already a pool of semen on the bed and that is what I'm in the mood for. But instead I try my best to keep the urge in and I clean up my mess without a word. Trust me . . . my dreams don't lie."

I couldn't believe what I said. I had kept that secret inside of me for so long, I felt like I just exposed my naked body to everyone. Silence grew . . . the only words that were made were our thoughts trying to block out the other's. I stared down at myself, but I have changed back into my clothes before I let Jacob come in and have a seat on the bed with me. My bad habit was coming back to me, but I couldn't do anything about it. It hurt but I couldn't risk unzipping the fly of my pants and taking out my stress reliever. I couldn't help it no more. I placed my hands over my eyes and leaned back till I lay back on the bed. Jacob looked at me like he didn't notice my stress.

"Xavier, are you okay?" Jacob asked nicely, probably trying not to piss me off.

"I'm fine. It's just that every time I think about it, my bad habits seem to take over my body and I'm afraid that..." I start, feeling depressed again. Jacob placed a hand on my forehead and moved my hair from my face.

I reached my hand out to Jacob and he grasped it. "I don't want to hurt myself, Jacob . . . but sometimes I can't help myself . . . and I masturbate . . . and I do other stupid things, and that's why I also don't like it so much when you watch me in my sleep," I said sounding a lot younger than I was with an innocent childish voice.

"Trust me, you won't hurt yourself like that. Not after you learn to love and accept yourself for who you are," Jacob said soothingly.

"How are you supposed to know? You have been a virgin all your life, Jacob," I said because we both knew it was true.

"Well, yes, but I know much more than you think. Just because I never engaged in sexual activities does not mean that I don't understand. Knowledge can profoundly change how you see things."

"Look, just forget about it. I'm sure I can handle myself," I said, sitting up because now I didn't like where this was going.

"No," Jacob grabbed my arm tightly and spoke in a strong serious tone.

"Don't forget about it. Don't ever forget. Remember all the tough times you have been through and push past it all. The past is what shapes today. The past shapes you . . . who you are. Do not forget who you are."

Jacob's eyes seemed to be staring into my heart. My heart raced and I knew not to ever forget. Not even the death of my family and friends . . . even the people I never knew who passed before my eyes.

Chapter Nine

The next morning, after an almost soporific sleep, I began planning out to move. Like Jacob said, there would be a lot of challenging work involved. To buy a home will cost some, and I must pay it all on my own. Not even Jacob was going to add in. Today, I was going to look for homes, oh and I must buy food from the market. It was not too poor around here, but you would find some homeless people here and there. The market was just simply shopping that people put outside their home to make some profit. They made everything by hand. In the case of food, they grew it themselves, though a high amount of the food was shipped to kingdoms. But here it was a bit different; we had no ruling kingdom. This was because it was mainly poor in this country and everyone rolled their own way. We had a government . . . but it was weak and was controlled by elderly white men.

Since I could already tell that it was super hot out, I decided not to wear much clothing. I slipped the leather cloak that Jacob showed me to make over my naked body. It was the first clothing I made, and it turned out beautifully. It goes down to my upper thighs, but I didn't mind wearing nothing underneath . . . the cool air feels nice.

Before I left the room, I grabbed my leather journal because

I had written a list and some notes inside that I need.

"Good morning, Jacob," I said once I got downstairs.

"Good morning, Xavier. Sorry I couldn't make anything special this morning. I really need some eggs, bread and—"

"I got it, I got it. I made a list," I cut him off, in a kind voice.

"Oh, okay. Good."

Before I could run out of the house, I made some tea for Jacob and me. I also ate some fruit that was left before I could go.

"Thank you," Jacob said as I was handing him his tea.

"Be careful it's hot," I said as I begin to take a sip of my tea.

Jacob gave a short laugh after taking a sip.

"I know, Xavier. You're acting like I am getting too old for this." I smiled without a word.

After my final bites of fruit, I was off.

"See you later, Jacob," I called.

"Bye, bye," he replied. "Don't forget the Amorad fruits that we need," Jacob called after me. I just laughed and left.

I walked out into the bright and shining star above, our blue star behind it. We have a binary star system, and we have fifteen moons. It was beautiful at dusk—the sky burst in colors, and you can point out almost all our moons in one sky.

As I walked through the market, I noticed two children playing tag. I sometimes wished I was young, like a child, so I could play. The first thing I noticed in the market was the Amorads Jacob was talking about. I walked up to feel them. They turned bright red when ripe and were remarkably like Vikrish fruit. I started to pick some out and other fruit as I walked around the market stand. Finally, I see the Vikrish fruit; they remind me of Dragon fruit. They were purple and the top faded into a green. It was sometimes called the man-fruit. This was because of its properties. There were chemicals in the fruit and juice that calmed male hormones. I ate them while I have my morning/night tea when I was stressed out. I put the fruits in a handmade bag, and I decided to move on to a different stand. Most stands that I saw were either food or clothing.

Next, I started to pick bread. I really liked the seeded ones. Right when I was about to decide, there was a tap on my shoulder. I turned around to see Bonesella again.

"Oh, it's you again . . ." I said confused and surprised.

"Yes, yes, it is . . . I never seen you around here before though," she said looking around like she was in a dream.

I clutched my hand . . . I didn't have the bread . . . where was the bread? I knew I didn't drop it . . . where did it—a flash of black in the corner of my eye. It looked like it was getting smaller . . . or it was moving farther away.

"What is wrong . . . are you okay?" Bonesella started. She noticed my expression right then.

"Wait, hold on a sec," I said. Her expression was confused but I was determined to find out what that was.

"I'll be back . . . I got to go," I said quickly, and I took off toward it.

People panicked as I ran toward them with anxiety that they could see in my eyes. It must have been a horror to them. I never acted like this in public; in fact, people in the village didn't always welcome me here. They thought I was strange. I took a sharp turn on the side of a bakery. The window was open, and I could smell every ingredient. As I looked closer, I saw bags of flour piled on the back counter, shelves full of sugar and corn starch and . . . I love sugar. I have a sweet tooth, and to see it piled up in the bakery makes my mouth water.

A grey hand popped out from under the table and reached for the bread. At the next moment I heard a door close and he popped up from under the table. Isaac! I almost screamed out loud, but he quickly put a hand to my mouth.

"Shh."

I nodded in agreement. Isaac motioned me to get in through the window. As I made my way through, I fell to the ground, and something fell beside me. But I didn't care to know what it was.

"Ow, I hit my head somewhere . . ." I let out somewhat painfully.

"Like I said, shh," Isaac said softly while kneeling over and placing a hand on my head.

His eyes glimmer as sunlight from the window hits.

"Isaac . . . why are you here?" I asked, which was the one question on my mind.

Isaac's eyes soften on me, his lips slightly parted. He looked as if he wanted something out of me . . . I wonder what that might be. Before Isaac can say anything, we hear the door. Isaac quickly shoves both of us down under the counter. Well, really it was under the cabinets that were under the counter, but they didn't reach all the way down and there was an amount of space left that surprisingly fit both of us. We heard footsteps of the baker . . . then we saw his footsteps. We were silent, but I really wished I could say something now. There was a lot of dust and it made me feel dirty and sick. I wanted to cry out, but Isaac wouldn't allow it. I had a feeling that if we get caught, Isaac would take the blame out of my chest and put it in his. True pain. I was shaking now; the baker moved in front of the counter.

"Hmm, where is that bread? I just had it here on the table . . ." the baker said out loud. Isaac continued to have a hand on my mouth, I had a feeling of biting his finger, but I really didn't want to. My anxiety was taking over.

I subconsciously moved closer to Isaac until I felt his neck beside my cheek. He was warm and when I start to hear his heartbeat, I could feel my anxiety calming down. I could feel Isaac's gaze at me. I still felt like coming closer. My back to his front, I was cradled in. The next moment we realized my foot was sticking out. Isaac quickly pulled it in before the baker knelt.

Isaac mouthed, "Close your eyes."

I did, and I came close as I could to him. I could feel the baker's breath and his gaze over us.

After an awfully long moment we heard the door close, and Isaac said we can get out now. I got up and out, my muscles all cramped up. The baker was gone.

"Isaac . . . why are you. . .?" I started.

"Shh," he cut me off. Then suddenly, he started to gather food that surrounded us, into a sack he had stuffed in his pocket.

"Isaac!?" I yelled out surprised.

"Shh!" Isaac put a finger to his mouth taping it twice.

"But . . ." I let out.

"Please, shh," Isaac let out once more. By this point I wanted to scream, but I held it in for as long as I could . . . until I could not handle it anymore. Tears dripped out from my eyes.

"Isaac . . . please," I said.

He looked at me in surprise.

"Don't . . ." I let out.

He stared at me deeply. He looked like he was falling apart. Fading away from me.

"I have to . . ." he finally said.

The next thing we knew, the door opened again. In a flash I was forced out the window.

The door quickly closed again. Maybe the baker forgot something. I was lying down now on the grass. Until I realized Isaac landed on top of me. He lifted his head up and realized the same thing. His mouth almost dropped and quickly got off me before I could confess. We both stood up staring into each other's eyes. Isaac's face is blushing bright blue...and I bet mine is bright red. I took a slow glance down, mostly not wanting too. I felt somewhat uncomfortable when Isaac fell on me, and now, I was dazed. As I looked slightly down, not really wanting too, I noticed something I shouldn't have . . . but then it happens to me all the time. Shit.

"Xavier, please . . ." Isaac burst out. I looked back up quickly, right into his eyes.

I could tell that he was nervous, and that I shouldn't have

done that.

"Um . . . I am sorry," I said honestly.

We are both blushing intensely.

"But why?" I said almost crying again.

"It's all I have," Isaac said softly to me.

His face wasn't red anymore, but a noticeably light pink. My bottom lip trembled. Isaac seemed to have heard something because, he looked around like someone was watching us.

"I have to go," he said to me.

I felt like I was about to have a break down. He placed both hands on my cheeks. We were both about to cry now. Isaac's eyes were sparkling now. I just wished I could hold on to them now. Hold on to them forever. My starry night.

"Isaac," I let out.

"I have to," he replied in a soft tone.

The next moment, we struggled to hold on. Hold on to all we have. After a long moment of silence and holding on for dear life. Isaac kissed me on the forehead. And it wasn't short. I shut my eyes tightly. His lips were soothing, and they moved elegantly. It was his way of making out with me. My heart tingled in my chest and I felt somewhat tight. I tried the best to hold on to it. The memory. But soon, it was over.

We just stared for a couple of seconds more. Holding on.

"Bye, Xavier," he said softly to me, starting to drift away.

I rushed in to throw my arms around him.

"Bye, Isaac . . . and thank you for everything," I said starting to cry.

"Aww, my pleasure," he said sweetly, hugging me back, stroking my hair a bit.

"Isaac . . . I . . ." I start.

"Yes?"

I couldn't say it. So instead, I forced out these next words.

"I will miss you . . . so much."

"I promise I will miss you too . . . Xavier."

Isaac's lips creased my cheek this time. I rubbed my head on that side into my neck. Then Isaac disappeared, with a sack of food, into the mist turning black and fading as he ran farther and farther away.

Walking all alone through the village, it was starting to rain. I pulled the hood of my cloak over me. I started to finish gathering food from the market. Oh, and I forgot to pay . . . so I did that quick, but the lady was mad at me for running away. By this point, as it started to rain harder, the shops were starting to close so now I started looking at houses around. I kept walking forward feeling depressed waiting to see something beautiful that would catch the corner of my eye. I tried not to think about what happened earlier. Once I got back to the market, Bonesella was gone and I felt hopeless, but I didn't want to see her anyway. I continued walking in the rain, feeling like I was going to fall apart and feeling guilt inside me. Soon enough I was right.

Something 'did' glimmer in the corner of my eye. I saw the beauty of it. A house that was one story, and it looked cozy. I walked up the three steps and knocked on the door. The rain was drowning me out. The door soon opened to a young woman wearing a long faded blue dress. She had brown hair and blue eyes, and she had medium tan skin.

"Oh, hello," she said.

"Hello, I was wondering if—"

"How about you just come in," she said quickly.

She probably thought that I was going to tell a long story, so might as well get comfortable.

"Have a seat," she said, motioning me towards the couch.

She took a seat on the other couch, at an angle from me

"Please be quiet, my mother is sick, and she doesn't like visitors. So, what brings you here? You look immortal, shouldn't you be a royal or something?" she asked, grabbing her tea from the coffee table.

"Oh, uh—"

"Martha, come get me some more of my medicine, oh and

change the water for me, please," an elderly woman calls from the room.

"Oh, that's my mother . . . I'll be back," Martha said and went off.

Soon, Martha came back and took a seat on the couch again.

"Sorry about my sick mother . . ." Martha started.

"Oh, no you don't have to be sorry," I said in return.

"By the way, I could help . . . I know a lot about medicine . . ." I continue.

"Oh, no thank you . . . like I said, my mother isn't happy with visitors," she said.

"Martha is a nice name," I said after a bit of silence.

"Thank you. And you?" Martha asked.

"Xavier. I think I might have given my name out to everyone already," I said thinking about how many people I just meet recently.

"Nice. So, what was it that you were wondering earlier?" Martha asked, reminding me about the real topic here.

"Oh, I was wondering about your home—"

"Oh, right I almost forgot. Since, my mother is sick and that it will be only me, I was going to move somewhere else . . . a smaller place," Martha said reading my mind.

"Perfect! How much are you selling it for," I said instantly.

"Oh, you wish to buy it from me. Wow, but I really am not sure about that . . ." Martha said in a lower tone.

"Oh, well that's okay, I am glad that you let me have some of your time. Thank you," I said getting up to leave.

"You're welcome," Martha said.

As I stepped down the three steps, the rain lightened up a bit, and some of the shops were opening again. But there were still some that were closed and done for the day. I begin to look through the shops. Before I could forget, I took out my journal to see if I have anything left. Just a few more, but not a lot. As I finished off with shopping, I began to make my way back home.

As I walked, barefoot in puddles of rain, the same two kids I saw earlier that were playing tag had come out to play again. As they ran chasing each other, they became close to me until, the kid running away ran into me.

"Ow, sorry about that," the boy who was running said to me. He looked a lot younger than the other boy. He had brown hair and wore a blue shirt. The other boy, who was older, was dirty blonde and wore a bright red shirt.

"Oh, that's okay. Don't worry about it . . . I am just going home now," I said kindly to the little boy.

"Come on, Mason. There's no point on talking to that freak," the older boy said, giving me a nasty look.

Mason looked at him then looked back at me. His eyes sparkled. He sure was precious. The older boy grabs Mason's arm and begins to pull him away.

"Excuse me, what did you just say?" I said out loud, looking down at my side. I could feel my blood rushing through me. Both boys stopped to look at me.

I continued, "Don't you dare call me a freak . . . not ever."

The older boy looked surprised, "And what are you going to do about it."

"Please . . . stop," Mason said softly. The older boy ignored him.

"You don't know what I been through . . ." I start.

"So . . . ?" the older one said.

"Please stop, Arson," Mason said, his fists clenched tight.

"Just shut up, Mason," Arson said as he hit him in the head. Mason landed on the ground. I rushed over him to protect him. Arson looked at me in surprise.

"Don't you ever dare to hit another child. Never," I said strictly.

I let my wings open behind me. I glimmered as I showed myself. Arson's mouth dropped open. "And don't go playing somewhere else, because you will pay for what you did. You might as well run off to your parents, before I have to chase you down . . . now leave!" I yelled out to the child. After a moment he ran off.

I sat in front of my house with a basket of medicine right beside me. I brushed the hair out of Mason's face. He was awake now, and he was lying on my lap as I treated a wound on his cheek when he hit the ground. Mason didn't mind it when I cleaned the wound, but he giggled a bit. He looked like he was five or six years old. He got up on my lap and placed a hand on to my nose.

"Are you a boy or a girl?" Mason asked.

"A boy—I mean, I am almost an adult, but you know what I mean," I said realizing what I was really saying.

"Oh." Mason then yawned and lay back down on my lap, allowing me to continue healing his wound.

After I finished up, I let Mason sleep for a little before I said that he should go back home before his parents started getting worried about him.

I walked inside to find Jacob on one of the lounge chairs reading a book.

"Hey, I brought back everything you needed for another meal."

"Oh, wonderful. Set it on the counter for me. It's almost time for luncheon," Jacob said looking up from his book, his reading glasses about to fall off his face.

"Is it okay if I take a little nap, I need some rest," I said. When Jacob nodded, I went off to my room recording the day so far in my journal.

I began to take off my cloak, plus it got wet in the rain. I lay on my back, completely naked on my bead. I really messed up today. It was great to see Isaac, but I really shouldn't have looked down. I regretted it a bit, but only a bit because it was an accident and we couldn't stop it from happening. It's natural and it happens to me all the time. It's just the fact that I saw it happen with someone else . . .

The memory began to fade out into my mind. I remembered when I began to look down at Isaac. It was an accident, and I didn't want to be rude about it. I started to see a small bulge appear in Isaac's genital area. I didn't exactly understand why I even started to look down there in that area in the first place. The bulge continued to grow bigger till I realized what just happened. I even started to notice wet stain appear. Isaac started to get extremely nervous about it. Even I was a bit freaked out by looking at it happen in front of my eyes. It was the first time I saw another man erect in front of me. Not just in an erect state, but the process of it. But of course, Isaac was clothed.

As the memory began to take over my mind, my face started to burn. I started to remember the part when Isaac began kissing me on the forehead and my cheek. I started to feel tight and I knew I erected too.

Isaac's kissing was extremely intense for me. His thick, full lips ran smoothly across my skin. If he would have kissed me on the lips, I would have blacked out and Isaac would have had to catch me before I hit the ground. Catch me as I fell in love.

I could already feel it happening again. I sat up to look at my penis. Its tip looked like it was dipped in semen. It was already high up, squirting a bit. After a moment of feeling a bit sexual about it, I decide to lie back down. I let my mind rest for a while after all that. From all of what happened back there with Isaac, I guess my penis does deserve to let some stress go. As I place my mind on completely nothing, I didn't mind it anymore. For some odd reason, I was appreciating it. And that was why I didn't fully regret seeing Isaac go erect in front of me. It was some way showing Isaac and I thought it was all natural and it was just our body's way of expressing themselves.

In this case, Isaac fell on me. If we weren't clothed, there would be penis to penis contact. We were lucky to be clothed. If Isaac didn't have any feelings for me, he would have not reacted the way he did. And I didn't think that his body would have reacted like that either. There was just something about us. Maybe Isaac really did like me. Better yet, love me.

I grasped my hands around my penis. Sometimes even my stress reliever got stressed. I start to rub the skin a bit. This was mostly why I masturbated. It was just another way to get rid of anxiety. It feels nice though; it really calms me down.

I turned on my side, towards the door to get a better grip. I closed my eyes and I kept my mind blank. I was using one of my meditation techniques, but it wasn't full though. I was really supposed to keep my mind blank and listen closely. I was supposed to be outside in the wilderness and I must listen to life.

I continued to sooth myself until I was interrupted. A quick and loud knock became present for only two seconds before the door opens to Jacob. I didn't even have time to make a move. My face burned red. Jacob stopped and started.

"Jacob, please . . . I . . ." I stutter a lot.

"Um, I just wanted to say luncheon is ready. Come down when you are," Jacob said cutting my stuttering off, trying to stare down at the floor and not at me.

The door soon closed, and my genitals felt thick and swollen.

My hand tightly gripped my penis. My body was burning, and I couldn't help it. I really wished Jacob hadn't walked in on me. If he just knocked, I would have been fine. But he had to open the door without me saying anything.

I didn't think I would even be ready soon for luncheon. My body was tight, and I wanted to rest more. I peeked my head out of my door.

"Jacob, you don't have to wait for me. I think I'll rest for a couple more minutes. Is that okay?" I asked, calling for Jacob.

"Oh, of course. Come down whenever you are ready," Jacob replied from the kitchen.

There was no stutter or pause in his words that suggests that might have freaked him out a bit. He seemed as calm as any ordinary day.

"Thanks."

I lay back in my bead, and this time, I decide to take a real nap. I soon woke up and I slipped on my shorts and just walk down to eat.

Before I even take a seat I warned Jacob, "Don't even say anything about it."

Jacob shook his head a bit and start to serve himself. We eat in silence. Just waiting for a conversation to spark up, hoping to forget what happened earlier.

Jacob looked up from his food to meet my gaze.

"Are you okay, Xavier?" he asked softly, hoping to not have disturbed me.

"I am fine . . ." I said as I looked back down at my food.

I knew I was lying. I hate to lie, but I do when anxiety comes over me. I was glad that Jacob didn't say anything, because my feelings were overly sensitive right now.

We continued to eat in silence. I believed that we both gave up on starting a conversation. We didn't even try after that. Soon I finished up, cleaning the dishes that I used.

"Jacob, I am sorry about earlier. Something happened this morning and it . . . pushed some buttons of mine," I said uncomfortably.

Jacob looked up after finishing his food. I began to fumble with the brush in my hand. I hoped I wouldn't break any dishes.

"Oh, well I forgive you. Well, I believe that you would be more comfortable if we don't talk about it, so you can go—"

"No," I cut Jacob off softly.

I didn't even think he heard me right because he was giving me a confused look.

"I want to talk about it. It really isn't as bad as it looked earlier . . . it is just that the situation was messing with my feelings. I feel the need to talk to you . . . I just hope you are okay with it. I know you are a one-hundred percent virgin and I don't want to make you nervous," I said starting to dry the dishes.

"Trust me, I won't become nervous. I am the one to talk to," Jacob said standing up sounding like he knows everything.

I could just picture him putting a finger in the air, sounding like he can do anything.

"All right when we finish here, we can head to my room and I'll tell you," I said as I start to collect Jacob's dishes.

Once Jacob and I were in my room, I took a seat in the middle of my bed, crossing my legs close to me.

"Jacob, promise you won't take this the wrong way . . . it is just that I like Isaac," I said trying to cool down.

Jacob nodded in return, I was only glad that he was trying. Jacob took a seat beside me and I start to tell my story.

"What happened earlier was just a reaction. I didn't mean for it to happen. I am glad that I already told you that I do it. It was just a mistake . . . when I saw Isaac again," I start.

I began to tell him everything to seeing Bonesella to Arson and Mason.

". . . And then what happened earlier . . . see it really isn't like what you saw, I was not feeling . . . well," I ended off.

Jacob gave a respecting nod before saying anything.

"I am glad you spoke with me. You know, you are getting better at it since you and your father . . ." Jacob began.

I didn't always like thinking about my father and me. We didn't have the best relationship. But, in this situation I appreciated it. I got to see the good things in life after the tough times in life.

"I am glad to see change in you. I think that we should continue this relationship and grow on it. We planted the seed, now with some water we can grow something magical," Jacob continued.

He really did have some wisdom and I really appreciated it.

"Thank you, Jacob. I am glad that you understand," I replied.

"Yes, it is my pleasure. I know this was an accident, but I really think your heart is trying to tell you something . . . and I really hope you do, but it is your choice. It is your choice to find the other," Jacob explained to me.

It took me a moment to process before I could say anything.

"Other?" I said out loud confused.

"Yes. You have two eyes. Two ears. Two hands. Two feet, but one heart. Why? That is because you are supposed to find the other," he explained deeper for me.

"Oh, the other heart. Wow, that really does makes sense. I also hope I can get it," I said fading in the end.

"Well, you found it. Now you must run after it and catch it before it flies away in the wind. You must pursue your dream," Jacob said giving me back my hope . . . and my strength.

Before I could think of anything else, I decided to go run after him. I loved Isaac.

Later, I went downstairs to see Jacob cleaning.

"Oh, and Jacob?" I called after him.

He looked up at me and nodded, "Yes?"

"Oh, I found a house for me . . . I think maybe later we could take a look . . ." I said leaning against the wall.

"Oh, great! I have been waiting to hear something about that," Jacob said sliding on the floor with the mop.

I laughed a bit. Jacob rarely showed some humor, but when he did, I had to laugh. Living in the moment. I closed the door of my room to change. I slipped off my shorts and pulled over my coat, grabbing my satchel with my journal in it and some other stuff. I zoomed downstairs and I almost fell over Jacob.

"Oh, my gosh are you okay?" I asked to be sure.

"Yes, I am fine . . . for now till I start getting really old," Jacob said with a hand on his head.

"You know you are always talking about you getting old, why is that?" I asked.

Jacob looked at me for a moment. He looked as if he was graying by looking at me. "Well, I am being truthful. Well, I am seventy-three years old . . . of course I am old," Jacob said in a matter-of-fact tone eying me.

"Well, fine. When you are finished cleaning like a figure skater, then catch up and let's go, old man," I said walking toward the door.

"No offense," I yelled out as I left the door.

Jacob must be so confused right now.

I walked out to the back of the house. Nightmare was there chewing a stick. Sometimes I really thought he had the brain of a dog. Nightmare was surprising for people. Many people tried to rob us, but Nightmare was in the back and he would just scare them away. So, we were safe . . . from most things. Nightmare didn't like strangers, but he soon got along with people, like Jacob. When Jacob found me, Nightmare didn't really like it, but they were forced to bond because Nightmare made his promise to protect me and always be at my side. As I approached Nightmare, he looked up puzzled for a moment, but he soon started swinging his tail around. I placed my hands on his nose and I pulled him in close. I loved Nightmare, but I didn't spend that much time with him because it was dangerous to play with him in the village. I asked Jacob if I could take him far away from here to play, but he still didn't allow me. Maybe I could when I moved out.

After a moment of Nightmare licking me all over, I opened my satchel to find a Vikrish fruit. I gave it to Nightmare, and he happily ate it. Nightmare liked fruit, but it was important to feed him an actual meal—meat. I didn't like meat, but I only got it for Nightmare. He liked it raw, which disgusted me. I didn't mind chicken, but I couldn't stand steak; it was even worse if it wasn't cooked all the way.

I tried to think of something else to cover the thought before I threw up or something. Nightmare looked up at me like Jacob might let me take him out. Nightmare had a leash and it was tied to a post of the back porch. If only Jacob would allow me to let him go.

"Xavier?" Jacob called for me. I noticed his face from the front of the house.

"Jacob, I am back here with Nightmare," I called after him.

"Oh, there you are," Jacob said relived turning around to see me here. Jacob came over. "Let's go, young man," Jacob said with a smile. I couldn't help but laugh out loud.

We walked to Martha's place. It was a wonder to see the place again.

"Wow, well this is surprising. This beauty is for sale?" Jacob asked amazed.

"Yah," was all I said.

"How much?" Jacob said still staring up at it. We were like two drunks staring up at a random sign. "She didn't say."

Soon enough, Martha came out of the house with her sick mother in a wheelchair.

"Well, a deal is a deal," Martha said as she passed by us.

"What do you do mean?" I was very confused.

"It's all yours," Martha said as she stopped next to me.

"What? I didn't pay anything!" I said.

"Don't worry, I didn't ask much for it anyway. I can make the money up," Martha said like it was no big deal.

"What? You can't just give this place away, you have to make something out of it," I said trying to convince her.

"Look, you can give whatever you want for it, but I got to go. I just don't want to take any money from you. You can pay it all back when you make it. I'll take any amount," she said as she left her mother here and goes back in the house, leaving the front door open.

"And?" I tried to catch Jacob's attention.

"What? Oh, sorry," Jacob said, finally looking at me.

"Please, pay attention. What do I do now, Jacob?" I pleaded.

"Do whatever you want. It is yours now," Jacob said, waving me off.

Before I could say another word, Martha came out carrying boxes and pulling others out. She really was on a move.

"All right, all yours. Come back tomorrow and I should be done here," Martha said continuing to pull out boxes.

"Okay, bye."

"Bye," Martha called back.

It has started to rain again. After all it was summer. We were walking back home. When we get home, Jacob started to cook, and I decide to go up to my room. Sometimes my feelings were completely mixed, and I must break the day apart in my head and write everything in my journal. After writing I decide to take a nap.

A couple minutes later, I awoke and head to dinner. I ate slowly but I didn't even make a word out. Soon enough I was asleep, and it was the next morning.

After eating a quick breakfast, I told Jacob that I will be checking in with Martha. As I walked, people give me strange looks. It happened all the time. That was because I didn't belong here. Sometimes I thought I didn't belong anywhere. When I got to the house of beauty, I made my way up the three steps and notice a piece of paper sticking on the door. I took the paper and flip it over. The handwriting of Martha was printed neatly in black ink.

Dear Xavier,

Thank you for your time, I appreciate you taking the place.

I wish you good luck and high hopes. Here is your entry not only to a home and a place to stay, but to a life ahead of you. Thank you very much for everything. (I left the key under the rug).

Wow, Martha must have really thought about this a lot. For a moment I closed my eyes for a small prayer for everything at this moment. Once I opened my eyes, I folded the paper and slid it into my satchel. I clutched the key that I grabbed from under the rug. I unlocked the door and it swung open.

It was time to get comfy. Everything had been cleaned out. The middle of the room was the living room. All the furniture here had not been taken out, but all their personal belongings had. I looked up to still see the chandler hanging above. Under the table and couches was a bright yellow carpet . . . which looked nice. One thing I really loved was the floors and walls of this house. They were wood, giving it a touch of nature. The walls were an even more complex-looking in design than the wood floors. The walls were logs and sticks of the same type of tree, but polished and cut a bit. The walls resembled the outer look of this tree and no part showed the center. With this look put together, I could enjoy the love of nature forever.

The kitchen was on my left. It was small, but it was quite nice. There were lots of cabinets and a front and back counter. On the left wall, above the counter was a window with shutters. Right on the sill were lovely flowers. Further past the living room (it was the same room, or one room) was the dining table, with a vase of flowers in the center.

On my right there one door. The only other door there was that was inside the house. I went in, and there was a bed with no sheets or pillows a sturdy wooden desk with a window next to it. On the far wall there was a closet, and, on my left, there was another door. I supposed it was either a bathroom or another room.

I went inside to find it was a bathroom. There were no other rooms. Did Martha share a room with her mother? Or did she have to sleep somewhere else? After a moment of thinking, I shook the thought out of my head. The bathroom was small but simple. The tiles were beige with small carvings. It was nice, just like a normal bathroom. A shower with a bathtub, the sink with a mirror and of course it was a water closet . . . who would forget the toilet?

I exited the bathroom and I decided to sit on the edge of the bed for a moment. I took out my journal to write the description of the house.

Soon, I began to head back home to give Jacob the news. And by then I was already making a home my home.

Chapter Ten

I picked up another item to put on the shelf. I went through about five boxes. I didn't own much, but Jacob has insisted that I take some of his stuff. So now I had more to unpack.

After finishing the box I was on, I chose to go to unpack some stuff in the kitchen. As I picked up some kitchenware, I heard a bush rustling. *Maybe it's just the wind. Not.* I began to pick another item and before I could get it off my hands Isaac popped up on the windowsill.

"Isaac!?" I yelled out, almost dropping the teacup on my feet.

Since I was barefoot, there would be some blood. But I was glad to catch the cup before it can hit the ground or my feet.

"Hi!" Isaac said cheerfully waving at me.

"Isaac! I almost dropped a teacup on my feet . . . and I am bare foot!" I yelled at him as I set the teacup aside, away from where I might hit it.

"Oops . . ." Isaac let out looking back.

"Isaac why are you visiting anyway . . . ?" I tried to ask nicely without getting pissed off, leaning on to the sill with my elbows and my hands in fists on my cheeks. I already was stressed. I hoped I could get this packing over with soon.

"Oh, well, I wasn't really visiting. I was watching nearby

and—"

"What! You were watching me this whole time?" I yelled, backing off. I really didn't like being watched.

"Yeah . . ." Isaac said in a tone that told me that he was backing away verbally.

"What? Were you waiting to see me become naked?" I asked defensively, crossing my arms.

"What?! I wasn't even trying to do that in the first place!" Isaac yelled back.

Isaac's next words came quick and were more to himself then to me, "Well, no, maybe I wouldn't have minded but . . . that wasn't the main purpose . . . well I have thought of it though . . .

"Isaac, are you trying to tell me that you would want to see me naked?" I asked leaning against the front counter that was behind me, trying to dig deeper, but a lot nicer than before.

"Well . . . I don't want to be rude . . . but I would not mind if you did . . ." Isaac said in an honest, calm tone.

He was looking down at his side, and his arms were crossed closer to him on the windowsill. I sighed and started to think about how I yelled at Isaac.

"Isaac, I am sorry. I didn't mean to yell at you," I apologize. "It's okay I forgive you. I shouldn't have been rude to you," he said still not looking at me.

"I accept your apology. Now, can you come in and we can talk this out?" I asked nicely. Isaac nodded and I let him in through the front door.

"So, what was the real reason that gave you the confidence to watch me?" I asked slowly to him.

"Oh, I was interested in you . . ." Isaac told me looking like he was embarrassed.

"So, you really did not want to see me naked? You know you could have knocked on my door and I would have let you in, right?" I asked Isaac.

"I didn't want to be seen. But trust me that was not the first thing I thought of about coming here . . . I mean I would not have minded though. Please, I just don't want you to think I am some crazy maniac. I really do respect you . . . it's that I like certain things about you. After you said that, it's kind of got trapped in my head," Isaac explained trying not to be disrespectful or hurt my feelings.

"Well, don't let that image be trapped in your head for too long. You haven't even seen me naked yet, so don't let it take over before the real thing," I said, taking a seat on the couch.

"What real thing? Are you waiting to trust me to get naked in front of me? Like I said, I don't mind . . . you can do it now if you want," Isaac said, taking a seat next to me.

"What? I just don't know when it might happen, okay?" I said.

Isaac didn't reply. I was glad, because I wanted to move on from this conversation already.

After a moment of silence, Isaac finally said something.

"Um, Xavier, I don't mean to be so awkward around you . . . but do you mind if I stay here a little while? And don't mean one night, I mean for as long as whenever . . ." Isaac said softly.

I could tell by the look in his eyes that he really was taking my feelings in consideration.

"Sure, you can stay for as long as you want," I said as soon as Isaac finished his sentence, but I continued his soft tone. My hand slowly found Isaac's hand, and I looked up to meet his eyes.

"Thank you, Xavier," Isaac replied, his eyes glimmering.

"It is my very pleasure," I said in return. Isaac gave me a sweet smile and somewhere in my heart was telling me that I was going to really enjoy Isaac staying here.

I rubbed my fingers on Isaac's palm till I jumped up with an idea.

"Isaac, I have the perfect idea!" I yelled out cheerfully.

Isaac let out a bright laugh.

"Well, what is your idea?" Isaac finally asked after laughing too much.

"Well, first you can help me finish unpacking . . . and then we can make biscuits!" I yelled out.

"Biscuits?" Isaac repeated, giving me a questioning look.

"Yes, I love biscuits! Why, do you not like them?" I asked after my excitement.

I felt like the party was dying down and it didn't even start.

"Oh, I do. I was just really surprised. You're so bright . . ." Isaac said slowly, at the end he sounded like he might pass out.

I knew he wasn't obviously, but it was almost like I was some bright light.

Isaac had been helping me with my packing. As a reward we are going to bake biscuits! We were unpacking for quite a while, and I was already getting hungry. Honestly my stomach growled a little too loud a bit ago and Isaac noticed it, but he said we should finish up first because we only had two boxes to go.

At that moment, Isaac had yelled out, "Ready or not, I am going to beat you!"

Pretty soon it was my turn to win.

"Done!" I yelled out. Isaac just breaks down and laughs.

"You're so adorable!" Isaac yelled out over laughing too much.

I blush just a little at the thought. I didn't mean to be.

"Here, get up. Let's go make some biscuits," I said, lending a hand to Isaac. I helped Isaac up. He cheerfully smiled at me, still holding my hands. I smiled back, hoping that it would last forever.

I got right to the kitchen with Isaac following behind me, not really knowing what he was doing.

"All right, let's get out the kitchenware we need, and we can get out the ingredients for the batter," I said.

"And . . . how do you make biscuits? I never baked before," Isaac said unsure.

"Don't worry, I am here to guide you, so don't be too hard

on yourself. Baking biscuits is easy," I said simply.

Isaac almost looked depressed still, so I gave a rub to his shoulder just to give him a hint that I would be there through his tough times. Plus, I wanted him to have fun and not hurt.

Once we got everything we needed out, I started to get out ingredients for the batter. I show Isaac how much he needs for each ingredient, the mixing part, and simply rolling up the biscuits to give them shape. Once, they were in the oven, the counter was a bit messy, but I know we can clean It up.

"Now the easiest part, cleaning up and waiting for the biscuits to be done . . . then you can put whatever you want on it," I said cheerfully.

"Plus, you did really well. Baking is fun right?" I added to cheer him up a bit more.

"Sure, I hope to do it again soon with you, but can we eat now? I'm hungry from making them," Isaac said, and we both laughed at the joke.

"Well, they are almost done, so let's clean up," I said. Once the biscuits were done, I took them out on to a plate and I start to grab out, butter cheese, and other stuff to put on them.

"Let's eat, you can put anything you want on it," I said placing the plate of biscuits on the table, in front of him. I started to put butter and cheese on mine, plus I sprinkle some sugar on it. "Mm."

Isaac and I ended up sitting on the couch, and I was tired.

"Mm, that was good . . . but I am so tired now. Sorry, If I fall asleep right now," I said yawning afterward.

"Oh, that's okay. You can lay on my lap if you want," Isaac offered kindly.

Instead of blushing, I was so tired, I lay on his lap immediately . . . and fell asleep.

Even though I was asleep, I could still feel him brushing his fingers through my hair. It felt nice to have someone to lean on (or lay on in this case). It was comforting to feel another immortal body.

After a while of resting, Isaac began to call my name.

"Xavier, wake up," Isaac called for me softly.

I peeked open my eyes. The room was dark. As my vision cleared, there was no light coming through the windows. Only gray. It was not complete darkness, I could see . . . but everything was gray.

"Isaac, what time is it?" I asked.

"About eighteen-thirty," Isaac replied softly.

"It is getting late, I think you should be in your actual bed by now," Isaac continued.

I sat up and I started to ask, "Where are you going to sleep, Isaac?"

"I was planning on staying here, on the couch," he said simply.

"Are you sure you are going to be okay? I don't want you to be uncomfortable . . ." I added.

"It is okay, I will be fine . . . you should get going to bed," Isaac said standing up with me.

He motioned me to get to bed. I went to my room and once I start to lay down, Isaac followed behind, slightly closing the door behind him.

"Do you mind if I tuck you in?" Isaac asked softly.

"What? I haven't been tucked into bed in forever!" I let out.

Isaac smiled, finding my excitement. Once I got comfy, Isaac pulled up my covers and placed a hand on my cheek, rubbing it slightly with his thumb. I giggled a little.

"All right, good night, Xavier," Isaac said leaning in for a hug. I hugged him back pleasantly.

"Good night, Isaac. Are you sure that you are going to be okay," I asked again to be sure.

"I will be fine. I hope you have a good night's rest," Isaac said, letting go of me and heading for the door.

"Wait," I called back for Isaac.

I just wanted to say one more thing.

"Isaac, thank you for everything. I glad that you're here."

Isaac turned back to me to give me an incredibly happy smile. Isaac's eyes glimmer and I could tell that I have made the most of it for him.

"And thank you for bringing me the joy I never had growing up in my life," Isaac said before he leaves my room.

I fell asleep with the usual scene, I lay in bed, staring at the ceiling, until a voice called my name. I sat up hoping to find who it was. A shadow, a figure standing in my doorway. I couldn't even see past the door; all was black. The figure with broad shoulders and large chest led me to infer that the figure was a man. I heard my name being called again, and this time I knew it was the man. The shadowy figure began to walk toward me, slowly. I sat and tried to make out the shadow, but no light was able to shed its own on his dark spirit. Soon, the man started to come on my bed, continuously calling my name. once his hand touched my knee, my body finally began to react. I began to scoot back against the back board. The man continued.

Xavier. There's no need to be frightened. I am not going to hurt you. Just let my fingers crease your skin in the most beautiful yet hidden places, where I may rest upon, the beautiful body of an angel who no man could resist.

"No," I simply said in return.

My body was still on the outside yet, inside, my body was shaking.

Xavier. I promise I won't hurt you. Not ever. I am not a new person to you. I just want to be blessed with your love.

The figure stopped coming toward me. The shadowy figure began to change slightly, almost as if the shadowing was fading off; I started to see more detail of the man, the hair was outlined better, also with his body, including abs. The color also stood out, but the shadow was not completely gone. It was halfway still there over the whole body, just half as strong as before. The man lifted his head toward me; I almost wanted to panic. I wanted to scream his name, but before I did, he covered my mouth.

Shh. You don't need to yell out my name. Xavier, you are fine. Calm down please. And if you can't, I will sooth you till you fall back asleep. Xavier.

I nodded. The man placed hands on my cheeks, and I began to blush . . . finally. I was brought into a tight hug, and he held me still. For about half an hour, until my nerves detected a different kind of touch. I opened my eyes immediately. The touch continued to appear and disappear. Wet but not sticky. Smooth but not slippery. The man's tongue slid against my shoulder quite easily. Not much friction, just a warm wet tongue sliding against my soft skin.

He began to thrust on me, but it was not what I feared. His thrusting was light, and I didn't need to panic about it. This was the kind of relation I wanted with another being. I wanted to be in a relationship with a person who would take it easy on me. Keep it light, yet comforting me when I felt the need to be loved the most. I opened my eyes again. All of it felt exactly right, yet, I felt that I should be evaluating my decisions and choosing the best choice for me. Yet, with a man's body thrusting on mine, does not mean I should just go with it. I chose to participate, gliding my fingers against his skin, wondering what life may be right now without him. What would I do if he didn't save me in the arena? Or what if he didn't show up in my life at all? I continued to enjoy my time, discovering what his skin feels like all around. Like when discovering a new planet that you have landed on, mapping the soil and touching the unfamiliar environment that surrounds you. I traced the darkest place of his body. The most imperfect places that can only be seen when a man chooses to show his most manly parts, above all his muscles and body build up. The part that defines biological man.

Xavier. Are you okay? You don't look so well.

"I'm fine, Isaac. I just need a break from all that thrusting we did," I mumbled, turning on my other side.

"Xavier? I did not have sex with you . . . yet. I just came in to check on you," Isaac said confusingly.

"You don't remember?" I said also confused.

"Xavier, that did not happen. I did not have sex with you yet," Isaac repeated himself. I turned halfway on my other side to face him.

"What?" I let out.

"Xavier, you were probably having a dream. I came to check on you because I heard you making some noise, so I wanted to make sure you were okay," Isaac explained to me.

"Are you sure—"

"Yes, I am very sure," Isaac gave a straight answer.

"Ugh, fine . . . I guess I am still a virgin," I said sitting up, not satisfied anymore.

Isaac took a seat beside me on my bed.

"So, you really don't like being a virgin . . ." Isaac started.

"I don't want to talk about it," I said, insisting that I could get away from this embarrassing moment.

"Okay, fine. I am sorry if I was bothering you—"

"No. It is not your fault," I interrupted Isaac's soft, sweet tone.

I dropped my head into my lap, sighing. After a long moment of silence, I finally broke it.

"I have just been going through . . . so much of these awkward and strange dreams that are either trying to haunt me or maybe they might even be trying to tell me something . . . or comfort me," I said out of the silence and darkness.

I lifted my head, tears wanting to make their way out, so instead I lifted my head high, and realize that it was still the middle of the night. Out the window, the stars glimmered in the sky, dark clouds floated above, and my heart seemed to drop deeper than ever, lost in a forest of my life. I dropped my head a bit again, and everything begins to fade, I was still unsure of my sexuality or anything or such. I think I have lost my mind.

"Xavier, please don't cry . . . Xavier?" Isaac said softly.

"What?" I let out.

"I think that you might have . . ." Isaac paused after his words.

"That I what?" I said.

"Don't tell me that you think that I might kill myself or something because of my depression or something," I let out fiercely.

"What?! No! I would not just randomly think of something like that. Xavier, I believe that you are better than that. You are my one and only real best friend I had ever had in my life. I was just trying to say that . . . there is kind of a lift of the sheet . . ." Isaac stated.

"What? —"

"Oh no. no. I am so sorry . . ." I let out, dropping my head into my lap once again, slightly after the sheet has fallen lower off me. I finally decided to cry about it because I felt helpless.

"Xavier, I didn't mean—"

"You did not see that, right? Or did you?" I asked over Isaac trying to apologize again. "Honestly, yes. I was not trying to . . . but—"

"It's okay. I just have been feeling strange an uneasy lately," I said.

"I am the one who should be sorry."

Without a word, Isaac brought me into his arms. The room filled with silence. My mind almost went blank, except for one thought. Isaac might be the only person in the world that I would need to survive the rest of my life with.

A little later, Isaac started to shift off the bed, I lifted my head off his shoulder.

"Where are you going?" I asked, afraid Isaac may even leave forever. Isaac stood in the middle of the room without a word.

"Isaac?" I repeated.

Without a word again, something flew through the window. Isaac caught it. Isaac then turned toward me.

"I am not going anywhere," he said. I felt comfortable again.

He came toward me, fitting something into my hair.

"What is it? Let me see it?" I said joyfully, while pulling it out of my hair so I could look. By the look of it, I wanted to scream with joy. What I lost for so long came back to me. A flower. Not just any flower. The Blossom of Life.

"Oh my god! I have been looking for this ever since!" I yelled.

"What? This?" Isaac asked confused.

"Yes," I said relaxing a bit, letting the blossom float over my hand.

"This flower was what came to me after my mother passed away. It was—or felt like—my protector. It was there through my depression, and I felt like I couldn't live without it. It means everything to me," I explained softly, even the cold nightly wind was louder than me.

"Oh. I never had something that important to me . . . that felt like it supported me though the toughest parts of my life," Isaac said.

After a while of silence, Isaac took a seat beside me. I automatically feel the need to lean against him, and I do.

"Here," Isaac said taking the flower and placing it in my hair again.

"You look amazing." My heart began to beat harder and faster than before. I blushed, unable to return the favor. Isaac smiled, noticing the reddening of my face.

"It is late you know. We should get some rest. I didn't mean to wake you," Isaac said after a while.

"No, it is fine. We should get some rest," I repeat. I lay back into my bed pulling the covers over me. Isaac stood aside, waiting but anxious.

"Are you sure you are going to be all right?" I asked again.

"Well, do you mind if I sleep in here?" Isaac asked, his eyes pleading.

"Where? On the floor?" I asked confused.

"Well, no. I rather sleep in with you," Isaac said simply.

"In bed with me?" I asked shaking a bit. I wasn't ready for this yet.

"Yes, but I was only planning on sleeping, nothing more than that," Isaac said.

I felt relieved.

"Okay. Good because I am not ready for anything that extreme," I said while Isaac jumped into my bed on the other side. It was a small bed but surprisingly it fit us fine. I pulled the blanket over Isaac, he shifted a bit to get comfortable, and we fell asleep, together.

Chapter Eleven

Bright sunshine reached my face. I opened my eyes, but squinted at the light. I turned around on to my other side to find that Isaac was still there, asleep by my side.

"Isaac?" I said softly shaking his shoulder a bit.

Isaac opens his eyes slightly, "Good morning, babe," he mumbled.

"What?!" I let out, unsure if what I heard him say was correct or not.

Isaac opened his eyes wide and shook his head.

"What? I didn't say anything," Isaac said quickly full of energy.

I couldn't even wake up and jump out of bed with that kind of energy. My mornings were "Xavier, it is time to sleep in."

I pushed the idea aside and instead I decided to think more in depth about this friendship.

I sat up, "Isaac, do you—" I paused. I couldn't believe I would take a question straight forward like that.

"Do you l-like me?" I asked shakily in a high-pitched tone. Isaac's face did not change from its calming, kind look: not a smile really but just a bit by like one or two degrees, and glimmering eyes that make me feel like I was something. Something amazing.

"Of course, I like you, why wouldn't I like you?" Isaac said quickly.

I thought he got what I said wrong. I just didn't want to say that other four-letter word that also ends in E, but its meaning goes far beyond any. If I had it, I would live by it for the rest of my life.

"I don't know. I just feel lonely sometimes. Nobody likes me here," I said shallowly after a moment of thought.

My words were like throwing my life away, maybe off a high cliff into the river below. The river of sorrow. Isaac's eyes opened wide in response from my response. Not in an energetic surprised way—but the surprise you get when you realize a loved one just died. Isaac's eyes were large enough. They were like the size that newborns have. Wide, round open eyes, but as you grow older, your eyes seem to shrink. It seemed exactly that, Isaac was still young. Lots of energy, wide eyes like a small child or a newborn, a tiny round nose, and that kind of body like a baby. They were chubby, but that was not Isaac. He was not skinny like me, but he was quite big compared to me his body was just larger than mine (he was muscular also). He was taller, his bones larger, and his body shape was hugely different from mine. But all together Isaac was like a child. A small child, that wants to give his all for me.

He looked as if he would be about to cry, but instead he held back his tears and started to speak.

"Xavier, you are not lonely anymore. Not while I am here. Do not start thinking that nobody likes you because then, it is going to get stuck in your head and you are going to start thinking bad about yourself. Don't do that to yourself, Xavier. I like you. I do. You should not be worrying about that while I am here with you."

I listened to his words carefully. It was like he really must hold on. I breathed for a moment, before I could say anything.

"I am glad that you are here and thank you. Anyways, what do you mean by "you like me"? how much do you like me?" I asked.

It took a moment for Isaac to respond, "Look, when I said I like you, I mean I like you . . . a lot. A lot or . . . okay fine, I really like you, Xavier," Isaac said, his eyes widening.

My heart was struck, but I still doubted it.

"Like a friend or—"

I could not go on. It made me nervous to go beyond that point.

"No, more than just simply friends . . ." Isaac started but stopped looking as if he was rethinking what he said. Isaac began to look as if he was sick.

"Are you okay, Isaac," I asked to be sure.

"Yes, I am fine, may I just use the restroom really quick?" Isaac replied quickly.

"Sure, go ahead."

Isaac said thanks and quickly rushed into my bathroom on the wall opposite to my bed.

I waited for a while hoping that Isaac would come out soon, but I ended up waiting a long time.

I walked over to the door, placing my ear against it, listening if anything was going on. I could hear Isaac breathing.

"It's okay, everything is going to be fine. Breathe, Isaac. Breathe," Isaac said to himself in a shaky tone. I continued to listen a little longer. I heard sniffles, then sobbing.

"Poor Isaac, what shall I do?" I whispered to myself. I tred to think of something while I listen to Isaac's sobbing. The sobbing got louder and soon enough I couldn't stay silent anymore.

"Isaac, are you okay? I really need to know if you are okay. Please be honest," I pleaded over the sobbing.

"I can't," Isaac said.

"What do you mean you can't?" I asked.

I tried to open the door, but it was locked.

"Isaac, please let me in. Please. I am not going to hurt you. I just want to make sure you are okay and nothing major is going on. Okay? Please?" I pleaded once again.

I backed away from the door. After a moment Isaac replied, "Okay, I just need a moment to myself first . . . I need to relax."

I nodded even though Isaac cannot see me. I backed completely away from the door giving him space, backing all the way to my bed and I leaned against it. A couple seconds later Isaac came out with a wet face, slowly walking toward me.

"Come here," I said with open arms.

Without hesitation Isaac wrapped his arms around me. After thinking of what I could say to help, I stopped. I thought it might be better if I left the situation alone, I was sure Isaac can handle it. If he forgot, it would seem like nothing happened in the first place.

"I am sorry for that," he whispered, letting go of me, with his hands close to his mouth.

"No, you don't have to apologize, if you ever need a moment, let me know and you can go . . . or if you want, I am here, you can cry on me whenever you need or want to," I suggested kindly.

Isaac nodded and thanked me.

"I'm starving," I said out of nowhere.

"Same, let us eat," Isaac agrees. We made our way to the dining room. I prepare a simple meal for this morning's breakfast. Salad, fruit, and eggs from an Endal bird. To drink I had made some hot tea. We ate, and no words were mentioned halfway through.

"So, what do you normally do? On a day like this?" Isaac asked after taking a sip of his tea.

"Oh, right. I was planning on going out to get some different threads to fix up an old pair of jeans that I wish to wear again. I first made them when I was twelve . . . my mother helped me make it, before she passed away," I explained slowly. Isaac's expression changed quickly from a calming smile to looking down at his plate like a child who wouldn't eat his veggies.

"I am so sorry for your loss, I'll do anything to help out,"

Isaac offered.

"Thanks," I said shallowly.

Isaac took a moment of thought and then continued the subject, "So, you lost your mother at such an immature age?" Isaac asked surprised.

"Yes, I did. My father too. He must have run away because of me. It is just that . . . I lost my mother. I hated living without her. I was twelve and still in need. I ended up pushing my father too much . . . to the point I lost him," I stood up and explained.

"So, you have gone through a bit . . ." Isaac said slowly, carefully crawling past my nerves.

"Well, more than that. I watched my mother die . . . and it was bloody," I said right before I picked up my plate to rinse it.

Isaac did not say a word after that. He knew to back off. Isaac stood up too rinse his plate after me. I grabbed my satchel by the door. I was already wearing my cloak.

"I'm leaving to get some things, are you coming?" I asked with my stuff ready.

Isaac was seated back down at the table glaring back at me.

"No, I can't go out. If they see me, they are not going to like it," he responded.

"So? I don't see the point why you can't go out. Are people going to try and kill you or something?" I said over-exaggerating.

"Yes. How did you know?" Isaac responded quickly.

I froze, as if Isaac were crazy. I didn't think he was, but there seemed to be a lot that I didn't understand and that I would not be able to fully understand it in the future.

"Okay, I am leaving. Bye. Make yourself at home," I said as I walked out the door.

I closed the door behind me after I heard Isaac's goodbye echoed out.

The sun was bright, shining right toward my eyes. I always had to look down when I was out—it just seemed that the clouds never block the sun's sharp rays. Loads of people were out today, shopping and walking about. Whenever I was out it seemed like everyone started to stare at me. I felt like a complete freak. Like I didn't even belong here. I continue to keep my head down. Usually those who were selling items right outside their own house were nice to me—though I felt like they were only being nice because it is the better thing to do. In their own minds, they must hate me.

I made my way to a stand, trying not to worry about what others think of me. I stood to look at the different colored threads. I grabbed the colors orange, red, gold, browns, and black for the main part. I basically picked out any colors that would match the fall leaves on my pair of jeans.

"Hey," someone said out of nowhere.

"What?!" I said out loud almost dropping everything. I turned around to see Bonesella tapping on my shoulder.

"Oh, hey," I said a little embarrassed.

"Hi, it's nice to see you again," Bonesella said in turn in a bright mood, giggling a bit.

"Yeah, so . . . what are you doing here?" I asked, getting out a small sack of coins from my bag.

"Well, I was thinking we could go to the central garden again, to talk and hang out," Bonesella explained, swaying a bit with her hands behind her back.

"Sure, why not. What time would you like me to come?" I asked casually as I was paying.

"Late afternoon would be fine . . . or tonight," Bonesella said as if she were slowly creeping up on the topic, but nervously.

"Well, I'll come around eighteen-thirty . . . Though, I should get home to put my stuff away . . . and I want to bathe and put some comfy outfit on," I added, also saying thank you to the seller.

"All right. You don't need to look that good. I just wanted to talk and hang out," Bonesella said a little surprised.

"So, what time?" I asked.

"How about eighteen-thirty . . . since you need to do some stuff," she said.

"Okay, see you then," I said before she left.

I walked back home after that; it was still early so I walked slowly to pass more time. When I got home, Isaac was no longer sitting at the table like I saw him when I left.

"Isaac?" I said out loud.

There was no response, but I was not worried. Isaac wouldn't run away from me like that. I walked into my bedroom to find Isaac fast asleep in my bed. I smiled. People look so young when they are asleep. I bent down right in front of Isaac, and I ran my fingers through his hair. Instead of waking him, Isaac wrinkled his nose. His tiny little nose. I placed just two fingers over it, pinching it. The bridge of Isaac's nose was concaved, while the tip was round like a little ball. I wondered over him like he was some new amazing creature. I slid my hand from his nose, to his cheek. I glided the back of my hand across it, back and forth. As I began to slide my hand to Isaac's chin, my hand was caught. Isaac pulled my hand right to his lips, where he tickled the back of my hand, then pulled my hand between his neck, where it was warm. Isaac did not let go. Nor that he wanted to. When I tried to gently pull away, he pulled back, right into the same spot. He continued to rest, while I started to fall asleep as well, sitting on the floor, head leaning on the mattress.

I awoke with the feeling of being lifted, soon feeling the soft touch that engulfed me, yet kept me floating high, with my body balanced out on the soft touch that now seemed to be inflated around me, comforting me until it all fades away, through the night sky, I see Isaac above me. Shining. Like the brightest star in the night sky, outshining all the others. At that moment I knew he was worth it.

"Good morning to you," Isaac said with eyes roving over me.

"More like good morning to you. It's the afternoon," I said, glancing around my room, while starting to wince because of the bright sun through my window.

"Well, get up. You look like you passed out on the floor next to me. I was starting to worry," Isaac continued. I started to sit up, but Isaac helped me stand without a word.

"I am going to take a shower. You can eat if you want," I mention tiredly, placing a hand on my head like I have a migraine, as I walked into the only bathroom, which was in my room.

I slipped off my cloak, letting it drop onto the ground, feeling too tired and lazy to pick it up. I turned on the shower, letting the water heat up. Once heated well enough, I stepped in rinsing my hair, while undoing the strands of hair that were grouped up. As I rubbed shampoo into my hair, I tried to remember what Bonesella was saying earlier. Something about meeting her in the main garden. I tried hard to remember when she wanted me to be there, but my brain failed me, and I continued cleaning up. A knock become present at the bathroom door, then Isaac's voice echoed in. "Can I use your restroom really quick?" he asked.

"Sure," I mentioned quickly, without even thinking much about it. Seconds later, Isaac's voice came up again. "Hey, what's this photo here?" Isaac mentioned. I knew exactly what photo he was talking about. The memory passed through my mind for a couple seconds, then faded, trailing out of my head. "Oh, nothing . . .It just calms me sometimes . . ." I muttered, stuttering a bit in the beginning. "It is nice though, I like it," Isaac responded quickly. "Thanks," I said under my breath. "So, do you have a camera?" Isaac asked after a moment has passed. "No, no, no. I don't have that kind of money. I'm poor, okay. It was something of my mother's," I said quickly, without really realizing how rude I was being. Isaac does not reply after that.

"Oh, hey, can you get me a towel, I forgot to grab it from the shelf," I asked trying to be kind this time.

"Sure," Isaac does not give attitude back, instead he still seemed to be in a kind mood.

"Thanks," I said poking my hand out to grab the towel, then turning off the water.

I should really have apologized. I was just so sensitive. First, I got pissed off, but soon after, I cried my eyes out. Except my tears didn't come, the shower already provided it for me. It was just that I push people away and I either cry, or sometimes not. I didn't cry really when my heart was already shattered and there was nothing to leak out anymore. Soon enough, I heard the bathroom door open and close. I sighed and I left.

Once dressed I found Isaac in the kitchen, making something. Something I was not sure what it was.

"Oh, Isaac. What's that?" I asked.

"I am making Schevons," Isaac said casually in a strange accent.

My eyes were wide.

"You can cook? I thought you didn't know how!" I yelled out.

"Sure, I just don't really . . . bake," Isaac said with his eyes trailing back to the food.

"Well, anyway, I never heard of that kind of food in my life," I exclaimed.

"It's a kind of spicy sea food," Isaac said while adding some spices.

"I don't really like eating the actual flesh from a once living animal . . ." I explained slowly.

"It's all right, I'll eat this all by myself," Isaac said finishing up and taking a deep gulp.

There was a moment of silence then. My anxiety started flowing through me. I could feel my blood flow, and the shaking of my body.

"I-I am sorry," I squeaked.

Isaac looked at me with confusion.

"What do you mean that you are sorry?" Isaac asked.

"I felt like I was being rude earlier . . . I want to apologize," I said shallowly.

"Oh, that is fine. Don't worry. I am not mad at you," Isaac replied kindly.

"Thanks."

"Of course."

"Come, I want to show you something," I said unexpectedly.

"Um . . . okay," Isaac let out as I grabbed his hand.

I lead Isaac to the front door.

"No, I am not going out there," Isaac said strictly, without moving a muscle.

"No one is going to see you, I promise," I told him through heart.

Isaac continued to look into my eyes if this was a sacrifice.

"You will be fine," I added. Isaac nodded, so I guided him through the door and off to the side of the house. Isaac bent over behind the bushes as we walked around. On the side of the house we got to a covered patio that was hidden by several sheets of unusual colors that were hung all the way around.

"Come," I said as I pulled the sheet slightly open.

"No one will see you here."

I disappeared into the patio leaving Isaac outside, walking straight to the back to open the sheet curtains. No one lived behind me, because there was a lake there—so it would be fine to let some light in from the back. Isaac walked in as I was tying the sheets to the wooden posts. Before Isaac could even make it to the center, he was greeted by Nightmare.

"Holy—"

"Shh." I cut in front of Isaac, reaching my hand out to Nightmare. He sniffed me, then started licking the palm of my hand.

"Nightmare, this is Isaac. Isaac, this is Nightmare," I said to start off.

"Come closer, he's not going to hurt you," I said after a pause of eye contact between the two.

Isaac reached out his hand just as I did. Nightmare started to sit up, slowly bringing in his nostrils—just barely touching Isaac's hand. Nightmare took a short sniff, then his expression completely changes, becoming defensive. He growled a low tone, backing slowly.

"It's okay, I am not going to hurt you," Isaac said softly, trying to bond with him. Isaac then came towards Nightmare, as he was backing up. Once Isaac reached in, just touching the tip of his nose, Nightmare let out a terrible, high-pitched roar.

I quickly pulled Isaac behind me, making sure he was clear of Nightmare's bite.

Isaac breathed heavily behind my neck.

"Nightmare, Isaac is not going to hurt you. He is my friend," I started slowly.

Nightmare cocked his head trying to understand what I was saying.

"Yes, Isaac is my friend. He is staying here with me for a while," I continued.

Nightmare straightened his head and then slowly walked forward. He wanted to make up with Isaac. I moved to the side, letting the two face each other. Nightmare continued forward till he sniffs Isaac from below at his feet, to above to his face.

"Hi, Nightmare," Isaac said in a cheer full tone.

Right at that moment, Nightmare came up and threw himself on top of Isaac licking his face.

"Oh, stop! You're getting your saliva all over my clothes!" Isaac yelled, laughing at the same time.

I giggled as I watched. It usually took an entire week for a dragon to bond with a person; it just took less than a minute between Isaac and Nightmare. After a while I told Nightmare to get off, he followed. Isaac, on the other hand, got up slowly, trying to wipe off all the dragon saliva from his clothes. Isaac broke into a smile, and before it even went past one second, Isaac broke into a hard laugh. I rolled my eyes as a joke.

"Wow, he really likes you then. I thought he might rip your arm off," I said as Isaac's laugh died.

"Well, I guess you can never tell with a dragon," Isaac responded, glaring over Nightmare, who was chewing on the wooden post next to him.

"Nightmare stop that. Chew on this instead," I said throwing to him some raw meat out of my bag that I bought earlier on the way back. He suddenly stopped chewing on the pole and immediately bit into the meat.

"Well, let's go inside. I have to get ready," I said walking off to the front door.

Isaac followed behind.

"Get ready for what?" Isaac asked, worried. Most likely worried about me leaving him.

"Nothing, I'm going out," I said hanging my bag and my cloak on the coat hanger.

"Going out where?" Isaac asked raising his voice as he follows me to my room.

"To the central garden," I said taking a seat at my desk. I threw my hands down flat on my desk, looking Isaac in the eyes, with full focus. Isaac's face was worried, while his clothes were a mess full of saliva. He reminded me of the homeless children and adults living on the streets in this town. It was extremely poor here.

"Xavier, I am sorry. I should not be yelling at you. I just don't like it when you leave," Isaac explained.

"It's fine. I'm just going to see a friend. She invited me there," I said finally.

"Oh okay," Isaac sighed and then went off to the shower.

I started to dress into a white dress shirt and pink straight-legged pants. To go along with it, I chose some old rundown boots that went up to the middle of my calf. Isaac was still in the shower once I was dressed. "Isaac I'm leaving, bye," I called out.

"Wait," Isaac said just barely over the noise of the shower, right before I walked out of my room. The shower turned off and Isaac poked his wet face through the door.

"I-I . . ." Isaac stuttered a bit, looking over at me, wide-eyed.

"I miss you," Isaac broke out.

"I'll miss you too," I said and Isaac smiled, bringing his head in and softly closing the door. Before I even stepped out, something glimmered, catching my eye. I stepped closer to my dresser. My cross necklace glimmered, laid out on top of some of my stuff. After a moment of staring at its glimmering diamonds, I put it on and left. I made my way over to the garden. The bright sun, that never seemed to get any dimmer, was finally setting under a pink sky. The closer to the sun you look, the more orange and yellow you see. When you look past the pink, furthest from the sun, it began to turn into purple—which then turns into a nighttime blue. Looking up at this as I made my way to the garden was just like a painting: the garden, the sun, and a sky of colors.

I soon found myself within the garden. It was like I never even noticed it until I was in it. I walked slowly through the twists and turns. After all, I knew this maze by heart. Once I made it to the center, it was no surprise that Bonesella was already there . . . waiting for me.

"Hi," she said shyly, gazing her eyes back at the sky.

I never seen her so nervous and shy before.

"Hello," I said taking a seat next to her.

Bonesella did not look at me, instead she continued to keep her head up to the sky. I started to watch with her. I could just fall asleep right here. A couple of moments later, she sighed and turned her golden sparkly eyes at me. They were a shiny golden yellow in the center, and on the rim, a deep glittery orange. And the iris was dipped in a deep glowing green—the rest of her eye. I suddenly realized that I wasn't blinking, so I blink a few times, then turned my attention back to the sky.

"Xavier," she said. I looked back at her.

"I am actually glad that you came," she said looking down at her lap this time. I looked up and noticed a fence, only about a foot wide and tall over our heads. Vines of roses were growing through it. And as I rolled my head over, the fence curved and so did the vines until the fence became straight down into the ground.

"Of course," I said finally.

"No but for real, thanks," Bonesella said once again.

"You know . . . I never really had a friend," she continued.

"Why not? You seem nice and incredibly open, I am sure you have loads of friends," I said in a more cheerful tone.

Bonesella giggled a bit, but it died down very quickly.

"Thanks, but I am quite alone," she started.

"People don't really like to hang out with me . . . by just taking one look at me," Bonesella said adjusting herself on the bench.

"You look fine and beautiful to me," I said kindly.

With her smile I could tell that she was blushing, but I didn't think she would be able to show pink on those black bones.

"Well, that's not what I meant," Bonesella continued slowly.

"Then, what do you mean?"

"Well, is in it obvious?" Bonesella said loudly, standing up with her arms out. I looked at her head to toe. Just a pretty girl in a dark grey dress with violet roses.

"No," I said after a moment.

Bonesella's face changes after that, it softens, and her anger dies down a couple notches. She finally took a seat beside me again, sighing.

"My family is royalty . . . when people look at me, they can already tell," she explained depressively.

"You're a royal!?" I yelled out, myself standing this time.

"Oh, so now you're going to act like everyone else who sees me," Bonesella said rolling her eyes; her head turned away from me and slouched over with a hand on her chin.

"Well, I didn't know . . ." I said slowly and much more relaxed, but not taking a seat yet.

"It's fine. Being a royal isn't all that, it's okay once in a while, but in the end . . . you really don't have any friends," Bonesella said.

"Oh, that seems kind of sad. I don't really have any friends either," I said, trying to make her feel better. Bonesella did not respond; instead she kept her eyes fixed on the sky.

"Well, considering that you are a royal, why do you even want to hang out with me? I am on the other side of the spectrum here. I'm super poor compared to you," I asked strongly, taking a seat beside her again.

She took a moment to respond.

"I don't just see money when I looked at a person," Bonesella finally said, looking down in her lap again.

"In fact, I don't see money at all when I looked at you," Bonesella adds meeting my eyes again.

"So, you fight in the ring here?" I change the subject to something more comfortable to talk about.

"Yeah, I really enjoy it. We should fight together sometime," Bonesella said, lighting up.

"Actually, I would prefer not to."

"Why? Don't you like it?"

I took a moment before I could respond. I only wanted to be honest.

"I don't like killing people."

"Killing people? That's the main point! If, you don't like fighting bloody wars, then why did you go?" Bonesella asked surprised.

I took a moment, longer than before. I tried to remember all the training I had with Jacob. I would practice shooting arrows at targets that he lined up for me, based on my weaknesses. I also practiced throwing weapons, like swords, knives, and axes. Some of these were heavy, so I had to use smaller versions of them. Weapon fighting was a mix of skills, Jacob wanted me to learn some of these tactics because he said I might need them one day. My training was mild. I didn't work overly hard all the time. It wasn't because I didn't enjoy it; I just felt that I rather do other things, such as reading and writing. Jacob was quite lenient on this.

"I-I don't know," I lied.

Bonesella did not respond. Instead of saying something negative about it, she said something that surprised me a bit.

"Well, I could always help you with it. It usually is fun; it is just that the ring is always bloody. It would be nice if we could do some fighting lessons together."

"Yeah, I guess so. Though, I don't think I am ready yet . . . the experience I had that day," I said slowly.

"Well, all right. My parents don't like me being out this late, what if we meet tomorrow night? . . . As a date," Bonesella said. The last words were even more surprising.

"I've never gone out with someone before . . ." I said. "Oh, don't worry about that. You will be fine," Bonesella reassures me. "But, where will we go out? Here?" I asked.

"A fancy restaurant—I was thinking," Bonesella responded quickly.

"I don't think I could do that." My anxiety was starting to grow. The thought was haunting.

"Why not?"

"I am poor, and I don't even know where this place is," I said a little more strictly.

"I'll stop by and we can walk together. It is not even that far . . . plus, I'll pay," Bonesella said calmly. In the end, I could not refuse.

Bonesella said she will do all of it. I just must get ready and wait till she came by. I said goodbye and left. I couldn't believe I had a girlfriend.

Chapter Twelve

I got home late at night. I walked into my room to find Isaac sleeping in my bed. I just loved it when he sleeps. He was lying on his stomach, hands tucked under the pillow, and legs apart. I took a seat at my desk and took out the strings to fix my jeans. I set all my materials out, ready for me to use in the morning.

When early morning came, Isaac wrinkled his nose and peeked open an eye.

"Morning, why are you up so early?" Isaac mumbled without moving from his previous position.

"I am fixing the pair of jeans that I planned on, I told you this the other day," I said like he should know all this already.

"Why so early though?" Isaac asked, complaining like, digging his head into my pillow.

"It's a lengthy process, I want to get it done this afternoon, so I can wear it tonight," I said casually.

Isaac did not like being up currently.

"What is going on tonight," Isaac asked, still sounding like he rather sleep.

"Nothing," I said keeping my casual tone. Of course, with Isaac this early in the morning, he did not argue back; instead he simply went back to sleep. Maybe he would forget that I ever said anything about tonight.

Once, Isaac awoke—for real this time, I was extending the length of my jeans. So far, I hadn't made any major mistakes.

"I am going to eat something; do you want anything?" Isaac asked, before leaving my room.

"Make me a tea and bring me a small bowl of fruit, thanks."

"Yes, sir."

Isaac got me the tea and fruit. I was not even sure if he would accept my request. Isaac began to watch me for a while. Taking old material and sewing it on to the jeans. Soon enough, Isaac seemed to have got bored and went to take a shower.

The day went by quick, even the jeans seemed to have caught up. I was finally finished in the afternoon, like I hoped for.

"Isaac," I called.

"Yeah, Xavier?" He said looking up from a book he was reading.

"I'm going out, I will see you later tonight," I said, ready in my fixed jeans and a comfy shirt.

"You said there was nothing going on," Isaac said strictly, standing up from the couch.

"Like last time, I just want to hang out with a friend," I said, rolling my eyes with caution.

"I thought I was your friend! Plus, I thought you said no one likes you out there!" Isaac yelled.

I was scared on the inside, but I wasn't giving up. I just felt that if I told him the truth, he would never forgive me. I had to lie a bit.

"You are my friend; I can have multiple friends if I want! Why are you so worried? You are afraid of going outside!" I yelled back. Isaac froze. He must have been trying to hide something also. We are now even.

"Okay, fine. You can go hang out with your other friends. I'll just stay here . . . hidden," Isaac finally said, shallowly.

"Thanks . . . but don't be like that. You are my friend. It is just that you won't allow yourself to go out. I want to be free;

you can't stop me when you are stopping yourself," I explained kindly.

Isaac nodded.

"Look I'll wait a little while with you, okay?" I added. Isaac just simply nodded again.

After a while of lying next to each other and reading, I went to check outside of the window to see if Bonesella was here yet. I did tell her where I lived right before I left. After a couple seconds of searching out the window, I spotted her coming up the steps.

I creaked open the door to say, "Hey, give me a sec. I am almost ready."

"All right. I will be here. Just don't take too long."

I went to say a warm goodbye to Isaac. I felt bad leaving him here. But that was his choice.

"Bye, I will miss you. See you tonight," I said hugging him.

"I miss you too. So much. Bye," he said, hugging me back a little tighter.

I went back out. Bonesella was wearing a cute top and skirt that match.

"You ready?" she asked.

I nodded and smile. We started walking together. When I spend time with her, I forget about Isaac, but when I was spending time with Isaac, I forgot about Bonesella. It was like my mind was purposely pushing other people out of my head.

As we walked, the poor village came out of sight, and the city came into view. There were buildings—shops, with glass windows you can see through. The city here was still not the fanciest. The fanciest were the six kingdoms, yet I was not a royal. Poor people had grown to despise the royals. The royal kingdoms got the largest imports of food and goods, so the lower classes blamed them for taking all their food. I didn't like taking sides; I rather stay neutral. Just because I belonged to the lower class did not mean I agreed with them. The lower class did not even accept me here, I wondered what other royals might think of me, besides Bonesella. This reminded me of the armor Isaac had. It was royal merchandise by the looks. Did Isaac break into kingdoms and stole gear? Was he a royal who was now refugee? Or did he run away on his own? I may never know.

We came up to the restaurant. Its glass windows revealed a nice dinner, with strings of lights around the bar, and hanging yellow lamps. I began to feel anxiety as we got in line to get a table. “Don’t worry, it is not that expensive,” Bonesella said, though I didn’t care about money now. Rarely.

Bonesella asked for a booth for both of us. We soon got to a table, and menus were handed to both of us. I asked for an Iced tea, while Bonesella asked for wine at the bar.

“Is all this money and royal stuff bothering you?” Bonesella asked after taking a sip of her wine.

“No, I am just not used to it. This place makes me a bit nervous,” I said looking around at the crowded place.

“Well, I am here for you. Let me know if it gives you too much anxiety, I will walk you out,” she said looking back at the menu. I nodded, silently.

When the waiter came, I ordered a salad. I didn’t feel too hungry. Bonesella orders dark violet sea food. I ate slowly in silence, while Bonesella tries to spark up some conversations.

“You know, you can be very quiet,” she started, another attempt to make me face her with some words. I stared down at my salad. Picking at it a bit. After another moment of silence, Bonesella fired up a bit.

“Are you going to talk or not?” My face flushed red.

“I’m nervous . . .” I said shyly.

Bonesella’s expression became calm again.

“Oh, sorry. I didn’t know,” she said sounding sorry.

“I am quiet when I am not okay,” I said.

She nodded with understanding.

I felt that I had to use the restroom, though I did not want to get up. This place became even more packed as time passed later in the day. Maybe I drank too much Iced tea, I was almost done with my second refill.

"Are you okay?" Bonesella asked, noticing that I was even more nervous.

"I'm fine, I just need to use the restroom," I said casually.

"Then go," she said with a tone that told me I was acting odd.

"I don't really want to . . ." I said slowly.

"If you are so freaked out, you should still go. You can't hold it in forever," she explained.

Bonesella was right. It would be better if I did.

After a moment I said, "Okay fine, I'll go."

I quickly stood up, yet I slowly walked over to the back. I kept my head down to avoid everyone close by. Before I knew it, I found myself there. Right when I pushed the door open, someone was coming out. My face burned. I just realized that I never used a public restroom before.

It was a nice restroom, though I did my best to ignore it. The restroom was packed too, and I was afraid of having a panic attack. People were talking, and, it was soft. But in my mind, it was loud. It felt that it was drowning my ears. I stared into the wall in front of me as I tried to do all my mind tricks to calm me down. So far, none have made much progress. Out of doing everything, I had only one thing left I could do, though I was trying my hardest not to. I was already holding it, yet I didn't want to start rubbing my fingers lightly because I know it would become something much more than that. After a while, the restroom grew silent, I turned my head a bit. The restroom was empty. Thank God. I finished up and washed my hands. I looked up into the mirror. My face was burnt pink. I splashed some water on me to cool me down.

Once I got back to the table, it might have looked like other things were going on.

"What happened now?" Bonesella asked sounding annoyed by now.

"Nothing that it looks like . . . I was just really nervous," I said looking down at my plate.

"Jeez, what's the issue with going to the restroom anyway?" Bonesella asked, still sounding annoyed.

"I never used a public restroom in my life. It was full of people; now will you please calm down. I have anxiety," I said quietly.

"Okay, fine," Bonesella stated.

"I know I have been a bit too stubborn towards you. That's just how I am. I'm sorry," she said, her voice dying down a couple notches.

"It's okay. I'm extremely sensitive anyways," I said honestly, making things even. Bonesella paid and we left.

It was late—and the night sky was beautiful. Bonesella and I were walking back to my place, but slowly.

"Well, I guess that didn't turn out the way I wanted it to . . ." Bonesella started, with her hands behind her back.

"Yeah . . ." I said a little shakily.

Bonesella continued, "Hey, if you are okay with it, I would not mind going out again," Bonesella said a little more cheerfully.

"All right, but this time I am going to choose what we do," I said in a playing tone.

"That place gave me the creeps."

Bonesella and I agreed that we would go out again. As we made other plans, the thought of Isaac faded away out of my mind. While I was making plans, Isaac was also making other plans.

" . . . Look, I don't want to harm you, okay?" Isaac started from going on about me leaving so much.

"I understand," I said trying to stay on the topic. The thought of Bonesella was still trying to roam my mind.

"I don't think I should stay any longer. If they find me, I don't know what will happen to you," Isaac explained.

The village people thought I was weird enough.

"Well, I don't know when I will see you again . . ." I started.

"I am thinking of leaving tomorrow morning," Isaac said, which finally breaks it. I had minor tears streaming down my face. I really was going to miss him . . . but tomorrow morning? I wouldn't be able to tell him things that I should have said when we first met. I knew I wouldn't be able to do it. I guessed if I would ever run into him, to tell him the truth about all of this.

I slept next to Isaac one more night. Most likely my last night with him. My face was wet from tears, as I shoved myself in my pillow. I scooted closer to Isaac. His warmth comforted me. That whole night I forgot about Bonesella, yet I remembered her in the morning when Isaac wasn't there.

He was gone. He must have left when I was sleeping. Shit, I sleep in way too much. And now I miss him so much. Everything will be okay, when I was with Bonesella, I could forget all about this. With this as my ending with Isaac, I started to go out more with Bonesella. When I was out with her, it helped me forget all my bad memories. It pushed them all aside. I was bonding better with her now. Her stubbornness died down, and I acted a bit more outspoken. Though, not all the time. I also started to learn how much she liked me. She didn't really talk about me in the way of being attractive or anything, she talked about me in the nicer ways. How kind and sweet I was. Mostly personality wise. As we bonded increasingly. I was also falling for her.

Chapter Thirteen

I picked the edge off a rose. Bonesella's gaze came toward my eyes. I was wondering how far this would go.

"Give me your hands," she said in a medium volume and a soft tone. I let out one hand to her.

"Both."

Then I gave her the other. She grasped them lightly.

"Stand up," she told me.

"Why? you're not going to make me ball dance with you, are you?" I asked, unsure.

It was the perfect environment for it, though I was not a dancer.

"Why? You don't want to?"

"I don't dance."

"Oh, come on!" She said happily, pulling me up.

I was only partially embarrassed. At least no one else was here . . . even though I would suspect there would be. It wasn't a major ball room, as what Bonesella said, though I thought otherwise; apparently it was a royal lounge room. The walls made up a dodecagon, while the ceiling was a dome with a chandelier at its center. Half of the walls were taken up by mirrors, and on the sides of each wall had long, violet curtains.

Bonesella showed me simple steps first. She said it got complicated when you were more skilled. As we went through the basics, I felt like I needed much practice with this. I almost tripped over Bonesella as I stepped forward. She reminded me that we had to be in sync. When she stepped back, I had to step forward and vice versa. She said I was a natural, I thanked her, but in the back of my mind, I doubted that.

"Do you want to go eat now?" Bonesella asked as I was just realizing that it was close to luncheon.

"Does that mean I have to eat properly?" I moaned.

"Yes," Bonesella joked, laughing.

I rolled my eyes playfully. Bonesella was my girlfriend, though I thought of her as my best friend. Just because you were in a romantic relationship with someone does not mean they cannot be your friend.

It felt strange being here. Bonesella did not want me to meet any other royals while I was here; plus her family was small. She was a single child. Her mother lived here, yet her father was someplace else. She didn't want to tell me what happened to him. She said she would tell me one day when she was ready. She said that she told her mother, I would be a visitor, yet I didn't meet her. Bonesella had an uncle living here also. She said that he was humorous and played with her as a child. Bonesella didn't tell me everything about her life. She told me most things were for later in life, when Bonesella and I were bonded even closer. Plus, we are just dating.

We sat at a small dining table to eat. Of course, it wasn't the main, large one that she sat at with her small family. The food was better than at the restaurant that we went to on our first date.

"My uncle cooks around here," Bonesella said taking a bite. I didn't make a right of way comment, I was waiting for more to hear.

"My mother is usually busy . . . royal stuff. Plus, my father is away somewhere. He pretty much disappeared from us," Bonesella explained.

"Oh, right," I said shallowly, but in my mind, I was more than happy about the food.

Out of Bonesella's life being a royal, the only thing that really struck me was anything dealing with her father. There must be something about him she didn't want to tell me now, but she said one day she will. I wondered what the story about him was. Who was her father anyway?

I tried to push the idea of her father out of my mind. I tried to forget most things and just enjoy the moment. It had been six months of dating, and it has been going well. I was wondering how long we were going to end up dating for. Now I was trying to figure out what Bonesella was up to. I lay on the gray staring up at the sky, in the center of the central garden in my village. Bonesella was not here yet. She was obviously planning something, but I still can't figure out why she was acting quite unusual.

"I am here," Bonesella called, walking in.

"Where were you?" I asked, laughing a bit.

"I have a surprise for you," she said instead. I froze for a moment.

"Really?" I asked, wondering what it might be. Bonesella's hands were behind her back like usual.

She laughs.

"It's behind your back, isn't it?" I said eying her.

"Nope. You are going to have to guess," Bonesella said showing me her hands. Now this was going to be a challenge.

"Tell me," I said about to give up.

"No, guess."

"But this is so hard," I whined.

"Well, you are going to have to try," Bonesella said, going an octave higher in the end.

"Well, I give up," I said simply, dragging my eyes back up to the stars.

Bonesella came and sat down next to me.

"I was thinking, that since things have been going well . . ." Bonesella started giving me a moment to think.

"Take a guess . . ." she said after my silence.

"I said I give up," I repeat depressively, not looking at her.

"Why so sad? You should be excited, it's a surprise," she said, surprised herself.

My excitement died out ages ago.

"Well, you didn't tell me anything yet," I said.

"Xavier, I want to marry you . . .what else would it be," Bonesella said like I should know this.

The words passed through my mind. I didn't realize after another moment of silence.

"Seriously?" I asked.

I looked back at Bonesella. She just nodded without a word.

"I'm sorry," I said.

"It's okay, I should not have been so hard on you," Bonesella said, picking at a flower.

"Hey, look at me," I said turning around, and placing a hand underneath her chin.

"I really didn't know, I'm sorry," I said again, pleading like.

"I forgive you," Bonesella said after a moment. I nodded, I was glad this did not come worse.

We walked around the garden. I had a tough time believing that it was true. She wanted to marry me. We just kept picking at the pretty flowers. It was so nice out here. Before I knew it, the wedding planning had begun.

~

"I don't really want to do this," I said, almost shaking.

"Come on, he is just my uncle. He's not going to do anything to you. Plus, he has his own humor," Bonesella replied almost at an instant.

Bonesella swung around me, swinging the door open, and revealing my face.

"Hey, Uncle!" Bonesella yelled across the room.

She ran up to the man and he gave her the tightest hug and started to swing her around.

"Oh, am I glad to see you!" he said letting go of her.

Bonesella looks as if she were about to be sick, clutching an arm around her torso.

Before I even make plans of sneaking away, I was spotted almost instantly after he has let go of his niece.

"Oh, what do you got here, Bonese? Your lover . . .?"

He was such a dramatic guy. His tone and volume always varied, from loud exited yelps to even low tone sneaky whispers. Since he had an over amount of emotion, not to mention his speech, he kind of scared me.

"Uh, yeah . . ." Bonesella replied, with still, an arm wrapped around her torso.

Before I could think otherwise, we were both brought into his gigantic arms. I began to have a tough time breathing, then I just remembered that I was claustrophobic. I pushed my way out of his arms.

"I'm sorry. It's nice to meet you. I am a bit claustrophobic," I said shakily.

"It's all right."

He turned right over to Bonesella, "What's the lad's name again? Xan-Xark—Zxarvixar . . . ? Oh, wait. That's your father's name. Uh—"

"It is Xavier," I cut him off.

"Oh, right! Xavier!" he yelled.

"I was so close I had it!" he exclaimed.

Not really, but I will give him some credit.

"Come, I want to show you two a special place of my own," he said, turning dramatically.

I looked to Bonesella to see if she knew what he was talking about, but she was looking at me with the same confusion.

"Oh, yeah. My name is Jashar, the God and Keeper of Light," he said as we follow him into a corridor off to the side.

"Did you ever hear of that!?" Jashar asked loudly. Bonesella continued to stay quiet.

"Yes, I have actually. I studied about you," I said in a low tone voice.

"Oh, really? What did you learn from those dusty, old books?" Jashar challenged.

"You carry light. You are the teacher for other light mages and alchemists," I said taking up my studies.

"Yes!" Jashar yelled as a victory.

"Well, I am also supposed to in charge of this place, if something were to happen to Bonesella's mother," Jashar went on.

I nodded without really thinking about it.

The castle soon turned to rock as we walked down stairs after stairs. I started to see reflections of light; I thought it was something of my imagination, until I saw millions of them. Inside the rock were pieces of gold. It shone brightly around us. There were some lit candles on the walls, though as the stairs ended and we were walking through a long corridor, there were so much more lined up on the walls now. After a while, Bonesella spoke my thoughts.

"Where are we going? And how long is it going to take?" Bonesella strictly asked Jashar.

"We are nearly there, just after this other corridor," Jashar said revealing an even larger corridor.

Golden statues of other similar gods floated above in a long row on both sides facing each other. A stone passageway—a bridge, passes between them. Under the bridge and on parts of the walls, Magma flowed. Between the statues, clusters of candles floated as well. This place was bright. Of course—Jashar was the keeper of light.

I walked down the carved stone in awe; I never believed that I would be here. Bonesella slowed her walk, till she was walking at the same pace, right next to me. Without really thinking about it, we automatically took each other's hand. We also began to walk closer together, a bit farther behind from Jashar.

"Xavier, this is amazing," Bonesella said watching all around her.

I was doing the same, taking in all the details.

"We are here. My beautiful home. My throne room," Jashar announced.

Bonesella and I walked up to it. It was like another cave within the cave we were already in. The inside was bright yellow by light reflecting off the walls. This smaller cave had its entrance, and a couple spaces though it, made naturally, showing glimpses of the inside of Jashar's throne room. As we entered, our eyes went wide. A golden throne sat in the middle of the dome. It was overly complex. Every hand carved symbol, at every edge of the seat. Spear shaped spokes stood out behind the back rest. On the floor, a map of constellations, planets, stars, galaxies and other related stuff in the universe, were carved in the beige stone. The closest to the throne, the stone was more yellowish, though it turned to beige as you go farther from it.

Waterfalls lined the walls around us. I looked back to Jashar who was standing aside from us.

"So, what do you think?" he asked pleasantly.

I spoke for both of us; Bonesella was too busy gazing over all this. "I think it's amazing". Jashar smiled.

Jashar was a sparkly gold man, with symbols written in a much lighter tone, almost white, but still yellow all over his body. His long wavy beard almost touched the floor and had golden rings around certain sections. He had relatively high cheekbones, and a generally round head. His eyes were round and silver. He wore gold cuffs, many necklaces, no shirt, and a red scarf wrapped around his waist. The scarf hung in the front and the back. As what I could see if the front, it looked as if it were dipped in gold symbols. They faded as you go up.

"Aren't you supposed to have four more arms—six in total?" I asked after a moment of studying, remembering my studies.

"Yes, I do have them . . ." Jashar started, showing his other arms, appearing from behind. "It's an immortal thing," he continued.

Oh, yeah. I forgot I do the same with my wings. Bonesella smiled at this.

"Yeah, I almost forgot about that too."

We laugh for a moment, then we all quiet down.

"So," Jashar said taking a seat in his throne.

"Who's the wedding planner? Oh, wait. That's me. I am going to be your party planner!" Jashar said excitedly.

"Wow, what a surprise," Bonesella said sarcastically.

"Are you always this sarcastic?" I said quietly. I could tell already that to be in this relationship, I was going to have to deal with Bonesella's hot temper.

"Well, . . . I get irritable often . . ." she slowly said. This ended up being better than I thought.

"All right, so what are your ideas?" I turned back to Jashar.

"Well, I was thinking we should find a place to host this of course. What about the grand hall?" Jashar quickly turned to Bonesella.

"I am sure your parents wouldn't mind," Jashar addressed both of us.

"So, what do you think?"

Bonesella and I looked each other in the eyes. She may be a bit stubborn at times, though I still admired her. I didn't care if she was not the best kind of person. All I cared about was that it was love that we strived for.

Bouquets of flowers tied with turquoise ribbon on the violet curtains across the large windows of the great hall. Tables were set nicely with long red cloths across and sets of clean dishes and silverware lined up perfectly. Flower petals lay scattered across the tables, making a perfect complement to the colored glasses and dishes. A gigantic chandelier hung above the largest dinner table in the center. The great chandelier full of glowing candles sparkled above the grand table of where Bonesella's closest relatives and family would sit. Though, I didn't have any family, so I would be considered an outcast . . . for now, until the wedding.

Chapter Fourteen

I stood surrounded by my own reflections. I was never vain. Not even today, when everything will count later. I cared for others too much, till I couldn't even care about myself sometimes. I glowed in mirrors. For some reason, mirrors show the best parts of me. Just standing insecurely nude, I still looked as if I were some holy blessing. I would let my wings out, only for gentle looks. I would flap them a bit, like a bird who fluffs up their feathers to get the attention of others. Just to mate. I have also found someone, but I tried not to think about that, yet I still contain the ever so clearly memories of masturbating. Deep inside of me, I really wanted attention. On the outside, I hid all that . . . only to show true kindness to people. To show how selfless I was, like I never cared for an inch of my own body. The fact was . . . that was a bit of a lie.

The truth was that I could barely care for myself properly. I could never just depend on someone. I could never depend on someone to make me happy if I couldn't even make myself happy. I know that I will depend on someone someday, I just can't do it all alone, without thinking of myself first. I masturbate hoping to get the feeling back in me, the feeling of being loved more than ever. I knew that one day I would have to expose myself. Expose all of it. Though, I knew I wouldn't be ready for it. Not ever.

Sometimes masturbating made me feel like everything, but sometimes it didn't make me feel any better. I would cry in bed, just hoping that I would be able to last another day. No matter how hard I try to please myself, I wouldn't be able to. My body just wouldn't respond. I knew why. There was nothing more that I could do. I remember all the times I would cry, hidden in the corner of my room. I knew my body needed attention, but it didn't need my own, it needed the touch of someone else.

Finally, my dreams became clear to me. Every time I would erect. Every time I would ejaculate. Every time I would cry. I was needy. I begged to be held. I cried to touch someone. I died to listen to someone's heartbeat. In the mirror, I saw someone. I saw someone that only wanted one thing in the world: to be loved in a way like no other. He wanted sex. He probably wouldn't even care what kind. He was in total need. He knew his secret was going to get out one day. For now, he must hold on. He must hold on to his penis.

That was who I was. I knew I wouldn't want to admit it, though I was sure that they wouldn't care about what I do all by myself. All they would care was that this was who I was . . . and that they would love me no matter what. No matter if it was all I had left.

The sound of some whining of an animal echo behind me. I turned away from the mirrors that showed my truth. Nightmare sat with his head cocked to the side. I smiled. I knew I wouldn't feel alive without him, even if he almost killed me. I went right ahead to kiss him between his nostrils. He looked at me as if the world was going to end.

"Oh, Nightmare. When all this is over with, I promise that I will spend more time with you, okay?" I said sweetly.

Nightmare gave a kind response, a certain growl that meant appreciation. I read it in a book. I looked back at the mirrors;

though, I looked in them as if it were the past. I knew I was a bit nervous about it; I tried to keep away from it though. I closed my eyes for a couple seconds, inhaling and exhaling, repeatedly. I reopened my eyes to Nightmare. His violet eyes glowed with the look of ember. I smiled; Nightmare might have brought me fear, yet he healed that fear with love.

I took a seat on the large, curved ottoman, which was aligned with the mirrors. I looked down into my bare lap. I tried to think of other things, but the same thought kept taking over my mind: I was making a promise, a wish to marry this person. *Is my choice true? Is it worth it?* I tried so hard to stay away from these questions and thoughts, it only made me feel worse. I wish this were to be over with.

Nightmare gave a low growl. At an instant, I looked up surprised, unsure what to expect. Nightmare gave his way of smiling: jaws wide open, tongue sticking out to the side, and glimmering eyes full of adorableness. Around his neck was a bowtie. He didn't have it on before. How did he figure out to put it on? He's a dragon. Not a person.

"Nightmare, how did you do that all by yourself?" I asked. Though with no words, Nightmare wagged his tail, without changing anything of his previous expression. I smiled even more. He was the one thing that brought me life and fire. He made me feel like I just might be the whole entire world to him . . . and that made me feel amazing.

I looked back to my lap as if the mirrors of my truth were swallowing me up. My smile faded into the darkness of the room. There were only a few lit candles. Nightmare looked at me with confusion.

"It's okay, Nightmare. I just want to be left alone . . . it has nothing to do with you . . . okay?" I explained shallowly.

He left after hesitating. He looked as if he really wanted to help me. I sighed. I was not sure if I was ready for this or not.

After a moment, I stood, watching the faces of myself watch me at every angle. In every section of mirror, I could imagine the faces of others that I knew, wanting me to choose wisely. After the fear that set me back, I stood strongly. I will. . .I will say yes.

I bathed in a bath full of bubbles with my feet propped up on the edge of the tub. From growing up in the Fawe jungle, isolated from everywhere else, to being generally poor, to marrying a royal and enjoying a great castle such as this. I loved it, from the gold floors to the fancy chandeliers. I never thought that I would make it here, I only thought that I rather be in the place I always was the lower class.

I sank deeper in the tub, till my eyes were just barely over the water. I tried to keep my mind blank, though everything was too overwhelming. I tried pretending I was used to all this for as long as I could. In the end, I was still with my mouth open in awe.

I started to dry myself off, wrapping a robe around me and wrapping a towel over my hair. As I got ready, I felt as if time began to slow all by itself. And as time slowed, I became increasingly nervous than before. I tried to look decent and wondered if it would be considered valid to the other royals. With the thoughts filling my head, I wanted to scream. My heart pounded, the air thickened, my lungs and my throat swelled and shrank, pain stretched across my head, my legs weakened, my knees buckled . . . I tried to scream but nothing came; I fell to the floor and everything turned black.

I awoke with a tight feeling in my stomach.

"Hey, are you alright?" a voice called.

It must be some fancy royal, I thought. Oh, fuck. This person must have found out that I was not one of them. They must have seen how clumsy I was. What if he told the others? Will I be able to make it through the wedding without being exposed to Bonesella and her family? Unlikely. My face burned as my vision was still clearing up. Once my vision was generally well, I found myself relieved; Jashar stood over me.

"Not really," I finally responded after a while.

"I heard some screaming, then some crying. I ran up here to make sure no one was hurt," Jashar explained.

"Oh, I had a panic attack," I said feebly.

"Well, thank God you are okay. I was really worried about you," Jashar explained. While he said this, I started to notice his outfit.

"What are you wearing?" I was a bit disgusted at the sight. Though I really did not want to be rude.

"I will be hosting your wedding!" Jashar announced.

"Wearing that?!" I said again looking head to toe at his outrageously glorious outfit.

"I thought this was supposed to be formal . . . not a costume party!" I whispered loudly.

"It is not, though this is what I shall wear," Jashar said trying to get me to like it.

I didn't roll my eyes this time, though it sure felt like I did.

"Well, I'll be off then," Jashar said finally while leaving.

I stood for a few moments looking at myself in the mirror. I wore an all-white suit, even white boots. There was something missing. Something important that I should keep a hold of. I walked across the room, to a silver corner table. As the table was reflective, shiny, and incredibly detailed, I paid not much attention to it. I hovered my eyes over a glass bowl of holy, sacred water from a guardian pool . . . in which the Blossom of Life floated upon . . . spinning in the slowest motion, calling my name. I gently lifted the blossom out of the water with both hands cupped around it. It glittered and shined as the holy water glided off the petals on all sides from filling in the center, leaving pin sized droplets sticking to the soft, lush pink petals. I lifted the flower up until it began to float on its own. In midair, the petals of this magnificent flower flapped gently, bringing it at the horizon of my head, gently landing in my hair above my left ear.

I pushed the nervous feelings aside. I wore minimum makeup; gold curls stood out from around my eyes. My lips were lightly covered in a clear lip gloss that glittered. A white and gold cape swung and glided behind me. My wings were properly opened behind me, curved, and fluffed up a bit. Speed walked across the floor, on the royal red carpet which was aligned with candles. It felt as if I was running, with wind hitting my face. I formally speed walked up to the podium.

"Well, someone's been working on their walk," Jashar said.

He was standing behind the podium, with an armed propped up under his chin. He looked as if he has been waiting a while for me. I felt that I was late, yet the large room was completely empty. It was just us, with our voices echoing off the walls.

"Yeah . . . I have been doing a bit," I said trying to hide my excitement.

"So, where's Bonesella?" I asked casually, looking off to the side.

"She's still getting ready," Jashar said in the same tone, until he went down to a romantic whisper.

"She said that she wanted to surprise you."

My face flushed pink. Because of this, I didn't respond right away.

"Oh, right. Of course."

I let my eyes roll around the room, from looking at the stunning chandelier to glaring at the long red carpet that I almost ran across.

"Wow, I cannot believe that I am standing in the middle of all this," I said to myself.

"Yeah, it's a lot to take in. well if you like this so much, you'll like being in the middle of all this tonight."

Jashar's words made me jump. I completely forgot he was there. I almost panicked and now I must take a moment to breathe, though I didn't relax all the way because I was starting to realize exactly what he meant.

"Oh no," I said aloud.

"Oh what?" I turned to look at him face to face.

"Jashar, you got to help me. When all the people come in, I feel that I might . . . I might . . ." I started frantically.

"What is it, boy!?" Jashar yelled, shaking me back to myself.

"I am claustrophobic; I hate being around so many people. If I pass out . . ." I tried to explain to him.

"Xavier! You're going to be fine. If anything were to happen, I would get you out here, okay?" I nodded.

I was too nervous to say anything.

"All right, will you calm down?" Jashar asked of me. I nodded again without a word.

I had been memorizing my lines for a while now, but I still read them over, trying to calm myself down. I sat at the edge of the stage with my feet on the lower step, holding a packet of parchment that has been tied together with some string knotted at the end through a small hole. After half an hour, I heard heels hitting the floor one at a time. I looked up to find a real shocking surprise. A surprise that were merely mentioned to me earlier; words that were passed on from Jashar.

I watched her glide across the floor. I suddenly felt all my nervous feelings disappear, yet I was still frozen on the edge of the stage, clenching parchment in my warm palms. Bonesella stopped right in front of me . . . watching me . . . waiting for a response. I tried to make out a couple of simple words, but nothing came. Bonesella giggled at this.

"You're so speechless," she laughed.

After that I was able to catch my breath again.

"Yeah, well at least I know to be more aware of the kinds of surprises you bring," I joke, standing up at the same time. Bonesella laughs again, but not as hard as earlier.

"Right, you should . . . I am on either side of the spectrum," Bonesella said looking around the beautifully decorated ball room.

I understood exactly what she meant, without her having to state it directly. I love finding context clues to solve a puzzle.

"Well, back to the first place, you look very nice," I said

kindly, getting back on track.

"Aww, thank you," Bonesella blushes.

She wore a sparkling gold orange long dress that matched perfectly with her eyes. A long red cape glided behind her. I smiled at her look. I noticed even the smaller unnoticed details, such as the earrings that hid under her hair, and every single glittering gold marigold on her dress and tied up in her hair that holds it in a ponytail.

"Okay, okay. I'll just leave you two alone for a while, I am going to check on some other stuff," Jashar said walking off.

I totally forgot that he was there. I didn't jump at his words though; I just kept my eyes staring deeply into Bonesella's eyes.

We didn't said any words for a while. We just stood there, enjoying the sight of each other. We already know how this day will end. She knew how I felt, she knows the best parts of it all . . . by heart.

The force of gravity began to pull me closer to her. Was it a black hole that I would never be able to escape from? No. It was a shining star that I would never be able to take my eyes off. My mouth was slightly open. I was longing for something. I knew it was coming. I closed my eyes as if it were a fantasy. I could feel our breath mingling together. Once our lips collided, my mind drifted away from reality. For a whole minute we kissed without even paying attention to our surroundings. Jashar did leave, but was he back and watching? Or was someone else watching? Bonesella's movement of her lips told me not to worry. I didn't matter.

I opened my eyes to the dimming candles around us and in the chandeliers. I held Bonesella's hands together in my own.

"We are doing this together," I said reassuringly.

She smiles in acceptance. Jashar came back rushing.

"All right, places people, places. It's about time. Everyone is gathering in the lounge room," Jashar announced.

I nodded to Bonesella and we went away to the back room. We both took a seat in two red cozy seats.

"Well, it's about time," I said to start off a small conversation.

"Yeah, too bad my father won't be here," Bonesella mentions.

"Why not? It's your special day. He's your father," I confronted her father to her.

"Xavier," Bonesella started.

She was looking down in her lap as if she lost someone.

"He may be my biological father, but he was never an actually father to me," she explained softly.

"Oh," I let out.

I could understand her pain. I remembered when my father suddenly disappeared. Even before he was gone, I felt the same feelings then. He never exactly felt like a father to me. He was like a figure I saw every day yet paid extraordinarily little attention to.

After a long moment of silence, I spoke again softly.

"I know that feeling."

I placed a hand under her chin, lifting her head up to face me.

"Look, everything is going to be okay. If I am right beside you, you don't need to worry. We are in this together."

Chapter Fifteen

I grasped her hand. The gentle touch of her fingers made me feel grateful; the warmth of her palm made me feel welcome; the blood running through her veins made me feel a part of her, and the touch of her bones made me feel like I was everything.

We glided together on the red carpet. Weddings differ depending on what religion or culture you were raised into. This wedding was based on Bonesella's religious beliefs and culture. I didn't exactly have too much of a culture because I was raised in isolation from the rest of the word in the Fawe Jungle. Even when I was raised by Jacob Soars, he didn't really have a religion or a vibrant culture to show me. I really don't think Jacob believes in any gods; he didn't do any kind of prayer or religious practices. In my opinion, I believed Jacob was atheist. If I had to say Jacob had a culture, it would be drinking tea and staring at the birds. I would call it bird culture.

Bonesella had been raised by the culture and religion of her mother. He father was very unknown to me. I wanted to find out more about him and what happened in the past. I was sure Bonesella would talk about it one day, but for now that door was shut.

So many faces were watching us. This was the time I got to

meet her family and accepted into the royal family. Of course, this wasn't the kind of royal family that tell you who to marry—which was another royal from some other family. No, Bonesella had a choice. In fact, I had never been a royal, not until this very moment coming up.

The large room was very dim. The only lights that were visible to me were the hundreds of candles that were floating in mid-air by magic, which were aligned with the red carpet. Before we reached the stage, we turned left to the royal table and took a seat with Bonesella's family. My face started to heat as I sat down at the table. There were just so many faces. I thought Bonesella didn't have such a large family . . . at least that was what she told me. I felt right away then that I was ready to pass out. My breath quickened and became heavy. It was right at that moment that I clenched on to Bonesella's hand.

"Xavier, what is wrong?" she asked me as she was starting to address her family.

"I am really nervous," I whispered to her.

I couldn't bear to look face to face at her family. I was really freaking out now.

Bonesella put a hand on my back and lightly moved her fingers as she spoke again, "It's going to be okay. Everything is going to be okay."

Now addressing her family, "I'm sorry about that. He's just nervous . . . that's all. Either way though, I am glad to be here with my one and only," she said as an introduction to a whole presentation or speech.

I wave shyly and said hi and hello quietly to everyone.

I after saying hi, I whispered in Bonesella's ear, "I thought you didn't have such a large family!"

"I don't, most of the people at this table are friends and acquaintances of my family. Some even have worked with them," Bonesella said showing me all their bright faces with cheer in her voice.

"Oh, well you should have at least told me that they would

be here," I whispered back.

Bonesella rolls her eyes playfully with a smile on her face; she goes back to addressing her family.

"Mother, I would like you to personally meet my becoming husband," she announced to the woman sitting right in front of us.

"It is a pleasure to meet you," I said kindly.

She did a single nod to me, "It is much of a pleasure to meet you too, Xavier. My name is Graditha."

Graditha was exceptionally beautiful; no wonder why Bonesella looked so good naturally. Her mother had white skin like mine. They were a bit bone-like but not completely. She looked more like a doll than a skeleton. Her eyes were gold-orange just like Bonesella's, except her eyes were not green behind them—in fact she had no glowing green in her at all—behind her irises was white like any normal eye. She had dark black hair like Bonesella's, with flowers in her hair. I also noticed that she had gold markings on her body that glittered like our golden star.

"That's a nice name. You look unbelievably beautiful," I said truthfully.

"Oh, thank you," she said quickly.

Then she continued, "Well, it is about time to go up there. Come on," she said as we get up.

Jashar stood behind the podium still wearing his funky outfit. I walked Bonesella up and stood to the left while Bonesella stood on the right with her mother right beside her. We held hands as if it were the last day of our lives. This was it.

Jashar spoke in Eidan, a language that Bonesella's family spoke. This language originated from their ancestors. I knew some of the language or understood parts of it at least. Though I never have spoken it before. We stood there listening to Jashar's words for hours. Some parts were speeches, and some were sited from the Book of Silar.

Finally, the religious parts could begin. All of us on the stage and the people sitting down below put two fingers to the center of their forehead and said a prayer in Eidan. After the prayers, Graditha must give forth her daughter into marriage and/or adulthood. This was the day that she was known to be with a life of her own and was no longer under the care of her parents. Graditha placed her two hands on top of Bonesella's head and they both lower their heads. A few words were spoken to finalize the practice. I would have had something similar, but that was impossible. I had no living family . . . and I was the only child.

It was time to bond us now. Jashar came around the podium with small red chest with gold symbols sewn into the red cloth. Jashar put on a pair of white fancy gloves and opened the chest. A needle glimmered in the candle lights. Bonesella's finger was pricked first, and a glowing green blood dropped into a large golden goblet—which I didn't fully understand because she was skeletal. It was my turn now.

"Ow," I let out as the needle punctured my skin.

My deep dark red blood was dripped into the goblet. Jashar rose it into the air, and we all prayed again. He brought the goblet back down to his chest level and swirled the blood a bit and poured it into a clear wine glass. The color of our blood that mixed was strange and I found myself a bit disgusted to see a dark black liquid. Bonesella gently lifted the cup, took a sip, and handed it off to me. Without a word I sipped it up and tried not to think of the strange thick metal taste. I gave the glass back to Jashar trying not to throw up.

Bonesella and I joined hands again and put our foreheads together as songs were sang by the audience. I breathed slowly trying to relax myself. There was just too many people around me. I could tell that Bonesella was a bit nervous too because she started to tremble.

"It's okay this crowed stuff is almost over. We will be fine," I whispered to her.

She nodded and didn't reply.

As the last song finished, Jashar began to speak a small paragraph that finished off the ceremony.

Finally, this was all that I have been waiting for. This was the time when I had something to keep my mind off all the people watching and just take my time forgetting everything else that existed. I closed my eyes and I truly felt ready for something. The first touch came. It didn't feel like much until Bonesella's lips started to make their way across my jawline. My breath became heavy, but I knew I wouldn't pass out this time. I grabbed the back of her neck and pulled her forth. This was all I needed to survive another minute. I just need to take my time. We kissed for about thirty minutes and kept the consistency of touch. Our lips didn't slip off or got tired. We both were hoping for this so, we gave it our best shot and went forth with strength and ended with strength.

I looked in Bonesella's eyes.

"When this is all over, we can start to plan things out," I said relieved for the first time in a while.

"All right, but before we rush away to think about ourselves, we should at least talk to my family a little while we eat dinner. Then if you would like, we could go outside and talk about things and relax," Bonesella explained. I agreed silently.

We trailed off to her parents.

"Congratulations," Graditha said cheerfully.

"Thank you," we both said almost exactly at the same time.

"It is a pleasure. I wish you both luck and a wonderful life. Feel free to stop by though," Graditha replied kindly, smiling over us as if we both were her small children.

We took a seat with her at the table while drinks were starting to be served.

"So, what have you two been doing or planning lately?" Graditha asked.

Before Bonesella could reply I speak before her instead.

"Actually, I was wondering about you." Graditha's eyes widened a bit.

"Oh really? My life is not even that important. You are the

ones who just married," Graditha explained.

I brought my tone down a bit, so that I would sound more respectful.

"Well, I was wondering about your family history or even just things in general about you. I mean . . . I just met you," I said.

"Oh all right. Fine," Graditha agreed as menus were being passed out now.

I was eager in finding out about Bonesella's father. But I couldn't rush that. I had to make a pathway to the answer, but not making it too obvious that that was my destination.

"I noticed that the biological family here is quite small," I started to dig away. Now I had to choose a direction based on my answer. This was probably how criminals get answers to what they want out of people without them even realizing.

"Yes, in fact not all gods have biological family that could be traced back. We are originals that start the family tree. Almost every immortal can be traced all the way back to some god. That is a fact," Graditha explained, taking her time.

It was interesting to hear her response. Now I knew that Graditha was a god, but what was her husband? What does that make Bonesella? I was guessing that he must have been a pure god as well.

"That's interesting. Jashar is your brother?" I asked trying not to go directly for the point.

"Well, he is more of a cousin to me, though we can't say that scientifically. There is no family background behind me. He just refers to himself like the uncle to Bonesella."

Wow. I was really starting to enjoy all this information that was coming to me. I might not be able to get my full and complete answer today, but one day I will find out the truth. I know I will. Even if it reveals itself to me in the end.

"That is about everyone I met so far in the family . . ." I slowly said trying to make myself not look like I was wanting to know something bad.

"It is really just us. Everyone else is people that I have been working with for a long time, servants and even some old-time friends."

"And it still looks like a lot of people," I said as a look around the room.

Bonesella finally spoke up again, "I know it isn't much. It is the only family I have now, but when we start to—"

"Start what?" Graditha interrupts her daughter. I think she started to take this all wrong.

"Planning things . . ." Bonesella said slowly as if she knows that she would get in trouble. I was not sure exactly what Graditha was thinking, but hopefully Bonesella isn't in a tough situation.

After a long silence, Graditha spoke up.

"Here's some advice to you. Plan carefully. Having children isn't as easy as you would like it to be . . ." Graditha started. By the last few words, I wanted to leave immediately.

"Excuse me for a moment," I said quickly, and I rushed off somewhere.

As I caught my breath, I started to see dinner being served. In the corner of my eye, I noticed Bonesella walking up to me.

"What is wrong? You have been acting so strange lately," Bonesella said.

"I am sorry . . . I don't mean to hurt you. I just don't feel entirely comfortable with this conversation. I am not ready to do it yet . . ." I said almost about to cry.

"I am sorry too. I shouldn't be pushing this on to you like that. Let's just go sit down and eat. Our food is here," she said, guiding me back to the table.

We were silent as we ate. Soon this would be all over, and Bonesella and I could talk things out. It felt nice to hear silence. I was embarrassed enough that I was glad to have a break. As we ate, I picked up on the fact that Bonesella was looking back at me every so often. She must be looking out for me, checking if I was okay. That was what I like, to feel like I was being taken care of. I just really missed having a family of my own.

As I finished I turned to Bonesella with a few words that have been on my mind.

"I was thinking that when all this is one here, I could talk to you about some of my feelings," I said shyly.

"Okay. I will keep that on my mind," she replied softly.

When both of us were finished we excuse ourselves from the table. "I think I know a perfect spot that we can talk without any disturbances," Bonesella said guiding me out of the castle.

I followed her to the entry of a forest. We didn't have to go too far; it was just outside the castle. Bonesella took a seat by a tree and I do the same.

"I know it is a little much for both of us . . ." Bonesella started.

"But I know we can get through this. I just hoped that one day we could have a family and do wonderful things together," Bonesella explained looking up to the sky.

It was dusk. A dark blue sky that was sparked with comets flying by, stars just beginning to poke out of the darkness.

"I would want that too, but I lost my family. Now, I don't have any. I don't even know if I would even make a good father. I have never really been raised by one anyways," I explained in the same tone, doing the exact same thing: staring at the sky.

"Xavier, you do have a family now. Even if it is just me, plus, I think you would make a great father," she said as she looked at me with disbelief.

Well, I guessed this was it. It was time to let go of the things of the past and create new memories. It was time to rise from sorrow and be the best versions of ourselves. Just in a few years we might be planning for a child. Anything could happen then. Maybe at that time I would be ready. I might as well accept it now for the future.

The sky was the future that we were looking at. You can only predict what was out there. You don't exactly know it all until you are up in space. From the ground though, you still are not sure what to expect. Just because you don't know what to expect doesn't mean to sit around and wait. Be prepared for anything that life throws at you. Even if it was a guy throwing a dagger, trying to aim for your head. Be prepared, but don't rush time . . . because time will take as long as it needs to take. Time was time.

One of the servants come out to call us in, saying Bonesella's mother was worried where we gone to. So, we went back inside, but before we stepped in, Bonesella and I looked each other in the eyes. We were bonded together now, and we forever would be.

Chapter Sixteen

Everything was a blur of nature. All green surrounded me. My head was still spinning after all that dancing. Flowers were blooming all around us. As flowers were caught in my hair, this place feels like another world. As if I was in absolute heaven. Or was I?

It was exactly what you would expect in the sky above you. Peace, happiness, and love. This would be the most important things you would find all around you. It was not the scenery that filled you up, but the impact of the social, emotional environment around you. Seriously, I should be a teacher of enlightenment.

I stood from rolling around in a patch of flowers. I walked slowly across the large field full of patches of flowers. The grass was tall; it was up to my knees. I stared up into the light blue sky as if I were encountering another being from another planet. It was all a painting, or I was in a painting. The clouds were pasty white on a pasty light blue background. The field seemed to be a blur of colors, mixed so spectacularly that you end up seeing the real thing once it was finished. I start to speed walk and then into a jog. I felt free. Like I would never have to worry about anything again or feel any kind of sadness or depression. That was exactly what heaven feels like. Then, I started to run. Straight forward. Into nothingness.

I stopped. Somewhere in this giant field. Bonesella came up from behind me.

"So? What's the plan?" she asked.

"I don't know. I just feel great and free," I said with an almost blank mind.

"Well, my mother has a surprise for us," Bonesella said.

Her hair was blowing in the wind beside me.

"Come," Bonesella pulled me along, out of this dream I was in. As we started to walk, we stopped, as we were greeted by Nightmare who swooped down and landed right in front of us. Nightmare gently bowed his head to us. Without a word we got on. "Have you ever even flown him before," Bonesella asked right behind my ear.

"No, but it would be nice to get a shot at it," I said as Nightmare prepared himself.

I felt Nightmare rise into the air after a couple flaps of his wings. We took off as a gust of wind hit us. Right at that moment we started to fly higher and higher. I looked down at the field that I ran in. it was huge. As we continued flying, I could not even find the end to the tall grass and large flower patches. I looked up this time. We flew so high, that the pasty white clouds floated near us. It was like we were trying to escape this giant painting that probably hung in someone's living room.

"How do you like it," Bonesella asked from behind.

"I feel free," I said, still in awe at the view and slightly falling off Nightmare's back. I really need to make a saddle for me. Bonesella wrapped her arms around me, leaning her head against my shoulder. We rested on the way to this surprise, though it was not even that long. Close to about an hour.

I opened my eyes, but I wasn't the first to wake up. Bonesella sat on Nightmare, her legs hanging in an elegant pose beside Nightmare.

"Good morning, sleepyhead," Bonesella said, still watching the pasty clouds pass by in the opposite direction.

"It's not even the morning, it is the afternoon," I said, yawning and still laying comfortably on Nightmare.

"Well, we are here, so you better start waking up," Bonesella said while leaning over Nightmare's giant wings to peer over at the sight.

I sat up unwillingly, but the sight caught my eyes as a white mansion or mini palace stood. Its white structure shone gold as the light hit it.

"Is this it?" I asked, way more surprised than I thought I would be.

"It's a small palace, what more do you want?" Bonesella joked.

After a nap I wasn't exactly in the mood for it. Maybe a cup of tea would be nice.

As Nightmare began to descend, Bonesella and I grabbed on to make sure we didn't slide off too soon. We felt a drop, but I wasn't ready to fall and hit hard on the ground. After a few more, we land safely as I least expected. Bonesella and I slid off. This so-called small palace still looked huge as we stood in front of it. Though, it was much smaller than Bonesella's home.

"Welcome home," Bonesella announced as she gazes up at the golden double doors. They were close to twice our size, and Bonesella and I were about the same height.

Once Bonesella opened the door, we walked into the dark room. Candles lit up all around us and the room suddenly became as bright as day. The floors simmered pure gold, but even the pillars had hints of gold covering its pearly white, stone surface. I looked around in awe.

"Oh look," Bonesella said pointing to the small table in the corner by the door.

"It's a letter from my family," she said as she looks at it.

"What does it say?" I asked.

"Just wishing us luck. Not much that is too important," she said quickly as she closed the letter neatly.

"Is there anything about your father? Did he said anything?"

I asked slowly, trying not to make it sound important for me to know.

"No . . . why does it bother you," Bonesella asked, looking at me strangely.

"Nothing, I was just wondering . . . because I never heard him said anything before," I said simply.

"Of course, he wouldn't said anything. He doesn't care about us. He pretty much abandoned us. Since then, I learned to care less," Bonesella explained sorely.

At that point, she didn't seem to be in a good mood, so I just stopped.

About moments later, I finally noticed a gold structure farther back leaded by a long red carpet. I walked across the carpet to get a better look at the structure. Shimmering gold. A medium-sized throne was shining in the candlelight. It looked as if no one has ever touched it. Like it was perfectly cleaned. I love when everything was clean. I just stood and stared into it as if I wish I could sit on it, but it would be disrespectful if I did. It was not the fact of sitting in it, I just loved how clean it looked.

Bonesella came up from behind.

"Well, someone can't take their eyes off of pure gold, can they?" she said a bit suspiciously.

"It's pretty," I said unexpectedly.

Bonesella giggled a bit.

"Yeah, but I don't like to be way obsessed with it. It's just a family thing. They always want to dress you up in gold . . . even your home."

I nodded. The last thing I would want would be to have a deep craving for gold till I would practically marry it . . . Not even.

"Let's go take a look around the place," Bonesella said taking my hand.

We walked across the floor of gold. We walked past the throne and a large staircase stood up high. The kitchen was on the behind and under the staircase. A large window with curtains was above the sink. The kitchen wasn't as large as I expected. It was quite small for a place like this. We walked up the stairs into a hallway. On our right, a pair of double doors stood. this was our room. It was quite large, with a queen-sized bed. A little semicircle balcony for one person was across the room and gave a beautiful view of the surrounding forests. I walked up to it and rested my arms on the decorated bar.

"What a view," Bonesella said as she stood beside me, also resting her arms on the bar.

"Yeah, I would just love to wake up to this every morning," I said as the sight took my breath away.

"Well, now you can."

We continued to stare in the distance. The sun was above the sky, brightening all the nature out there. I bet it was wonderful at night too. The sight was so breathtaking that Bonesella and I lay down in bed and rested for the rest of the day.

The next morning, I was the first to awake. I had some good rest. I guessed I shouldn't bother waking up Bonesella, so instead I went down to the kitchen to make some tea for us both. Tea was the best invention yet and it has been around forever. Not only that it was good for you, I read in some books that in certain cultures that tea was used in rituals. As I was still making the tea, Bonesella made her way down.

"Good morning, Sweetheart," I said as I finish the tea.

"Good morning . . . you're acting a little so happy," Bonesella said eyeing me.

"Why? Does it really bother you?" I asked, feeling awkward about the situation.

"It's not you, it is just that I haven't been cheerful much because of problems that my father and I had when he still lived with us," Bonesella explained, taking the cup of tea that I made for her.

"Did that happen recently?" I asked concerned.

"No, of course not. That was a long time ago. It just has been bothering me for years," she continued.

"I remember the times when my mother could not stand the fighting we did. She would cry her eyes out," Bonesella said sipping the tea slowly.

She looked as if she were that simple. First it was one thing, then it was another. It all piled up in the end till we could not stand it any longer . . . then my father just left," Bonesella finished, pushing her tea aside.

Her eyes were filling with water. I opened my mouth to ask why, but Bonesella stopped me.

"Don't even ask another question," she said softly.

I quickly shut my mouth, finished my tea, and brought her into a hug while staring out the window.

It's all going to be okay. Everything will be fine. Bonesella laid comfortably in my arms. Her warmth spread through me, and I felt her pain. To have a father leave you behind. To have nothing left. In the end, you end up having to find love out of a stranger. I held her close as I thought about my own life. It hasn't been all well. Losing your family was probably the worst pain that you can ever feel, but it all changes when you are not the only one in that situation. Instead of all the pain being pounded on one person, it felt better when that pain was spread out among other people. With the same amount of water, one bucket will be full . . . but when you must fill multiple buckets, one bucket was not all the way full. So, one person wouldn't feel as much pain as if they were completely alone. That is the most important thing to remember: you are not alone. You are not the only one feeling this pain. Have hope. Never give up on yourself. God is watching over you . . . And the Angel I Am is too.

Our bright stars shone above. Blue and gold heated the white sand. Angel's Beach it was named. It was not on an ordinary map on the country of Ejyne, instead it was on maps of the same place as Ejyne, but different dimensions. Bonesella taught me more about the travel of the soul to different dimensions. I read a bit about it, but according to Bonesella, many books do not have much information on the study of soul transfers and soul travel. She said that the first text to have talked about it was founded and written by the First Alchemists. They were a group of alchemists that discovered not only soul transfers, but they founded basic schooling that was taught in the field of science and magic.

To get to Angels Beach, we had to do a religious practice. It wasn't too long, and I was glad for that. I read about religious practices that span over the course of months . . . some even years. We both pressed fingers of one hand on the other's forehead and spoke the words in a foreign language. The words were not that hard or long to remember. Sources said that because it became a popular tourist's destination, the process became easier because it was practiced more often.

We held hands and walked across the sand. We both wore white clothing. This was technically our honeymoon, but it differs for everyone and diverse cultures and religions. The beach was empty just for us. It was the most perfect day out, yet it was just us. Bonesella smiled at me, twirling in her white dress. She laughed and I smiled back.

"Isn't this fun! Just you and me. No one else. Just you . . . and me," she said grabbing a hold of my arm right before she fell into the water from twirling too much.

"Yes, I find this more pleasurable than I even expected!" I said laughing after she almost fell.

We played and danced all day and let the water come up over our bare feet. We sat next to each other watching the suns began to set.

"I really hope this lasts long . . ." Bonesella started after a long moment of silence.

"I really want us to be happy and grateful."

"Why do you said that?" I asked, looking back at her glimmering eyes reflecting from the suns.

"I just feel that I need to release the stress of my father and me. I really don't want this to end up the same way. I want to forget about what happened in the past," she explained, still staring up into the almost night sky.

"Well, I believe that it is impossible to forget, but . . ." I pause and Bonesella stares into my eyes with a craving for my response.

"It is still possible to heal those wounds," I finished. Without a word, Bonesella scooted closer to me, wrapping her arms around me. After a moment of unexpecting, I finally felt the feeling that I have been hoping for. Her warm lips touched mine. They held on tightly as if she were afraid of falling into an abyss of her past. I also held on tightly because I wanted to release her pain . . . plus, I wanted to release my own.

Chapter Seventeen

Everything seemed more like home now. I was like a child which became homeless, then unexpectedly became a prince. Well, not actually. I just became . . . rich and not poor. The truth was that nothing here was mine. The things that were mine were the few clothes I have made on my own and just a few things I keep with me . . . like my journal.

I never really made a full saddle. I made bits and pieces to sell off to other small shops, but I never tried to put them together. I gathered vegan leather (I was an animal activist), tools, and jewels so I could make it look pretty. I decided to set up a work bench outside, away from the garden (yes, we had a mini garden maze with benches like the one by my old home). Nightmare sat beside me so I could take measurements. As I was working, Bonesella came up from behind.

"It's early, Xavier. Did you even eat breakfast?" she asked me.

I froze from my work. "I just realized that I didn't . . ." I said slowly.

"Well, why didn't you tell me?" Bonesella asked bending down next to me with a hand on my shoulder.

I put down the tools I was working with and kissed her on the forehead.

"It really would be a pleasure if you can do that for me," I said, looking back at what I was doing.

"Okay, I'll let you know when it is ready," Bonesella said making her way back to the mansion.

As I continued my work, I felt the table move. I looked down; Nightmare's head was under the table. I started to feel Nightmare smelling me.

"Hey, stop it! Stay still," I yelled out to him. He didn't get out immediately, so I pushed his head aside with my foot. Nightmare came out with a look of confusion.

"What are you doing?" I asked in the same confused way. Nightmare came around to my side. He looked at me for a moment, and then began to sniff in my lap for some odd reason.

"Stop it!" I yelled and Nightmare backs off. I had no idea why he does that, but he had done it a few times before.

Nightmare showed a face of fear and sadness. I looked at him with curiosity. Was it a good reason that he was sniffing me? Why did he do this so much?

"Why?" I asked.

Nightmare made a low tone noise, but I was not sure what he was trying to tell me. "I don't understand," I said. Nightmare made the same tone again, but I still had trouble figuring out what it means. Nightmare looked at me one last time, then he went back to his original spot in front of me so I could continue working.

Just minutes later, Bonesella came to call me in. I washed my hands thoroughly first. I couldn't stand not being clean. I couldn't even go a day without taking a good shower. I took a seat and Bonesella handed me a plate. I was sure, if I could travel anywhere, that the food there will always be diverse by two hundred percent. Basically, breakfast, luncheon, and dinner were always changing and complex.

"So, how's the saddle going?" Bonesella asked, taking a seat beside me.

"Very well, but it is going to take a while," I said simply, taking another bite.

"That's good," Bonesella said in the same exact tone.

As I ate, I noticed more about Bonesella's expression. She stared down at the table; there was no plate place in front of her.

"What is wrong?" I asked her softly.

"Nothing, I was just thinking about other things," she said, not looking up at me.

I knew exactly what she meant. I needed to show her that everything was going to be fine. She needed to trust me with her heart.

Later in the day I finished the saddle. Nightmare was over-excited, jumping around in circles, not even letting me put the thing on. The saddle was completely in a medium brown vegan leather. Along the sides I made geometrical holes into it that I fitted the gems into. I used all sorts of colors . . . and the finish was amazing.

"Slow down," I said, laughing my heart out.

Nightmare finally settled down a bit for me to at least put the saddle on . . . though, Nightmare still tried to move a bit. I buckled the saddle on and let go of him. Nightmare stood in front of me, gleaming in the light.

"You want to take a ride?" I asked happily.

Nightmare wagged his tail a flapped his wings hysterically.

"Okay, I am going to change. I'll be right back," I said while Nightmare started rolling in the grass.

I ran quickly inside and rushed to our room to change. I zoomed past Bonesella.

"What are you doing?" she asked as I got on an outfit.

"Flight lessons," I replied as I rushed out of the room.

I made my way out and Nightmare looked prepared.

"Are you ready?"

Nightmare roared and bowed down so I could get on. I got on and I suddenly felt comfortable in the saddle. Nightmare seemed to like it too.

"All right. This time don't try to rush it. Just come up slowly so I could get the hang of it," I reassured Nightmare.

I wore my old hunting outfit. I always reused the clothes that don't fit me anymore by making extensions. Plus, it was easier and uses less materials than making the whole thing again.

Nightmare started off with a jog, then into a run. The wind was already hitting my face and I knew it would get harder once we were in the air. Nightmare stretched out his wings and with a couple flaps we lifted into the air. Nightmare continued to go higher and higher. I held on tightly to the handle I made, and my feet were slipped into the stirrups. Nightmare's wings flapped so hard; I could feel the wind come up from underneath them . . . which also hit me in the face.

We ended up going so high up, I put down my metal face shield for protection against the wind. Nightmare's angle of flight got steeper and steeper. At some point, we were going straight up into the sky.

"Nightmare!" I yelled.

Nightmare roared into the air and started to change direction; it felt as if we were falling backward. I held on tight as the sky turned and the wind pushed against me. I wanted to close my eyes as my hair flew violently in my face. With a lurch in my stomach, we began to fall backwards.

Nightmare's roar was deafening. I was ready to pass out. I continued to hold on, even though I wished I could let go to get off this violent ride. Wind began to swipe in-between my hands and the handlebar. I latched on as tightly as I could. No. I couldn't give up. I had to learn to control him.

I scooted up and I grabbed a hold of Nightmare's thick and large neck.

"Nightmare, now!" I yelled as we fell straight forward down near a giant lake.

Once I thought I would be engulfed and submerged in water, an instant came. I could feel myself floating. A lift in the air, with Nightmare's wings high around me. They relaxed down. Everything was blue, but I wasn't wet. My hands ached from holding on. I slowly let go of the handle, but I didn't fall off. I felt balanced. I lifted my face shield and rubbed my hands together to release the pain.

"Nightmare?" I called breathlessly.

With a loving low growl, Nightmare popped his head up and smiled. I smiled back like it was the best day of my life . . . even if I looked like a total mess.

I peered over Nightmare's wing. There was lots of blue, but I was safe. Nightmare and I soared right above the lake that we almost crashed in. When I looked up, the sky was as blue as ever with only a handful of clouds that were spread out in great distances. "You did it," I choke out. I suddenly felt that my throat was dry and closed. I put a hand around my throat and begun to cough. At that moment, Nightmare swopped down to the edge of the lake. Without the slightest bump, we were on the ground safely.

I got off shakily. I really had to get used to this, so I guess for now, we will practice. I grabbed on to Nightmare's side to keep myself from falling into the grass. As I stared at the ground and my vison blurred, wet finally touched my face, but stickier than I expected. I looked up to Nightmare's smile. I gave the weakest smile back and I fell forward without even realizing it.

I awoke with water splashed in my face. This time, it wasn't Nightmare's saliva, but actual water from the lake. The grass tickled my skin as the wind came over. My vision cleared up and more water came to my face. I wiped my eyes. Nightmare was taking the water from the lake into his mouth, then spraying it on me. I must have passed out like the usual.

"Thank you," I made out.

Nightmare sprayed more water in my face.

"Hey, you alright?" I hear a familiar voice call out to me.

I was too exhausted to reply. Bonesella appeared over my head. Well, at least she was blocking the bright sun. She placed her hands on my sore, wet cheeks. I bet it looked like I was blushing . . . or maybe worse. I still couldn't reply, but Bonesella knew exactly how I felt. Without a word she kissed me on the forehead gently. Nightmare sprayed both of us this time. Bonesella came out in laughter, but I couldn't even make out a word. She looked back at me and smiled. I smiled back the best that I could. Bonesella still didn't said another word to me, instead she began to play with my soaked hair. I never liked when people would mess with my hair, but I was too tired to bother about it, instead I rested with my head on her lap.

I woke with a wet and warm feeling on my lips. With the sight, I immediately closed my eyes again. Bonesella's lips were warm and comforting. I didn't think I could live without being kissed like this. It was not like I had known anything better. I pulled her closer by gently putting a hand on the back of her neck. We kissed for minutes without realizing how much time was passing. I didn't feel like an hour. Maybe half? Less than that? I wasn't fully sure, but I was enjoying my time. I didn't even know if Nightmare was still nearby. We let go and gasp for breath. Her eyes glowed and glittered over me. I was speechless and so was she. After taking a short break, Bonesella leaned in a pressed her lips on my neck. Here we go again.

I opened my eyes again.

"Stop. Let's just stop for a moment," I said, putting a hand on Bonesella's chest.

She backed off slowly. The bright yellow sun came into view again, almost blinding me. Behind me, the gigantic blue sun shone, but was further away so it was not as bright looking. I finally sat up and Bonesella scooted next to me. I looked across the lake and found Nightmare eating a fish he caught.

"What a beautiful day out it is . . ." I said to start things off.

I looked back at Bonesella. She looked as if she was about to kiss me all over again. ". . . Just like you," I continued.

Her eyes softened and she leaned her head against my shoulder.

"You know. I had a dragon of my own before," Bonesella said, breaking free.

I began to listen with my heart. "I found him when I was a little girl. He was a Bone-Snapping Dragon," Bonesella continued, looking across the lake to Nightmare. Automatically the memory of myself in the ring came up. The Bone-Snapping Dragons that teared people to bits, the men fighting each other. Jax, who prepared me for the entrance, and some mysterious man in the ring that saved me . . . twice.

Holy. Fucking. Shit. Before I knew it, I was standing. My hands were in fists and my palms were sweating.

"What's wrong?" Bonesella asked me, standing up as well.

The memories of Isaac began to flood my head. I put a hand on my forehead, losing my balance.

"Xavier. Hold on to me," Bonesella called out to me, grabbing a hold of my arm.

I leaned against her for support, and I tried to calm myself down before I cried my eyes out. I sat down and Bonesella did too.

"Are you alright?" she asked me with a confused face.

"Yeah. I am sorry. I just had a bad memory come to mind, but I am fine," I lied.

Bonesella took a deep breath and continued with her story.

"I named him Bone Crusher. At the time, he was only a baby. When I got old enough to fight in the ring, I used to take him with me all the time. He would help me win. But, after times of risking Bone Crusher's life, the managers of the ring wanted to take him away from me. I tried to do the best I can to keep him, but they put him in a large cage and hid him from me. Once I went to the ring again without him . . ."

Bonesella slowly paused. I was filled with so much suspense I was about to burst out like a child: A then what happened?!

"Bone Crusher became my enemy," Bonesella finished. After a moment I shook out of it, and I realized that I was biting on to my sleeve that went over my fist. Bonesella shakily sighed. I knew it must be hard, especially after what I went through. To see people die was the worst, but it also stabbed you in the back to see your friend on the opposite side as you.

It started to get late, and it was time to go to bed. I took a good shower and slipped in bed. Did I just leave Isaac? What did I do? I couldn't help myself anymore. I slept on the closest side to the door and cried myself to sleep silently.

Chapter Eighteen

My dreams were about my memories I made with Bonesella and Isaac. I loved Bonesella, but I missed Isaac. He was extremely sweet and my first best friend. I wished I would have given him a proper goodbye. Or maybe I could have taken him with me. Just maybe Bonesella wouldn't mind me having a man in the house . . . or maybe she would get jealous. Why would she be jealous? Isaac was my friend, and it was not like he was competing for me. I suddenly remembered the time he slept with me and kissed me on the forehead. That's what best friends do, right? Then I just give up. My heart just shatters to the ground. There was no feasible way that Isaac loves me. I cried lots, but silently.

Plus, if he did, he would have told me that. What would I tell him? Would I leave Bonesella behind for him? If I would have told him yes, would that mean that I should have told him something? I asked him if he liked me. He said yes, but as a friend. Was he really trying to tell me that he loved me? Was I trying to have the same? Did I just give everything up for someone else and not him?

I couldn't breathe with all these questions and worry running through my mind. If I were to ever meet up with Isaac again, I would apologize for everything. That I wish to be friends again and that I was sorry for leaving him for someone else. I just wish it were easier to do.

I awoke with tears sticking wet to my face and something sticky beneath my waist. I moved and my thighs ached for some reason. I slipped the sheets down a bit to reveal magenta glowing through my body. They were like veins like I first saw them. But when I looked further down, they cannot possibly be veins. The most of them were where my abdomen was. They branched out from a glowing center all the way through the rest of my body. What was this? The magenta glowed brightly down my penis. Was this normal? I have glowed like this before, but not this much.

I scooted back toward my pillow, from sitting in a ginormous pool of semen sticking to the bed and me. You got to be kidding me . . . I rubbed my thighs to release the pain. The magenta glow branched out all the way down to my toes. Wow, I really haven't had this bad of an erection or ejaculation in a long time. When I first started puberty, it was the worst . . . and I mean the worst pain ever. After that though, it had stopped being abnormal . . . until now. Now that I think of it, I should have visited a doctor in the area. I was poor at the time, so I didn't have the money. Even if I could pay the doctor, I was already embarrassed about it. It would be worse if I had to tell an adult about what I have been feeling and such.

I looked around the room to make sure I wasn't going to be laughed at . . . like when I lived in the village. People made fun of me all the time. I had to duck my head down to stop myself from seeing other people's faces. Good . . . no one was in the room. I must have slept long. I took a warm shower to clean myself off, even though I took a longer shower than usual, I was still very well erect. Fuck. Now I must worry about wearing clothes. It usually goes down after a couple hours, but if it surpasses a certain amount of time, it would be a medical emergency. When I was not having abnormalities like this, it usually went down sooner, though it was more continuous when I was in pain. I already knew that none of my clothes were going to hide it. I could either embarrass myself or wait for it to go down. I chose to scrub the bed first, just waiting for it to stop filling with blood. Even after I cleaned the bed, I kept waiting and waiting.

I ended up lying in bed like I was before, like I never even got up. A knock became present on the door.

"Xavier, are you up yet?" Bonesella asked while walking into the room slowly.

"Yeah, I guess I was knocked out from yesterday," I faked again.

I was pressing my penis down under the sheets like it should be.

"Yeah, you slept pretty long," Bonesella said, letting her eyes catch on to the clock on the wall next to her.

Once she turned back to me, I nodded. I was just trying to contain myself. I hated lying and I knew I was bad at it, but I didn't feel that I should embarrass myself. I really was not sure what Bonesella's reaction would be if my erect penis slipped up from the covers . . . just like when I was with Isaac that one night.

The thought of Isaac made me shake and Bonesella noticed it. She came over and sat on her side of the bed. I pulled the covers more to my chest to make sure I wasn't going to be exposed on accident.

"Are you okay? Sick possibly?" Bonesella asked me.

I guessed on the outside I didn't look too well. If so, I wouldn't mind staying in bed all day to get rid of this pain I have.

"I don't feel too well.," I said slowly.

"Yesterday was probably a bad idea."

"Well, I'll bring up some tea and something to eat," Bonesella said getting up.

"And you can lay in bed for now if you want."

When Bonesella left, I slipped down the sheet to check on myself. My penis had gone down a bit, but it was still elevated a bit. Good. I pulled the sheet back up just in case. The memories of yesterday passed through my head. The flight, Bonesella's lips, the saddle I made, and . . . Nightmare sniffing me struck me. Nightmare has been a bit odd with sniffing me so much near my genital area. Did he predict my abnormal erection? I wasn't sure, but maybe if I could see him, I might be able to get an answer.

Bonesella came back with a tray of my tea and breakfast.

"Here you go. Rest well," Bonesella said . . . and she was off.

Once I finished eating, my body was back into a relaxed state. I looked outside to find Nightmare. He was still sleeping on the side of the house.

"Nightmare?" I called to him.

He peaked open one eye to me. I came close and sit next to him, putting him on the head. The familiar low growl came again. This time, when Nightmare sniffed me, I didn't push him away; I let him. After a while of sniffing and staring at me, Nightmare got up and started to walk to the forest.

"Where are you going?" I asked confused.

Nightmare motions me to follow, with a movement of his giant head . . . just like he did when I first met him.

We walked deeper and deeper into the forest. He must be taking me somewhere special because his behavior with me isn't normal. The forest became sharper and the smell of pine was entering my nose. It would be a different feeling if I was in a jungle or rainforest. Here, the smells were sharp, and it looks as if we were walking through an environment full of needles that will pinch every blood vessel of mine and leave me unconscious on the ground. Nightmare was still leading me, and the picture became foggier. Was I going to pass out again? As I walked, everything was patched with grey. I shake my head to see if I was dreaming, but the picture remained. As the trees thickened, my ears caught on to a fuzzy sound. It became clearer and clearer as we walked. The patches of grey wet my face. It was mist and we must be headed toward a waterfall.

The trees finally opened to a clearing. I was finally able to breathe. Sometimes I completely forgot that I was claustrophobic. My eyes widened at the sight. Another guardian pool. I fell completely in love with the sight. A ginormous waterfall splashed down from a far height. Rocks broke the fall of water, which was straight, then it broke off from there. The giant pool of water was surrounded by the rest of the forest.

"Wow," I said as I turned to Nightmare.

He sat down by the water. *I guess I know what that means.* I stripped off my clothes and tied my hair up. Nightmare gave a strange sound once I was completely nude. I faced the other way, so I turned my head and the top of my torso to him. Nightmare got up and walked around me.

"What is it?" I asked him.

Hopefully in the end I will have an accurate explanation for his strange behavior.

Nightmare pointed his snout from my penis and up.

"Oh all right, will you stop judging me by the way my penis looks? Geeze, I know it's pale like the rest of me; you can't even barely see my lips either," I joke as I step into the water.

I try to step into the water carefully, but my foot lands on something rough and sharp. I try to grab on to the rocks beside me, but my foot slips down.

"Ow," I let out.

I think I cut open my foot. Once I was fully in the water, stepping in the soft sand, I turned over to Nightmare. He stood at the edge of the rocks looking at my curiously.

"What? Do you want to cut yourself too?" I asked kind of harshly.

Nightmare gave another strange sound in return. I was sure that meant no. I came toward the edge, but I wasn't on planning on cutting my foot open again; instead Nightmare pulled me out of the water on the ledge above the rocks. I sat down next to him, and I put my foot over my lap. I had a large gash with blood continuously pouring out. The waters couldn't even wash it off.

"Oh, what do I do?" I complained to Nightmare.

I thought he would sniff at my foot this time, but my foot was pushed away.

"Hey! I thought you were going to help me!" I yelled at him.

Nightmare did what he did all the time before: sniffing at my genital area. Nightmare gave an apology growl and a sad face.

"Then why aren't you helping me?" I asked strictly.

This time Nightmare backed off and sat beside me, Looking out into the water.

I just didn't understand him. I didn't know how to understand him. I propped my foot back up on my lap. I guess I should let it dry. Maybe it will stop bleeding soon. I pressed my fingers on my gland's penis. I didn't understand, but I wanted to. I already knew I was different from the others. Everyone in the village would laugh at me time to time. By this time, I was ready for answers. I had come this far, and I knew that there was so much still to uncover. I just hoped I would live long enough to find out about the rest.

I pressed harder, then began to massage myself. I masturbated to calm myself. That was all. It was the only thing that seemed to help when I have anxiety, or I was just simply out of it. It was the only thing that made me feel that I would be all right. I loved myself for all the times I should have been loved by someone else. I pressed and massaged to a point that semen started to leak out. It dripped everywhere and I totally forgot that my foot was bleeding. Before I could notice in time, my semen reached the gash on my foot. The mixture between semen and blood stung. I couldn't just wipe it off. Maybe I'd dip my foot into the water so the semen could come off. Before I decide to get up, I knew I was risking myself again. I looked down at my foot and could not believe what was happening.

The blood was dripping off, but less and less came. The gash began to shrink as skin grew over it. The semen sunk in, and I suddenly felt relieved. The pain in my foot vanished and the gash was just a mere cut.

Oh. My. Fucking. God. My foot was starting to look as if nothing happened.

"Nightmare, are you seeing this?" I called him.

Next to me Nightmare watched.

"Was this what you kept trying to tell me?"

Nightmare simply nodded his head. I just wish he could have spoken words to me . . . but of course, dragons have their own language. I couldn't believe I somehow healed my own foot. I read about healers, but they were exceedingly rare, so it was hard to study them. The healers were typically angels who lived to help others. They healed for a living and tended the wounded in battle. I just never thought I would be one of them after all the hate I felt from others.

I stood up, with a healed foot and began to stretch my wings. I hadn't flown in a long time because my parents and Jacob didn't like me flying around the house. They said I might break something, so lots of times I completely forget that I had them hidden away. It felt nice to let out my wings. The wind caught on to them, and I almost was about to ride them. I picked up my clothes and put them in the compartment on Nightmare's saddle. As the wind became stronger in my direction, I flapped my wings and rose into the air. My wings were beyond huge. They were so oversized; I really thought I needed to see a doctor for multiple reasons. My wingspan was about eighty-five yards long. That was way more than the average length I had read about.

I flew back to the mansion with Nightmare by my side. The wind was hitting my face again, but this time it felt good. I felt free. I made it back to the mansion in no time. Once I was inside, rushing up to Bonesella to tell her the news, screw the fact that I was bare naked.

"I really, really, really need to tell you something. You won't believe it!" I burst out.

Bonesella stared at me awkwardly and with a hint of fear. I took a deep breath before I could explain.

"Yeah . . . sorry. You should know by now that I prefer to be nude often. Anyway—"

"Calm down, Xavier. You need to relax. Take a seat, then tell me from the beginning," Bonesella said, pulling a seat out from the table.

"Okay. Just don't freak out okay," I said, and Bonesella nodded.

As I explained through the story (as slow as possible), Bonesella started to make me some tea. Once it came, I carefully wrapped my hands around it, trying to keep myself calm. Bonesella's eyes widened once I got to the surprising part.

"I know, I couldn't even believe it myself!" I said excitingly.

"Well, maybe if you start practicing that some more . . . you can help others along the way," Bonesella said slowly, staring at her own cup of tea.

"Well, yeah. Doesn't every immortal have powers?" I asked.

"Yes, usually," Bonesella said in the same slow tone.

"They usually have their elemental and their main special power—which is different from everyone else's," Bonesella explained, looking around the room.

"And the elements are fire, water, earth, and air, right?"

"Yes, but not everyone necessarily falls under those. They are basic, not everyone is basic. Like me, for example. I don't fall under any of those. And you are—"

"Fire," I filled in for her.

Bonesella continued, "Your main power doesn't always correspond to your element. Healing can either be fire or earth, even if it is more strongly associated with earth."

"And what is your main power? If you had to be put in a category, what element would you most likely fit into?" I asked curiously.

Hopefully this didn't involve any business with her father.

"Well, I can't be put into any of those elements. I am

olonic—or one who does not fit any element. Some people are just so diverse they don't fit the standards . . . And my main power? Your main power is called your faculty. My faculty is something that must be kept a secret between you and me." Bonesella dropped her tone into a whisper at the end.

"But why?" I dropped my tone just like hers.

"Just don't let it spread. If my father . . ." She paused. "Just please keep a secret," she said. I nodded.

"I am the connection to the dead and evil spirits. I can communicate with them and unleash a devastating and controlling power that is only written about in ancient text," Bonesella barely said.

"What do you mean?"

Bonesella sighed.

"I have never done it before—"

"Then how do you know," I cut her off.

"My father told me when my mother refused to talk about it. I used to have nightmares because I could hear the voices of spirits in the night. My mother said it was nothing, but it kept happening. I never really liked my father, but I asked, and he responded. For some reason, he knows exactly what I am. My mother doesn't even have a clue," Bonesella explained.

The room went completely dead silent. The candles were not even disturbed by the talk. I almost expected to hear what she could hear, but nothing could break the silence. It hurt deep inside of me. Bonesella's father knew something that no one else should know. Her father must have a reason to hide other secrets about Bonesella and her family. There must be more that was hidden beneath the earth. This planet, Adrean, would soon break open to reveal a devastating secret kept from all of us.

Chapter Nineteen

As time passed, Bonesella refused to speak of her father. I never even knew his name . . . or do I? Even if I did, I couldn't even remember. Everything had been kept hidden from me, and it still was, but this was just the beginning of these things that have started to open a little. I tried my best to keep my mouth shut about it. There was just something that was bothering her, like there was more to her father than I might think.

The night sky was full of stars, but clouds were beginning to block the view. There had always been something inside me that I wanted to disappear. There was something empty inside of me, and only one thing was going to full fill my want. It was something that masturbating did not satisfy. It was something that could not be fulfilled by my own love for myself. It had to be someone else giving me it. I had the feeling of emptiness. What the poor, starving, and hungry kids feel without food. I felt empty without someone loving me deeply. Kissing me on the forehead was one thing, but sex was on a whole new level.

"So, you have been looking a bit confused lately. Is something wrong? What's on your mind?" Bonesella asked, walking up slowly behind me.

"I have just been having a lot on my mind, lately," I said simply, trying not to disturb the creatures of the night.

"Well, do you want to talk about it?" Bonesella asked keeping the same whispering tone.

"I don't know. I feel embarrassed about it," I said, turning toward her.

Bonesella's hands were wrapped around each other, close to her chest as if she were afraid to let something go. Her eyes were pleading like, glittering in the moon light. Her nightgown was see-through, so it had a layer underneath. The under layer was light blue with an outer layer full of stars, like the night sky . . . like the eyes I have missed for so long . . . of my long-lost best friend: Isaac.

"Come, let's sit," Bonesella said, taking a seat of the edge of the bed. I sat down with her, hoping to relieve my feelings.

"So, what is it?"

I thought before I made out a word. I didn't want to show how insecure I was. I was already quiet enough; my wife didn't need any more of this. I was supposed to be strong, but I was weak; I was supposed to be brave, but I was scared; I was supposed to be worthy, but I was nothing.

The tears started to stream down my face. I could see Bonesella's pursed lips and concern in her eyes. It was not just Bonesella's past with her father, it was also my own. I was supposed to be more than this.

"I am just . . . scared for the day that everything is going to be taken from me, just like the day I lost my family. I don't want this to happen to us. I want everything to be okay like nothing could go wrong. I feel like I don't have the power to change anything . . . not even our fate," I make out.

Bonesella opens her mouth to say something, but the words don't come. Instead, I must speak again. "I feel like your father is going to come and curse both of us . . . I feel like he will try to take it all away . . . he must be planning something. . ."

Bonesella's eyes went from fear to anger.

"I said don't ever dare speak—"

"I know!" I cried.

"But I have the feeling that we won't be like this anymore. I feel like I am so insecure and that I can't do anything about any situation. I am a fool." I pressed my hands to my face and fell back on the bed. Bonesella sighed. "I always thought you were better than that."

"Then you have always been wrong about me."

"I am sorry thinking that way . . . I should have known better."

I closed my eyes as if I were afraid to look at everything here as if I didn't want to live this life anymore. I had two options and I threw away one . . . an important one. What if Isaac thought the same of me. What if he put me down for everything. What if he wasn't right for me at all. What if this was the life that I must live . . . or what if this was the wrong life I shouldn't be living.

"I have always felt that I have been missing something," I started.

Bonesella looked up at me again. She was ready to listen.

"I feel like I have been missing a large amount of love from others. I lost my family; I never really had any friends and here I am with you . . . begging for more than this."

I could tell by the look in her eyes that she knew exactly what I meant. My body was shaking now. I was completely lost and out of my mind. I was nervous and I didn't like showing it to her. Bonesella didn't seem to mind it though . . . or even pay attention to it. What a fool I was. I moved her hair out of the way and unclipped her bra. What was I doing? I wanted to feel like the world. Like no one could ever bring me down on the soil ever again. I was doing this for myself. Did I even care about her anymore? I tried to make it seem like it. I was just afraid to come out to her. I was afraid that I would start to hear Isaac's voice in my head telling me: *Xavier, choose wisely. Do you want to be loved and accepted, or do you want to love someone who doesn't love you back. It is your choice. I still love you.*

No. I needed to act better than this. I tried to push my going on depression and anxiety out of my mind. I tried to focus on what I was doing. Nothing else mattered now. Just Bonesella and I.

Once we were both bare naked, I sat shakily on the bed. I had masturbated before, but I never had sex with someone else. Maybe this would heal our wounds, maybe we could be bonded forever. I want to at least believe it. I looked at her in the eyes. I was putting my trust into her . . . and she was putting her own trust into me. I nervously looked toward a wall for this. I forced my head down though, so I could at least do step number one: Insert. Penetrate.

"I never actually done this before," I squeaked.

"Don't worry, I'll help you," Bonesella said last before magenta crawled over me, making lightning designs that were able to be seen through my skin. When it hit, I found myself in another world.

Waves hitting the rocks on shore in an ongoing pattern. The movement of water was smooth, but the rocks break its smoothness, causing water to splash everywhere. These represented orgasms. Our regular pattern was the water and the rocks were—the rough parts of our trip? Obstacles in life? No. It was none of these, but perhaps one represents the other. I was the water: gentle, broken easily by obstacles, and I took the shape and form in whatever people want for their own amusement. I was a follower. Bonesella was the rock: rigid, not broken easily by obstacles, and never took the form of what people want. She was a leader.

I wished I was like her sometimes. I wished I could be the one sticking up for both of us if we encountered her father. I wanted to be the brave one, but instead . . . I was the weak one. And because I was weak, I wished and dreamed of a lifestyle instead of living it. I needed to change my thinking pattern. I needed to take a stand. If war ever came, I had to be ready to fight. Either way, war came whether you were ready or not.

I stood, looking out into the open water. Did I accidently soul travel here? I wiggled my toes, sifting the sand. It all felt real to me. I walked along the beach, thinking about the same thing repeatedly . . . I felt that I left Isaac behind. I needed to forget. This wasn't the place for him and I. This was just Bonesella and I.

I continued walking till something in the ocean caught my eye. I couldn't tell if it was just a rock in the sticking out in the middle of water, or a structure that used to be above the water. It was so intriguing that I just must do something. I was curious and I had to quench my thirst for answers. I slowly got into the icy water and started paddling. As I kept swimming, it looked as if it were miles away. In the beginning I thought the site was a couple yards. Once I seemed to be getting closer, the suns were beginning to set.

Come on! I was almost there! I finally felt the edge of the rock. Before I even thought of going on top of it, I examined the sides. It was a mix of both a rock and a structure. It was an ordinary rock with symbols carved into it. As I swam around it, I noticed that some of the edges were geometrical. This was very strange indeed.

I climbed on top of the rock. Mist floated right above the water. Miles away were groups of other rocks that came up at sharp angles. Wow, there really was quite a view up here. I sat down tiredly from all the swimming I did.

Minutes later a strange echo caught in my ears. I sat up, but nothing new came into view. The echoing made a presence again, but this time with more power. I looked around, but I still couldn't tell where it was coming from. In the end, I investigated the water. I saw a clear reflection of myself. When the sound came again, my reflection blurred, and my eyes focused on the deep ocean. Sharks and other strange sea creatures swam by. Soon, as I continued searching for the origin of the sound, A large scaly ocean blue tail passed by. What was that?

I didn't realize it until I was face to face with the creature.

The echoing sound had stopped . . . for good this time. I stared into a face full of hair that had the blue tail. A silvery aquamarine blue hand came over and pulled the hair back. Her face was finally revealed. The echoes belonged to a siren.

Her hair was a blue with white streaks of a mess. Some of her hair was in braids which had silver clips at the end. Overall, her hair was wavy, soaked, and all over the place. I guessed this was what happened when you come out of your comfort zone.

She first spoke in a strange language that I didn't understand.

"Excuse me?" I asked confused.

"My name is Lavina," she said with a strong accent.

"It is nice to meet you. What were you trying to tell me?" I asked slowly for her to understand.

Lavina explained the best she could, even though she had a super strong accent.

"There is a legend of a violet stone, that can protect you against evil spirits. It is called The Stone of Refuge. It lies in an underwater cavern in the Uja jungle," Lavina explained.

Before I could ask any questions about it, she spoke again in the unfamiliar language then told me something that I could understand. "You must find the stone. It will help you along your journey," Lavina finishes as she slips back into the water leaving me here . . . as if nothing had ever happened.

Sweat drips from my pores. I blink a couple times to clear my vision. I couldn't breathe. My lips were continuously being smothered. I kept trying to make out the words stop, but they can't come. Over and over, I tried. I tried to push her off, but I was weak; I adjusted to what people wanted; I was a follower. Without warning, I bit Bonesella on her lower lip.

I was finally let free. Automatically felt guilt for what I did. I never wanted to do that, I just felt that there was no other way to get out. I was about to panic. Bonesella patted two fingers on her lower lip. It has already become swollen, and droplets of blood were making their way out. "I-I didn't mean to. I am claustrophobic. I'm sorry," I said.

Bonesella pressed her lips back together, rubbing them back to normal.

"I wish you would have told me."

"I tried to."

I looked around the room. It was still completely dark, except for the moonlight coming into the window. Every night, a different group of moons shed light over us; it was ridiculously hard to keep track of which ones. A wall to my side glows gold without warning. I turned to that direction, Bonesella was lighting a candle on my nightstand and hers. I guessed it was my time to break the news.

I explained everything to Bonesella at once. She didn't look surprised about the story. It seemed like she had heard it before, like she had been waiting and anticipating for this moment.

"So, what should we do about it?"

Bonesella glanced around the room, like she was making sure that no one was near. She looked at me directly in the eyes with determination, like she was about to risk her entire life just to get to that stone. She needed it, she starved for it.

"I have a plan."

These were the last words in the night. We both fell asleep like we knew exactly what was going on in our minds, but the truth was . . . I wasn't exactly sure about anything that we were going to do for the next few days.

Chapter Twenty

Before we went to get the stone, Bonesella wanted to see my powers. I had never actually shown her how I could heal. I really wasn't planning on cutting myself with a knife for a demonstration. I kept trying over and over to see if my semen could do anything else. It was already good that I could heal wounds, but this wasn't something that I would attack people or monsters with.

I lay back in the grass, thinking over and over the same thing.

"Hey, Xavier!" Bonesella called from far away.

"Come over here, I want to show you something."

I sat up, Bonesella was walking over here, wearing a shiny new set of armor.

"Whoa, were can I get some of that?" I said, not believing my eyes.

"The armor . . . or me?" Bonesella joked. She took my hand and pulled me along.

"I opened up a weaponry and an armory. Here, let's measure you."

Bonesella led me to the back of the mansion, which was right in front of us. Bonesella came up to a golden sliding door and pulled it aside.

“Here it is,” Bonesella announced.

The forge was organized and clean, but it would not be like this for long if it was going to be used.

“I have never seen a forge this classy before,” I said looking from the ceiling to the floor.

“Of course not! This is an original,” Bonesella joked again.

Bonesella got out a tape measure and went all around me.

“So, what type of armor do you want?” Bonesella asked me. I didn’t know that many types of armor, but when I looked back at the ones I knew, Isaac’s armor came to mind. It became popular around the world. Skintight armor, with flexible aluminum plates. It was lightweight and the design made it possible that the impact didn’t hurt you that much . . . just like some of the older vehicles in Eurquence.

“I want the worldwide skintight armor,” I said proudly.

“Whoa, well that’s going to be kind of tricky, but I will do my best. Its worldwide name is aldine armor. It means flexible in some language of where it originated from,” Bonesella explained to me.

“Well, do whatever you can to make it happen,” I said simply.

It was a lengthy process, but I waited patiently, trying out my skills that I had so far, and trying out new ones. In a couple of days, the armor was finished, and I was still trying to figure some stuff out.

“Here it is, finished and ready to put on. I also have some weapons I made with it,” Bonesella announced.

I was sitting here, in the middle of the forest still thinking about the time I healed myself.

“Great . . . that’s good,” I said slowly, a bit out of it.

“So, what have you been up to lately?”

I sighed, unsure of what to do now.

“I am just so confused. First, I found out that I was able to heal, then I got information about a stone from a mermaid, and now I am wondering why all the creatures of the forest like me," I said stubbornly.

"I just don't get it."

Bonesella took a seat beside me.

"Well, I am sure that the answers will come to you one day. Always remember that. Everything has a purpose," Bonesella explained.

The words were not coming directly into my head, but into the wind, then carrying it gently to my ears and then my head.

"Yeah, I guess you're right."

My feet were dipped in the guardian pool I came by last time. Fish swam over and stayed, floating by my feet like they never want to leave. After sitting a while, an alench came by and sniff me. It's a sort of large, low-standing mammal with thick armor and a hard head with skin covered horns. They were typically red with yellow patches. They were made to blend in bushes of that color. Once it came near enough, I petted it gently on the head. I was surprised that it even came close to me. These creatures were usually aggressive if you came near them, but then this one came to me. They usually ignore people, why me?

The alench started to sniff me near my genital area, just like Nightmare did. He knew too. "Yeah, I know. Is there anything else new to me?" I said, talking to the creature. The alench made a sound in response. It was like I could speak to them or something. I thought long and hard about this. Finally, something came to mind that I almost forgot about: The Blossom of Life. Did it have anything to do with this? I started to run fingers through my hair. It isn't there. Where did it go? I looked toward the alench. It was facing the opposite direction. I looked closer to what it was looking at. Something was glittering and floating in the air. I went up to catch it and opened my hand. The Blossom of Life lifted into the air and tucked itself behind my ear. I looked back at the creature. The creature turned to look at me with the blossom in my hair. After a long moment of staring the alench looked as if it were going to lay down. Though I noticed something different. The front legs were bent while its back legs were straight. Also, the alench's head was pressed down to the ground. After a moment of studying the creature's posture, I realized something astonishing: it was kneeling to me.

I stood and looked around to spread the news, but no one was there. Bonesella was gone. I didn't even realize when she left. I guess I was a little too caught up with this. I flew back in a rush. When I got back, Bonesella had her own armor on.

"Hey, I thought you preferred silver," I said walking up.

Her gold armor glimmered brightly in the sun light.

"And I thought you preferred gold."

We both laughed the next moment.

It was true that the opposites would have looked best on us. By this point, it didn't matter. I chose silver because, one, Isaac's armor was silver, and two, I didn't want to look rich and evil. I like things a bit plainer than what Bonesella likes.

I placed a hand on her shoulder.

"I swear, for every day that passes I am going to find out something new which is going to add up on the pile of this," I said looking at the detail of her work.

Silver armor. Skin-tight with plates. Just the way I liked it. Bonesella's armor was also skintight. The only different was the metal. Gold can be molded in almost anything. So, when it came to this kind of armor, it was either silver or gold. But the silver was just the color, we really mean aluminum, but silver sounds more appealing.

"Well, if you keep finding out stuff, then we might as well be on our way so we can find out more stuff when we really need it," Bonesella said with determination.

"I rather be safe than sorry," I added in contrast.

I fitted on my armor. It slide on perfectly like a suit, clenching on my sides nicely. No, I was not implying that I was sexy. I was not trying to look good for myself or for someone else. I equipped myself with the weapons that Bonesella made. She seemed to be well taught in almost anything and everything.

"You ready?" Bonesella asked.

I nodded. I wasn't sure of what to expect. Should I be scared or brave? Safe or at risk? Weak or strong? Every situation has its advantages and disadvantages.

Bonesella knew exactly where we had to go. I just followed behind, looking around me so I didn't run into anything unexpectedly. I had a bow over my shoulder and arrows in a vegan leather case on my other shoulder. I also had a sword slipped in the belt on my waist. Nightmare walked beside us. If anything happened, he would be here to protect us.

The thick jungle looked as if it were devouring us. Green was everywhere. I felt that I might pass out here. As we walked deeper in this lush environment, I felt as if I were walking through a passage of time . . . and it was taking me to the past. It was the time I met Nightmare. I was frightened until Nightmare made me feel that everything was going to be fine. I lived after that day . . . and in another life I would be able to tell that story. I would be able to tell others how to not always be afraid, but to take the unexpected into consideration. To not just be afraid of everyone but have some hope. Life may go one way or the other. You may never know.

"So, it's in an underwater cavern?" Bonesella asked.

"Yes, I mean that is what she said," I replied, trying to catch up.

"Well, hopefully she's right." As I walked beside Bonesella, something seemed different about her. Her eyes were stern, and she wasn't walking so upright like she usually did. Was she tired, yet determined to stay focused?

"Are you okay? There's something about you that seems different. Did you not sleep last night?" I made out shakily.

I didn't like being that honest to people in their face. I usually preferred to keep my mouth shut about things. I never wanted to make someone feel bad about something that I noticed about them.

"I'm fine . . . it's just that . . ." Bonesella paused.

I wondered if I went a little too hard on her.

"I'm sorry if I was a little outspoken about that. I couldn't help the fact that you seemed different," I said in honesty.

"It's okay. I don't blame you, plus I should be a bit open about this anyway."

"Be open about what?" I asked wondering what she was talking about.

"It is just that . . . well, I am . . ." Bonesella started to make out, giving bits and pieces slowly.

"You are what?"

Bonesella's eyes went from surprised and open to giving up everything. Her eyes fell on the ground as if she suddenly became depressed . . . or maybe she was. I looked at her with confusion. There was no way that I could help her if she can't tell me.

"I don't know how to make out the words," Bonesella breathed out in a low tone.

"Fine. You can tell me. Whatever it is. If it is super important then tell me now," I said strictly.

Bonesella sighed.

"I am pregnant," she said barely in a whisper.

Without any surprise in my tone I asked, "How do you know?"

"Magic."

I grabbed ahold of the saddle on Nightmare for support.

"So, then I guess there is magic for everything?"

Bonesella slowed down to walk beside me. She had been a bit in a rush lately.

"If you know the spells. I could have gone to a doctor, but I felt that I was a bit too embarrassed for that. I rather just check on my own and let you know instead of having someone else do it," Bonesella explained to me.

I guessed she's right. It would be better to keep it personal than to have it known to others.

We continued our path. Since I knew now, I began to keep a close eye on her. Of course, it would be many months later till we had a newborn child, but just in case I chose to be a little overprotective around her for now on. After a while of stepping over sticks and fallen branches, the ground became steeper. Without really noticing I immediately put a hand in front of Bonesella.

"Stop. Be careful."

I leaned forward to get a closer look at what was down there. The ground sloped down, but then it finally evened out to what we were used to.

"Careful now, give me your hand," I said reaching out for her.

With my left hand, I held on to a tree for support. Bonesella made her way to me by doing the same. With Bonesella grabbing on to my arm I took a couple steps forward, then holding on to another tree. Bonesella was still attached to me. Once I tried to do it again, we both slid down to the bottom for about three to four seconds. At the end, Bonesella shakily grabbed my arm tightly. I looked straight into her eyes. She was afraid, she was portraying exactly how I felt right now . . . the difference was that I refused to show it.

I was hiding my feelings inside. I knew I was weak. I was not worth anything near as what she was worth. I refused to show because I felt that I would just put both of us in danger. I need to learn to be better than this. I couldn't be myself anymore.

Just as we were getting on our feet, walking as normal, the ground dropped. Not as a normal slope, but as the ground has holes in it. It looked as if a sinkhole or two had taken place. I walked around the depression to my left. The hole opened and revealed water. It looked exactly like the description Lavina gave me.

"I think this is it."

It wasn't exactly a hole on this side. It opened, which gave us a shore. It was an odd slope, but this was better than jumping into a hole with which we didn't know exactly what was even down there. I stared into the water, unsure of what to do next.

"So—"

"We get in," Bonesella finished for me.

"With all this armor on?" I asked finally.

"Well, not duh," Bonesella throws back at me.

Maybe I should be careful on what kind on tone I was using. Bonesella started to strip down first. Once she was finished, she eyed me with concern.

"Are you coming or not?"

I didn't exactly like to be pushed at doing these kinds of things. Without a word, I undressed looking in the opposite direction. Once I finished, I meet with Bonesella in the water. Right away at the looks of it, we had to put our heads under water because the ceiling was d0wn under.

"All right. At three."

I inhaled as much air as I could.

"One . . . two . . . three."

I thrust my head under the water after Bonesella. The pressure built up around my head, mainly over my ears. After a moment of staying completely still in the water, I opened my eyes and pushed myself forward to catch up to Bonesella. Some people's eyes were made to adapt in water better than others. I think I was included in that category. Everything was a blur at first, but after a moment, everything became clear. My chest was pounding with the amount of air supply I had to carry myself. I thought this trip was short, but I didn't know how wrong I was. It has been minutes of swimming in a dark tunnel and I was ready to get some air. I followed Bonesella still, ready to pass out. As I looked below me, small fish gather in the weeds. This cavern was empty. By this point, my vision blurred, and I couldn't swim no more. The last few bubbles of air released, and it looked like I was stuck in time.

I felt a jolt of movement. Something was tightly wrapped around my wrists. My head breaks though the water and I felt frigid air sticking to my face. My vision began to clear. "Xavier, are you okay?" Bonesella panicked.

Her face was with so much worry. I felt as if I was going to fall into the water, but Bonesella was holding me up.

"Where are we?" I asked trying to look around me.

"We found a point to stop. The ceiling here came a bit above the water," Bonesella explained.

As I looked beside her, I began to understand what she meant. We were in a cramped dome of rock above the water and there was only space for our heads and parts of our shoulders. The rest of our bodies were underwater.

"I can't be in here," I said.

I was ready to go under again. I couldn't bear being in tight spaces. I never wanted to be here again. Just as my head was going to break the water, Bonesella grabbed me hard on the shoulder.

"Just relax, okay? I need you to breath. Who knows where the next stop will be," Bonesella explained to me.

I looked at her. I was shaking all over, yet she was calm as ever. She was brave and I was weak.

Without warning, despite the frigid air, heat ran over me. I was looking down into the water, trying to watch my feet float, but the water was too dark to see beyond that. Hands grasped around both of my shoulders. I tilted my head back to breath. I couldn't be in here. I was just about to have a panic attack when I couldn't scream no more.

Warm lips touched mine and moved smoothly across. I wanted to scream before, but now I want to fall asleep with this as my dream. What if I was asleep? What if all of this was a dream? What if I couldn't wake up? What if I would never know of anything else? I closed my eyes and eagerly pressed my lips on hers. If this was the only thing left to keep me sane, I will take it. I kissed like I was fighting in an arena. It was a battle . . . and we both wanted to fulfill our thirst for each other.

Instead of myself having to pull away, Bonesella did. We were both out of breath and it was worse for me right now. I took deep breaths until my breathing was regulated. Once I had a hold of myself, I was the first to hit the water. The blue vision has come back. Everything I saw had a tint of blue and or green to it. This time, I was better at swimming through the tunnel. It was exceptionally large and deep. As I looked down again, the floor began to come up, little by little. We better hope that soon this cavern would open. I continued the path, the first to lead the way. Be a leader, not a follower.

On the trip, we found other stops. The tunnel was long and turned in many directions, but it didn't split up into other pathways. Finally, I could see the water above me reflecting. I could see the top layer of water; there was no rock above it. That must be where the stone was, in an open cavern. I pointed up, signaling Bonesella. She nodded and we both made our way there. We both broke the water at the same time. We gasped for breath; our faces soaked with water. I opened my eyes . . . wide.

"This is it . . . the cavern," I said, trying to hold myself together.

Bonesella nodded, still gasping for breath. I looked all around me. We were in a giant cavern. Waterfalls were scattered around the area. There was no dry land; the cavern was flooded with water, only giant rocks poked out of the ground.

"Wow," I let out.

To my right, there was a group of waterfalls, closely running next to each other. In the middle of the group, there was a flat, smooth rock. Perched on it was a violet stone that looked like it had been placed there simply on purpose: for us to find it.

Chapter Twenty-One

I stepped out from the deep parts of the water into the shallow. Bonesella followed slowly behind me. I kept on toward the stone.

"I can't believe we made it this far," I said.

I didn't hear a response right away, which suggested that Bonesella was still shocked just as I was.

"Yeah, no kidding."

From being so clueless, I continued walking toward the stone as if it were my destiny. On and on, until I finally noticed something slithering around my legs. A slimy body tightened around my ankles. I looked down and all around. This water was full of serpents. I yelped. Bonesella echoed back my call. I fell to the ground. I struggled to break free of the thick, black snake like body that slithered in all directions. I tried breaking free, repeatedly. Every time I got one part of my body out, it would be devoured by the serpent repeatedly. I should have known that this would all be a trap.

I looked back at Bonesella who was being swallowed by the mess. Her head was just barely above it all. Her face glimmered in the dim light. She wheezed and coughed. She was choking . . . and I had to do something about it. If only I had my sword which was away with my armor which laid at the entrance of the cave . . . waiting for us.

I had to do something. The mess of snake bodies was tightening around my shoulders. I couldn't just let us die . . . so close to that stone. My body was numb inside of all this. I couldn't move and I could hardly breath. A pain came from within. I looked toward Bonesella again. I felt like I was dying. The mouth of this monster must be under its body, taking a bite out of me our something. I watched Bonesella. I couldn't lose seeing her face again. Her eyes widened as my pain grew.

"You're glowing!" she screamed.

The magenta glow was so bright, I could see it peeking through the serpent bodies. I must have been doing something. What was happening?

The serpent bodies started to glow themselves from the inside. Between pigments, the magenta grew. The pigments started to separate and split one by one. The entire body in front of me split apart. Everywhere I looked around me, the serpents split open. My body loosened up. I began to slip out of the mess. I stood up over it all. My body glowed in pain. All the lines across me were glimmering with magenta. The serpents continued to split, their purple blood oozing out. I was free . . . and my body glowed bright enough to give light to the whole cavern.

My vision blurred, and I hit the serpent bodies unexpectedly. I blinked a few times. No, I could not fall now. I had to save Bonesella. I stood weakly, my body no longer glowing as it was. I flapped my wings behind me, stretching a bit. I first attempted to pull apart the serpent bodies from her. Bonesella was well passed out by now. As I pulled, they tightened back again just like they were before. I next attempted to find a sharp rock to cut them open, but there were none. I suddenly light flame to my hands and grasp on to the serpents. They glowed red and split apart, just as the others did. Bonesella's body relaxed over the serpents. I had to wake her up. Soon something else might happen and I wouldn't know it till it did.

I placed a hand behind her neck and shook her a bit. With a jolt, she coughed, and her eyes opened in a flash. I immediately felt relieved; I hadn't realized how up tight I was. I pressed my lips to her forehead. Thank God my baby was safe.

After a long moment, I released. Bonesella's face looked as if it were burnt red. I really don't understand why you could see blush on an exoskeleton, but whatever. This was not the point. She was alive, and that was what matters most.

"You did it," she choked out.

I nodded heavily. My pores were full of sweat. I was so worn out; I couldn't respond. I help Bonesella up silently. The cavern was quiet except for the running waterfalls. I stood with Bonesella uneasily.

"Let's get the stone, but quick. I don't want anything happening to us, okay," Bonesella said.

I nodded. It was now or never. I ran to the perched rock. I didn't look around to see if anything was lurking in the dark, I just wanted to take it and run. I made it to the perch without a single scratch. I kneeled in front of the stone. It glowed and looked like someone's spirit must be locked away in it. I cupped my hands in front of me to grab it, but before I could grasp them around the stone, I looked around me. Bonesella stood, mouth opened, in the shallow water. I had to take it now. I must. If I didn't, Bonesella may be doomed for good . . . and her father might take over.

Before I could do anything, I noticed something in the shallow water. Sirens, all around swimming, their heads were underneath the water. Were they good or bad? They must be protecting the stone. As I encircle my hands around the stone, the sounds of the sirens began to echo all around. I placed my hands softly around the stone. The sounds of the sirens continued to grow louder and louder. I didn't know what was going to happen, but I took a run for it.

"Come on, no time to waste," I said breathlessly as I run past Bonesella.

As we both made our way deeper and deeper into the water, the sounds of sirens became louder and louder as we made it farther and farther away. Are they following us? I finally threw my head under the water and the sounds all stopped. I began to lead the way this time, with Bonesella right behind me. Hopefully the stone would be safe . . . for now.

I swam deeper and deeper into the water. My ears became muffled and the pressure built up around my body. The waters were quiet except for us breaking the water. We continued to press on until we were right outside of the mouth of the cave. I just barely got myself out of the water by latching on to a rock. I pulled myself up and sat breathlessly on it. Bonesella came up from behind and sat down on the rock right beside mine. We sat in silence looking out into the forest. I let the stone rest safely in my hands. It continued to glow brightly as if it were a candle that would never burn out. I looked over to Bonesella. She didn't look to well. She was soaked, tired, and breathless . . . holding a baby inside.

With the little energy I had left, I stood and walked over to her with caution. I placed a light hand on her shoulder and rolled the violet stone into her hands.

"You are safe now. There is no need to worry," I said softly.

Bonesella looked up at me. She still seemed to be surprised that we even made it this far. It seemed too unreal. Without responding right away, Bonesella looked at the stone in awe. She brought it right to her face and turned it in every direction. There was nothing in the world that would displease her from the fascinating find that we made.

"Thank you . . . you know, for being there for me," Bonesella said in a soft tone that I could just barely hear.

"Of course, I would do anything for you. Are you sure that you're okay?"

I give my honest response. I really hoped she was doing well. After a moment of silence, she finally responded.

"Yeah. I am fine. So, about the thing of me being pregnant . . ." Bonesella started.

Without a word I give her my full attention and sit on the lower rock right in front of her. I leaned closer to her as she began speaking again.

"Are you mad at me? Did I hurt your feelings in any way? Does it—"

"Shh." I cut her off grasping her hands with the stone between them.

"No. I am not mad at you. I am fine. You don't need to be worried about me. I am more worried about you," I explained, pulling her hands towards me.

She looked to the side as if she were hiding something, then looks back at me. Her face was wet as if she were in the water again. Her eyes hold pain in them. The kind of pain I felt as a child when my mother died. I know that pain. And it was my job to take that pain away. Bonesella was crying, and I couldn't help but bring her into my arms and give her all the love I have to offer . . . and I mean all of it. I would do anything to help those in need, especially loved ones.

I pressed my lips to her forehead and held her body against mine. She was still a bit cold from the dive, hopefully I could warm her up and maybe also lighten her mood a bit. As the time passed, the time between Bonesella's sniffles became shorter, and I had a feeling that she was starting to feel worse. I held her tighter and pressed my lips to her cheek as near as possible to her lips. As her crying became louder, I pressed the palm of my left hand onto her other cheek. I would do anything to keep her safe. I finally broke out the truth.

"I can't stand seeing you like this . . . I need you to be strong and brave. . ."

I sniffled, trying to hold back my own tears which I knew would come down anyway. "I need you to stand up . . . because from the inside I can't do the same. I am weak and would hate to see you fall by my side. I know that you expect me to be the strong one in this relationship, but I can't. My brain was full of anxiety and insecurities, while my heart was full of pain and suffering." I had already started crying. I cry my eyes out continuously as I try my hardest to get the next few words out.

"I-I . . . just need you . . . to be strong."

Without word, I felt warmth reach my lips and I began to kiss back, taking all I could make sure the moment lasts. Bonesella releases after pressing on my lips as hard as she could.

"Xavier, I know that you are better than that," I finally hear her said as she brings me into a hug.

She sounded like she just fought a tough war that she had won even when she was expecting a loss.

After minutes passing, an unexpected roar came from behind. Bonesella and I were too exhausted from crying to be scared. I turned my body slowly toward Nightmare. He sat happily with his tail wagging. Bonesella pulled out her hand which tightly grasps the stone and releases the pressure. I lightly took the stone from her hand and held it in the air to reflect light. Nightmare's eyes dazzled at the stone. Without a second thought, I threw the stone to him as he caught it between his teeth. I smiled down at Bonesella. I guess we did it after all.

Bonesella and I rode on Nightmare's back as he walked. There were too many trees in the area for him to fly. I leaned against Bonesella's shoulder. Neither of us said a word till we got back home. It was late and I was ready to slip into bed for the night. We jumped off Nightmare's back and we headed inside while Nightmare flew up into a nearby tree for the night. Sometimes Nightmare acts like something else other than a dragon. I pressed my head heavily on the pillow. My head hurt too much to think before bed. I closed my eyes lightly, telling Bonesella good night sheepishly.

I awoke tiredly with a ringing in my ears. I opened my eyes, and my vision clears. It was still night. I moaned and rolled over hoping the ringing in my ears would stop. With time passing, the ringing continued, and it sounded more realistic this time, like I wasn't imagining it this time. I looked over to Bonesella, who was still fast asleep then to the glowing stone one her nightstand. For once she was protected and now, I could focus more on other things. I banged the side of my head furiously for the ringing to stop. It persisted, and I lean over Bonesella's side to take a closer at the stone. The ringing got louder. That stone must be causing the ringing in my ears. It hurt just by staring at the stone. I slipped out of bed so I could finally let my ears rest. Do Bonesella's ears hurt? Probably not because she was fast asleep. I go downstairs and make myself a cup of tea. The ringing finally vanished. I breathed in relief. Once I finished my tea I went to sleep on the couch.

A warm, soft, and wet surface touched my cheek.

"Xavier, good morning," I heard Bonesella's voice in my ear.

I opened my eyes to her confused, yet worried face.

"Bonse, I am fine."

Without pressing the issue more than it needed to her, I responded.

"Still, you could have at least told me you were going to be down here. I got worried. Why did you come to sleep down here in the first place?"

I knew the answer straight forward, yet I pretended to think about it.

"Well, at first my ears began to ring . . . and I thought it was nothing until when I got closer to the stone it got louder and more painful . . . so I came down here to get away from the sound," I explained casually trying to not make it sound like a big issue.

Bonesella had other things to worry about just as I do.

"So, let me get this straight, the stone caused your ears to ring?" She asked concerned, most likely for my sanity. I wanted to straight out tell her that I did passionately believe it.

"Well, I don't know," I said instead. Bonesella's somewhat tense shoulders relax and she came around to sit by me.

"So, what's your conclusion?"

It took Bonesella a moment to answer.

"Well, I didn't hear anything last night, so I am trusting that what you are saying is true."

"Why would I lie?"

"I am not saying that," Bonesella said.

"I am just saying that I am unsure what this means for you."

My mind was left blank, waiting for Bonesella to have another response.

"I am not sure how to put this," Bonesella said as she placed a finger on her temple.

"Not sure about what?" I pressed on this time.

"That this stone is supposed to protect me from dark energies . . . and somehow it made your ears ring. Your sensitive ears must be picking up the forces that the stone puts out to stop the dark energies from coming near," Bonesella explained.

I suddenly understood the situation much better, but I still had questions.

"What kind of dark energies? How do you know this?"

"Various forms of it. I know stuff about the Stone of Refuge because I read about it," Bonesella said in a way that made me feel stupid for asking such a question.

"Well, you didn't inform me of your knowledge before we embarked on our journey," I stood for myself.

"You didn't ask."

Bonesella looked toward the wall next to her trying not to piss me off. I could already tell.

"Still, we could have gotten in much trouble if you still hadn't said anything. You are lucky that both of us made it out alive," I pushed forward.

My eyes fell on the exact opposite wall of the one Bonesella was looking at. I needed this information. Somehow this stone might be able to protect Bonesella of what I fear. Her father.

Chapter Twenty-Two

I knew that Bonesella was safe with the stone. I knew that she was in danger of dark energy, and in my gut, I had a feeling that her father maybe sending out this dark energy. Though without further thought, months passed on as we lived a normal life. Bonesella moved the stone further away from me so my ears wouldn't hurt at night. Now we didn't think nothing much of it. I wanted to believe that everything was fine, but I still feel that something will go wrong eventually.

I wanted to go back to the rock formation out in the ocean where I received my information, but Bonesella told me to forget about it. She said we were going to be fine, but I still don't think that was true. I close my eyes at night and roll onto my back. I just wanted to escape from reality, I needed more information. With so much on my mind, I got up and quietly snuck into the library down the hall. It was quite large, and the shelves were filled heavily with books. I walked around each shelf slowly, examining the titles along the spines. I kept going around till I caught a book with my eye titled: Energies and spirits.

I glided my hand across the smooth, leather cover and opened the book gently. I skimmed through the pages till I found a chapter called Dark Energy—The Allia. I didn't understand what The Allia meant, so I read on:

The Allia is the ultimate Dark energy that exists in the universe—founded by Esnar Waliegh in Amar 34, 72441. The Allia exists in many different forms as it is transferred to different holders. The Allia is harvested by a holder by one of two ways:

The Allia can be taken into the body through digestion from one holder to another (See pg. 324) or

The Allia can be cursed upon and individual by no means of religious practice—although this is exceedingly rare (1 out of 8,467) (see pg. 782)

Before I read on, I finally noticed how dark the library was. There were only a few candles still lit, many have burned out. I also was very tired, so I slip a bookmark into the book and go off to bed.

Sunlight touches upon my skin waking me up. I sat up, taking the book from my nightstand. Bonesella was just waking up as I was finding my place in the chapter.

"Good morning, Xavier. What is that you are reading?" Bonesella asked while wiping an eye.

I decide to speak openly about my findings.

"Reading up on some information that you forgot to mention to me."

"What information?" Bonesella asked as if she really didn't know what I was talking about.

"The Allia," I said simply like it was not a big deal at all.

"So, what did you find out?" Bonesella asked slowly.

"Well, I didn't really read much, but The Allia is the most powerful dark energy out there which can take control of an individual. So, I was starting to make some theories and connections."

After a moment of silence, Bonesella spoke up again.

"Tell me about them."

"Tell me more about your father first, then I will tell you what I think."

I could see the anger flaring up in Bonesella. He face changed immediately like she was ready to explode.

"You really want to know?" Bonesella said through her gritted teeth.

"Yes. Yes, I do," I said firmly.

Bonesella scooted close from across the bed with her face in my own.

"If you tell anyone, I swear I will tear your heart out."

I nodded as my heart skipped a beat. Bonesella leaned back into a more relaxed position, but her poster was still stiff.

"My father has had The Allia since he met my mother . . ."

Bonesella started roughly.

"I knew he had it since I was a little girl, yet at the time I didn't really understand what it was. When I went to bed, I heard horrible things. I wasn't sure if the sounds made out words or if they were just sounding. I told my mother the things I heard at night, but she told me it was all in my head, that they never even existed. I trusted my mother even when I really believed they were real. I didn't dare tell my father what I heard. I didn't trust him . . . and I still don't. Him and my mother argued all the time and I knew they didn't get along well. I had asked my mother why they didn't like each other, but she just told me that they had agreed to stay together so they could take care of me. During their arguments I heard my father mention The Allia, but I really don't remember what he had said about it."

Bonesella paused. I looked at her with eager eyes. I needed to know what had happened.

"Now that I am older, I know that my father is hiding secrets from me. I just don't know what those secrets are. I can only imagine him using the Allia against me, but for what purpose? I don't have anything he wants. I was born because he raped my mother. But once I was born, she wanted to take care of me . . . and that is when my father agreed to stay to help her, even when they were married and absolutely hated each other. I was the only reason they decided to stay together."

I thought long and hard about it. Her father had to have a reason to stay. He wouldn't have done it just to take care of Bonesella. Plus, where was he now?

"I still wonder what is going on inside his head," Bonesella said.

I didn't know either, but I know that we need to figure this out, before Her father does something mad.

"So, you can't remember of your father saying anything about or related to The Allia, besides mentioning the name?" I asked while we ate breakfast at the table.

I sipped my tea while Bonesella answered.

"No not that I remember. If I ever do, I will tell you."

I placed my tea down on the small plate as I brought up another thought.

"Why does he hate your mother? Did she do something to him that made him rape her?"

Bonesella didn't respond right away, leaving the question hanging and me in the silence.

"I don't think that she did anything to him, but after harsh arguments she would sometimes talk with my uncle about him . . . but it was rare. They hardly mention him at all. My uncle simply pretends that he had never existed in the first place."

I was already ready to respond, so I broke in before the silence took over again.

"So, none of you like him at all because he raped your mother, right?" I said.

"Well, yes of course, but I am sure they don't like him for other reasons too. I mean think about it, my father didn't show up at all at our wedding . . . and even if he did, I am sure they would kick him right out," Bonesella said defensively.

Without thinking any further, I had a conclusion based on my analysis.

"Well, the Allia doesn't make your family like him anymore. I think you should go talk to your mother and if you could get some information out of your uncle that would also be great . . . and don't worry I'm coming with you."

After the shock drained out from Bonesella's face, she agreed to go back home to talk to her mother. We gathered our gear and climbed on to nightmare's back.

"You ready? Or are you nervous?" I asked Bonesella before taking off.

"A bit of both."

The wind caught underneath Nightmare's wings and we rose taking flight. I still find it hard to ignore the wind hitting my face, but Bonesella seemed to not mind it at all. I was surprised she was doing well, because she was already a few months pregnant. Holy shit.

"Bonse?" I said uneasily.

"What is it now?" Bonesella responded as if I might ruin her day.

"How are we going to tell your family that you're pregnant?" I said carefully not to piss her off.

"Shit!" I could tell that Bonesella was ready to explode.

She really did get angered easily.

"Sorry," I mention, but it didn't sound truthful.

After a few inhales and exhales Bonesella finally said, "Oh well, I guess it is time anyway. Hopefully she doesn't get mad at me for it."

I paused for a moment.

"Why would she be mad at you?" I asked into her ear as the wind increased.

"She's sometimes a bit overprotective."

"Is she trying to protect you from your father?" I suggest.

"Does everything have to be related to him?"

"Sorry."

We made it to the palace by luncheon. I knocked on the double doors anxiously. As we waited to be let in, Bonesella wrapped her hands around mine. She really must have been nervous by now. I turned to her to meet her gaze.

"Everything is going to be fine, trust me," I reassured her.

She didn't respond but smiled instead. The doors opened and we were greeted by two guards. I could tell that they were shocked to see Bonesella have her belly sticking out.

"Uh, hello. May we come in and speak to Bonesella's mother?"

One of the guards nodded and we walked into the royal hall. As we find our usual grounds, one of the guards calls out behind us that Graditha would be right with us as soon as possible. Bonesella and I found lounge chairs by the double doors with a small table in between and we take a seat there. I reopened *Energies and Spirits* and continued reading where I left off while Bonesella looked around the room anxiously.

Once a person has control of The Allia, or The Allia has control over them, the person has the power to use the Allia for their will but must make a sacrifice (Such as another soul) to get what they seek (see pg. 336). The Allia is typically used to take over kingdoms and take control of people, though other motives of harnessing the Allia also exist.

Once a sacrifice has been made to The Allia, the host may use The Allia for their wishes and they will be granted, but there is a limitation to this power. What you sacrifice must be at a certain level of importance to fulfill certain wishes of certain power. For example, for a wish to take control of a kingdom will take a sacrifice of a high level of importance that will be accepted, such as the death of a handful of important people to history, or with souls of high worth (see pg. 591).

I went to page 591 and bookmarked it for later reading. Bonesella shook my arm hard, grabbing my instant attention.

"What? Is she here yet?" I asked almost panicking.

"No, but she will be in about three minutes," Bonesella said trying to keep her cool.

"Do you want me to talk to your mother, because I think

you are a bit too nervous to handle this," I mentioned honestly.

"I can handle it. I just need more time to relax."

Without further note, I trusted her word and waited the three minutes with her, holding her hand tightly.

Her mother walked into the hall with the two guards beside her that let us in.

"Hi, Mom," Bonesella said trying to sound happy to see her could tell that this isn't going to go too well.

Bonesella got up fully revealing her large belly. Her mother froze about a yard away. "Surprise!" Bonesella cheered. I was still seated with my legs crossed. I didn't want to interfere.

"Why didn't you tell me before?" Graditha gasped.

"Because we were busy with stuff.," Bonesella started.

"Busy? Busy with what? You should have come by months ago," Graditha claimed.

"Well, we came by now to talk about that," Bonesella said sounding sorry.

"So, what is it then?" Graditha said with concern.

"Xavier and I . . ." I got up and stood next to Bonesella, supporting her.

"We found the Stone of Refuge and we want to know why Dad has The Allia and what is he planning to do with it?"

Graditha's face changed quickly from surprise to anger. No wonder who gave Bonesella her short temper.

"Your father is gone and that should be the last thing that matters," Graditha said strictly.

"The last thing that matters is my father trying to kill us," Bonesella fired back.

"Where did you hear this from?"

I could see the anger and the questioning look in Graditha's eyes.

"Xavier was worried about what he was planning since he found out about him."

Graditha switched her attention to me and I knew it was my turn to say something.

"And how do you know this?"

"He has The Allia and to use it he needs to sacrifice someone to use its powers for whatever he wants. I believe Bonesella is his sacrifice."

Graditha's expression changed back into shock. For a whole minute she couldn't say a word. Graditha looked toward Bonesella with worried eyes.

"And what would you like to know so that you could stop him?"

"Everything," Bonesella firmly replied.

We sat down at the grand table with Bonesella's mother. She looked as if she might have a break down any moment now. I held on to Bonesella's hand and kissed her on the cheek occasionally to make sure she was okay. She looked as broken as her mother, but she did her best to hide it.

"Your father only wanted you so that he could activate The Allia. I am not sure why he needed The Allia. He refused to tell me anything, but he said that many were going to die, including me."

Bonesella's mouth dropped open and tears were already streaming down her face. She buried her face into my shoulder and cried loudly. I hold her as her mother continued to speak.

"You need to find out why he is going to use The Allia and protect Bonesella. Her father could show up anytime now and take her away for good. I should have warned you two about this a long time ago," Graditha explained.

"What else do you know about his plans?" I asked eagerly.

"Not much else. You are going to have to find him and find that out yourself."

I thought back to Bonesella's and my previous conversation.

"Does your brother know anything else?"

"No, nothing else. Do you want something to eat? It's luncheon."

"Yes, please."

I looked over to Bonesella who had lifted her head and was

now wiping her tears with the back of her hand.

"Do you want anything?"

She shook her head.

"I am not really that hungry."

"Well, you can share with me so that you eat something at least."

Graditha told the guards to tell the kitchen staff to start making food. We waited in silence. I couldn't think of anything else to bring up. All I could think of now was that when we finished eating, we would said goodbye and leave. When we get home, we could think of what to do next. After about thirty minutes, food came, and I began eating right away. There was fresh salad, chicken, and some other food that I couldn't name. Graditha and I ate happily while I started to notice the depressing look on Bonesella's face. I didn't think she was planning on eating.

"Bonse, are you going to eat anything? I don't want you to starve on the way back."

Bonesella sighed, "I'll eat if I feel like it. Right now, I can't take this situation off my mind."

We ate silently as Bonesella shared occasional bites.

Finally, Graditha spoke, "So the baby . . . is it a boy or a girl?"

Bonesella looked up from our plate. Finally, a hint of excitement rushed through her. "To be honest I am not sure," she said smiling. "I really want a girl." Bonesella turned toward me. "Xavier, hon, what do you want?"

I thought about it for a moment. I didn't see why a baby's biological sex was so important.

"To me it doesn't matter. I would like both a boy and a girl."

Graditha and Bonesella both smiled at the thought.

"Well, that is good news. Just be careful, your father is out there, you know," Graditha added.

"Yeah, I know," Bonesella responded less excitingly.

Once we finish eating, Bonesella gave her mother a tight hug.

"Good luck with the baby."

"Thanks, Mom, love you."

"Love you too."

I gave Graditha a hug too and she wished me luck as well. We waved as I took Bonesella's hand and headed out. Bonesella and I climbed onto Nightmare's back.

"So, you ready to be a mother?" I asked full of ambition.

"Yes, I am, and I really hope that my child is going to live a normal life and that my father doesn't interfere with that," Bonesella explained.

"I hope so too," I said as I kiss her on the cheek.

I wanted nothing more than to have a child who was going to live a happy and normal life with us, even if we were not the greatest first parents there were. Bonesella kissed me back on the cheek while Nightmare was taking off. We didn't talk much on the way back; we just held the most important conversations till we got home.

Once we were home, I took my book and sat on the couch. Bonesella came over and sat with me, leaning her head on my shoulder. I opened my book to the page I marked earlier.

Sacrifice and Receive

Soul(s) for ultimate power

Any soul has great worth to some extent and every soul has a certain scent. The rarest souls of divine scent were usually sought after by demonic creatures to fulfill their hunger and craving. Only demonic creatures can smell souls and find them. For a host who wants to find one of these divine souls for a wish should have a demonic presence with them. The host itself cannot find these souls.

Once the host has found a demonic presence, the hunt for souls begin. Once the soul(s) is found, the proper spell can be cast with these words (See pg. 413).

Souls were usually traded for ultimate powers such as control over others or even for other souls.

I skipped over the part that talked about the power to control others and marked the part about exchanging souls for later. Right now, I was too tired to read more.

"Bonse?"

I was not sure if she was sleeping or not. She moves from my shoulder and sat upright.

"What is it?" She responded tiredly.

"Do you think your father wants to have control over other people or does he want to exchange your soul for another?" I asked.

"Why would my father do that? The only logical thing he would do is to take control of other people—probably you and the rest of my family so her could rule the country," Bonesella explained.

"Yeah, I think your right. There can't be another reason why your parents would fight so much."

Bonesella nodded. We both knew that our fates would depend on what her father has planned for us, but for now we hoped to raise a healthy boy before we could continue any further on our journey.

Chapter Twenty-Three

My head spinning in circles, hands pressed on my temples. I didn't know how I was going to get through this.

"Bonesella, I don't think I am going to be a great father," I said.

Bonesella dropped her book and looked at me with disbelief.

"Xavier don't say that. That's not true."

I went on with the heavy feeling in my chest, anxiety crawling over my skin.

"But seriously, how am I ever going to be a great father if my own father never even . . ."

I paused. I wasn't sure how to put it.

"Xavier, I am sure that your father did his best to protect and take care of you—"

"No, no he didn't. If my father did his best, he would still be here for me. He would have never disappeared," I yelled.

"Are you sure that he was busy doing something and that you are the one who ran away?" Bonesella asked eyeing me.

"What? How could you said something like that! My father would never be busy. He just liked watering my mother's plants in the garden and keeping the house clean. He didn't work at all," I exclaimed.

A moment of silence came but was broken by Bonesella's voice.

"Did your mother work at all?" I thought about it for a moment.

"No, she would be home every day to take care of me."

Another moment of silence came.

"So then how were your parents able to afford such a huge house if they didn't work?"

The question filled my head, and I wasn't sure how to answer it.

"I am sure they got the money from my grandparents or something. It's not a big deal," I pushed the conversation aside, but another question came up.

"Who were your grandparents?"

I had never meet them. In fact, I never knew anything about them. I was sure that I do have grandparents, but I was never told anything about them. I was sure they must have passed before I was even born. Maybe they had a disease or something.

"I never got to meet them. They must have passed before my birth."

Bonesella gave a sigh.

"I don't know if I have grandparents either."

We both felt the same now. As the silence grew, we knew it was just going to be us, and that maybe Bonesella's mother might help for the new child.

Bonesella got up as I sat down on the edge of the bed. She walked over to my side and placed a hand on my cheek while kissing the other.

"I am sure you will make a great father. I know you have it in you."

The words fell inside me and made my heart feel a little heavier than before. I simply laid my head on her shoulder, and she brushed fingers into my long hair. I close my eyes and let the wave of silence pull over me like if I pulled the sheets over my head. It had been another month, and I was becoming fearful of the future.

From downstairs a loud knock became present. The wave of emotion, silence, and fear freed me. I felt relieved to take those off my mind. I ran downstairs to get the door before Bonesella, who was walking slower now that she was carrying more weight. I swung open the door to see Graditha waving at us. As I let her in, Bonesella finally made it to the last step.

"Come. It's a pleasure to see you again," I said as I guide her to the table.

"It's a pleasure to see you too," Graditha repeated.

As Graditha took a seat, Bonesella placed a hand on my shoulder.

"Let's not mention anything about my father, okay?" she whispered in my ear. I nodded with understanding.

"So, how's the planning been going on?" Graditha asked while Bonesella went off to make tea.

"Great—I'm nervous," I said by accident.

Graditha giggled lightly.

"Well, I hope you not only prepare for the child, but yourself too."

I looked off into the kitchen. "Yeah, I really need to keep up with that too."

Bonesella quickly came back with the tea. Graditha changed her attention from me to her daughter.

"So, how's the child, darling?"

"Well, though it's a bit more pressure on me doing normal things such as getting dressed in the morning and going up and down the stairs," Bonesella said setting the tea in front of her mother.

"Well, shouldn't your love be helping you with that?" Graditha asked looking over at me.

My face flushed with minimal embarrassment.

"I have helped her quite a few times recently, although she is getting pretty good at doing these things herself despite the extra weight she's carrying," I mentioned, putting the topic aside. Bonesella and I sat as we got ourselves our own cups of tea.

"So, Xavier . . ." Graditha started.

I lift my face immediately, flushing red again. I really hated being the center of attention. I rather stand aside and let Bonesella do all the talking . . . Yet again, that just proved that I was weak.

"Yes?"

Graditha looked around the room before continuing.

"So, I heard about your special powers recently . . ." Graditha started.

My face burned red this time and I was ready to have a panic attack. My breathing became heavy as she continued.

"Healing it is, correct?" I could only nod.

"It is an exceedingly rare talent to have. You should really investigate it more. Maybe you could help take the pain away for Bonesella's first birth," Graditha suggested in a calm demeanor.

At that point I couldn't take it anymore. I let my head fall on to the table as the very thought haunted me. I couldn't hide my tears this time. I was weak and that Bonesella might not deserve me in the first place.

Warm arms wrapped around my shoulders. Soft lips touched my ear. Fingers ran through my hair. I pressed my eyes close as I turned to hide my face in her chest. I couldn't bear the thought anymore. I was absolutely embarrassed about healing with my semen. I didn't know why Bonesella would ever tell her because she did and now my secret may just end up to the public. I could hear the stuttering of Graditha trying to put her words together. I let go of Bonesella and run upstairs without warning.

I pressed my face into my pillow with tears streaming down my face. Bonesella swung open the door after me and slamming it, though meaning to close it softly.

"Xavier, what's wrong?" Bonesella yelled in question even though she should already know the answer.

"I can't stand being embarrassed like that!" I yelled between sobs.

"How is that embarrassing? It was a question!"

I cried harder knowing that it was for no good reason.

"You know I have anxiety . . . I don't like openly talking about my healing semen . . . and who knows what else is going on inside me. That isn't something you ask out of thin air. You know I have panic attacks. I told you this before and yet, you decided to tell your mother about my insecurities," I explained loudly.

A moment of silence came over, as Bonesella stood with her mouth open. I took this advantage to get away from this and dig my head further into my pillow as my sobbing increases.

I could hear the struggle in Bonesella's breathing pattern. I knew that deep inside I didn't want to hurt her, yet I hated being nakedly exposed. I hated to show how vulnerable I was. Like having my clothes magically stripped away by others' will and having no control over it . . . and once that I realize that I have the control of my reactions . . . that too was stripped away, and anxiety took over. Anxiety filled my bloodstream and overflowed my head with unwanted thoughts. My hands shook, and I could no longer keep myself afloat. I suddenly lose my breath and drown in the depths below, but I awoke soon, on the shore with weakness. the mind of overflowing thoughts empty the shaking hands stiff as stone and anxiety stripped away leaving me in a new awakening.

Once I was released from my trance, I suddenly realized my sobbing has stopped entirely. I laid face down into my pillow, grasping in lightly with my hands, with empty thoughts. As I lift my head up, only seeing a blur of color, I feel the sudden gain of weight on the bed and a hand stroke through my hair. Bonesella laid aside from me on her side with a hand in my hair.

"Xavier, it's okay to be afraid . . . nervous and anything in between," Bonesella said softly so I could just barely hear her. I looked away noticing how rude I was.

"I am sorry for what I said," I said in the exact tone.

"No worries. It's okay. I just want you to know that I am sorry too and that next time I won't push you too hard, but you got to let me know if this anxiety started to show up again," Bonesella explained.

I nodded releasing breath that kept pressure in my chest. I felt more relieved now.

I looked back at Bonesella again.

"Can you not tell anyone again?" I pleaded quietly.

Bonesella nodded, pulling me close to her and then kissing my cheek.

"Of course."

After a moment of silence, I had to break it.

"Should we go back down and tell your mother that I am fine and that nothing happened?" I asked.

"Sure, I'll help you out with the conversation this time."

"Thanks."

We got out of bed and made our way downstairs. Graditha waited patiently for us.

"Sorry for the inconvenience . . . Xavier kind of panicked. He has major anxiety." Bonesella explained simply.

"Oh," Graditha could only make out.

As I came back over to the table, taking a seat, I wave with a short smile to Graditha who looked extremely worried.

"Hi . . . now what were you saying?" I said as I took a seat as I were before.

"Hello," Graditha started slowly.

"I was wondering about your healing powers. How does it work?"

I thought for a long moment about this. I couldn't even flush red because I was too busy building a starting sentence.

"Well, I am not exactly sure of the biological mechanics of

it, but there is something about it that is strange. . ."

I continued to think about how to word my healing semen in the most non embarrassing way that might hide the truth. I decided there was no substitute for the words, and I might as well spill it.

"My semen heals wounds," I said like it never bothered me.

Graditha's eyes widened and Bonesella placed a warm hand on my shoulder. At least no matter how degraded I felt about it, Bonesella would be here to support me in my flaws. Silence came over us.

"So that's all I really know about it . . . I would still like to find out more," I said slowly to brighten the conversation.

Instead of a response from Graditha, Bonesella broke in.

"I guess it would be a clever idea to see if I can have a painless birthing, right babe?"

I nod and smile. If I could do anything for her, it would be to take the pain away.

Graditha nodded and I could see the focus regained in her eyes.

"Well, that sounds like a promising idea," Graditha paused for a moment and then continued.

"What also sounds like an innovative idea is if you can maybe help stop some diseases that have been spreading recently. We have been having a decrease in the population in our country. If you can come back to the palace, we can communicate about this situation more, and I can also give you a station in Mala, a poor community in the northern Vermir deserts where these diseases have been spreading from. You can make a lot of money if you take this opportunity that I am giving you," Graditha explained.

I gave myself a moment to think about this, but I couldn't find much progress because this would have to be something that Bonesella and I need to talk about.

"Wow, that sounds great. I would take the opportunity right away, but Bonesella and I need to talk about this first. So, while you are here, I think we should change the subject so we could . . . end on a happy note," I explained.

Graditha nodded happily and gazed upon the clock on the wall behind her.

"Oh, I am afraid that this conversation is going to have to end early. I must get back to the palace at this time. It wonderful to see you both," Graditha explained as she got up.

She quickly gave both of us a tight hug and went off out the door.

I turned back around to Bonesella, who was picking up the tea dishes. "Well, it sounds like you're going to actually have your own money," Bonesella stated.

"Yeah, it sounds like a really great deal."

"Of course. No kidding. Working for royalty pays a lot."

"Yeah." The words echoed in my mind.

"So, are you willing to agree with me taking this path?" I asked out of my thoughts.

"Well, of course. What you must take into consideration is the fact that this child needs your support too and not just the diseased people out in Mala," Bonesella explained.

I sighed.

"Right, so how are we going to organize this?"

Suddenly Bonesella's father came to mind and fear struck me. I knew that Bonesella didn't want me to mention it, but I couldn't help the fact that I was worried about not just my safety, but Bonesella's too.

"What's wrong?"

Bonesella seemed to have recognized the concern that I had been presenting in my expression including my nervous posture.

"I am afraid for the future . . . that 'you-know-who' is going to come and take our life away from us," I said shyly.

Bonesella's expression turned into disbelief, but before it could become anger, I finished my thought.

"I don't know if we are going to have all of this anymore," I said as I looked around the dining room.

Instead of anger, Bonesella's expression became soft and somewhat understanding. Whiteout a word she came up and wrapped her arms around me. I hugged her back as well as my fears wondered my mind. Bonesella spoke finally.

"I think we should just live the best life that we can and then we will figure out how to deal with it when the time comes."

I thought about it. Right now, I just didn't feel that was the safest thing to do, but I didn't want to argue with her. I thought for now I should trust her word and forget what the future might hold.

Chapter Twenty-Four

The next day, I began to get dressed. I was heading to the palace alone this time with Nightmare. Bonesella was going to stay here and take care of herself. I told her that I was not sure how long I was going to be gone, but I will send frequent notes and maybe a palace worker to come and check on her for me. I put on nice clothes that were acceptable for the palace. I didn't like dressing too fancy, but something that will not be disrespectful to the royal community.

Bonesella was still lying in bed, but she was clearly awake, watching me carefully as I got dressed.

"So, you're going to let me know when you're coming back, right?"

I turned to face Bonesella for reassurance. "Of course. I will send a note."

She nodded in understanding. I really do hope that she was going to be okay all by herself.

"Well, have fun and let me know how my mother is doing."

"I will."

I went over to give Bonesella a hug and kissed her goodbye.

"If anything, send a note," I said as I let her go.

"I'll let you know."

There was nothing much to say. I waved as I walked out

from the room. I was already dressed, and it was time to head out to get Nightmare ready to fly. I headed down and walked out the front door. I blow a whistle to call Nightmare over. Bonesella and I let him sleep outside and he even hunts for himself. Nightmare enjoys being high up in the trees and hunting fish, rabbits, and bird eggs. Nightmare would hunt larger animals, but I didn't allow him too. It leaves a trail of blood through the forest that I was extremely sensitive to the smell of. I whistle again, this time I hear a rustle in the trees toward my left. "Nightmare! Come on we got to go somewhere," I called. I few seconds later, Nightmare flew out from the trees and landed in front of me with blood-tipped teeth. Once the scent reaches my nose, I pressed my fingers on the sides of my nostrils.

"Eww, Nightmare. You know I hate the smell of blood," I exclaimed.

Nightmare gave a low growl. I'm sure he didn't mean it. I took a few steps back from his mouth and let go of my nose.

"All right, here's the plan: We are going to have to fly to the palace. Once I am there you can come back here, but I am going to need you to come back to pick me up in a couple of days. Bonesella will let you know when, okay?" Nightmare nodded.

It was a bit awkward speaking to a dragon, but Nightmare understood me. I settled myself onto his back, adjusting myself accordingly. Once set, I tapped Nightmare on the shoulder and in response he took flight.

The wind picked up all around me. Before I know it, we were soaring higher than the clouds. The magenta sky gaped down at me. I let the wind hit my face and mess with my hair. I closed my eyes to feel everything from within. With a thick heart and a steady mind, I opened my eyes in the new awakening.

As we flew, I looked down passed Nightmare's wing. Small villages scattered the area. I noticed how bare they were and suspected that we were passing my old home. I hadn't thought about my old place in a while. Now that I was trying to remember exactly how I left it, I began to miss it. The two comfy yellow loveseats, the wooden coffee table, the shelves full of books and small plants and decorations, to the open kitchen with an island, to my small, only bedroom with my desk, bed with all white sheets, tiny closet, and a tiny bathroom. In my head I began to compare my home now with my old one. Living in a mansion was so much more different than a small comfy house. The thought of large rooms as refreshing, but I found it too large to what I was used to. I did hate tiny spaces; it gives me claustrophobia, yet large spaces gave me the feeling that I would get lost. I enjoyed where I lived now, but I wished I could go back to my old home some time . . . to embrace the memories I had there. To embrace the fact that I lost a friend who stayed in my old home for a while . . . and slept with his arms around me . . . making me feel safer than ever.

I gazed back down again. The small villages vanished, and large colorful towns and cities appeared. Bright lights filled the streets, and the suns' light reflected the broad structures that scraped the sky. I looked down with awe. It was such a large city that I was afraid to go down there. I never actually been very deep in it. Just the outskirts, I did find it very thick with small spaces and streets. I was terrified, but I really wanted to explore more. Nightmare began to fly lower, taking us closer to my fear, yet also to my curiosity.

The air began to become thicker as we soared close enough as we could get without touching the tops of the buildings, but I wasn't ready to pass out yet. Nightmare glided across as if he were on ice and the buildings were nonexistent. I grasped the leather handle on the saddle even tighter. Nightmare flies lower as we find an open spot between the buildings. I looked down to observe what was there. Other dragons who I assumed flew right by us were landing faster than we were. As we neared the ground to find a spot, I recognized dragons and people traveling in and out through the port for travel and trade. As Nightmare landed between two posts, as did the other dragons, I sat and waited. People were unloading goods from dragons' backs and checking in to the city. After a moment of scanning there were people scattered around wearing a red and orange uniform. I suspected that they worked here at the port. I slid off Nightmare, walking pass the other dragons between posts. They all had a rope trying them to the post. Nightmare gave a short roar, and I realized that I should be doing the same. I grabbed a rope from the saddle carriers, tying Nightmare to one of the posts beside him. As I finished up, one of the port workers walked over to me.

"Hello."

"Uh . . . hi," I said as I scan a male worker's face.

His face looked as if it were painted over to look like a sugar skull, but I knew better. It wasn't paint, but his actual face. It represented the main culture here in the country of Nelam.

"I'm Alex, and I'll be your port assistant for today. Now, are you traveling? Or importing goods?"

"Traveling," I said quickly.

I couldn't wait to go back into the palace.

"Okay." Alex took out a screen and looked over to get the post number. "And do you have an ID?"

"Yes." I reached into my pocket to get out a shiny card with a chip. Alex took out a scanner from his belt and scanned the chip.

"Xavier?" Alex asked looking up at me from his tablet.

"Yes."

"Last name: Goldaire, is it?"

"Yes," I said slowly.

It was Bonesella's last name that I took when we officially got married, on document of course. It was because I didn't exactly have a last name before. I never knew the family last name; my parents never mentioned it around me. There really was no talk about the family around me. It was a good thing that I was able to get her last name before I applied for my ID. Or else I wouldn't be acceptable to receive one, then of course, I wouldn't be able to travel or pay electronically for things. The only reason there were electronics at the ports was because of the different people coming in, that don't have anything on paper. Same goes for those coming from other planets in the solar system. Once you're in the palace, all that goes away. Royals really like to stick with the traditional cultural ways that they have been sticking to since the beginning of time.

"Okay. Is this the correct information?" Alex asked while passing me the tablet.

I scanned through all my information, from my name and date of birth to insurance and other stuff as I scroll down slowly.

"It looks good," I said passing Alex back his tablet.

"Okay, wonderful." Alex made a few more taps on the screen and passed it back to me.

"I am going to need you to place your finger here so I can confirm your information."

I pressed my finger on to the tablet as it scans my DNA mark. I passed the tablet back once it fully confirmed that I had a legal fingerprint. Alex tapped some more, but then his face changed from confidence to uncertainty.

"I believe that your information does not correspond with your fingerprint. I am going to need you to review your information again."

I got the tablet again and I scroll through the same screen I checked a moment ago.

"It's correct," I said loosely as I pass the tablet back again.

Alex did some more tapping.

"The system still said that your information is incorrect. Would you like me to check with the system manger to make sure that nothing is working unproperly?" Alex asked kindly.

"Yes, please that would be great," I said feeling impatient.

"I'll be back. If your dragon is a bit hungry, you can get one of the staff. They have treats," Alex explained.

"Okay, thank you."

As Alex left, I leaned over on Nightmare hoping that this wouldn't take long. I gaze at the sky above. The port started to become even more full of travelers. I looked over at Nightmare who was resting now. I guessed that sometimes I did make him feel tired of flying so much. I could fly with my own wings, but it wasn't ideal for long distances. If I ever decide to do that, my shoulders and back would kill me. I'll start feeling old before I even become old. As I wait, I continued scanning the area, seeing knew dragons and people all around me.

About half an hour or more later, Alex came back over to me.

"So?" I asked.

Alex's face still seemed to be full of uncertainty. Alex exhaled.

"I checked with the manager. There is nothing wrong with the system, and it still said that your information does not match your fingerprint."

I sighed heavily. How was I ever going to get to the palace if I couldn't even get into the city? Alex reviewed my information himself this time.

"You don't have a last name for your parents?"

"I don't know the family last name. My parents passed away when I was a child," I said slowly.

"Have you lived with someone that knows you personally?"

"Yes."

"And who is that?"

"Jacob Soars. He raised me after my parents passed."

"Okay," Alex said as he taps the tablet.

"Is this his correct information?" Alex asked while passing me the tablet. I reviewed the information. It included Jacob's picture, date of birth, and address.

"Yes, it's correct." Alex's face looked more relieved now.

"Which way would he prefer me to notify him?"

"By written letter," I said.

"Okay. Well, it is going to take a long time, at least a couple of days," Alex said.

Now I was questioning how I was going to get into the palace.

"So, I could lend you a room in that hotel . . ." Alex started to explain, pointing to the tall, silver building behind me. "Which you can stay in until I receive your correct information. You will only have to pay a small fee. Was that okay with you?" Alex explained to me.

I breathed out, releasing my anxiety build up.

"Sure, that's fine."

"Can I see your ID again?"

I passed my ID to Alex, who scanned it and tapped a few times on the tablet. A buzz sounded from a machine on his belt and a small paper with printed writing started to come out. Alex swiped with paper from his belt and passes it to me. I scanned the information while he spoke.

"So here is your ticket to get the room. Just take this over there . . ." Alex said while pointing to the long desk full of different receptionists separated by tinted windows.

"And then just let them know that you need a room for a short stay, and they will tell you what to do from there."

I smiled after hearing this information.

"Thank you so much."

"Of course," Alex said smiling at me.

I waved as I made my way off to the receptionist. I placed my ticket flat on the desk, leaning toward the speaker on the window.

"Uh, hi . . ." I said slowly, trying to figure out how to address the person.

"Hello," the person responded.

"Uh, I am sorry to bother you, but what are your pronouns?" I asked slowly.

"They/them please."

"Sure. I use he/him by the way," I replied simply with respect.

"Of course and my name is Wyndu. How can I help you today?"

I slowly study their face. Greenish-blueish skin with a sort of yellow, green, and purple hair and ocean eyes.

"Yes, I uh need a room for a short stay," I said as I slide the ticket underneath the window.

Wyndu took the ticket, scanned it, and typed some stuff on their computer.

"Okay, you're in the system. Let me print out your ticket and get you your key."

"Thank you," I said kindly.

"Of course," Wyndu said while giving me a key and a ticket with my room number on it.

"It's that tall building right behind you," they point out. I turned around to a silver building with many windows and balconies.

I smiled at them.

"Thanks."

From there, I went straight to the hotel. I walked through the glass doors. The main floor was wide and full of lounge chairs. I showed my ticket and key to a receptionist and found my way to the elevator. As I stepped on to the tenth floor, I slowed my pace, scanning the room numbers. I checked my ticket once more. Room 139, 10th floor.

I unlocked the door, pressed my hand on the handle of my room number, and pushed forward. Sunshine hit my face before I could even open the door all the way. On the far wall, a single, giant window let the sun's rays light the room. Not a single electric light was on. Beside the window was a door to the balcony. I scan the rest of the room around me, letting the details sink in. Everything was white and clean. The furniture was silver. The bed was to my left, including another door which leads to the small bathroom. On my right, a clean, silver desk stood with a tiny vase with a Monserk—a quite common violet flower. I sat on the white sheeted bed and took a few minutes to myself.

The sunshine to my left shone in my eyes. I looked down to possibly block it. I was not sure that I would make it in the palace at all. I slowly started to doubt everything as the feeling of emptiness began to devour me. I began to take my clothes off and then I hang them in the closet on the side of the bed, closest to the door. I guessed I wouldn't be needing these anytime soon. Once the sun light was able to scan my whole naked body, I decided to take a warm shower. I thought that the warmth would help cheer me up a bit, but it didn't last long. Too soon, I found myself lying in bed on my side, facing away from the window, with a towel wrapped around my wet hair.

After taking a short nap, I was able to get myself up to write a note to Bonesella. I slipped on my shorts and grabbed parchment and a pen to write with. I stare at the blank page, unsure of what to start off with. I didn't feel like writing to her. I preferred to deal with the news after the trip, but she needed to know what was going on. I start to write, but I didn't get into any specific details. I said hi, state the issue, and tell her where I was staying for a while. The result was very bland and emotionless. I couldn't make it more real for her.

Dear Bonesella,
Hi, I know you are wandering what is going on now, but I will just update you on what is going on so far. I am here in the capital, but I have been having some problems trying to get to the palace. I am still at the port, but I am in a hotel. I could not be let in because there was some issues with my information. I told them to contact Jacob, the man who raised me after my parents. Hopefully he could get back to them soon, but for now, I am here in my room waiting for news. Other than that, I am fine. I hope you are fine as well. Let me know if you need

anything. Tell me how the baby's doing. By the way, I would appreciate it if you can send me some more clothes with Nightmare. Thanks for understanding. Love you lots, Xavier.

After writing the note I sealed it off and got fully dressed, so I could have it sent to her. I quickly went to the mailing post and had a dragon send it off immediately. Once I got back to the hotel room, the suns were gone, and it was getting late. I went down to the lobby to eat dinner and then I went back to my room to undress, update my daily journal, and go to bed.

Warmth surrounded my naked body. I pulled the sheets over my head to block the sun from hitting my face. After about a minute, two loud bangs echoed across the room. I threw the blanket off my face and looked in the direction of the noise. Two loud bangs echoed again, from the door. I slipped out of bed to answer it. I popped my head out the door to see an unfamiliar face at the door.

"Uh, hello?" I said confused.

What time was it anyway?

"Hi, I have a letter and a little . . . gift for you," the woman said.

"Oh."

The woman was in a red and orange uniform, holding a letter out to me in her hand and a suitcase by her foot.

"Xavier, correct?" I looked her right in the eyes.

"Yes."

"Here you are then. Have a wonderful day."

"Thanks. You too."

I brought the letter and my suitcase in the room. I put my clothes away first, which half were casual, and the other half were fancy. I slip on some casual clothes and I took a seat on the bed with the letter in my hand. I opened it slowly trying to bear myself for any unexpected news.

Dear Xavier,

I am glad that you wrote back to me. I hope you are doing okay. Just let me know as soon as possible when you can get in the palace. If you need anything or any help, please let me know. I am always here for you. I also brought you some extra clothes. Other than that, I am doing fine. There's no need to worry. I still have a few more months to go. Never worry, I always love you . . . and I mean it. I really do love you, Xavier.

Love, Bonese

Relief filled me. I put the letter on the desk and lay back on the bed. I was not sure if I was going to get a reply from Alex about Jacob, but I thought I would go check on him to see how everything was going. It's fine and all to stay at the hotel, but it does feel a bit boring not being able to get into the palace. I wish I could have something to be excited about right now.

I put on my brown boots and go out to the port in hope to find Alex. I ran in between dragons and people, but every time I saw a person in uniform, it wasn't Alex. Finally, I went to Wyndu to ask about him. I wait in line eager to see Alex passing by me. Quicker than expected, I was at the front of the line

"Hi," I waved eagerly.

"Hello, again," Wyndu said slowly.

"What can I help you with today?"

"I am looking for Alex. He helped me out when I first arrived," I said.

"Okay, let me check where he is at."

I watched Wyndu type on their computer up to when they started responding to a voice in their earpiece.

"Alex? Hey. I have someone here, who I believe, needs your assistance."

At this moment of silence, I was sure that Alex was responding back.

"All right, thank you. I'll let him know that you are on the way. Okay. No problem."

I smiled as Wyndu's attention came back to me with positive feedback.

"Thank you," I said finally.

"Of course. If you need anything, you are welcome to come back and check in with me."

I moved away from the desk and walked about the port, watching dragons carrying goods and visitors arrive. Toward the end of the reception stations, a tall glass wall stood, acting as a fence. I walked over and press my hands on the glass. It was another port, but this one held spaceships and visitors from neighboring planets, possibly from other galaxies too. I gazed over the neon and silver ships, watching people and goods exit them. I didn't think in my entire lifetime I will be one of them. Traveling by spaceship was super expensive, and not to mention how much the spaceship itself costs. After about two minutes of being brainwashed by the sight, I felt a soft tap on my shoulder. I turned around to see Alex smiling at me.

"How do you like the sights?"

"Amazing," I said with relief.

"I was wondering about something, I wanted to ask you first," I said unsticking my hands from the glass.

"Have you gotten anything from Jacob back?"

Alex bit his lip. "No, not yet."

I exhaled to keep my cool.

"Hopefully soon," Alex added to help lift the weight of my concern.

"Well, then, I was wondering if I should pay a visit. To check on my information plus, I haven't seen him in a long time," I explained.

I had many thoughts starting to circulate inside my head.

"All right. Well, you may leave and come back if you like, but we will have to go through the same process again, okay?" Alex explained.

"Yeah, sure."

I went to the reception station to ask about transportation. I was planning on getting a train ticket. I made the front of the line again.

"Hi, Wyndu. I'm sorry to bother you again. I was wondering if I can get a train ticket to Serq."

Wyndu smiled.

"Sure, may I see your ID?" I slipped my ID out of my pocket and handed it to them. Wyndu scanned the chip and typed a few things up.

"All right, there are only two times available. There is ten-fifteen and seventeen-thirty."

I checked the time on my watch. It was 09:32 right now.

"I'll do ten-fifteen," I said.

I was planning on finishing this up and going back to the hotel to eat, get my stuff and wait for the train to come.

"Okay, here's your card back and I will also give you a print-out, just in case something goes wrong."

"Okay, thank you."

I left with a smile and I took a seat in the lobby's dining area. There wasn't too many people. I looked on the board with a handwritten menu above the steaming, hot food. You just grab whatever and pay at the end of the line. After looking over the menu three or four times, I finally got up and went over to get some coffee. I usually don't drink or crave coffee, but today I wanted something more rick in flavor than tea. I poured myself a cup and added cream and sugar. Even after I gave myself something to be excited about, I still had wandering thoughts that were passing against the sides of my skull. Would I get to see Isaac again? What would I do if I see him? Would he hate me forever even after I apologize? How would I react? What would I do with the feelings left over? Would I throw them away? Or hold on to them till my death?

I stood by the counter sipping my coffee, absorbing all of this. I sighed and went off to get food, to get my mind off it. I quickly went through the line, getting salad, fruit, and some biscuits. As I sat down with my food, I suddenly remember showing Isaac how to make biscuits. I felt as if my heart just dropped. I ate what I could and saved the biscuits for my trip. After throwing my food away, I took my coffee and the bag of biscuits with me to my room to get the rest of my stuff. Once I packed everything up, I went off to the main gate that I couldn't pass before—which technically I still couldn't pass.

"Hello," I said to the person in uniform.

"I have a train ticket for ten-fifteen," I said as I show them the printed copy.

"All right, pass the spaceship port. Should be the station to your left."

"Okay. Thank you."

As I walked, I could see just the palace afar, and the popular city full of tourist right by me. Wow. I gazed at the people passing by and the shops which lined up on the streets. Soon, that will be me. I turned to my left, into the station.

I took a seat and gaze at my watch. It was 9:50. I lay back on the seat and gazed at the ceiling. Thinking about seeing Isaac just made me feel like crying. I didn't hate him. Of course, I want to see him again, but I didn't think I could handle it. It's been almost five years already. I was afraid to face him again.

After my overwhelming thoughts, I fell asleep, but woke up right before the train would get here. I wiped my eyes, noticing that my face was wet. I must have cried for the time I was sleeping. I try my hardest to keep myself awake and alert till my train gets here. I looked at the time once again. It was 10:15. Not long after, the train came roaring and I finally got to my feet, ready to pass out on my trip. I scanned my ID and walked right in going toward the back to find an empty seat. The train was the most modern and looked nothing like the classic. It was sleek and could go faster than what was thought previous of its invention.

Luckily, there were not too many people, so I was able to get a seat all by myself with no one sitting next to me. I gazed out the window watching trees, buildings and other structures pass by. I sipped the rest of my coffee and then I finished my biscuits. As trees grew short and thick, the green grass become sand, and the hills become flat, I couldn't help myself from thinking repeatedly about Isaac.

His face was clear in my mind: soft, curved hair; round face; chubby cheeks; tiny, round nose; large eyes and pupils; and a soft loving smile that I had been missing for so long. I focused on my face in the window. My eyes were pleading, and my face was wet from my tears. I was too busy thinking about him, that I hadn't noticed that I was crying. I lean my head against the window. My heart was throbbing in my chest and I didn't know how to handle it. I felt like I was choking. I wasn't ready to pass out yet, instead, I found myself obnoxiously crying. I was too attached to the man I hadn't seen in years, opposed to my own wife, who I didn't remember crying for.

Chapter Twenty-Five

The train slowed to a stop. Out the window, I could see my entire past right before me. I slowly stood to grab my stuff. I really couldn't believe that I was really doing this. That I was really going to see my old friend again. If he hated me or love me, I was here, and I was here to take it all in.

I stepped out into the bright sun and still air. The environment stuck on to my skin and I could tell that it was real. I took a deep breath and I let it all out. I walked up to the kiosk, and I scan my ID. From there, I decided to go to Jacob's house to ask about my information, then I planned to see Isaac.

I found my way through the small town. I traced back to the old paths I walked on every time I went out. I watched the small children play in the streets and the people selling goods at the stands. As I walked by, people gave me surprised looks and whispered to one another. They must have thought I was from the city.

I finally made it to the front steps of Jacob's house. I placed my fist lightly on the wooden door. It was exactly how I remembered it. It didn't seem that anything has changed. The wood was a dark orange with an uneven surface; the cuts were deep and wide enough to slide my fingers through. I pulled back my fist and lightly knock on the door, just enough that you could hear across the quiet rooms. I stepped back after three knocks and waited patiently with my hands behind my back. I focused on the cuts through the wood. It looked too real. I felt that I had just traveled back in time.

The doorknob slowly turned, and the door opened with a creak, the face I hadn't seen in so long appeared with such surprise.

I couldn't say a word. I just stood hoping I would be welcomed here again.

"Xavier?" His voice was raspy, and I almost want to get him a glass of water.

"Yeah?" was all I could say.

"Where did you go?"

My heart dropped and I wanted to cry all my feelings out. I bit my lip.

"May I come inside first?"

"Sure."

I walked into the warm room. A scented stick was burning in the kitchen and the scent of frilia—a type of red poisonous flower that released a strong scent, fills the living room. I took a seat at the kitchen table, where tea was already made. Jacob goes to fetch an extra cup. All the colors of the room stood out to me. I felt as if I was trapped within a painting. I couldn't stop thinking about it.

"So?" Jacob came back slowly, taking a seat across from me.

I started to pour tea into my cup, unsure on how to start.

After finishing with my tea, I begin to speak.

"After I met someone in the garden one day, everything kind of . . . flipped upside down. I was dating her and now we are married. And now there was a lot going on. She was pregnant and I was about ready to get in the palace for a job and my information was apparently screwed up and here I am asking about why it's not correct."

Jacob gave me a confused look.

"There are two things I don't understand. First, I want to

know about what information you are talking about."

"My ID card that I got not too long ago isn't working. Like my information isn't correct, yet how can that be? It's my name, date of birth, and current age. The only thing that could prove that it's not right is my birth certificate."

My mind pondered around the thought.

"Can I see my birth certificate?"

Jacob kept his eyes on me without saying a word for a moment.

"I don't have it."

I continued to look at him with concern.

"Why? Where is it?" I urged.

"When I first picked you up, I couldn't find it at your old house at all. I pretty much gave up after that," Jacob explained.

"Well, then let's go back. I can't get into the palace if I don't have this fixed," I said.

Jacob and I walked beside each other with our feet crunching on the forest floor. My past just inches by me, absorbing me. The familiar forest pans down on me. Everything was just the way I remember it. Nothing changed since. The difference was Jacob beside me, making me feel a bit more open to exploring what I had already experienced in my childhood. I had just a bit more confidence this time to go back, than when I had thought about it before. I looked to my side as we walked through the dense forest. Jacob keeps his eyes forward toward the vast number of trees he could see in front of him.

"Jacob?" I called for his response.

"Yes?" He didn't look at me.

He kept his eyes straight forward still.

"Jacob?" I called again for his full attention.

Silently, Jacob whipped his head around to me with a stern look. I looked him up and down innocently.

"Are we really going to find my birth certificate?" Jacob attempted to roll his eyes, but he ended up relaxing on me.

"Of course, Xavier," he said sounding annoyed.

“It’s just that I am nervous,” I said trying to hint what I was really thinking about.

“Why are you nervous?”

“Maybe . . . just maybe we might not find or will find something that we maybe should not be looking for . . .” I said slowly, without giving away the horrible feeling in my stomach.

“Xavier, you are not making any sense,” Jacob said, turning his head back to the dense forest ahead.

“That’s not what I mean,” I whispered to myself.

“Well, then be specific.”

I looked up, surprised at Jacob who I didn’t expect to respond to my self-comment. My lip quivered.

“What if I don’t have one?” I said shakily, tears welling up in my eyes.

Jacob looked at me with concern.

“Why wouldn’t you have one?” Jacob just barely whispered.

“Because I never belonged here in the first place.”

I placed my hand on the door. The erratic designs mesmerizing me.

“Shall we?” I said as I apply pressure to the door.

As we walked in, the air was still, dust cluttered between the furniture. Everything was left just like it was when I ran away.

Without a single mention to Jacob, I slowly climbed the stairs, hoping to find what I missed in years.

“Xavier?”

I didn’t respond. Instead, I continued up the stairs and then to my parents’ room. The room was a mess. The sheets were used, boxes scattered the floor, items lay on all the tabletops, and the window was open. I walked over boxes to close it; the cool air was turning the room to ice. I bend down to the boxes on the floor. They all were heavy, covered with leather, and were locked. I moved them out of the way in search of the key. I opened my father’s nightstand. Besides some random objects.

There was a letter at the bottom. I pulled it out and sat on the bed.

To Margal,
If you do receive this letter, please do not write back.

. . . Xavier should be free of injury. If not, please take diligent care of him. He doesn't need to know about the dark side. Let him enjoy life freely, don't expose him to my greatest fear. Please, take care of the little angel for me . . . take care you as well.

There was no signature at the bottom. I sat still as stone. What did this person mean, "Take care of the little angel for me"? I stare at the page with a blank mind.

"Xavier?" Jacob calls.

"Did you find it?"

"No, but my fear has become real."

I handed the note to Jacob, who took a seat beside me. After a moment, Jacob turns to me with wide eyes. Tears start welding up in my eyes again.

"Am I . . . adopted?"

Instead of responding, Jacob pulled me close to him. I cried lightly on him. It was all turning into a lie.

After minutes of crying, I started to dig for more information in the room, while Jacob went downstairs to look in my room. I opened my mother's nightstand. The first thing I saw was a photo of us. Just her and me together. My mother had a camera, but it wasn't new. She took the photos she could with it. I still have no idea where all the money came from.

I slipped the photo into my pocket to take back with me, whether I was adopted or not. I still loved her.

Next, I found what looked like a check of some sort. I looked over the small paper. 782,648,000 was written on it in pen. Finally, one of my questions had an answer. This must be why my parents had a lot of money, because they were given this, but by who? The person who wrote the letter to my dad. I collected these papers and laid them out on the bed. Next, I looked on top of the dresser. My mother's jewelry was laid out. I looked through what was in the jewelry box, but nothing else was stored in there but her other jewelry. I looked in the drawers next, but there were only clothes. I looked elsewhere for keys to the boxes but found none. I collected the papers and make my way downstairs. I knocked gently on my door to catch Jacob's attention.

"Have you found anything?"

"Nothing yet, but this box of stuff is quite curious."

I knew exactly what he was talking about.

"Oh, yeah. I had that since I was little. That's the box I had gotten my journal out of. Other than that, it is just a bunch of random stuff that I never knew what to do with," I said quickly like it's nothing.

"Well, possibly, if we take another look, it won't be just a bunch of random stuff anymore," Jacob said slowly, kneeling by the box.

I went over to kneel beside him. I started to take things out one by one. Some powder, a small box with some gold rings, some silk woven blankets, some nice trinkets, and underneath all of that was a folder full of papers—which I didn't ever remember looking at.

"Maybe I might have either a birth certificate and/or adoption papers here. If not, the certificate I will take the adoption papers if I find any here," I said opening the folder.

"And what if there are none of those?" Jacob added.

"Then I will take what I have so far and try to do my best to get in. If that doesn't work, then I guess I will have to have Bonesella come with me into the palace, for me to get in." I thought for a moment then continued.

"You know, it said on my ID that I am married to her and that I have taken her last name, but I don't understand why they won't just take that."

Jacob didn't respond. I opened the folder slowly to really take in all the information. I looked closely at the first paper.

"Xavier Anudi of Shakina Anudi and Margal Anudi," it stated. Those were my parents who I grew up with, and I finally had a last name with them.

"Wow! I think this is it! An adoption certificate!" I exclaimed. I turned to Jacob kneeling next to me. He smiled brightly at me. I could feel some remnants of tears coming up from inside of me. I leaned over and hug him with excitement.

"Thank you for helping me."

"Of course, I will do anything for you."

Jacob's words entered straight into my heart.

"You are the best father I could ever have so far," I said looking at him in the eyes.

Jacob tilted his head.

"So, are you saying you want to find your real family who birthed you?" he asked slowly.

"Of course, I do," I said smiling.

After seeing Jacob, I took all my information and stuff it into the folder I found. I just wished I could have found keys to the boxes, but I looked again after finding the folder and there were none I could find. Jacob did say he will keep looking for me and would send me a letter if he finds any keys or anything else. I did really appreciate seeing him. I took a key out of my pocket, and I unlock the door. As I walked in, the smell of wood circulated to tell me that I was back home.

I walked into my room and place the folder on my desk. I had not been here in a long time. I let the feelings sink in. I was truly back; the only thing missing was Isaac. I left shortly to get some food and I quickly come back to eat. I was constantly thinking about Isaac . . . and I needed to find him. After I finished, I went to the arena where I first met him. I thought he went there all the time. Instead of walking, I found myself in a rush, eager to talk to him and see his adorable face. I grabbed the hot metal bars and scanned what I could see into the arena. I first saw a buff man who was being cheered on by his fans. He held his hands up into the air. The crowd went wild. I continued to scan for the opponent. I saw a smaller figure of a man in a full suite of silver, skintight armor. Isaac. My heart started to beat twice as fast. I was about ready to yell his name out, but I stop myself. I didn't think he would be able to hear me. I clenched the metal bars which burned my skin and watch as Isaac got ready to charge at the man who was not even paying attention. He was too busy adoring his fans. He must have thought that he won, that meant that Isaac had fallen before I got here. Luckily, he seemed perfectly okay.

As the man waved to his fans, I saw Isaac run towards him in slow motion. With his sword clenched in his hand, I knew that he was prepared to take him down, but such as strong buff man, I was unsure if he can take him down in one shot. I didn't even blink for a second. As Isaac put full force on the thrust of his sword, the very tip passed right by the man's neck . . . and before I know what was going to happen, Isaac was hit and flying across the arena, with his back hitting the wall; I screamed his name as loud as I possibly could. The man who stuck him had black blood across his sword, and from that moment I know what had happened.

I shook the metal bars, screaming still, as loud as I possibly could. As I yelled, I saw no movement from Isaac. *He must be hurt badly. I hope he can hear me.* Anxiety built up in me, and I was about to have a panic attack. Tears burst out from my eyes. I needed to get in there to help him. As the bars finally were lifted by the end of the fight, I ran in straight toward Isaac. I knelt next to him and shake him as hard as I could.

"Isaac!" I screamed into his helmet.

No response. I pulled it off immediately. Isaac's face was full of blood, including a busted lip and several bruises across his face. I looked down across his body. Black blood seeped through a hole in the armor. *That must be where he got stabbed.*

"Isaac?" I said with tears pouring out.

I was already going to explode with emotion.

"Isaac! Talk to me!" I yelled this time. His eyes were wide and stare straight into my eyes.

"I need you to say something."

Isaac made a noise, then I could hear it more clearly as he repeats it.

"Xav . . . Xavier," he said, struggling to make my name out.

"Isaac," I repeated back.

I place a hand right onto his bruised cheek.

"You are going to be okay. I am going to heal you," I told him.

Isaac closed his eyes for a couple seconds, then reopened them.

"Help me," he said.

"I will. I promise."

I started by trying to pick him up, but then realizing how heavy he was again. I wrapped my arms around his chest this time and dragged him under the archway. As I pulled him up into a chair for a moment, Isaac started to talk to me.

"You came back? Why?" he said slowly.

I was too into the fact that he was hurt, I almost didn't catch what he had said.

"Listen, I got to get you back to my house so I can help you. We can talk after, okay?" I responded, trying not to seem rude.

Isaac nodded. After a moment I spoke again.

"I can't just drag you to my place, so I need to know if you can walk a bit."

Isaac attempted to get up but lost his balance immediately and fell into my arms. I helped him sit back down.

"Okay then. I guess I am actually going to have to pick you up then."

I slid my hands underneath him and pull toward my chest. He was extremely heavy; I just hoped that I didn't lose my balance and fall. As I found a better grip on him, I walked out of the arena, and I headed straight home. As I walked, Isaac lay his head on my shoulder. I could hear him crying softly.

"Isaac. You're going to be okay. I got you," I said to comfort him.

He slowly started to cry harder on me.

"Isaac. I promise I am going to heal you. When we get in the house, you will have nothing to worry about," I said sweetly.

Isaac continued to cry, tightening his arms around my neck. He pressed his cheek onto mine and places a hand on my other cheek. He lightly touched his lips to my cheek this time. "Shh, it's okay," I said softly.

Soon, we were home. I went straight to my room and placed him lightly onto my bed.

"I'll be right back. I need to get some stuff," I said quickly and went off to get some stuff to clean the wounds out of the cabinet in my bathroom and then I washed my hands.

I came back and I looked over Isaac's body. "I need that armor to come off."

Isaac nodded and lifted his head up so I could take the armor off. I pulled on the flap and slipped the armor off. I pulled off it slowly around the wounds, trying not to scratch them with the broken metal plates. I pulled it down all the way off him. The wound where he was stabbed was the lower area where his intestines were. My face burned slightly red. I guessed I might have to take off more than the armor.

"Isaac?" I asked.

He opened his eyes and looked up at me.

"I might need to take off your underwear so I can clean the wound. May I please? I promise I won't touch you on purpose," I said a bit shakily.

"Sure. It's fine if you touch me. If you help me get better," Isaac said quickly.

I grabbed onto the elastic band and slipped the underwear off slowly. I tried not to look, but it's kind of hard when the wound was right above the abdomen. I looked up at Isaac instead.

"It's fine. You can look. I don't mind," Isaac said.

"Okay." I got a cloth and start to apply pressure of the wound. The cloth turned black immediately.

"Are you okay?" I asked to be sure.

"Yeah, I'm fine. Now, can you tell me why you came back? I've been wondering where you have gone."

I thought about it for a moment. I really didn't want to tell him everything that had happened so far. I knew that he was going to be mad at me and I really didn't want to handle it right now.

"Is it okay if I talk about everything after this?" I asked slowly.

"Can I ask why?" Isaac asked in the same tone.

"Because you are going to hate me after. I rather help you first with your injuries."

"Hate you? Why would I hate you?" Isaac exclaimed.

"You will find out after," I said strictly.

Instead of responding, Isaac sighed and lay back all the way. I grabbed another cloth and applied pressure again.

"I do still have to tell you something," I said a moment later.

"What is it?"

"When I said that I am going to heal you, I mean in a way you are not expecting," I said to start.

"What do you mean?" Isaac asked while giving me a confused look.

"Well," I started as I began cleaning the wound.

"I have recently found out something that I think is crazy and weird and I know you will too."

I took a breath. Isaac listened intensely with both eyes staring straight into mine.

"How do I say this without embarrassing myself?" I said out loud.

"You know, you can tell me anything. I promise I won't laugh. I respect your voice."

I relaxed a bit after those words.

"Well, I have been noticing something strange about Nightmare recently. He keeps sniffing me near my genital area. So, he started doing it again after I cut my foot on a rock. And then I kind of got a little weirded out by it and had a bit of anxiety so I . . ." I paused for a moment.

"Please don't laugh at me for this, but I started to kind of . . . masturbate," I said slowly.

"It's okay. I do it too. I wouldn't laugh at you for that," Isaac said.

I released a breath of pressure.

"Seriously?" I asked to be sure.

"Of course! Almost every guy does it," Isaac responded a bit too cheerfully.

"Thanks for being so supportive."

Isaac smiled at me.

"Anyways, I got semen on my foot, and you won't believe what happened to my cut after that!" I said a bit excitingly.

Isaac continued to listen closely.

"The cut on my foot healed completely, and all of the blood went away."

Isaac blinked and his eyes became wider.

"So, you're telling me that your semen can heal wounds . . ." Isaac said slowly.

"Yes!" I said firmly.

"Wow."

"So now I have to ask if it is okay for me to heal you."

Isaac's wide eyes closed for a moment, then reopened.

"I would be happy to be healed."

"You're weird," I said.

"Well, what do you expect? I'm homosexual," Isaac stated.

"Yeah, no kidding. Now am actually a bit scared to do this."

"Don't worry. I don't bite."

"Fine. Enjoy yourself while I'm at it."

"Of course, I will."

I stripped of my clothes quickly and place them on my desk. Isaac smiled at me.

"What? you want this?" I joked.

"You're pretty," he said in a cute manner.

"Thank you, I appreciate that a lot. I am usually laughed at instead," I said honestly.

"I respect you."

I started to masturbate slowly until I could get some out. Once I got a small squirt, I let it stick to my fingers.

"All right, I am going to put this on your cut lip," I said walking over to him.

I could see his face burn and I could feel mine.

"It's going to sting just a little bit, but it's going to go away quickly." Isaac nodded.

With my left hand, I pulled his lip out towards me, and with the other hand, I tapped the semen on the cut. Right away I could see the blood returning to the wound and skin forming over it.

"It's working," I told him.

I could see hope in Isaac's eyes. I continued to hold his lip out as the wound closes. I let go of his lip once the wound closed all the way.

"Better?"

Isaac licked his lip and smiles brighter than before.

"It's sweet," Isaac said.

"Really?" Isaac licked his lips some more.

"Yeah, like candy!"

Wow, this was weirder than I thought.

I masturbated some more to get a lot for where he was stabbed.

"Okay, this is going to sting a lot more," I said as started to rub it lightly on the edges of the wound. I guessed I was going to need a lot more. I pressed some more till I could get a lot more on my hand. Once I looked up, I almost panicked.

"Isaac!" I yelled.

"What? I can't help it!" he yelled back at me.

I placed my hand on my face. I couldn't believe it. This was obviously going to happen. I dropped my hand and looked at Isaac again. He was holding his penis down from sticking up. "Okay, now your arms are over the wound. I need you to let go."

"Um . . . I think it might be a bit disrespectful to have my penis up in your face as you heal me," he said slowly.

"Well, hopefully you don't mind me touching you," I said with a sigh.

"I already said I don't mind it."

"Fine."

Isaac let go and I pressed my hand gently over it. I was not telling my wife about this. I rubbed the semen lightly on the edges of the wound. Isaac flinched a bit.

"Relax, I know it stings," I said calmly.

The wound slowly started to shrink, but I could tell that Isaac was going to need more than a day to recover.

"Damn, that hurts."

I did my best to cover up the entire wound without having to touch it.

"Isaac, I think you might have to get some rest a couple of days because this looks like it might need more time to heal and for you to make a full recovery," I explained.

"All right, but as long as you tell me why you left."

I sighed as anxiety slowly crawled through me.

"You are really going to hate me now."

"I promise I won't."

"Well, I left because I started dating this girl and well now years later, we are married and she's pregnant. I came because I have a job in the capital and they wouldn't let me in because my information was screwed up and I went back to my house with Jacob, so now I found out that I am adopted and then I came here to see you," I explained quickly. Isaac's mouth was dropped open, and I could see how frightened he was. Tears streamed down my face.

"Just say it. I know you hate me," I broke through tears which came down harder and harder.

After a moment Isaac finally responded.

"I don't hate you. I can never hate you, but I am extremely disappointed."

"Isaac, I'm sorry. I know you really hate me now for leaving you here," I pleaded.

"Like I said: I don't hate you! I'm jealous . . ." Isaac yelled out then his voice became soft.

"You're jealous? Why? Because I'm married? I can help you find someone . . ." I started.

"I already found someone! It's just that they are already taken, and I will never have the chance to love and be with them."

Isaac's words echoed in my mind. I knew that he wasn't talking about someone else; he was talking about me.

"Are your serious right now?" I asked softly.

"Of course, I am. I love you, Xavier."

I was not the only one crying now. Isaac was too. I took a seat on the edge and leaned over, hovering my face over his and my arm beside cheek.

"You really feel that way about me?"

Isaac nodded and broke out into more tears. "Yes, but I don't think you will ever understand. You don't love me back. I know you don't."

Isaac's words stung.

"What?! I do understand! I do love you back! What are you talking about?!"

My heart raged with anger. I wanted to choke him. Just for a little bit, until he apologized.

"Wow, I can't believe you don't hate me," I said with hate in my own words.

"I don't because I want to love you still. I want to hold your hand. I want to wrap my arms around you when we go to sleep.

I want to kiss you. I want to spend my life with you. I want to have sex with you—"

"What?" I said.

Isaac nodded again.

"You really find me attractive?" I asked to be sure.

"Yes. I really do," Isaac said honestly.

I could really tell that he meant it. I looked into his innocent eyes. There was no way that he hated me. He just wanted me to be in his life, that's all.

"Do you want me to kiss you now?"

"Sure," Isaac smiled.

I touched my lips to his for about a minute, then released.

"I really do care about you. I do love you. I came all this way thinking about you. In fact, I cry every single night having dreams about you. When I took the train here, I cried so hard for you. I have panic attacks for you. I do care, it's just that I made a stupid mistake without considering how you feel about me."

Isaac thought for a moment.

"I should have told you when I first met you."

I closed my eyes.

"No, I really have made a stupid mistake. I am terribly sorry," I said through more tears.

"You know, it scares me that you actually got your wife pregnant," Isaac said with a bit uncertainty.

"We wanted a family," I said trying to bring hope.

"Fine, but . . ." Instead of continuing what he was going to say, Isaac turned his face away from mine with disgust.

"Isaac," I called.

Isaac turned back to me with tears streaming down his face still.

"Will you have sex with me?"

I thought for a moment. Honestly, I would love the thrill of trying something new, but I was still terrified. "One day. I promise," I said.

I got up and check the wound. It had gotten better, but it still looked bad. Luckily, Isaac's erection had gone down. Now I didn't have to stare at it as much.

"Isaac, I think you should rest while I go get some ingredients and make us something to eat. It's way past luncheon by now," I said about to walk out the door.

"Xavier," Isaac called after me. I turned around.

"Yes?"

"Will you stay with me?"

"Isaac, I will stay with you till you get better. I have to go work at the palace," I explained.

"But what am I supposed to do? I don't want you to leave again because if you do leave, I might commit suicide," Isaac whined.

I froze in panic. After a couple seconds I ran up to Isaac again and held his face in my hands.

"No, no, no, no. Don't do that. Please, don't kill yourself. I promise I will visit again. I swear on my life. I'll write you letters every single day. I promise," I plead to him.

I looked at his watery eyes then I give him a light kiss.

"I am not going anywhere right now, okay?"

Isaac nodded and I went off to buy some vegetables and other things I needed to make soup. I quickly got what I need and came back. It didn't take that long to make it. Once I finished, I brought the bowl to the room to find that Isaac was asleep. I placed the bowl on my desk and shook him lightly on the shoulder.

"Hey, I made some soup. Also, you can put your underwear back on if you like."

Isaac peaked open one eye.

"Can you hand me them?"

I passed him his underwear, or what I called shorts usually, to him. Isaac slipped them on and sat up.

"Here it's hot," I said, passing him the bowl.

"Thanks," he said.

"Anything for my sweetheart," I responded.

I went into the living room to sit on the yellow sofa. I drank and ate my soup while looking around the room. It was quite peaceful. I try to think about how I was going to adjust back to being with Bonesella. Luckily, I was going to work first, but soon when I got my first vacation, I was going to have to deal with all of her. For some reason, I was not that happy to be seeing her again soon. Honestly, I would rather be here in my house with Isaac, but I knew I couldn't do that. If she ever found out about all of this, I might be exposed to the whole palace and I might not even be able to go at all. As I thought about it more deeply, I didn't mind being kicked out. Like I just thought before, I would rather be here.

Once I finished, I placed the bowl on the small table between the two couches. I lay back and stared at the ceiling. I was afraid to leave Isaac. What would I do? After moments of blank staring at the ceiling, I went to check on Isaac.

"Hey, any better?"

"Yes. Your penis magic really works."

"Oh, shut up," I joke.

As it got late, Isaac pulled the covers over him. I went and gave him a kiss.

"Good night, I'm going to rest on the couch, okay? If anything come get me or call my name," I said as I was walking out.

"Wait," Isaac called.

"What is it this time?" I asked a bit annoyed.

"Come here."

"I am here."

"No, come *here*" Isaac emphasized. I walked close as I can to the edge of the bed and lean forward a bit. "More."

"I can't go any more *here*," I said, reaching for his hands. He started to pull me toward him. I place my knees on the edge of the bed beside his feet. Isaac pulled me more.

"Come on," he said gently. I crawl up on the bed till I was on my hands and knees, face to face with him.

"Sit."

"What? Why?" I asked.

"Sit," Isaac repeated.

I sat right on his pelvis. Isaac put his arms around me and pushed me till I lay down on him.

"There."

I was completely naked and ready for bed. Isaac slid the cover down and back up again till it covered both of us. "I want you to sleep here with me," he said.

"Okay." I didn't object at all.

I placed my face into his shoulder blade and wrapped my arms around him. Isaac rubbed his warm hand on my bear back, calming me. I quickly became sleepy.

"I love you," Isaac said softly into my ear.

"I love you too," I said into his shoulder.

The next morning, sunshine hit my face through my window. I squinted and tried to stretch out a bit.

"Xavier, you awake?" Isaac said in a scratchy voice.

"Yeah," I said in the same tone. I placed my hands on both sides of Isaac and lifted myself to my knees, upright.

"Good morning."

"Good morning to you too," I repeated while stretching my arms.

Isaac placed his hands on my thighs.

"Your skin is soft."

I opened my eyes.

"Why are you touching me?" I asked concerned.

"May I not?" Isaac asked while his eyes opened wide.

"It makes me feel a bit uncomfortable. I'm not your babe."

"You can be, for now."

"No."

"Well, not yet," Isaac said while giving bit of a sexual look.

"Please don't do that. Not when I have a wife and a kid on the way."

"Oh, come on! I can't help myself," Isaac whined.

"Isaac, are you always like this? Or is it just because of me?" I asked seriously, concerned about his sexual behavior.

"I have always been like this, why?" Isaac said confused.

"Well, I was just wondering if something is wrong."

"I really don't get what you are saying," Isaac said honestly.

"You are hypersexual, aren't you?" I said to confirm.

"Oh."

I could hear the drop in Isaac's voice. I remember reading about it in a book.

"Please tell me the truth," I pleaded softly.

"I had it for a very long time," Isaac said softly.

I lean over and kiss him on the cheek.

"It's okay. You can tell me these things," I said.

I sat back up and feel something that I hadn't noticed before. I looked between my legs. I had a bit of an erection, luckily it isn't too bad. Isaac moved a bit to stretch and I felt something again, and it wasn't me. I lifted one of my legs and noticed that Isaac had one too. My face burned a bit. I couldn't believe I was sitting on it. "I'm sorry about that," I blurted. "It's fine," Isaac said, trying to calm me. I was already off, and I started to get dressed immediately.

"What's wrong," Isaac asked.

"Nothing, I'm fine," I said quickly. Isaac got up finally and could stand.

"No more pain?" I asked to be sure.

"None," Isaac said happily.

"Good. I guess I tomorrow I should get going then," I said. Isaac and I both got to the kitchen.

I started to make something to eat.

"About yesterday . . ." Isaac started.

"Yeah?"

"Not only that I am sorry for arguing with you and all, but you said that you are adopted. How do you know?" Isaac asked slowly.

"Well, I did tell you the story, right?" I asked to be sure.

"Yeah, but you weren't that specific."

"I found an adoption certificate when I was looking for my birth certificate. I guess overall it makes more sense now why my 'dad' didn't get along with me too well."

"What happened with your parents? Did you tell me before? I think I forgot," Isaac asked while messing with a fork on the table.

"My dragon Nightmare killed my mother. And I still have no idea what happened to my father. He was just gone one day," I said softly.

Instead of thinking, Isaac responded quickly.

"Well, that's not a normal way to lose your parents. I can't believe you decided to keep Nightmare as a pet. Are you okay?"

I sighed.

"I'm fine, I guess. There was just something about him that I couldn't just leave behind. He's a good boy. I trained him," I said to brighten the conversation a little bit.

"You sure? He's not going to kill someone you love again?"

I thought about it for a long moment. Overall, it was strange. I guess everyone has a reason to call me strange.

"No. I'm sure," I said.

Something deep inside me told me that Nightmare was more than that.

After I finished making breakfast, I placed the food on the table and sat down in front of Isaac.

"So there seems to be a lot of strange things about you. Don't you want to discover what is really going on? I mean, this all can't be some major coincidence. There has to be something behind it all," Isaac explained in a convincing tone.

"Well, I am exploring it actually, but just very slowly."

I almost forgot to tell Isaac about the stone.

"Speaking of which, I soul traveled and found out something strange a while back," I started.

Isaac leaned in listening to me.

"I was told about a stone that can protect Bonesella from danger—"

"Who?" Isaac cuts in.

"My wife."

"Oh," I could hear the depressing drop in his voice.

"This stone," I continued.

"I believe can keep her safe from her father, who I believe is planning something very evil."

"How in the world do you know that?" Isaac exclaimed.

"I have been doing some research. I fact I brought the book with me and wrote a lot down in my journal . . . let me go get it and I will show you what I mean," I said as I rushed to get my stuff from my room.

I came back to the kitchen and place everything on the table. The folder full of my information. The book I was reading on about The Allia and my journal in which I had written everything I experience down.

"That's it?" Isaac asked.

"Yeah, it's not a lot, but I hope to find out more when I start working in the palace."

Isaac nodded and I start to go over what everything means.

"So Bonesella as the stone to protect her from the Allia that her father has and that he might use it against you two?" Isaac recalled what I just explained to him.

"Yes. I just don't know why he wants to attack us with it."

"Probably because you got some special powers and who knows what he might want to do with his own daughter," Isaac suggests.

"Yeah, that sounds about right, but about the second thing, Bonesella did tell me that she is the result of her father raping her mother," I said.

"Well, he probably doesn't like her or her mother for some reason," Isaac suggested again.

"Yeah, who knows what that might be."

"So, you're leaving tomorrow then?"

"Yeah," I said even though I rather not.

"You know I would help but if you're going to leave me again, then I guess you will be on your own."

"Yeah," I said again but this time I hated the word even more.

"Well, tell me what happen please, whenever you visit again."

"I promise to write to you every day once I leave," I promise.

"I hope to hear from you."

After we finished eating, I washed the dishes and moved my stuff on to the coffee table and I took a seat on the couch. I scanned through all the information I collected. Isaac came over and took a seat next to me.

"You look nervous."

I almost jumped at his words. I didn't expect for him to say anything.

"I'm fine," I said.

"No, you're not."

"Well, I have anxiety to hide, so I have no choice," I said turning back to my stuff.

"Actually, you do. You have the option right now to tell me everything that is bothering you."

I took a few breaths to calm myself.

"I just don't understand any of this. I feel that something bad was going to happen if I didn't figure this out soon enough. I felt that I was going to be murdered if I didn't do something," I explained through heavy breaths.

Isaac placed a hand on my shoulder.

"Look at me." So, I looked.

"I promise you are going to be fine."

"No. No I am not," I objected.

"I need you to just pretend that everything is fine right now."

"What? No," I refused.

"Please," Isaac pleaded.

"No. I will not rest till I figure all of this out," I said strictly.

"Xavier—"

"What?"

"I want you to be safe."

"I know," I said getting up.

"Seriously, listen to me," Isaac said while getting up after me.

"Isaac. I am going to figure this out. I promise I will stay aware of danger," I explained more calmly.

"I'm coming with you," Isaac said quickly.

"What? I thought that you are an illegal immigrant. If I bring you with me. We both will be thrown in the dungeons," I explained strictly.

"I don't care. I want to be with you," Isaac persisted, placing both hands of my shoulders this time.

"Isaac, I can't," I said shakily. Without a word, Isaac placed both hands on my cheeks and pulled my face forward into his chest.

"I don't want you to get hurt," I whined with tears.

Isaac kissed my forehead.

"I know. I know," Isaac repeated while stroking his fingers through my hair.

When my tears finally dried, I decided to change the subject.

"So, while I was gone, what did you do?" I asked.

"Did what I always have done. Stealing foods and fighting," Isaac said.

"Did you do anything different?" I asked wanting to hear something a tad bit more exciting.

"Well, I made some art too . . ." Isaac said slowly.

"What?" I let out. "Yeah, I kind of borrowed your sketchbook. Sorry," Isaac said apologetic.

"Let me see it."

I followed Isaac into my room, and he pulled out my old

sketch book out of my desk and flips through the pages. Isaac passed me the sketch book. I placed my fingers lightly on the brightly colored paint. I scanned the details of my own face; it was like looking into a mirror. I wouldn't doubt a single proportion. My face in the painting was no different than my own.

I looked up at Isaac.

"I didn't know you are artistic. It's so lovely. You can paint better than me," I said with a chime.

"Yeah, I haven't done a lot of painting recently," Isaac said sounding a bit sad.

"Is it okay if I take this with me when I go back?" I asked holding the sketch book close to me.

"Sure, but then I don't have anything to paint on."

"I can buy you some canvases now if you want from the local shop," I suggested.

"Yay! Wait, really?" Isaac said.

"Yeah. Of course," I said.

"Thank you."

After I bought some large canvases, I sat on my bed, watching Isaac sketch light lines with his left hand on one of them.

"What are you going to paint?" I asked.

"You again," Isaac said casually.

"Really? Why don't you want something else?" I suggested hoping to see him paint something different.

"Don't worry, it will be different."

"How?" I asked eagerly.

"You will see."

I went off to make dinner, Once Isaac finished sketching. After a while, I came back with my plate and a plate of food for Isaac. I placed Isaac's food on the desk and sat on the bed with mine on my lap.

"Hey, I made lunch," I said. Isaac turned around, revealing the painting.

"Is that . . .?" I could barely make out the words. Isaac nodded as he took a seat beside me on my bed, taking his plate as well. I am sitting in a grass field looking up into the starry night sky.

"I . . . I love it," I said.

"I knew you would."

I looked up at Isaac.

"The night sky looks just like your eyes," I said as I investigate them.

"Well, that's a first," Isaac said while breaking out a smile.

"A first?" I asked as Isaac got up.

"Yeah, no one ever tells me things like that."

I wanted to ask how come, but Isaac was already in my bathroom washing his hands. He came back and started to eat; I did too.

As the day passed, Isaac fully completed the painting and hung it on the wall nearest to the couch. I started to pack my things and I also started to make dinner.

"I know you are leaving, but I really don't feel comfortable letting you go," Isaac said messing with a fork again.

"I promise everything is going to be fine," I said calmly.

Once finished, we both ate in silence. I knew Isaac was scared, but I couldn't risk putting him and myself in danger. I really don't want anything to happen to him, just like Isaac didn't want anything to happen to me. Once I finished, eating I washed my dishes and headed straight off to bed with a heavy feeling in my chest. Minutes later, Isaac followed me and crawls under the covers.

"Are you okay," Isaac asked.

I lifted my face from my pillow a bit.

"Yeah."

"You don't look to good," Isaac said worriedly.

"I am just upset that I have to leave you here," I said letting my face drop into my pillow.

"I love you, Xavier."

"I . . . love you too."

"Promise me one thing."

"And what is that?" I asked tiredly.

"That no matter where you go that you always will keep me in your heart."

"I promise," I said before I knockout completely, unable to see the start night sky through my window.

Chapter Twenty-Six

I looked over the files full of notes and sketches of the widespread epidemic. Hundreds had died and thousands were sick. It was a new kind of disease which didn't have a common name for. Scientists and doctors called it J-39. Every folder I looked through had different notes and sketched from every different scientists and doctors. I skimmed through a very particular set of notes.

J-39 spread through liquids—mainly bodies of water. Is a bacterium that multiplies rapidly and attacks the brain and lungs—causing bodily functions to perform at uncontrollable rates and the inability to breathe properly.

I canned the rest of the notes, then skimmed through another set. After taking two days to absorb the information, I prepared to nurse those who were infected with the disease. I scanned through the notes once or twice after I finished getting dressed. I hurry out my room and go downstairs to see Jashar. "Hey, Jashar. I guess it's time," I said a bit nervously.

"Yeah, it's been getting worse by the minute! Luckily, we have you. Without you, the entire population could be infected, and we would all perish," Jashar said with much enthusiasm.

"Yeah, about that . . . I am not sure how I am really going to do this. What if I get sick with it?" I asked with anxiety pushing through me.

"Xavier, you are a healer! You are the child of God himself! You should have absolutely nothing to worry about, not even .00000000001 percent!" Jashar exclaimed.

"Well, I guess I better be on my way to the medical emergency room," I said as I rush off nervously.

I placed the notes on the desk beside me as a patient was brought in. Doctors laid her on the bed beside me. I nervously bit my lip. She looked awful. This brown stuff was covering her entire body. Parts of it were black, especially around the mouth. I never expected the disease to be this bad.

Soon, I was left alone with my patient. I put on gloves and a white surgical mask. I touch the woman's damaged skin. As I gently rub my fingers against her cheek, the skin started to peal. I opened a drawer full of tubes and attachments. I pulled out a tube of medium length, about double arm length. I then took out an attachment with a needle and another that I had specifically designed to fit over my penis. I screw on the attachments, and I put the device on myself first, before inserting the needle into my patient's arm. I guess it was a good thing that she was under anesthesia and not awake because this might be a bit frightening. I pressed the head of my penis till I could get my healing semen flowing through the tube. I pulled a chair up and took a seat as the semen started to get sucked into the tube.

Soon I was not the only one in the room (besides the patient). A few doctors entered the room. I waved nervously at them. One of the doctors came up to me and placed a hand on my shoulder.

"Are you doing okay?" the doctor asked.

I smiled nervously.

"I think so. . ."

The other doctors examined the patient quickly and started working. The doctor beside me pulled up a chair and kept his hand on my shoulder.

"If you start to feel lightheaded or something, please let me know. I am here to assist you," Said the doctor.

"Okay," I said nervously. I watched as the doctors did what they can. I didn't know if I could last through the entire operation. As I sat and tried to calm myself, the doctor didn't let go of me, instead he does what he can to help me stay calm.

"How much longer?" I asked.

"Possibly not too long," the doctor replied.

"Can I get your name?"

"It's Arkrae," he responded.

"You must be Xavier."

"Yes. It's a pleasure to meet you."

"You too."

I could finally see the brown and black layer start to peel off the woman. She was starting to look much better. As hype built among the doctors everything started to turn slowly. My body started to shake, and I grabbed on to Arkrae's shoulder.

"Are you alright?" I heard him say.

I couldn't see because my vision was blurred, and once I hit something, everything turned black.

I awoke on a bed beside the patient. I looked down and notice more tubes were connected to me with semen flowing through them and they were much longer than the one I started with. I looked at a few of the doctors that surrounded me. "It seems that your body is working extra hard. You must relax for now so that you can recover," one of them said calmly. I closed my eyes again. I couldn't bear the fact that this was happening. I just wanted to disappear then come right back when I felt better.

As I healed, I started to feel the pain of it. My thighs and genitals were killing me. I felt uneasy and my anxiety increased. As the pain got worse, the doctors were preparing pain medication for me. As I was given medication through another tube, I passed out again.

I awoke. Everything was a blur. I focused on the vision. I was in a castle, but the walls, floor and ceiling were moving . . . as if it were water. I took a few steps forward observing the dark colors of this haunted place. Every step I took, the colors of the floor moved like paint in a glass of water. Like the paint left from when I picked up my paintbrush and then placed it back in the glass, causing a disturbance among the water molecules.

Before I knew it, what looked like black paint entered the glass, but there was no paintbrush to be seen. The black paint dropped slowly, spinning till the bottom tip reached the bottom of the flowing floor. Once it touched the violet paint representing tile, the black paint spread, forming an unfamiliar shape. A figure I had never seen. Tall, skinny, and large evil man with sharp fingers and a cruel crown. The shadow started to appear larger. My heart began to beat twice as fast. At this moment, I realized that the shadow wasn't getting larger but getting closer. My heart began to beat even faster. My vision began to blur again, but before I could black out, another figure appeared.

This shadow was smaller and not as skinny as the other. He ran with leaps every few seconds. Before he could merge with the larger shadow, he took a larger leap and with a shadow of a sword, he stabbed the shadow, causing it to slowly separate into nothingness in the glass. My heart began to slow. The other shadow gave me no sense of fear. Instead, I felt no longer alone. The shadow walked up to me. As I reached for his face, the black paint shadow left his true self. Isaac.

I placed my hands on his soft cheeks. His eyes glittered as he places his hands on my own cheeks.

"Xavier," he called me.

"Isaac," I called back.

"What is this?" I continued.

"I don't know, but you need to get out of here. This is a dangerous dimension to be in. Go. I need you to be safe," Isaac explained.

I knew I needed to leave, but I hated the thought of it.

"I just have one more thing to ask you," I said.

"Be quick."

"Please don't forget me," I said. "I am coming back for you. I promise."

Isaac smiled.

"I will never forget about you."

He pulled me in and kissed me on the cheek.

"I promise that I will never forget about you. I love you, Xavier. No matter what the future holds. I promise to never stop loving you even in the darkest of times," Isaac said with the most truthful heart I ever heard in my entire life.

I couldn't even imagine Bonesella saying those exact words. I kissed him back and he started to fade into the black paint that engulfed him before. I could feel the tears dripping from my eyes. I knew that it was no longer safe; no longer safe to exist.

I awoke again. I could see the concern on the doctors faces. We knew that something needed to change.

I got moved to a different room. A room that was much larger than the one before and has white walls and curtains. Of course, all the beds were white. I still had many more tubes connected to me, but the doctors pulled the covers over me so that I didn't have to see them and plus I was more comfortable that way. On the other hand, the patient was still in another bed next to me, but a curtain separated us, which also makes me feel more comfortable. As time went on, my first patient made an almost full recovery, and the doctors continued to comfort me. They lit scented candles around the room to lower my anxiety. As I healed many more patients, Arkrae stayed with me day and night. I healed most of the day but had a break once it was time to eat something. The doctors gave me soft foods which were easy to digest, such as soup.

At the very end of the day, I had Arkrae help me get out of bed. I noticed how I tended to lose balance after healing for so long. Doctors insisted that they help me in the shower, but I refused kindly. I wasn't ever used to people doing things for me. I made my own clothes, hunted and gathered as a child. Though as I showered, I still had trouble, even when holding on to one of the bars, I fell anyways due to trying to bathe myself and hold myself up. After doctors wanting to assist me too much, I accepted a shower chair rather than one of them coming in the shower with me. I felt better after being able to get myself clean easily. After my shower, trying to brush my hair, teeth and general grooming, I had to accept the help of Arkrae holding me since I had to have both hands occupied. I brushed my hair and teeth, washed my face and hands and rubbed lotion across my whole body. I left my hair down instead of trying to take hours to gel the groups together, plus I needed as much sleep as possible for the next day. It was nice having my hair naturally down; it was incredibly soft.

I slept comfortably during the night. I enjoyed having Arkrae wake me up in the morning. I knew he didn't leave the room at night, but I wasn't sure where he slept, or if he ever slept at all.

After lots of healing I found time to look over the notes more. I needed a break anyways. Doctors and scientists said that they finally were able to get a sample of the bacteria. I had asked them if I could look at it. Surprisingly the doctors and scientists agreed. I sat in the laboratory with a microscope in front of me. A scientist gives me the slide, I first look at it with my naked eye. It looked like the black stuff that covered the patients. I placed the slide under the microscope and adjusted it accordingly. As I looked through the eye piece, it was hard to believe this was even a bacterium. No, it can't be. What looked like a growing bacterium to scientists, looked like something I had been taking an awfully long time to study. I sat up and grab the whole bottle of it, which sat right next to the microscope. The doctors and scientists stood behind me silently.

"This," I started, holding the bottle up to them, "is not a bacterium. This is something else . . ."

I breathe in, hoping I wouldn't have a panic attack.

"This is traces of The Allia."

After about a month, I started to pack my things. I guess I finally started to enjoy work, but now I must go home to take care of Bonesella and her child, which was soon to be born. After sending multiple letters throughout my medical journey, Graditha decided to stay with her. I heard that she took diligent care of Bonesella and that she even started decorating a room for the child. I had told Bonesella of a name for him. She agreed and so we were naming him Alexander. I was planning on calling him Alex for short. After thinking of the name, I thought of Alex from the port shortly after. I didn't mean to name my kid after him or something, but it was a nice reminder of my journey so far.

With all my things packed, I walked downstairs into the main hall to say goodbye to Jashar. Jashar noticed me immediately before I could say anything to him.

"Oh, Xavier! I wish you good luck!" he cheered with a charm, hugging me tightly.

"Yeah," I said uneasily. My medical journey seemed like a partial nightmare. I was glad that it got better toward the end.

"I really hope to be seeing you soon," I said with a final note.

"Of course. I will be seeing you," Jashar waved as I left the hall.

Nightmare lay at the port tied to the pole. His head was over his crossed legs, and he was dragging his tail side to side. I walked over with a light smile. Nightmare continued to lie down as I approach him. I knelt and petted him on his head.

"How are you doing, Nightmare?" I asked softly. Nightmare

gave a slow growl. He looked a bit depressed. I gave him a kiss on the side of his head.

"It's okay. I know I have been gone for a while," I said.

"I promise I will start spending more time with you." I got on Nightmare's back and one of the people working at the port removed the rope. I waved to them, and Nightmare and I were off, off to a new beginning.

Chapter Twenty-Seven

"Bonesella," I started. She looked at me.

"I need you to believe me," I said.

"About what?" she asked.

"This black stuff was covering the patients; it is not a bacterium at all like the scientists and doctors thought," I said.

"Then what is it?"

"It is what I fear for us," I start.

"It is The Allia."

Bonesella's expression dropped. She looked pissed at me.

"Don't you care about the wellbeing of this family?" I asked.

"I don't give a shit about this fantasy of yours. I had already told you to stop bringing up this mess about my father, and here you are again . . . telling me about some evil plan he has," she said with straight up disgust.

"So, you don't believe me," I said.

"No. I don't believe in any of it anymore."

Before I could bring up the stone, Bonesella continued.

"You better promise me that you will never bring up any of this fantasy shit about my father ever, as a parent in front of our children. Not even if they are not nearby. I don't want any of this crap ever again," Bonesella said with a very nasty tone. I nodded slowly. I felt as if was about to shatter into a billion pieces.

Seventeen years later, Bonesella and I had a total of three children: Alexander, Jenifer, and the youngest, Rosetta. Alexander had been not easy to get along with, especially since he was our first child. Not that he was a troublemaker, but he had been always quiet and didn't really like to hang out that much. I tried to visit his room often to see what he was up too. He usually was either doing homework or reading a book on his bed. I even asked him if he was okay, but he always said that he was fine and asked me to leave him alone. I even asked Bonesella if he was okay. She told me that it was no different with her and that I should probably let him be.

I found it hard to ignore Alexander, but Jenifer and Rosetta were usually always up to something. I checked on them quite regularly. Jenifer was sixteen (one year younger than Alexander), and Rosetta was fifteen. They usually hung out together a lot, even though they both were almost complete opposites. Jenifer had black, straight hair (like Alex), but she did have a strand of blue and pink in her hair. She typically dressed in only black clothing. Rosetta, on the other hand, had curly pink hair with blue accents and no black. She typically dressed in all pink dresses. All three of them had pale skin like me, but I knew that their bones looked like Bonesella's exoskeletal structure. I usually find Jenifer Hanging out with Rosetta in her room. They enjoy making clothing and jewelry for themselves. I had already told them how when I grew up that I did that a lot too. Jenifer and Rosetta did fight a lot, but they usually made back up quickly. Though, few times I would find Jenifer in her own room lying in bed. I was told by Bonesella that she had bad period cramps. I offered Jenifer my help usually, but she told me that I didn't understand and that she rather have mom help her.

After checking on the girls I continue to walk down the hall. I knew Alex didn't like being bothered, so I guessed I would turn into our room instead of going towards his. As I walked closer, I could hear sniffling from Alex's room. I continued to walk toward it. As the noises got louder, I gently placed my ear on the door. I had extremely sensitive hearing, so I could hear pretty much everything I the room. I knock softly on the door.

"Alexander," I called softly.

I continue to listen as I hear some movement, then silence. I wait by the door.

"Yeah," I heard a moment later.

"Can I come in?" I asked softly.

"Yeah," Alex repeated.

I walked in, Alex stood in front of the doorway.

"Are you okay? It sounded like you were just crying," I said continuing speaking with a soft tone.

"I'm fine," he said.

I could see the look in his eyes. I placed both hands on his shoulders.

"Alexander, why are you lying to me?" I asked.

I could see some shock in his eyes, but it went away quickly and turned into sadness.

"Why are you crying?" I asked again.

Alex moved away from the door and took a seat on his bed; I went and sat next to him. I noticed his hand wrapped in a bandage.

"Are you hurting yourself?" I asked in shock.

"No, no. I was being made fun of in school for being so quiet and not wanting to hang out with anyone and someone pushed me outside and so I cut my hand on a rock," he explained.

"Let me heal it," I said without really thinking.

"No, it's okay. You don't have too," Alex said softly.

"But I want to," I said eagerly, pulling his hand close into my chest.

"Dad, I'm okay," he said, pulling his hand away.

I exhaled and took both of his hands this time.

"I only want to help you. I would never do anything rash. As a father, I want to be the best that I can be for you," I explained slowly. Alex didn't take away his hands this time.

"Do you understand that?" Alex nodded slowly.

"Am I allowed to heal you?" I asked finally. Alex took a moment, then he responded. "Sure."

As I rubbed the 'medicine' on the wound, Alex spoke.

"You know, you're a lot different than Mom," he said.

"How?" I asked.

Alex continued.

"You are more open and kinder. Mom, well, she . . ." Alex stopped.

"What is it?" I asked.

"It's fine. You can tell me anything."

"She keeps her distance. She actually leaves me alone, but you—"

"I choose to not shut you out completely. I rather keep this connection between father and son. I don't ever want to break this," I cut in.

Alex grinned and looked down at his hands.

"No wonder why you're kinder."

I smiled as the words ring inside my head. *Kinder*. Yeah, no wonder.

As I gave Alex a kiss on the forehead and walked out his room, the words continued to ring in my head till I stop completely in the middle of the hall. I was kind because I had a responsibility to take care of people. I continue walking to the end of the hall to the library. I let the door close softly behind me, then I skim through the books on the shelves. This time, it was not about the Allia or Bonesella's father. This time, it was about me. I skim through, till I found something that might shed some light. It was a very heavy book, so I wobbled over to the nearest table, letting the book drop on the wooden surface. I took a seat and I drag my fingers softly against the old, torn cover. *The History of Angels*. I opened the book slowly, so I didn't tear the cover on accident. I skimmed through the table of contents. I found a chapter about healing, and I flipped the pages. As I read, things started to come together for me. There was so much more than just healing. With my head full of new information, I was tempted to try some new things out, but before I could close the book, the library door opened and Bonesella walked in.

"Hey," she said as she softly closed the door behind her.

"Hey," I repeated.

"So, what are you up to this time?"

"Just wanting to learn more about myself and my ancestors," I said slowly to hide my excitement.

"Like what?" she asked as she pulled up a chair next to me.

"Healing," I said simply.

"So, what did you find out about it?" she asked.

I smiled brightly as I looked her in the eyes.

"You won't believe it."

I grabbed her hand and pull her into the forest. I ran until I found an open spot surrounded by tall trees.

"You see this?" I said.

"This is the center of all healing. It is life. It is the nature that surrounds us. Angels have direct access to this. We are like portable ecosystems. Healing is so strong it can literally create life from scratch. It can form and repair cells, create tissues, then organs, and ultimately creating an entire animal. I have that ability; I just need to learn how to use it. You understand?" I explained with enthusiasm.

Bonesella nodded with her mouth still open.

"Angels heal in many, different, unique ways. And apparently semen is mine. The guardian pools are where we energize ourselves. It is where we collect ourselves and control our powers. And I believe that I am the last one. Based off my reading there was some kind of war. All the angels died. I am all that is left. I have a responsibility. I have to help people, but I don't exactly know what my objective is. I don't really know what this journey is all about."

I paused, taking in all my thoughts.

"I need your help," I pleaded.

Bonesella finally closed her mouth and walked up to me. Without a word, she wrapped arms around me.

"I promise to help you." She soon took her head off my shoulder and pressed her lips on mine.

After about a moment, we let go. I went to find the nearest guardian pool and Bonesella followed behind me. Once I reached the rocks that I cut my foot on before. I undressed and stepped in carefully. Bonesella took a seat on a flat, rock edge, watching me carefully. As I entered the water, the Blossom of Life floated off from above my right ear. I caught it in my hand and blew on it. It floated in the air and landed gently in the water. It glowed magenta. I touched the shimmering petals. The glowing magenta crawled into my fingers and traveled up my arm. I touched the flower some more till my whole body started to glow. I finally bent down in the water till the water got to my neck. My hair gently flowed around me as I moved. I went under the water and observed my surroundings. The flower floated above me. Fish were gathering around my body; some even swam through my hair. It was like they knew. They were attracted to me. I was some kind of holy spirit to them.

I rose from the water and look at Bonesella. She was on her knees watching me patiently. I stood on my feet and cupped the flower in my hands. I walked over to Bonesella. She didn't said anything, she just waited for me.

"I feel a lot better," I said softly, unsure how to explain it. She nodded.

"Um . . ." I took a seat beside her, to try and start a conversation again.

"Are you okay?" I asked.

"Yeah, I just am having a hard time processing everything," she said.

"Oh."

"So, I guess maybe this isn't the time to try and create something new," I said slowly.

"Well, it is your privacy."

Right. It would be kind of awkward, yet I suddenly remembered having to masturbate in front of Isaac so I could heal him. He didn't mind. Most likely because he was also a man and homosexual. "So . . .?"

"I'll leave you be," Bonesella said quickly. She got up and started to walk off.

"Wait!" I called after her.

Bonesella turned and looked at me. I didn't said anything. I just got up and kissed her again. I just wanted more attention. She let go and placed her hands on my wet cheeks. She smiled.

"I know you will be able to do great things," she said.

"I want you to stay with me," I said quickly after her.

After a moment of silence, Bonesella spoke again.

"I'm not as comfortable with that as you think," she said glancing shortly at my sexual parts.

"Why not?" I asked eagerly.

"Listen. I love you as much as possible, but I think it would be better to keep my distance. Plus, even though I imagine myself with a man, I don't think it would ever be my place to keep my eyes and hands too close to it," she said softly.

I sighed softly. I wanted attention.

"Please," I said.

Bonesella scanned my expression closely.

"You are very needy," she said.

"I've always been this needy ever since I lost my parents," said.

"All right, fine. I'll stay with you," she said finally.

Bonesella sat about two feet away from me for my privacy. To not bother her, I kept my knees up to hide my hands and parts a bit. Bonesella stared over the water. She must have been thinking hard about something. I glided my hands across my penis. I was unsure how to create some kind of animal. I just know that this stuff could build tissues and stuff. I didn't really like how far away she was; I just really felt that I needed her constant attention and affection. So, I decided to talk a bit.

"Why don't you like it?"

"I already told you. It is not my place."

"But why is it not your place?"

Bonesella sighed.

"You really do this a lot do you? Why do men do it so much?"

"Well, I don't know about all men, but for me, I do it because it relaxes me. It took away my anxiety, loneliness, and even my depression," I explained.

"So, it makes you feel better?"

"Yes. But don't women like you do it too?" I asked.

"Well, sure, but it will never feel as close to what you feel. I don't think it is that pleasing for us," she explained as she gazes off into the sky.

"You sure you don't want to come here with me?" I asked again.

"Like I said, I really don't think that I should," she said.

"Please?"

"No, really."

"Please?" I repeated. I just needed attention. Tears start to stream down my cheeks. I wanted to be loved.

Bonesella turned toward me this time, her face was suddenly surprised. "Are you . . . crying?"

I nodded.

After a moment Bonesella finally said, "All right, fine. I'll sit with you."

She came up and sat as close as she can to me. She slowly guided my head to rest on her shoulder. She kissed me on my forehead and held me close. I couldn't help but cry some more.

"Thank you."

"Of course."

I opened my eyes. I must have fallen asleep for a little on

Bonesella's shoulder. She was still kissing me on the forehead and brushing her fingers through my hair. I really don't like when people touch my hair, but this time I let it slide. I reached up and touched her cheek. Bonesella looked down at me.

"You're awake."

"How long have I been asleep?" I asked.

"Not long. Just for about thirty minutes or so," she said.

I sat up and stretch my back a bit. I wonder what to do now. I looked down at myself. I made quite a mess.

"I'm not sure how to do this," I said to Bonesella. She looked at me in the eyes.

"What did the book say?" I thought for a moment and recite the pages in my head. It was magic that was learned over time.

"What kind of magic is it?"

I was confused now.

"What do you mean, 'what kind of magic is it'?"

"There are different types of magic. They are not all the same. For example, there is controlling magic which is to control certain things like water and wind. It is one of the most basic types of magic used by elementals. Like you are a fire elemental, that means you can use fire controlling magic," Bonesella explained.

"Oh," I let out. I tried to think again to see if I could remember it.

"I think it is bio creation or something like that," I said.

Bonesella thought for a moment.

"So, it is creation magic then. Lucky for you I have read about it before. In general, creation magic involves taking material of what you want to create with and move it in specific ways." Now I was really lost.

"I don't get what you are saying."

Bonesella brings her palm in front of her.

"Take it in your hand and bring your hand in front of you, like this." I scoop up some of the semen and bring my palm in front of me.

"Now close your hand."

I close my hand.

"Now, I'm not sure if this works with creating animals, but it has been used with other materials to create other things. Bring out your other hand facing down in a fist. You are going to turn your hand with the material over and slide it against your arm, let some of it out of your hand but not too much."

I followed along, but I was unsure if this was really going to work. I continue doing what she said for the past few minutes. My hands were starting to sweat now.

"Now open your palm."

I opened my hand and my heart raced. A small, tiny butterfly was sitting in my hand flapping its wings gently.

I looked at Bonesella with complete confusion.

"I told you, "she said with a laugh.

"I don't get it still. How does movement make cells form?" I asked loudly.

"Not sure. I guess you are going to have to do some research."

"Yeah. I don't think we have any books that have answers to my question at all."

Later, Bonesella and I went back home. While Bonesella made something to eat for all of us, I went to check on the kids. Jenifer and Rosetta were together like always, making clothing. I once thought they wouldn't get along to well, but things really did turn out different. The only one who didn't get along to well was Alex. He never gave too much attention to the girls. It was always hard to talk to him. Both Rosetta and Jenifer gave me hugs. I really enjoyed their love. They were both so bright and open . . . just like me.

I walked over to Alex's room. Every time I walked over there, I always started to worry a bit. It was like nothing would change. He usually didn't said much. I knocked on the door slowly as my anxiety heightens. I really don't want to mess things up.

"Alex?" I called.

"Come in."

I opened the door and slowly walked in. Alex wasn't doing much, just reading like usual.

"Hey, I don't mean to bother you. Just wanted to let you know that Mom is making something to eat, and I was just wondering if you are doing okay."

I waited for an answer.

"I'm doing fine," he said casually.

"Did you do anything today?" I asked.

"I fed your dragon."

"What?" I didn't like the term *your*. It made me feel sick. It made me feel like throwing up.

"Yeah, I fed him. He was a little feisty though."

An idea ran through my mind. I thought maybe there was a way to bond with him more. "Do you want to ride him?" I asked.

"I don't know how to ride a dragon," he said.

"No worries. I will show you. It is not too hard. It just takes some practice, that's all."

Alex agreed, and we all ate together. Soon, we finished eating and I told Bonesella that Alex and I will be outside.

"Nightmare!" I called.

After a few seconds, he came soaring down.

"Hi!" I said in a high-pitched tone. Nightmare wagged his tail and started licking me.

"All right, you want to go for a fly?" I asked him.

Nightmare became excited and started jumping around. I looked towards Alex.

"You ready?" I asked.

"Um . . . I don't think so," he said.

"Don't worry, I promise Nightmare won't go crazy," I said.

"Okay."

"Nightmare, lay down," I said. Nightmare lay down on the ground. I climbed on top and motioned Alex to get on too. Alex shook his head.

"Come on, what's wrong?" I asked.

"I'm nervous," he said.

I suddenly froze. Alex must have anxiety. That could explain why he does not like to talk to people. I got off Nightmare and walked up to him.

"Do you feel nervous when you are around people? Do you not like to socialize with people because you have anxiety?" I asked.

Alex looked me in the eyes with a surprised face, but it quickly goes away and became sad.

"Is this true?"

I could see tears streaming down his face as he looked toward the ground. Without another word, I hug him tightly. He started to cry into my shoulder. I should have known. I pull away and place my hands on his cheeks.

"Alex, you should have told me," I said softly.

"I d-didn't want to."

"Shh. It is okay. I have anxiety too."

"How?"

"I don't have social anxiety like you, but I do have major anxiety when embarrassed or in a really unpleasant situation, I also get anxiety when I am in a small, tight space. I have claustrophobia," I explained.

"How do you cope with it?"

I coped with it by masturbating mainly, but I did not want to tell him that. I did not want him to follow after my bad habits.

"I take deep breaths and try to think about good, calm things."

"You forgot about something," Alex said.

He was not crying anymore. His face was serious. With realization, I let go of him and back away. My face burned red. I was not embarrassed this time. I was angry, but I could not take it out on him. I could not. I do not know what to do.

"That . . . that is besides the point. I have issues that I struggle with. I don't want you falling down the same path, okay?" I said instead.

"Okay," Alex said calmly.

I released a breath of tension.

"How do you know about that anyway?" I asked.

I was kind of scared to know the truth though.

"I pay close attention to detail. I guess I felt that if I paid more attention to you, I might figure out how to talk to you better."

My heart stopped for a moment.

"Are you serious?"

"Yeah, I am sorry if I upset you. I was just trying to make things better."

I closed my eyes for a moment and breathed. It helped keep me calm at times like this.

"I forgive you," I said.

I reopened my eyes and hugged him once more.

"You know, just because I struggle with things, doesn't mean you can't come and talk to me about anything. I just want to be here for you," I said softly into his ear.

Alex finally got on to Nightmare, while I tried to keep Nightmare calm. I placed my hands on his snout and I looked into his eyes. Most dragons can be calmed by their owner this way.

"Let me know when you are ready."

"I'm ready," Alex called a moment later.

I released Nightmare and I climbed on behind Alex.

"All right. I want you to hold on to the leather strap. And what you want to do is always keep yourself centered and balanced," I explained.

"If Nightmare is turning right, then you lean toward the center, which will be on your right and vice versa," I added.

"Okay, I think I get it," Alex said.

"All right. You tell Nightmare what to do," I finally said, patting nightmare's shoulder to signal him to fly.

Once they were off I stood back to watch out for them. Nightmare took off not too rough, but enough to get him into the air. I kept a close eye on Alex as Nightmare soared across the open field. I watched for minutes, but Nightmare flew nice and steady the whole time. Alex seemed perfectly fine in the air. Once they landed, Alex slid off Nightmare.

"How did I do?"

"Not bad for your first time. With more practice you will be able to fly much smoother," I explained. We went back inside and Bonesella met up with me. Alex went off somewhere else.

"How did it go?" Bonesella asked a bit excitingly.

"Very well. Now I know why he's so quiet."

"You do?"

"Yes, he has social anxiety. Probably got it from me," I said softly.

"Ah, no wonder why," Bonesella said a bit mockingly.

I ignored the tone and I went off into the office. It was getting late, but there was still much sunlight. I hadn't realized we have been outside for more than an hour in total. Almost two, I think. Above the desk was a window that opened horizontally with two sides. The window was left open. Behind me, there was a small shelf of books and two chairs with pillows and a blanket. I looked back toward the desk. An unopened letter laid on the dusty wood surface. Nightmare would send letters for me and bring some back. He must have picked this one up for me earlier today. I took a seat and look over the envelope. It was from Isaac. Usually, I wrote to him first, but this time Isaac was the first to write today. I opened the envelope and read the letter.

Dear, Xavier

How are you? I hope you are doing well. I missed you a lot lately and have been waiting for your return. I've slept and cried in your bed. I have also masturbated in your bed too, but hopefully you won't be mad. I clean after myself. (giggles)

Anyways, I've been wondering if you are okay. I can't help but wonder what you are doing right now. I wish I could hold your hand again. If I can look into your eyes again and tell you that there was nothing to ever worry about and that I am here for you. I want to tell you how I feel. That I need your love. (Crying now) All I ever wanted was to be with you forever. But I know I can't have that. You already have a life. I constantly dream of you. I want to be in your arms. I want to cry on your shoulder. I want you to be right here with me. I can't stand being alone like this. I need your attention and love. I want to love you. I Want to touch you. I want to have sex with you. I want to do everything with you. I am actually crying right now while writing this.

I love you so much, Isaac.

Tears streamed down my face. I couldn't help but crying. I wanted him too, but I had already made a decision and I didn't think I could ever break away from it. No, not now and most likely not ever.

I took out a pen and more parchment. I didn't know how to respond. I just wanted to be in his arms right now.

Dear, Isaac
Your words have made me cry heavy tears. I wish I could embrace you right now. I'm not sure how to tell you how I feel, but I will try. I feel like I need you. I don't feel right in this relationship, especially without you. I'm not sure how I will ever tell her or how this will affect my own children. I don't know anymore. I am just feeling more depressed than the days before. Just know how much I appreciate your writing and how much I love you too. You are my best friend, and I don't ever want to leave you behind like this ever.

With all my love and heart that I have, Xavier.

I pushed the two letters aside and lay my head on the desk. I continued to cry and let out all the feelings I had. I hated this feeling that I had trapped inside of me. I wanted to kill it. I heard the door open as I continue to cry.

"Xavier, why are you crying?" Bonesella asked softly.

"I don't want to talk about it," I burst out.

"Why not?" Bonesella continued in the same tone.

"You are going to hate me," I burst again.

"Why would I ever hate you?"

Bonesella places a hand on my shoulder. I didn't know how to respond. I didn't want to tell her.

"Who is this from?"

I quickly lifted my head and snatch the letter from her hand.

"It doesn't matter," I said.

"Well, clearly it does, so please tell me why you are upset," Bonesella said seriously while taking a seat in one of the comfy chairs behind me.

Everything hurt inside. I felt like I was dying.

"I left my friend behind," I said in a raspy voice.

"Can I see the letter?" she asked.

"No. It's personal to me. My friend wrote it. He misses me and wants me to go back home," I said quietly.

"You know, by this point, your life shouldn't be kept personal from me. I am your wife, and I should know everything. I am supposed to be here for you," Bonesella said softly, looking me directly in the eyes.

"No. you won't be here for me. You will hate me forever and leave me," I said.

"But, why?" Bonesella pleads.

"You know, as much as I feel like telling you everything because it is the right thing to do, I also feel that this is just about me and my friend and that no one else should be involved. It only has to do with us. I would appreciate it if you respected that," I explained.

I turned back around to place the letter I wrote in another

envelope. I noticed the sketch Isaac drew of me on the back of his letter. It was the most beautiful artwork I had seen. As I sealed the letter, Nightmare dropped another letter through the window. He flew off into the trees nearby. The letter landed softly in front of me. I could tell that it definitely was not from Isaac.

Chapter Twenty-Eight

"This-this letter," Bonesella started formally while holding it up above her head. "is what you were talking about all along."

Fear and truth come over me like a wave. "What do we do?" I asked.

"The Stone of Refuge is going to help keep me safe from this danger. So that means you have to fight if necessary. I can't be sure what lies ahead, but if I have to use my powers to help you I will. I promise," Bonesella explained.

I nodded, unable to speak at the moment. My throat was tight and dry. Bonesella and I suit up in armor and grab as many weapons as we can. Nightmare waited patiently.

"What's going on?" Rosetta yelled in a high voice.

I walked over to talk to her.

"Rosy, sweetheart, there's danger coming for us, and we have to fight it," I said as calmly as I could.

"We're not leaving you out to go get in trouble. We're coming too," she said strictly.

"Rosetta," I objected.

"Please," she begged.

"Alex, Jen, and I can help as back up. I promise we will stay safe. Plus, I've been training so hard lately to learn to sword fight. I want to help."

I scanned her face for a moment and decided to let it slide. "Fine, but I need you to be careful."

I looked up at the other two who stand back away from Rosetta.

"Same for you two. Got it?" They nodded. I walked back over to Bonesella. She stored the stone in one of the pockets on Nightmare's saddle.

"I guess it won't be just us two," I said leaning over Nightmare.

"I just wanted the kids to be safe," Bonesella said stressfully.

"I know, me too, but if this is what we have to do then fine. I just don't want any of this to be a disaster."

I could see the look in Bonesella's eyes. The terrifying letter she read. How she was going to be killed if he didn't achieve his goal: acquiring me. I guess word of my healing powers got out there and now Bonesella would be killed if I didn't do anything about it. This was why she needed to be protected. I needed to speak with Lavina again. I needed to find the sirens. To save her.

We traced our steps back to the cave that we found the stone in. We entered the familiar dense jungle. Nightmare was walking beside us. I couldn't believe that everything was true. I was right and Bonesella didn't want to believe me. I let out a sigh. I really hoped this would be over soon. When we took breaks on the way, Rosetta would practice fighting on a tree. She really was the most determined out of the three. She even might be more determined than Bonesella was. We continued on until we reached the cave. This time I decided to keep my armor and my sword on me. Nightmare would stay out here waiting for us to come back.

"Rose, Jen, Alex, I need you to stay with Nightmare in case something happens. Keep him fed and give him attention while were gone. I'm not sure how long this is going to take."

They nodded. Bonesella took the stone and we hit the water without undressing. With our swords on our belts, we swam till we could find stops to breath air.

After multiple stops and a long swim, Bonesella and I came out from the water. We heard the sirens all around us.

"Lavina!" I yelled.

The sirens became louder, their tails moving through the water sliding past other tails. I noticed the same rock that the stone was on.

"Bonesella. Stand on that rock I found the stone on and call out to her," I said.

"Okay."

She walked through the water slowly. She climbed on to the rock and raised the stone above her head.

"Lavina, siren of the sea. Here is your Stone of Refuge. We are in great danger, and we need your help. Call out to us if you can hear us!"

Her words echoed through my mind as The Sirens screeched loudly. The familiar face of Lavina appeared above a rock not too far from the rock that Bonesella was on.

"That's her," I said.

Bonesella stepped off the rock and walked up, holding the stone out to her. I slowly came closer as Lavina placed her hands around the stone.

"Keep it with you," she said.

"I will help you on your journey, but I cannot go with you. You can consider this as a gift," Lavina finished as she vanished into the water below her.

The water started to churn as the sirens swam in circles. Their screeches became louder. I covered my ears and Bonesella and I were sucked into the water.

Bright sunlight reached my face. I was floating on my back. The water was warm. The sky was blue. *Wait . . . I'm no longer in the cave.* Where was I? I got up and my feet touched the sand. The water was murky. It appeared I was in a small lake but surrounded by beach sand. There was a wooden shack with some surfboards lying against it. As I looked past the tall palms and the shack, I could see the ocean. It looked like Angels Beach because I could see the white sand, except over here the sand was golden yellow. I looked behind me. Branches spiked out from multiple directions. There were no leaves, just dark, skinny branches of what looked like dead bushes. I spotted Rosetta laying in the water with her clothing caught in the branches. I swam over to release her. Panic rushed through me as I took her out into my arms. I swam to shore.

"Rose. Rosy. Wake up," I said as I laid her on the sand.

She opened her eyes.

"Where am I?"

I turned to see the others coming out of the water. Bonesella, Jen, and Alex came out together.

"Didn't I tell you to stay with Nightmare? How did you get here with us?" I asked strictly.

Instead of the two answering, Rosetta responded, "We came after you. We were worried. I thought it would be better if we stuck together."

I looked at her innocent face. "And where's Nightmare?"

Jen responded this time.

"We told him to come and find us if something happens."

Her strong voice shook my spirit.

"All right. Well, let's figure out where we are then," I said getting up.

As everyone started to make a fire on the sand, I walked up to the shack. The door was wide open and a yellow tail with a fluff of fur at the end pops up from under a table. I jump at the sight. A girl with cat ears stood up.

"Uh, hello?"

"Oh, hi!" she said. "By the way, I'm Cathryn."

"Hi, I'm Xavier."

She was a feline girl with yellow fur and orange stripes. Her hair was short and yellow, also with orange stripes. She has ocean blue eyes and she was wearing a blue shirt with a light blue paw print that was falling off her shoulder and light tan shorts. I looked beside me and see a surfboard placed upside down on the longest table.

"You surf?" I asked.

"Yeah, of course! If you go out far enough you will hit some really good waves," Cathryn exclaimed.

"Wow. I, uh, never surfed before," I said a bit shakily by trying to imagine me doing that.

"Well, I can show you."

I brushed off the thought of trying to learn and centered my focus on what was important at the moment.

"You know, right now, I have a bit of an issue and I would like your help," I said more seriously.

"Sure!"

"My family and I are in danger. Listen, my wife's father is pretty much trying to kill us."

"What?"

"Yeah, seriously. He's trying to take advantage of her so he can go after me," I finished.

"I've never heard anything like that before in my life," Cathryn said with a depressing tone.

"That's why I would like your help. I am worried that I can't take him on my own."

Cathryn now walked up to me. Without a word, she wrapped her arms around me.

"I can only promise you that everything is going to be okay," she said with a soft voice. I hugged her back and laid my head on her shoulder. I did really hope everything was going to be okay.

Cathryn and I left the shack and go to meet up with the rest. Bonesella and the kids were gathering wood for a fire. I introduced them to Cathryn. They didn't seem super thrilled about having another member. Once they were gone, I took a seat on a log around the fire. Cathryn shook out a sandy towel besides me.

“So, is there anything I should know about you before you get a little too involved in our journey,” I said to start conversation.

“Well. I am very cheerful and hyper. Besides that, though, I am pansexual. I tend to focus more on people’s personality rather than gender,” she said. “How bout you?” she asked while laying out the towel on the log and taking a seat on it.

“Uh . . .” I let out. The memory of Isaac appeared in my head. He was so kind to me. He respected me. He loved me more than anyone. More than my wife.

“Well, I kind of am a bit confused, but I will only tell you if you promise not to tell anyone else.”

“Okay, sure!”

“Besides my wife, I like someone else. Someone I have been friends with before I met her. Isaac was so kind to me. He even respected me in every way possible. It has been so hard to live without thinking of him. When I went to visit him, he told me that he loved me. I told him that I loved him too. I gave him my love while I was with him. I now give him all my love when I write to him,” I explained softly.

“Bisexual, maybe?”

“No. that doesn’t seem right. I feel that Isaac has my heart more than anyone else. I feel that I truly love him. I think I am homosexual and not heterosexual.”

I felt worried on the inside. I just wanted to cry into my pillow in a room by myself. I wanted Isaac to come and hug me and tell me everything was going to be okay.

“I think you should tell your wife.”

“No. I’m scared. She’s going to hate me. Isaac told me that he loved me when I visited him without telling her. She’s going to rip my guts out.”

After a moment of silence, Cathryn spoke again.

“Well, whenever you get the chance, you make up your mind. I’ll leave the rest of this to you to think about,” she explained softly.

Cathryn got up and walked off. I continued to sit on the log and tried to find the words to my confession.

I felt my insides torn into pieces without him. I felt that I was choking. It was like having a heavy weight in my stomach and a chaotic fire spreading around my brain. I shoved my face into my knees. I felt heavy tears flowing down my cheeks. I was choking now through my own tears. I wanted to hide away from the world. I wanted to disappear from reality. I hated this feeling. The feeling of loneliness. Because I didn't find any company among my own family.

As I bawled my eyes out, I could hear sand shuffling near me. I lifted my head from my emotion breakdown. Instead of Bonesella finding me like this, it was Cathryn who had come back to check on me. Maybe she was better than what I expected.

"Do you want to come over to the beach with us? It's okay if you don't want to."

I wiped my face. My head really hurt, and I still had a giant weight in my stomach.

"I would, but I don't feel to great right now. I'll catch up with you all later."

"All right, you can go chill in my house if you feel like. It was that blue building over there."

I looked among the various trees and find the blue building standing out among them.

"Thank you."

"Of course," she responded giving me her hand.

I took it and she pulled me up. Once she waves to me, I start following the path to her house. Once I open the front door, fresh air and a bit of relief hit me. I navigate my way around the vibrant house till I found Cathryn's room. I could tell it was hers because of all the cat items and furniture she has. I found a comfy blue blanket to wrap around me. I took it and sat on her bed. At least her room has a very welcoming look to it. I grabbed one of her pillows once I felt my tears pushing through.

"Isaac," I called.

"If you can hear me, please listen. I need you right now. I want your love. I hate feeling this way without you. This anxiety that keeps me from sleeping at night. You're the only one who can make me feel calm. Please, love me," I whined. I lay back and pull my knees to my chest as I closed my eyes.

A soft whisper came over my ear. I opened my eyes. I couldn't make out what it was. I heard my name being called, but by whom? I blocked out my thoughts to hear the voice more clearly. The familiarity of the voice was locked in my brain. My heart skipped a beat. This wasn't a voice coming from the house. It was in my head. Isaac was calling out to me. I shed more tears on the pillow.

Xavier. Darling, don't cry. Please don't cry, I hear echo through my brain. Was Isaac actually speaking to me, or was my brain playing tricks on me to help me cope with my anxiety? Most of the time, I couldn't tell reality from my brain in these situations. I just give in and play along, hoping that I felt better.

"I can't. everything hurts and I can't," I responded shakily.

Everything began to fade away and I found myself within my own mind.

I was surrounded by my best and most memorable memories from when I was first taught how to bake and paint to heartwarming talks with the people I love most. The strong feeling of warmth touches my back. I turned around as the familiar touch sinks into my skin. His eyes gently looked upon my face. He was slightly see-through though. My heart raced as I wrap my arms around him.

"Isaac, I need you," I cried out once again. Isaac wraps his arms around me.

"I know you do. You can cry all you want on me." I looked up at him. His appearance was strange. He looked unreal.

"Isaac, please tell me you're real. Please!" I begin to raise my voice.

"I'm as real as your heart desires. Just close your eyes for about five seconds. Forget what is in your head. Feel what is around you. Then open your eyes," Isaac explained calmly.

I did what he said and let his warmth take over me. This was the only way I would ever be happy. I opened my eyes.

We were back at my old home in the living room. Isaac's warm hands were distinct as ever and Isaac was no longer see-through. I touched his cheek. This was the reality I wanted to get back to ever since.

"I don't ever want to leave you."

"You can stay with me forever. As you know I'm in love with you."

I took a step back to make sure I could fully navigate my surroundings.

"Of course. You are all I dream about." I started to walk towards my room.

I felt free, like I broke the metal bars in my mind. I opened the door. The room was the same as I left it, so was the air. I walked in as Isaac hugged me from behind. His lips touched my neck gently. I combed my fingers through his air. My anxiety was lifted up for now. As my blood pressure rose steadily, I could feel the heat in my cheeks. Isaac came around and pressed his lips to mine. I let the feeling of love and comfort overtake me. Once I found an exit to my mindless state, I finally realized that I was on my bed. My clothes were being stripped off. His hands glided across my body. I let the mindlessness take over again. My heart controlled me now, not my brain.

Isaac's eyes meet with mine. Pure pleasure was all I felt. He touched my bottom lip with his thumb.

He kissed me for about a minute and said, "I love you. Never forget that."

"I won't," I said as his hand slid between my thighs.

The burn spread down my legs.

"Ahhh. Please be gentle."

He touched his lips again to my neck as he gripped my genitals.

"I promise. I would never hurt you."

We continued to grind as we breathed each other's breath, lips to lips. A shock moved through my body till I let out a high-pitched moan. I quickly opened my eyes. Everything I wanted had disappeared. I was back in my reality, crying in a cat-themed room.

Chapter Twenty-Nine

I felt numb and hollow. Everything I wanted was gone. I cried my eyes out so much that I felt empty. My body ached even though none of it was real. My shorts were wet and sticky, and I had a really bad erection right now. Maybe I needed some fresh air. I pushed up off the bed to get up. My legs shook, and I fell onto my face. Still on the floor, I crawled up into a little ball so I could recollect my thoughts. I needed to get out of here. Minutes later, I made the struggle to get up and get out. I pushed the front door to a gust of salty wind. It was much later than I thought. The sun was setting, and I could see from a far the campfire. I rushed to the group as soon as possible.

Once I reached them, Bonesella stood.

"Where were you?" she asked strictly. Cathryn's cheerful expression dropped. Bonesella waited with her arms crossed.

"It's none of your business," I said walking toward the beach.

"Uh . . . actually it 'is' my business. Where were you?" she barks.

I roll my eyes.

"Why does it matter?"

Bonesella continued to chase after me and grabbed me by the shoulder, swinging in front of me.

"Because I was worried sick." I looked her dead in the eyes.

"You were worried about me? I was the one who was worried just now." I tried to continue walking, but she stopped me.

"Worried? About what?"

"None of your business."

"Tell me."

"No."

Bonesella rolled her eyes.

"What is wrong? Why are you acting like this?"

I brushed her off my shoulder and I turned away.

"Everything. Everything is wrong."

"What do you mean 'Everything'?"

Bonesella dropped her anger a bit.

"I have a lot on my mind right now. You won't understand."

"Of course, I will! I'm your wife!"

I turned to her.

"No. you won't. Trust me."

After a short moment of silence. Bonesella finally responded.

"Well, then, help me understand then."

"That's the issue. I don't know how."

"Xavier . . .?"

"When I figure out my feelings I will tell you. Just give me some time."

Cathryn's cooking actually wasn't bad at all. The seasoning was just enough and the fish was pretty tender. I didn't eat seafood often, but I didn't mind it. It's not like eating a bloody steak. I looked up at Cathryn, whose face was glowing orange from the fire.

"So, how is it?" she asked cheerfully.

"Very good, thank you," I replied first.

Still the feeling of silence overtook us. Bonesella and I were sitting opposite of each other; we refused to look up. About two minutes later into eating, Rosetta spoke up.

"Are you okay?" she directed toward me.

I mouthed the words, "I'm okay."

"How about, we focus on the issue at hand here?" Jenifer spoke.

"Well, all right. What can I do?" Cathryn chimed in.

"Help us find my father and fight with us," Bonesella finally said.

"Where do you think he is?"

Bonesella stayed silent for a moment. Cathryn waited patiently for an answer. She looked somewhat nervous and drowned out in my peripheral vision. "We also need to find Nightmare," Alex adds before Bonesella spoke.

"He's at the Albraekia ruins," Bonesella finally said.

"How do you know?"

Cathryn's face was full of confusion.

"I can sense him. He's waiting for us. For a fight."

"Waiting's kind of dumb," Jenifer spit out. Bonesella gave her a look to stop. I kept my eyes on Cathryn's gentle manner. She sat calm as her ears twitched and faced different directions.

"The ruins are very far from here. I guess I'm going to have to teleport you all there."

"You can teleport?" I finally said.

"Well, not on my own. I have a little something that can help," Cathryn chimed as she got up.

I quickly got up and followed her into the shack. Cathryn knelt and pulled on a large gray tarp that covers a medium sized, mysterious object. I bent down to take a look. Cathryn let the tarp fall on the floor next to her.

"What is that?"

The black and gray oval shaped object was nothing I had seen before. "Did you build this?"

"Yep, but I haven't really tested it yet. It's a teleportation device that is supposed to work better than my gauntlet. By the way, I went to Lebaki University to study mechanics and electrical engineering on my home planet," Cathryn explained confidently.

"Wow, what planet?"

"Wynzca. It's where most furries like me come from."

Cathryn then pulled out a chair and her tools and began to work on the device. I slowly walked out of the shack to give her space. The salty air hits my tongue. I smack my lips as I sat back down on the log. I looked up and find Bonesella staring at me.

"What?"

"I need to talk to you."

We found ourselves at the beach again. The cold water passed by me on the shore.

"Are you going to tell me what's wrong or what?" I asked.

I was already sick and tired of the arguing. *Why do we have to be here again?*

"You like her, don't you?"

My heart stopped beating for a moment.

"Why would you assume that?"

"She's the only person you have been giving attention to lately."

"Uh, yeah because you have been pissed off with me lately. I don't want to hang out with people who can't even stand me at the moment."

I could see the fire in her eyes. *She must want to choke me right now.* Right when she opened her mouth, I spoke first.

"You really think you are right about everything, but you're not. I know more than you about me."

"And you won't tell me what's wrong."

"Because you won't understand! I don't even understand it! Trying to explain myself is only going to ruin all that I have right now! You're just going to push me away . . . Like everyone else. . ."

I collapsed on the sand. I couldn't help my tears. I felt like broken glass. So fragile. I couldn't stand anything anymore. Silence lingered in the night. Bonesella knelt by me. I pulled my knees closer to my chest and looked away.

"I'm hurting you, aren't I?"

"Yeah, no kidding."

"How about we focus on our mission and forget about this. I'll give up on the thought that you like Cathryn and I apologize about yelling at you like that. Is that okay with you?" Her voice was calm, but I was still decided whether I should trust her or not.

"As long as you be on my side rather than against me. I don't want to fight anymore. Promise?"

Her hand touched my shoulder and her lips gently touched my cheek.

"I promise."

I guessed that this wasn't too bad, but I knew it could be better . . . to have Isaac by my side. The good thing was that I know Isaac cared, and that he would always be thinking about me. *I know he loves me. I love him too. Isaac knows that I'm hurting right now. He has me in his heart. I know it. I could feel it.*

Chapter Thirty

The salty air blew into my face. I opened my eyes. It was sunrise. I couldn't believe Cathryn decided to stay up all night to fix that thing. I knock on the door of the shack. Cathryn was cleaning up her tools.

"You're done?"

"Yeah, want to check it out?"

Before I could respond, Cathryn jumped in. "I'm kidding! I'll start prepping it up."

"You're coming with us, right?" I asked to be sure. "Yes. I'll be right by your side every step of the way."

"Thanks."

"No problem."

Once the sun started to beat its rays above us, Cathryn started to cook. Bonesella finally decided to sit next to me on one of the logs. Jennifer and Rosetta were chatting as if we were home. Alex went to help Cathryn with catching some oysters and fruits to eat for breakfast. Everything seemed to be going back to normal. I'm actually starting to enjoy my time here. Sadly, we will be leaving this place soon.

"You ready to do this thing?" Bonesella asked while packing her gear.

"Yeah, A lot more prepared than any of the days before."

"I guess I freaked you out a bit then."

"Yeah, that arguing really distracted me."

About thirty minutes after we prepared what we had, Cathryn and Alex came back. Food was cooked and eaten. Cathryn pulled out the device from the shack. It dragged slowly against the sand. "All right, it's time," Cathryn announced. After few seconds of fumbling with the power source—which stayed in the shack—a burst of energy shook the area around us. The space inside the oval ring gaped open. It was sort of like a black hole.

"Are you positive this will work?"

"Yes. I know what I'm doing," Cathryn responded.

"Well, then you go first."

Cathryn was wearing some mechanical suit, with glowing blue gaps between different parts. She also had a belt with her own tech weaponry. Cathryn nodded and jumps right through. My eyes widened; she definitely went somewhere else. Hopefully it was the right place. I decided to jump through second as everyone else followed behind.

A gravitational pull was all around me. Everything disappeared quickly, and then an entire new place appeared right after. My feet touched the ground. Green grass was everywhere. I looked up. I was at the edge of a forest. In front of me was an open field with the Albraekia ruins. Huge blocks of unevenly cut stones scattered the area. Beside me, Cathryn stood with her hands behind her back.

"Here we are," she said.

The rest of us came from behind. We looked around to make sure we weren't missing anyone. We were all here.

"What are we going to do about Nightmare?" Rosetta asked.

"I'm sure he will get back to us. We need to focus on finding my father," Bonesella responded.

I nodded. We needed to focus.

We walked toward the stones. I had heard that this used to

be some sort of religious building. Most of it was in pieces, but there was still a standing tower, and what looked like a main hall, where the entrance would be. The tower was missing about a fourth of the wall, which reveals two floors and stairs that follow around the existing wall. I could even see a chandelier hanging from above the top floor. We all make our way to the entrance hall. We sit down on the torn red carpet. The whole entrance was gone, but there was still three walls and a ceiling. The back wall was severely damaged though. I wonder what happened here.

"It's a very big place, where do you think he is waiting?" Cathryn asked.

"He should find us here." My anxiety started to creep in. I started to play with the ends of my hair to distract myself. Bonesella and Cathryn were very alert. The kids seemed a bit worried. I was on the verge of a panic attack.

I slid out my sword from my belt. I clenched the handle. If I panicked, I might kill. I closed my eyes. My breathing was becoming heavier. I was shaking. I wanted to scream. Suddenly Bonesella whipped her head around at me. My breathing had become noticeable. She quickly came over to me.

"Are you alright?"

I shook my head. I didn't think I would last a chance here. She wrapped her arms around me. I leaned my head on her shoulder. Cathryn stayed at the missing entrance as a look out. I hoped Isaac was okay. My anxiety increased as I thought about him. I wrapped my arms around her. After about a minute or two, Bonesella suddenly froze with wide open eyes. She felt cold. I shake her.

"Darling!"

"I-I . . ."

She was unable to finish her sentence.

An unsettling feeling started to linger in the air. Cathryn's ears twitched. She must be sensing something too. I shook Bonesella more violently this time.

"Babe!"

"Mom?" Rosetta let out.

"Xavier!" Cathryn screeched.

"What?!" I yelled.

"He's here."

Bonesella finally started to come to her senses. My fears were becoming more real by the minute. We ran out of the hall. This black dust swirls in the air, they reach out like giant tentacles. In the center of them all, A sort of tornado forms and fades as it reaches out toward us. I clench my sword even tighter and pull it in front of me as his figure appears. He's way taller than me. Piercing neon green eyes on such a dark face. A suit of armor I had never seen before. And a long cape with torn edges. He was the very thing that scares me the most. The form of my anxiety. The name Bonesella refused to speak. Bonesella walked up in front of me. I lowered my sword.

"Zxarvixar."

The name stung inside me. Who was he? I needed to find out more.

"Why are you here?" I demanded.

"Why do you think I am here?" His dark voice echoed all around.

The ground shook.

"To take advantage of me and my powers," I said.

Bonesella looked at me with disbelief. She was expecting me to say something about her. I looked straight into his piercing eyes.

"Clever boy."

I stepped in front of her, pulling my sword up at a higher angle.

"Why? To destroy this world and become all powerful? To never die?" I raised my voice as I spoke.

"I don't need to stay alive. I have already wiped out an entire population of people through disease. I need to strip away everything you have. All of it, and let you die all alone."

The words struck me harder than the ones before. I felt like I had been broken into a million of pieces.

"You are so cruel! Why would you try to do such a thing?" I said as my voice became dry. I could feel the tears rolling down my cheeks.

"You know nothing of what I'm doing. It's better off if you don't know."

My brain went into an empty state of confusion. *You're right. I don't know anything.* "What I do know is that I have to defeat you, so that you will stop hurting everyone."

"Go ahead, try."

Everyone was looking at me with disbelief. I had to do something. I took a single step back to propel myself forward. As my sword broke with wind, swirls of green mist and black dust spread out from Zxarvixar. Before I could hit him, his hand raised. A green shield appeared, and I froze. I looked at him, through the shield, dead in the eyes unable to move. The front of the sword touched the shield of magic but did not pass it. Zxarvixar closed his hand, the shield disappeared, and I fell to the ground on my face.

"Xavier!" Bonesella yelled.

I could hear Cathryn running up to me. She grabbed my arm and pulled me up immediately. Bonesella pulled out her own sword and stood prepared to fight. Cathryn pulled me back and away from Zxarvixar's reach. I grabbed on to her shoulder, having a tough time standing. I thought I might have hit the ground too hard.

"All right, That's it!" Bonesella yelled, but before she could charge at Zxarvixar, the black dust quickly reached the entire ruins and falls, forming an army.

"What is happening?" I screeched.

Cathryn pulled me away even farther this time. She brought me to the last tower standing. Cathryn touched my head.

"You are bleeding."

I could see afar that the kids were trying to fight the dust warriors as well. I couldn't even bother thinking about my head. I needed to help them.

"Forget about it. I'm going back."

Cathryn shook her head at me.

"No, that is definitely not a promising idea. You need to stay put, so that we can keep you alive," Cathryn stated.

"Alive? To stay alive, I have to fight. There's no point in being alive if I don't do something!" I yelled back.

"Xavier. . ." Cathryn let out with tears in her eyes.

"Do everything you can to stop him."

I closed my eyes.

"Okay." I calmed myself before doing anything crazy yet.

I slowed my breath to lower my anxiety. I looked up at Cathryn.

"Just go, I will be there soon. I need a minute." Cathryn went off to help.

The blood stuck to the side of my head. I touched it with two fingers. I could heal myself. There was no need to worry about my health. The rush of my bodily fluids flowed through me. I could feel the power of the magenta glow even though I was almost fully covered in armor. I continued to touch my head as the wound closed and the blood disappeared. I gripped my sword and forced myself to get up. I was still in pain, but I felt much better now. As I got closer to the scene of the action, everyone was fighting the dust warriors and ignoring Zxarvixar's presence as he ignored them as well. The only person he was worried about was me. With my sword drawn now, Zxarvixar made his way towards me. As he got closer, I stepped back till I was almost touching the tower I was at. He brought up his hand and green magic surrounded my neck. I rose about two feet. The power around my neck choked me. I gasped for breath, struggling to fight back against his power. With weakness filling me, I stopped. Zxarvixar's hand clenched, and he swung his arm, throwing me across the field. The thin grass didn't accommodate to my weight. I hit the ground harder than I did earlier. I forced myself even harder to get up. Pain grew inside of me. I continued to push off the ground.

"You're weak. I knew you wouldn't be able to even stand a chance. Pathetic. I wish you would just die already! But first . . . I need to suck your powers out of you."

One last push, and I found balance on my feet. With my left hand, I clenched my side, which I had fallen on; with my right, I held my sword up to Zxarvixar.

"No! I won't let you do any of that. I refuse to let you hurt others and myself. Even if I value my life way less than what you expect. I won't let you take that away from me," I firmly stated.

"Very well." Zxarvixar opened his hand.

A large, wide black sword with glowing green designs outlining the blade appeared. Once he clenched the sword, I started to run, making my way around the tower. I needed time. I couldn't do this yet. I bent down behind a large structure. I pressed the metal plates of my armor. As I pushed the plates aside, I could see the magenta looking veins tracing me. My abdomen felt as if it were on fire. I could feel Zxarvixar's presence coming slowly close to me. As I looked behind me, just over the wall, his head was distant scanning the area. He continued to walk slowly not only looking for me but observing the others. I didn't know if I will ever be able to strike him with my sword. I rubbed myself just a bit, to get the juices flowing. As I started to feel the rush of adrenaline through me, Zxarvixar crept beside me. I jumped and stepped away from him.

"You said I'm weak but want to take away my powers. What's the point!" I yelled as I gain distance away from him.

"You're weak because you don't understand anything yet. It would be better if you stayed that way."

The words echoed through my head. Zxarvixar lifted his hand. I braced to be thrown or hit. Green magic surrounded me. I concentrated on the power that flowed through me.

"I won't let you take advantage of me!"

The green magic continued to surround me. I felt numb. My body hurt. My feet were still planted into the ground. I didn't understand what was happening. The glow of magenta started to outshine the green magic. I focused harder. Zxarvixar's shocked expression said it all. I might not know what I was doing, but I could be sure that I was stronger than him. I directed my stare into his gaze. The numbness started to fade. Freedom touched my body. Zxarvixar was clenching the arm of his magic hand. I must have reflected his powers back to him somehow. I felt pain free. My body was loose. I was ready to fight hand-to-hand combat if I must.

Zxarvixar's sword appeared in his hand again. I grabbed my own and let my wings open freely.

"Come at me," I announced firmly.

As he swung, I blocked. Another swing, another block. As we went back and forth, I could feel my feet sliding on the thin grass. His hits were pushing me away little by little. I swing once more hitting Zxarvixar's shoulder, but only to be hit by his own sword into my side. I found my back to have hit the same tower. Pain shook throughout my body. I touched the gaping wound in between the broken plates. I was bleeding all over. I didn't know if I would be able to make it. As Zxarvixar walked up to me, I could see Bonesella running up to me from the other direction. She was fearing for her life. I couldn't even move. Before he could put a hand on me, Bonesella came up in front of me. I felt like fainting.

"Don't you dare hurt him anymore!" she yelled.

My vision started to blur. I could only make out a few words of the conversation between them.

"Father!"

"Try to stop me and you'll die too. I don't need you anymore."

"Dad! No!"

Everything was black. I couldn't hear anything either.

Maybe I would die. Maybe this was it . . . and there was nothing I could do about it.

The pain in my body became more distinct. I could feel the blood pouring out of me like a punctured sac of water. My vision started to come back. Instead of finding Zxarvixar above me, I was alone. I let the rest of my vision clear up, as I sat up with my back against the tower. In the distance, all the dust warriors were gone. Everyone, including Bonesella, was fighting Zxarvixar. They must have taken him on to protect me. I actually had time to heal.

I closed my eyes. I couldn't believe this was happening. I didn't even have time to think about what was happening earlier. I could finally feel my depression creep in. The only reason I felt confident was because of Isaac. I only wanted to do it for him. To make myself feel like I deserve every bit of him. That I was fighting for him. Now that I saw the fight ahead, I knew that I was only doing this for my safety, and everyone involved. I just wanted to go back to my old home and cry my last few tears left on Isaac's shoulder, but I didn't think I would even get the chance to.

I wished he were here. I could only imagine what he would have done from the beginning. All he would do was protect me consistently. That was all I needed. Him to show me that he really cares. That he wants me to be alive to receive his love, and answer to it.

I could have done so much before this. I could have told him that I loved him. I could have turned Bonesella away. I could have stayed with the man I loved. I could have loved him more. I could have stayed up all night, giving him all my love. I could have taken his hand and become his beloved husband.

My face was soaked. I felt tired and sick, but I still want to fight. I need to finish this, or else I would never be able to go back home to my love. I knew what I had to do. I got up slowly. The wound was still healing, but it was much better now. I pick up my sword and make my way to the fight.

As I come up, Zxarvixar stopped fighting and looked my way. He didn't seem to be surprised. Bonesella came rushing up to me.

"What are you doing? I left you behind to take care of yourself. Let me handle it." I continue to stare in the eyes of death.

"This is my fight."

"But Xavier. . ."

"No. Worry about yourself."

This time, I confronted Zxarvixar.

"I am so sick and tired of—"

"No more speeches. I have had enough of those already. Instead, let me show you something."

Zxarvixar then snapped his fingers as Bonesella disappeared.

"What did you do?!" I yelled.

"Look up."

I looked. I soon spotted her figure at the second exposed floor of the tower. She was chained to the wall.

"Pick and choose."

I looked at him with disbelief.

"You son of a bitch, I am going to tear you to pieces eventually!!" I screamed. I could see Cathryn's confused and lost face beside me. I looked back up, seeing Bonesella struggled in the distant tower.

"I refuse to let you hurt her."

I ran. Zxarvixar watched as I quickly zoomed across the field. I opened my wings allowing the wind to take me up to the tower. I couldn't believe this. I flapped them quicker to slow my decent to the floor.

"He's just trying to mess with you. Forget about me. Go fight him." She looked exhausted and tired out.

"But I can't leave you here," I said anxiously. I turned to see Zxarvixar right behind me. "I thought you were. . ."

"Time to suffer the consequences."

Zxarvixar walked in front of Bonesella. I took a step back. Zxarvixar pulled up his hand and closed it. Instead of something happening directly to me, I heard the tower start to crumble.

"Xavier!" Bonesella screamed.

I looked around. The floor behind me was collapsing. I stepped away.

Zxarvixar took his sword and pointed it at me. I was right at the edge of the crumbling floor.

"I'm done with you."

Before I had time to react, Zxarvixar kicked me in the stomach. I fell back. My weight plunged me down. I reached out my arms as far as I could. Before I could go down further, I caught a hold on the edge of the floor. I pressed my elbows on the floor. As Zxarvixar was looking down at me, I was hanging on to the edge of the floor . . . and below me, a pool of green, fizzing acid where the first floor was.

Chapter Thirty-One

I watched Zxarvixar as he looked down at me, with a greedy expression. Tears streamed down my face.

"I'm not ready to die."

"I think otherwise. . ."

Bonesella screamed. I looked down below. The green acidic liquid was splashing high. I spread my wings to flap them, but as I did, I felt a large splash of acid hit them. I flapped harder and looked at them. They were turning black as the acid ate the feathers. It continued to burn to the bone all the way up to my back.

"Ahh!"

The acid hit the skin on my back. I looked up at Zxarvixar. He created this mess and he was controlling it to make me suffer.

"Xavier!" Bonesella screamed.

I couldn't help her. I didn't have the strength to pull myself up. Something glimmers in the corner of my eye. I looked to see what it was. The beautiful Blossom of Life landed on my right hand.

Magenta veins glowed around the flower and trace down my arm to the rest of my body. The flower must be helping me heal my wings. As I slowly started to feel better, Zxarvixar lifted his foot to step on the flower and my hand with it. Before he crushed it, I was hit with a force of gravity that pulled me away from the tower. Everything quickly zoomed away. I looked up to see what was holding me.

"Nightmare!"

He looked down at me with a smile. He must have known.

"I miss you, buddy!"

Nightmare roared as he descended. I hopped on to the ground as Nightmare landed behind me. Zxarvixar appeared before me.

"I'm not dead yet, bitch," I announced with a harsh tone towards him.

I couldn't see Bonesella in the tower.

"Nightmare, go save her," I called.

As Nightmare soared into the air again. Zxarvixar built his dust army again, which started to shoot arrows at Nightmare. Nightmare struggled as arrows struck him and touched the ground again knowing he couldn't fly.

"No!" I yelled as I saw the blood dripping from his wounds.

He came over, blocking me. The arrows stop. I place a hand on Nightmare.

"Okay. No more flying. Stay here with me," I told him.

All the dust warriors point their bows with arrows at us.

"This is it. No more playing around," Zxarvixar stated.

I sighed as I realized how ridiculous this was. I couldn't heal Nightmare as I was being attacked. I looked down at him. He still smiled at me. I was sure that he will be okay. He was strong, plus the arrows were small.

The Blossom of Life blows in the wind and attaches itself into my hair.

"I don't think I'm going down that easily," I respond to Zxarvixar.

"Sure. Why is that?"

Cathryn and the kids came up behind me. Cathryn placed a hand on my shoulder.

"It's six to one right now," I said with confidence.

"Dust army doesn't count. It's not real."

Zxarvixar took back the army.

"Fine."

I opened my wings, even though they aren't fully healed yet and pull out my sword once more.

"Come at me, bitch."

Swords clashed as Cathryn pulled out her laser gun again. The other three kept a distance from the fight and took out bows and arrows to shoot. Zxarvixar created a shield to block those attacks as he fought me. I dodged attacks more quickly now and my quick moves caused inaccuracy in Zxarvixar's attacks. I sprinted left and right. Anywhere I could cause confusion. Cathryn did the same. Zxarvixar used more shields. My healing powers rushed through me. My sword collided with one of the shields and broke it. Cathryn attacked directly at the shields to damage them for me. As I started to glow, my sword slashed through three shields and sliced Zxarvixar in the neck.

All the shields disappeared. The arrows stopped flying. Cathryn stopped shooting. I took a step back, gazing at Zxarvixar, who was injured. Maybe If I could hit him once more, just like that, all of this can be over. I prepared to charge at him. Green glowing goo started to ooze out from his wound. I had no mercy.

I ran toward him with full force. I pulled my sword back and swing forward. Before I could see the results, my neck was caught. Zxarvixar tightly closed his hand around my neck. I started to choke. I couldn't breathe. My anxiety was starting to attack me. I continued coughing as he pulled me up, face to face. Our noses were almost touching. He really looked pissed at me. So pissed that he wanted to snap my neck right now. I braced for the injury as I had a panic attack. I couldn't see anyone else because I couldn't turn my head.

"You little son of a bitch, who do you think you are?! I'm about to snap you in half and eat your soul! So, you better hang tight as I enjoy your suffering."

I wished I had the strength and the guts to do something. I wished Isaac were here. I had the bad feeling in the beginning that I was going to die. I might actually be right. If I died, Isaac wouldn't get to see me. He'd start to worry and eventually kill himself due to depression. I couldn't leave him alone. I needed to reunite with him. I needed to protect him, while he protected me. With his other hand, Zxarvixar grabbed my jaw. He continued to press his fingers until I yelp do to pain. He continued to add pressure to my neck. My vision quickly started to blur. Right before I passed out, I heard Bonesella yelling out my name and cursing at her father to let me go. After that, I passed out completely.

My vision was fuzzy. I felt a warm hand on my face.

"Darling. You're okay. I got you. I promise nothing is going to happen to you," Bonesella said. I reach out and touch her face. I was laying down.

"You escaped?"

"Yeah. I did. I should be more worried about you right now."

I closed my eyes to rest. My entire body ached right now. Her lips hadn't touched mine in a while. It was strange now. Now that I knew my heart was with someone else. I kissed her back anyway. She deserved affection from me before I went to search for my true love, even if it wasn't real. After a moment, she let go and let her warm check rest against mine.

"I really love you, even after all of this."

Her words made my heart drop. "I know," I replied sadly. I opened my eyes.

Bonesella lifted her face up. I could see the sad confusion in her eyes. "And. . .?" She waited for the actual answer.

"You know what to say."

I looked at her with tears in my eyes. I didn't know how to respond anymore.

After a moment or two, Bonesella finally placed her hand back on my cheek again.

"It is okay. I am sorry for all the arguments and such. I have been just really worried about you lately. You may think I am annoying or whatever for it, but I need to know why. Why you have been like this? I just want an answer so that I can help you."

Bonesella's concern for me was understandable. I didn't blame her. I really wish I could simply sum up my feelings, but it was complicated for me. I didn't know how to express these feelings to her. I was also worried about what her reaction would be. She might make me feel a lot worse than I was already.

"I appreciate you. I'm just worried that you are going to take all this out on me. I don't want you to feel what I feel. I just want to make sure that you can live life more comfortably than me."

Bonesella started to comb her fingers through my hair.

"That's not how you should be thinking. You need to care for yourself and talk things out. You can't live life in these kinds of feelings."

"I know. I know. I really want to benefit both of us right now. I want to feel just as loved and cared for as you do . . . I just . . ." I paused, unsure of how to go on.

Bonesella's face looked more depressed than ever. I didn't know how to tell her this.

Before I could go on, Bonesella spoke.

"I think, you would be better off taking care of yourself right now as we are out on this battlefield. I need to fight for you now. You need to rest because you are severely injured. I don't want anything to happen to you."

Bonesella kissed my forehead as she got up.

I sat up as she left. I was in the hall where we first settled in. It was late in the night now. I leaned my back against the wall. That was close. As I looked out from the missing entrance, Bonesella confronted her father with everyone else by her side. Above, Nightmare was flying toward me. He landed right at the entrance and walked up to me.

"Hey, love." He laid his head on my lap to comfort me. He also laid the rest of his body next to me. I petted him on the head. His three eyes facing me glimmered. At least I had someone I could count on.

Isaac wandered in my mind. I wanted to cry my eyes out. I couldn't stand living without him. I need to feel his lips touch my soft skin again. I started to cry again. My tears dripped from my cheeks and hit one of Nightmare's eyes. He shook his head a little, then started to lick my face.

"Aww. I love you too," I said as I hugged his face.

As Nightmare comforted me, Zxarvixar seemed to be looking around. He must not know that I was here. Something must have happened when I was out. I tried to get up. Nightmare got up with me to support me. I held on to his back as we walked out of the hall. As we walked up to the scene, Zxarvixar gave me a nasty look. He was still injured badly.

"Don't hurt him."

Bonesella said as I walked up next to her.

"Oh, that's not what I'm worried about now. You, my child, have done your job, so therefore I don't care what happens to you."

My eyes went wide as Zxarvixar spoke to his own daughter that way.

"What do you mean?"

"You were made with a specific purpose for me. Your powers were used to find Xavier by sensing his soul—which is a demonic trait. Demons can sense souls, so that they can hunt and eat them. And so, I sent you to find that soul for me. So, I can suck the healing powers out of him, use them if I like, and eat Xavier's soul to fulfill my hunger."

My body shook at the words. Bonesella seemed even more terrified than I was.

"I can't believe you would use me like that!"

I started to tremble at those words.

"Why me?" I asked.

"You're . . . extra special. You see, you have an exceedingly rare spirit. Those powers make it more so and so that makes you an incredibly attractive meal for any demonic presence."

"No. I won't let you get the chance to eat his soul! Take me instead!" Bonesella yelled.

I pulled her to my side immediately.

"No don't you dare do that!" I yelled at her.

She tried to pull away from me.

"No. I want you to live. I deserve this fate. He's my father. You shouldn't have to die with that fate."

Before I could react, Zxarvixar spoke.

"Well, I can do that."

He used his green magic again. It surrounded Bonesella and lifted her in the air. Her arms were closed tight behind her back. She was unable to move.

"No! Don't take her!" I screamed.

"Oh well. She chose her fate."

She started to suffer for real. She tried to move and started to scream.

"Let her go," I demanded.

"I will let her go if you give me your soul to trade."

"No. I won't do that."

"Fine. She dies."

I focused on the energy inside me now. My body glowed bright magenta.

"I won't let you do that." Everything glowed so bright it was white. I couldn't see the surrounding area anymore. I outstretched my hands in front of me. After a bit, everything reappeared, and Bonesella lay on the ground. Zxarvixar's green magic was broken. I took my sword in my hand, ignoring Zxarvixar's surprised expression. I struck him before he could react. I stabbed him in his wound. He didn't make a sound. He started to fade. The dust of his body went up into the air and went as far as time. I had finally done it. I defeated him. Everyone was safe, including me.

Chapter Thirty-Two

I couldn't believe it. I couldn't believe any of this. I dropped my sword and pulled Bonesella up. I looked at her with disbelief. I couldn't stand the fact that she was used to draw me in like a fish catching on a fisher's hook. By now, the line was reeled in, and I was exposed to the outcome. The air I couldn't breathe, outside my home. That's how I felt right now.

"You didn't know about any of this?" I asked. I had tears in my eyes. Cathryn and the kids were more shocked than ever.

"I swear I didn't know."

I couldn't tell if I believed her or not. My stomach had an unsettling feeling that told me I couldn't trust her completely.

"If you are hiding something, tell me now," I demanded.

"Tell you what? I wasn't trying to do any of this!"

Bonesella and I had tears in our eyes. We were both shocked by the truth and now we wanted answers.

"You have a demonic trait. How do you feel? Hungry for me?" I raised my voice.

I couldn't trust someone who was reeling me into a boat with a fish killer.

"I don't understand any of this. I know no more than you do. Why don't you trust me no more?" Bonesella's eyes were watering up even faster than mine were.

"You almost got me killed."

"And I saved you! What else do you want?! I did everything I could for you!"

The words sunk in. The more I thought about it, the farther apart we seemed to be.

"No. That wasn't enough."

Bonesella's eyes lit on fire. I expected her to choke me. She stomped up to me.

"You are acting like the most ungrateful, greedy man in the world!" Her spit landed on my face.

"Greedy? I'm depressed . . ." I said, about to have a panic attack or a mental breakdown. I covered my face with my hand.

I stepped away to put distance between us. I started to cry.

"Why are you depressed?" Bonesella asked nicely.

"Because I have been hurting someone this whole time and I feel like a horrible person." I cried even harder and take a seat on the ground.

Bonesella came and sat next to me.

"Who are you hurting? Hurting me?"

"No. I am hurting someone else."

"Who. Do I know them?"

"No. I knew them when I lived in the village."

"Was it a friend?"

"Yes."

"How are you hurting them?"

"Emotionally. He misses me. The more time I spend with you, the more upset he gets that I am not there."

"You want to go visit your friend?"

I could see by Cathryn's expression that she knew exactly what I was talking about.

"Yeah."

Bonesella took a moment to think.

"Was that who was writing to you in the letter that you wouldn't let me look at?"

The clear memory came back to me. How scared I was if she

were to know that I had feelings for someone else. It was time to explain myself.

"Yes."

"So, you started writing to him when we left together?"

I decided to spill out everything by this point.

"No. When my information was wrong to work at the palace, I went to the village to get my information from Jacob and visit him. I gave him the address to write to. I stayed an extra day there because he was injured. I didn't want to tell you because you would have gotten very upset and start asking me a bunch of questions. I just felt like I couldn't handle it at the time."

Bonesella looked me up and down. She placed a hand on my shoulder.

"I'm not mad at you. I'm just curious about this friend of yours."

"I know. He saved me before. He was always there for me. He became my best friend and the last time I met up with him, he told me that he loved me."

I sunk my face into my knees. I didn't want to deal with this now. I really wanted to get this over with. Bonesella's hand came off my shoulder. Tears quickly poured out from my eyes.

"Zxarvixar was being controlled by The Allia, that must be why he went all crazy about wanting my soul," I said to change the subject. I was freaking out already.

"Right." Cathryn said slowly. I looked up and wiped my face. I slowly stood and took a good look at my surroundings. The clouds were a dark grey, and I could still see dust floating in the air. Something tickled my nose. Then I felt it again. It was about to rain. As the rain started to pour, we all went to the hall to keep dry. Nightmare curled up beside me. Bonesella took a seat on the other side of me.

"You know, all I want is to help you."

Now were back on to this conversation again. All I felt like doing was running away like I always had.

"I know. I appreciate that you do. I just feel like you are going to hate me just as I thought he was going to."

She thought for a moment before responding.

"You think he hates you?"

"Well, he said he doesn't. he was disappointed though. I just feel like I stabbed him in the back . . . And if I tell you why I am going to be stabbing you in the back to."

We all fell silent. The only noise was the rain hitting the old ceiling. Nightmare fell asleep to the sound while drooling on my armor. I took a close look at his wounds. They were small, but quite a few of them. Nightmare managed to pull the arrows out of him. All that was left were a bunch of holes with violet blood spewing out of them. I got my powers going and I put a little of my semen onto his back. The holes started to close on their own.

I scratched him behind the ears while my thoughts wonder off to find Isaac. I closed my eyes. The fear of exposing myself crept inside of me. I was right on the edge of a cliff, with clipped wings, unable to fly anymore. This was it. This was the end of me. May God let me burn in this feeling of anxiety. I want to scream as every minute goes by. I don't want to, but I kept stabbing people in the back. I've been stabbing myself since the beginning. This hell will keep haunting me till I completely break away from it. Till I decide to jump off that cliff unable to fly.

This feeling of emptiness grows inside me. Lightning strikes, and the thunder rolls by. I open my eyes. Nightmare was fully out. Everyone else waited eagerly for the rain to pass.

"How are we going to get back?" I asked to lighten the mood a bit.

I just wanted to help my own feelings by this point.

"Well, I don't have another portal, but I am sure we can make it. Walking is good exercise," Cathryn stated.

I was glad she spoke cheerfully about any situation. Her nice smile always brought me to feel better.

I adjusted my position off the wall to sit forward.

"We don't have any injuries, right?"

"Nope. You're the only one who experienced pain today," Bonesella responded.

I almost jumped because I forgot she was sitting on the other side of me.

"I guess we can go when the weather lightens up a bit," I said.

I closed my eyes to rest again, but Bonesella's soft tone made a presence.

"Are you going to tell me what it is? Why I am going to hate you?"

I reopened my eyes and stared at the pale ceiling.

"Only if you don't hate me."

"Well, I can't hate you for anything besides the fact that you are accusing me of trying to kill you."

The words stung. I could tell this was not going to go down well. I might as well explain myself, throwing myself off the cliff, unable to fly. I moved Nightmare's head aside and stood up. Bonesella stood after me. Everyone else leaned in on our conversation.

"You know, I had no idea what to expect when I met you. I didn't know about any of this. You told me few things about your parents, but you refused to tell me too much. I have perfectly good reason to accuse you of trying to kill me."

"What?"

"You barely told me anything. You lied to me!"

"I didn't know any of this would happen!"

"You ignored everything I said. You told me to forget about it! Now, how do you think I feel after almost being killed!" I fired back.

Bonesella's face expressed anger, hate, sadness, and even a bit of confusion too. I didn't think I could forgive her for this.

"I hate being lied to. My family lied to me this whole time. I had to figure out on my own that I was adopted. You know how much that hurts!"

Tears streamed down my face. I couldn't stand the feeling. I wanted to die rather than be lied to. The only person who had been the most honest and respectful to me had always been Isaac.

"I can't believe you anymore. I refuse to trust you by this point," I said walking right out into the rain.

Bonesella chased after me, grabbing my shoulder.

"Why can't you just trust me!"

"Because you don't understand anything. I can't communicate with you. You don't even open up to me about any of my problems! You act like you care but don't even help me with how I feel!"

We were soaked, arguing at each other in a storm. I could tell that Bonesella couldn't stand me anymore. I was about to hit the ground after my fall from the cliff. I felt empty and broken. I didn't even think I still have a soul no more. It's like I was dead. There's no life left. Our tension was just the hope of being alive and breaking free from the coffin without even realizing it because I was dead. We were dead.

"The only full support I have had was him. And of course, Cathryn. He was the only person who actually told me that he cares about me. Totally cares about me," I explained as I started to cry.

I couldn't control my feelings by this point.

"When he told me that he loved me, I knew he was being serious. I knew he really cared that much. And I feel horrible for not knowing it before. So, when I left him, he missed me and tried to connect with me. I love that because he actually showed me that I am worth more than just your husband or a father. He showed me that I am his friend and true love. Don't you get it? I love him now . . . I just want to reunite with him. But I don't want to hurt you no more and I know it sounds like absolute shit, but please, just listen to me and care about my feelings. I want you to understand that I have as hard time loving you back. I have someone else on my mind now. Please just understand."

"I-I don't understand . . ." Bonesella admitted.

The rain started to slow down and everyone else got out from the hall. Nightmare came over to me. I patted him on the head. I guessed I had just hit the ground from my fall, completely lifeless. I didn't think I could shed anymore tears, like a tree in the winter that has lost all its leaves.

"So, this is it? You're leaving me?" Bonesella asked in a high pitch tone.

She was about to lose her mind. I was done with crying. I thought it was time for me to accept who I was.

"Yeah, I am. I feel better this way. I love someone else. I was just afraid to tell you all this time because I didn't want you to hate me forever and do something rash," I stated calmly.

Bonesella was lifeless. She crossed her arms to keep warm from the freezing rain. Surprisingly, I felt better now. Instead of feeling horrible and broken, I felt numb . . . but in a good way. It was like bathing in ice on a scorching summer day. It makes you feel cool and refreshed. I felt refreshed right now. I let a small smile grow on my face. Bonesella was a train wreck. I walked up to her nicely.

"It was nice knowing you. I hope you feel better soon. Are there any last few things I can do to help you feel better?"

After a moment, she finally spoke. "No. I don't think so. I think it would be better if you talk to the kids."

"Okay, sure." I let my hand slide over Bonesella's shoulder as I walked up to my own children.

Before I reached them, Cathryn stopped me by placing a hand on my shoulder.

"You did the right thing. I hope to see you again sometime," Cathryn said softly.

I could see sadness in her eyes, but I could tell that she was happy for me. She knew how I felt. She understood what I had been going through. She was proud of me.

"Alex, Jenifer, Rosetta?" I started.

"It's okay. I've noticed you weren't too happy lately. I also like the same gender. I'm Bisexual," Jennifer said. Her kindness shone brightly through her eyes.

"Thank you for understanding. I love you all," I said hugging them.

"Me too. I like girls. I'm homosexual too," Rosetta stated.

I let go and looked at them all.

"I'm glad you finally told me."

"So, am I going to have a stepdad?" Rosetta asked.

"I'm sure you will," I said with a smile.

"So, are you coming with us?" Cathryn asked from behind.

I looked up at her. My heart was telling me otherwise.

"I think I am going to take my own path. I promise I will come back eventually."

Cathryn nodded. I looked back at the kids.

"I love you all," I said as I kiss each of them on the forehead.

"I love you too," they said.

I walked back over to Bonesella to check in on her. "Are you going to be okay?" I asked as I scanned her face.

"I think so. I will have my mom to support me."

I wrapped my arms around her one last time. I just need to say goodbye before I move on. "I guess this is my goodbye. I will probably see you soon, just not that often. You don't have to worry," I said.

She hugged me back twice as hard as I was.

"I will miss you," she said through tears.

"You too."

I placed my hand on Nightmare and looked at everyone else. I waved with a smile. Nightmare gave a low growl, and we headed towards the forest. This was it. The battle was over. I felt free, but not complete yet. The only thing missing was Isaac. I needed to find him.

The forest started to devour and swallow me whole. Everything that happened started to fade away. My memories were shattered, but now must heal. I was becoming a new man. After my memories healed, I would be able to heal my soul and become a new person. I had found a better purpose. I knew more about who I was than I ever had. My goal was to find myself and to find happiness.

I want to be loved. I want to feel like I am the world to someone. I want to be someone's best friend. I want to be someone's soulmate. I want to be someone's everything.

The more I think about it, I already am someone's everything. I belong to Isaac and only Isaac. I won't let anyone ever control me. I have found my place. I found love. I found myself. I found hope to be finding more that is out there. I found the greatest thing in life and that is who I am and who I love. I know much more than ever now. I know life won't ever be the same again for me. Isaac will be my companion through the rest of my journey.

To be continued in *The Legend of Xavier: Drowning*

Printed in the USA
CPSIA information can be obtained
at www.ICGtesting.com
LVHW021325140724
785413LV00010B/224